HARRY CARRY

CW01496951

HARRY CARRY

BRIAN MCDONALD

The manufacturer's authorised representative in the EU for product safety is Authorised Rep
Compliance Ltd, 71 Lower Baggot Street, Dublin D02 P593 Ireland
(www.arccompliance.com)

This is a work of fiction. Names, characters, businesses, places, events
and incidents are either the products of the author's imagination
or used in a fictitious manner. Any resemblance to actual persons,
living or dead, or actual events is purely coincidental.

Troubador Publishing Ltd
Unit E2 Airfield Business Park,
Harrison Road, Market Harborough,
Leicestershire LE16 7UL
Tel: 0116 279 2299
Email: books@troubador.co.uk
Web: www.troubador.co.uk

ISBN 9781836281931

British Library Cataloguing in Publication Data.
A catalogue record for this book is available from the British Library.

Printed and bound in Great Britain by 4edge Limited
Typeset in 10.5pt Garamond Pro by Troubador Publishing Ltd, Leicester, UK

To my sister Eileen

CHAPTER 1

Wyllie had insisted on Harry's attendance, which was unusual, particularly at 4.45 on a Friday afternoon. Harry supposed it might have something to do with the fundraiser scheduled for that evening, but sensed something was wrong.

Although it was high summer, and the interior of the bank felt chilly, Wyllie dabbed at his face with a handkerchief as beads of sweat trickled down to his jowls.

He motioned for Harry to sit, cleared his throat and came straight to the point. "Head Office is on my back. Unless you can redeem your overdraft within four weeks, we will be obliged to foreclose on you, Mr Carey."

'Mr Carey' – that was a new one, thought Harry. When Wyllie had been practically shovelling money at him, it had been 'Harry' this and 'Harry' that, with a lot of back slapping and friendly chat.

"It will be OK," Wyllie had kept telling him. "Don't worry about it," and of course, as with everything else concerned with money, Harry had chosen to go along with that. Now, however, Wyllie's attitude had become frosty and aggressive.

Harry was finding it difficult to breathe. "Could you repeat that, please? I don't think I heard you properly."

Wyllie repeated what he'd said before enquiring, "How do you propose to deal with this? Do you have any means of clearing your overdraft; stocks, shares, insurance policies, any other assets that could be liquidated?"

You know very well that I don't, thought Harry, but kept silent as Wyllie continued. He extracted some documents from a folder and passed them to Harry.

"This is a statement of our intentions regarding the steps the bank will take to recoup the money you owe. I cannot stress how important it is that you give it your full attention and be prepared for vacating the premises within the time frame specified."

Wyllie stared at Harry with ill-concealed hostility. The banker's florid face had deepened in colour as he shuffled papers on his desk.

"Is there nothing I can do to prevent this?" Harry enquired.

"The bank's position is quite clear. Unless you can pay off the outstanding balance of £150,553.59, in the time specified, you will lose your croft, Mr Carey. One possibility is that you could find a buyer for it, but as we both know, the land has little value, some of the buildings are run down and will need expensive repairs. Your neighbour Joe Burns has been trying to sell for years but even with the filling station and plant nursery, nobody wants to know. Your property is not very desirable, is it? It's marginal land fit only for grazing and even that is very sparse and unlikely to be able to support livestock on a commercially viable basis. Your only income from the van delivery business has dwindled away to nothing over the last couple of years, following the death of your grandmother. I'm sure you can appreciate that this cannot go on, Mr Carey."

With a deepening sense of futility, Harry could only stare dumbly back at Wyllie, unable to respond in any way that would persuade the manager to reconsider his ultimatum.

Wyllie spoke again.

"I do not think there is anything else for us to discuss, then. Use the little time you have to prepare for relinquishing the croft. Goodness knows, you will need every spare moment to dispose of the stuff you have accumulated over the years."

He pressed a button on the intercom. When a female voice answered, he instructed Miss Smith to show Mr Carey out.

Still in shock, Harry barely acknowledged Sally Smith entering the room. She touched his arm as she ushered him out and, in the corridor, asked if he was feeling all right.

"I think I'm done for, Sally," was all he could say as he exited the bank.

She stared after him, deeply concerned. Sally had known Harry all her life and had lots of reasons to care for him. This was the man who had been her childhood playmate, protector in the schoolyard and fellow campaigner in saving the local hospice from closure. Something must be terribly wrong if he did not even ask how she was keeping.

As Harry crossed the main street of the little market town, another pair of eyes watched him intently. They belonged to a dark-haired woman, who retreated into an off-street lane as he came towards her. She examined a crumpled poster taken from the local inn and knew immediately that the face on the pamphlet belonged to Harry. She would have liked to run to him and introduce herself, but his expression deterred her from making an approach. He was clearly troubled, and this did not seem like a good time to approach him.

As he made his way along the street, she looked again at the handbill and reread the notice that proclaimed Harold Carey aka Harry Carry would be performing later that night in the Crown Hotel. It went on to reveal that the final draw for the 'Save the Hospice' campaign would also be held then.

Maybe she should wait until after the event before engaging with him?

Across the street a four-by-four screeched to a halt outside the bank from which Harry had recently emerged. Tristram Grant leapt from the vehicle and proceeded to enter just as it was closing. He was met by a stout man, attired in a pinstriped suit, who looked furtively around before urgently ushering the newcomer inside.

While this was happening, Beverly Smart had removed an old photo from her haversack and was comparing it to the poster.

CHAPTER 2

As Harry trudged onwards, head bowed, he was unaware that a car was crawling along beside him. The driver tooted his horn and shouted to him. He looked round to see his best friend behind the wheel.

Mark Brown was shouting something. Harry's puzzled expression made him repeat his enquiry.

"Are you all set for tonight?" he said.

When Harry didn't answer, Mark stopped the car and got out.

"What's wrong, Harry? Got stage fright?"

Harry just shook his head and found that he could not speak.

Concerned, Mark put his arm around him and enquired again.

"What's the matter, you old bugger? Cat got your tongue or something?"

Still, Harry could not form the words to explain how he felt.

By this time, Chris Collins, who had been travelling with Mark, had climbed out of the passenger side and was also looking on with concern.

Eventually Harry managed to blurt out, "I've lost the farm, Mark."

"What do you mean – lost the farm?" Chris wanted to know. "It was there when we passed a few minutes ago," he replied in a jocular way, although he too was concerned about Harry's demeanour.

But the words wouldn't come, so Mark bundled him into the car and drove to the Crown.

As they entered the bar, a cheer got up from the drinkers gathered there, although it was only just after five on Friday night.

There were cries of, "Sock it to them, Harry!" and "Tonight's the night, Harry!" "You'll make the target tonight, Harry."

Harry barely acknowledged them as Mark and Chris led him to the lounge bar.

"Come on, buddy, tell us what's wrong."

They waited patiently and eventually, Harry managed to relate what had happened at the bank.

Chris was the first to speak. "I hate that bastard banker – he's nothing but a wanker. And well named too, although his name is back to front – the creep. He should have been called 'Wily Willie' not William Wyllie, as he was christened – although that may never have happened. I don't think he ever knew who his father was. The big, fat, scheming turd!"

Chris might have continued to voice his dislike of Wyllie but Mark adopted a different tack.

"How much are you into with him, Harry? Does it amount to much?"

When Harry told him, he whistled softly.

"You owe the bank £150k? How did that happen? You're busy enough with your van deliveries, aren't you?"

"I've not been keeping up to date with my accounts," Harry admitted.

Mark looked at him fixedly and asked him how far behind he was.

"I've hardly sent out any invoices since Gran passed away," he confessed.

"But that's almost two years ago," Mark marvelled.

"I know, I know! Somehow, all I could focus on was saving the hospice. They were so good to Gran in her final weeks. I couldn't think of anything else except trying to save it from closing. It was her dying wish and that has been all I've been able to think about. Wyllie was so supportive at the outset but now it's like he's an entirely different person – the way he treated me today."

Chris was about to launch into another monologue concerning Wyllie's character, but Mark stopped him before he could get going.

"How long did you say you have to square things?"

"Four weeks was what he said. Here are the papers he gave me," he said, producing them from his inside pocket.

Mark took the documents and began to examine them.

After a quick scan of the papers, he said he would like to take more time to inspect them.

"Is that all right with you, Harry? Will you leave them with me to see what can be done?"

Harry nodded agreement.

"I'm not promising, old friend, but if I can help you get over this, I will. Wyllie won't get away with this if I can help it!"

"You can count on me too," Chris confirmed.

They were interrupted by the arrival of two men carrying a set of record turntables.

"Where do you want these, Chris?" one asked.

"Take them through to the marquee," he replied. "Put them on the stage beside the microphones where we will be performing."

"Really looking forward to tonight," the technician told Harry.

His sidekick agreed.

"The whole county wanted tickets for tonight," he added. "I'm glad to get in free but will pay the £25 ticket fee just the same. It's a great thing you're doing, Harry. I take my hat off to you. What an achievement. The half million is within our grasp. How much do you need to take in tonight?"

"He's already done it," Chris responded. "Anything extra will be the icing on the cake because it can provide all sorts of extras that we never thought we could afford – but keep that to yourselves, boys. We want to keep the money rolling in tonight. This will be a great opportunity to put the closure beyond doubt, for the foreseeable future, anyway."

As the men proceeded to the marquee, a squad of catering staff came into the lounge followed by Sally from the bank.

Mark grabbed Harry by the shoulders and shook him hard.

"Listen to me, you old sod. We'll sort it out between us. Just concentrate on tonight. It's everything you've been working for. I want you to give the best performance ever. You owe it to your gran and all the other poor souls that need that hospice to remain open. I really have to go and deal with the caterers and Chris will have to set up too, but I'm sure Sally will join you for a drink to set you up for the show."

"Look after him, will you, Sally? Your boss has given Harry a right shake-up today. It was the last thing we needed tonight!"

Sally looked enquiringly at Harry but decided not to press him for information.

"Let's have that drink, Harry, I know I could do with one and if the landlord says we should have one, who are we to decline?"

CHAPTER 3

William Wyllie looked at his visitor with unconcealed annoyance. The arrogant Tristram Grant swaggered into his office and dumped himself in a chair.

"What the hell do you think you're doing here? Carey left only seconds ago. He might have seen you!"

Grant sneered at him and said in the superior fashion that echoed a privileged background with public school overtones, "Don't be so stupid, Wyllie, I watched him leave before coming to the bank."

"What about Sally Smith, my teller? She was still here when you arrived and might wonder why I'm receiving visitors after hours. She's in thick with Carey. Any connections between you and me might alert her that things are maybe a bit dodgy here."

"For heaven's sake, man, don't be so timid. She's only a stupid little girl whose only interest in life is likely to be pop music, bingo or reading romantic novels."

"Don't underestimate her, Tristram. She might look a bit mousey and timid but she's as sharp as a tack. You took a chance coming here. Never do that again. We shouldn't be seen together except during normal banking hours. There's too much at stake for both of us if there's the least suspicion over

what we're up to. In future, use your mobile phone or text me
– or the whole thing is off."

Tristram looked at Wyllie pityingly.

"You could never do that, Wyllie. You have too many pressing reasons not to be able to back out now or ever. Do I need to remind you of the gambling debts I've settled on your behalf? I wonder what the bank would think if they were to learn you had to offer me a loan for a bogus project, just so that I could settle your debts with some of it. Let me remind you, if we do not manage to acquire Carey's land, you will be in big trouble with your employers."

"And you too, Tristram Grant, especially if you are unable to service the loan and we can't prise the croft away from him. You have just as much to lose as me, especially since you forged you father's signature on the loan application."

The two men glared at each other. Wyllie, the taller and heavier built of the two men, took a step closer to Grant and looked likely to strike him.

Tristram could see that Wyllie was likely to attack him and decided to placate him as best he could.

"I'm sorry," he conceded. "It's just that I'm so anxious this should work. We shouldn't fall out. That's madness, especially since we have so much to gain if we can pull it off. Forget what I said. It's just nerves. If we handle this right, we'll make millions and never have to worry about money again."

Wyllie's face had drained of colour; his eyes were pinpricks of pent-up fury. Gradually, he appeared to recover his composure. Tristram was relieved to note that the whites of his knuckles resumed normal flesh colour as his fists uncurled.

"So, what did Carey have to say for himself? Is there any chance that he can come up with the money?"

"No, none at all. I think we should expect to make him an

offer that he can't refuse within the next three weeks and the deeds should then be safely in our hands."

As the two men pondered a possible outcome to their scheming, the silence that ensued was broken by the sound of children's voices from outside, followed by a jazz band approaching. Wyllie went to the window and looked out at the procession passing the bank. People in costumes were rattling collection boxes as the parade continued along the main street.

"It's the Hospice Carnival," he told Grant. "I have to be at the Crown tonight to receive a cheque from the fundraisers. If Carey hadn't immersed himself so fully in trying to save that hospice and paid more attention to his business, we wouldn't have been able to pressure him like we have. He loves that croft and would never part with it if he had any choice in the matter."

"More fool him then!" Tristram Grant concluded.

"You'd better leave by the back door," Wyllie instructed. "There's too many people going about just now."

CHAPTER 4

Mark was buzzing around, organising various activities that needed attending to. He would have preferred to spend more time with Harry, to reassure his friend that all would be well, but as proprietor of the hotel, he had to ensure everything would run to plan tonight.

In the marquee, Chris was fussing around the audio equipment, while the two techies were checking lighting rigs and other performance equipment.

"Are you about finished here, Chris?"

"Almost," he replied.

"Will you have time to take Harry back to get changed?"

"Sure, I'll be free in a minute or two."

"Here's my car keys. Try and buck him up if you can, he's had quite a shock and you know how easy it is to upset him. We want him at his best tonight with no distractions."

Chris nodded, saying he would do his best.

In the lounge bar, Sally was running through some of the financial details concerning the fundraising. Harry was trying to concentrate on what she was saying but found it difficult not to let his mind wander to the prospect of losing the croft. It had meant so much to his grandparents and himself. Abandoned by his mother, while still an infant, it was the only home he had ever known. Nestling in the lee of a hill, sheltered by trees from the cold north winds, it was the kind of place that wealthy weekenders would love to own.

His thoughts were interrupted by Mark's arrival.

"Chris will drive you home in a minute or two. Freshen up while you're there and get ready to put on the performance of your life, Harry! Everything will be all right. You'll see."

As Mark turned away, he collided with a young woman, knocking her to the floor and spilling the drink she was carrying. Mark was appalled.

"I'm so sorry!" he began as he bent to help her up.

She took his hand and gingerly got back on her feet. Sally noticed that Mark, not normally at a loss for words, was staring like a loon at the woman he had bumped into.

She was very attractive, Sally noted, the kind of woman that would look good in any outfit. Her current attire was that of a hiker, but she had the fine bone structure of someone that would look elegant in any form of attire. She, too, appeared embarrassed and snatched a glance at Harry but he was oblivious to anything going on around him.

"It's OK," she finally managed to blurt out. "I'm fine!"

Mark found his voice at last. "That was so clumsy of me. Are you sure you're all right?"

"I'm fine, I'm fine," she responded self-consciously.

Sally thought she detected a slight antipodean accent and wondered what this traveller might be doing in the village.

Mark still seemed unable to string two words together as he offered to replace her drink. Could he offer her a meal to make up for his clumsiness?

By now, Harry had also taken notice and was surprised to

observe Mark was behaving like an awkward adolescent. The jangling of car keys in front of his face alerted him to Chris's presence.

"C'mon, Harry, I'm taking you home to get changed."

As Chris and Harry departed, Sally and Mark noted that the new arrival stared disappointedly at their departure.

"Please," Mark persisted. "Let me help you get dried off and make you more comfortable. I would be delighted if you would allow me to make amends. I don't usually treat my customers like this."

She dragged her attention back to him and gave a little smile. Mark felt the room had just become very bright and very warm.

"That would be very kind of you," she replied, "but I can see you are very busy."

"Nothing could prevent me from trying to atone for that clumsy move of mine. Would you like to take a seat with Sally here? I'm sure that she will look after you until I get free, won't you, Sally?"

He turned to go, almost barging into a waiter bearing a tray of glasses, before turning back to enquire if she was on her own or if she was with someone.

"No, I'm on my own," she informed him.

That seemed to boost Mark somewhat. He went on to ask if he could join her for a meal and a glass of wine when he had finished what he was doing.

She thought about it for a moment but then accepted. "I would like that," she said, and Sally got the impression that she was not disinterested in getting to know Mark better.

The lounge got noisier as more people arrived. Sally noticed a lone figure approaching their table. Unlike the others, this individual edged through the crowd with almost apologetic movements. Liam Forbes, the local solicitor, approached and said, "Hello, Sally. I like that dress you're wearing. Did you get it especially for tonight?"

"Just something I picked up from a chain store, nothing special," she replied, blushing from her neck upwards.

"I think you look great in it!" Liam went on. "It really suits you."

The new arrival noted that Liam had also coloured after complimenting Sally. Then, as if it had all been too much of an ordeal, he retreated, muttering something about needing to talk to Mark. The disappointment on Sally's face as Liam departed was quite apparent but she rallied and enquired if Mark's guest would like something to drink.

"I'm Sally Smith, by the way," she added. "And you are?"

"Beverly Smart," came the reply.

Sally studied the newcomer's face as they shook hands. Beverly was a good six inches taller than her and sported the kind of suntan that hinted at a life spent in a warmer climate. Her dark hair was tied casually back in a ponytail. She fingered it self-consciously as she gave Sally a friendly smile, accentuated by dazzling white, evenly spaced teeth. Beverly's hazel eyes twinkled as she held Sally's gaze.

"Let's go to the bar and refill your glass," Sally invited.

Beverly followed, lugging her rucksack with her.

"Are you here for the fundraiser?" Sally enquired.

"I didn't know there was anything like that going on," she replied.

"Just passing through, then, or are you planning to stay for a while?"

Beverly said she hoped to stay for a few days at least but did not say why. She enquired what the fundraising event was about, and Sally explained they were trying to raise enough money to save a local hospice threatened with closure. "It had been championed by Harold Carey," she continued. "He was one of the men that left just when you were knocked over by Mark – that's his best friend by the way and the guy who owns this hotel."

CHAPTER 5

Chris drove quickly through the village but had to slow to a stop when they met the carnival procession as it made its way to the Crown. Seeing people dressed in a variety of brightly coloured fancy dress costumes seemed to bring Harry out of himself.

Several of the participants, on seeing Harry and Chris, waved and danced around the car.

"They look really up for it!" Chris observed. "You must be the most popular man hereabouts, Harry. It's just incredible what you've managed to achieve."

"Come on, Chris, if it hadn't been for your radio programme and all the plugs you gave us, it wouldn't have been nearly so successful."

"Maybe so but that was only a small part I played and was easy to do."

"Sally, Liam and Mark have also contributed such a lot, along with so many others," Harry went on. "We couldn't have done it without everyone who has given their time so generously."

"And tonight will be the icing on the cake," Chris went on. "Sally tells me that, apart from the money we'll pull in tonight, she's had donations from all over the country and from abroad as well. It seems that many people have reason to be grateful for the care their loved ones received at the hospice."

When the crowd moved on, Chris drove forward and soon they had left the village, passing old Joe Burns' place and now entering the short driveway that led to Harry's croft. They got out of the car and made their way to the Portakabin that was Harry's home. The build-up of items acquired at auctions and other paraphernalia filled every room of the house, causing Harry to seek accommodation in the Portakabin. The farm buildings, too, were jam-packed with stuff from his grandfather's time. Chris knew Harry had other lock-ups around the village and in other buildings around the area.

"Have you ever thought of getting rid of all the stuff you've dragged home?" Chris enquired.

"I've always meant to get round to it, but there never seems to be enough time to do that."

"What exactly are you storing?"

"All sorts of stuff. It's mainly items no one else wanted and was given to me – and before that, my grandad – to dispose of. Like him, I kind of stuffed it into anywhere that could house it, until there was time to sort through it. Somehow or other, I could never be bothered to do that. But I'm going to have to now unless a miracle happens."

Chris shrugged his shoulders and said, "You never know, Harry. Miracles do happen."

CHAPTER 6

The Crown Hotel was full of revellers in party mood now that the parade had reached the inn. Sally and Beverly were making polite conversation about things in general when Beverly enquired about the evening programme.

Harry, Sally informed her, had an incredible ability to memorise music and lyrics having only heard them once. This was going to be the star attraction tonight because he was going to be singing a selection of songs, as yet unknown, from the 1960s through to the 1990s. A competition had been organised on the Chris Collins Radio Show with people ringing in to make their selections. Each entry was charged at £1. Ten of the entries would be placed in a box, which would be drawn to test him. If he was unable to perform any of the chosen songs, the person that made the selection would receive £100.

Beverly was astonished to hear this and said so.

"He's always been like that," Sally confided. "He only needs to hear a piece of music once and it is memorised exactly – words and all. It's just a pity he wasn't so good at operating the van delivery business."

"What business is that?"

"It was started by his grandfather who started doing house

removals with a horse and cart. When he passed away, Harry kept the business going but they had acquired a van by this time. That's partly why locals call him 'Harry Carry', not just because he can carry a tune in his head."

"So, what prompted Harry to get involved in this 'Save the Hospice' event?"

"Harry's grandmother contracted a terminal illness. She was admitted to the hospice where they looked after her really well. Before she died, she begged Harry to do all that he could to save it from closure as they had run out of funds. Tonight is the culmination of that crusade and why everyone here tonight will be seeking to make that target a reality."

"Do you think that he will be successful?"

"Oh yes, we have already passed the £500,000 that was needed and tonight will only add to that."

After a short silence, Sally asked if Beverly had somewhere to stay.

"Not yet but I'm hoping to."

"You don't have much time to find anywhere tonight. I could ask Mark if he has a spare room. Would you like me to enquire for you?"

"I think I'll hold off for the moment," she hedged.

Mark joined them just as they had been discussing Beverly's accommodation, apologising for having left them for so long.

"I'm afraid I'm going to have to pass on joining you for dinner but would like to extend that offer to you tomorrow, if you'll still be here."

Beverly thanked him and said that she would like that. Sally allowed herself a little smile on hearing this.

CHAPTER 7

Across town, Chris and Harry were returning to the Crown. On the way there, they saw Joe Burns walking down his drive. Chris stopped and offered him a lift.

"You'll be going to the Crown, I guess?"

"Too true!" he growled in his distinctive gravelly voice. "Wouldn't miss it for the world. Are you ready for the challenge, Harry?"

"Of course, he is," Chris was quick to reply. "Although he's had quite a shock from Wily Willie today."

"What's that creep been up to now? I wouldn't trust that swine as far as I could throw him."

"He's trying to force me to sell up, Joe," Harry confided.

"You too, Harry? He's trying to make me sell too. He came round my place a couple of months ago with the little 'gobshite' Tristram Grant, telling me that he was interested in buying me out. The offer he made was an insult, to say the least, and I sent them off with a flea in their ears. Since then, he's been back a couple of times with other derisory offers, but I told him plain – Grant would be the last person I would sell to even if he gave me five times what the place was worth."

"How's business just now?" Harry asked. "This should be a busy time for you just now with plant sales?"

"No, it's been a disaster. For some reason or other, the tanks that feed the watering system have been contaminated. Thousands of plants have been poisoned and are unsaleable. Come to think of it, that seemed to happen after my last run-in with Grant. I never made that connection before but now something else comes to mind. That wastrel Jake Butcher was lurking about, soon after my falling-out with his boss. Am I being paranoid, or could there be a connection there?"

Further conversation ended as they arrived at the hotel and made their way to the marquee.

Everywhere, people were in party mood. The tent could only hold two hundred people. Probably three times that many were preparing to picnic on the grass meadow in which it was pitched. All had paid a fee to support the cause. Ahead of them, a local band was being cheered as they made for the tent, but an even louder cheer erupted when Harry and Chris appeared.

Beverly was standing alongside Sally when Mark reappeared.

"Has Sally been looking after you?" he wanted to know.

"Indeed, she has," she replied.

"I don't suppose you'll have a ticket?" he enquired.

"I'm afraid not. Are there any going spare?"

"No, they've been sold out for weeks. But, if you would like to stay, I can find a place for you although it might only be a standing one. Would you like that? If anyone challenges, you just tell them that I authorised it."

CHAPTER 8

Beverly watched from where Mark had directed her to stand, but a kindly elderly couple invited her to sit with them, as there was a spare seat at their table. One of their friends had been unable to attend due to a breakdown with their car. It was only two tables from the stage, and she was able to get a good view of all that went on.

Chris Collins got the evening under way and acted as MC throughout. Several bands performed before he finally invited Harry to come on the stage. Accompanying him were Mark and Sally. Mark carried a guitar, Sally sat at a keyboard and then Chris and Harry joined them. Chris sat behind a set of drums and Harry carried another guitar onstage. The crowd clapped and whistled enthusiastically before, on Harry's nod, they started playing.

The quartet started with a medley that included Irish, Scottish, Welsh and English folk music. The audience joined in, following the lyrics beamed onto a screen above the performers. Beverly found herself joining in.

The next set included music from the sixties with the Beatles, Rolling Stones, Hollies, Searchers and other Mersey-beat numbers being reprised. The next selection was a medley of hits from musicals that were also very popular with the audience, with Harry performing as lead vocalist in each rendition.

Then Liam, clearly uncomfortable at being in the spotlight, stepped up announcing that he would be drawing the song contest entries which had been sent to test Harry's knowledge. He stepped up to a series of boxes, from which he selected one entry for each of the four decades, from 1960 onwards.

Chris then announced that Harry had been challenged to play and sing the words to the selection that Liam had picked.

Through a laptop connected to the screen behind where Harry stood, the words of each song would be beamed up for all to see as he performed each in turn. His performance was faultless and received the biggest cheer of the evening.

Chris then announced that the draw would be held. One jubilant lady received a cheque for £5,000.

Followed by speeches from various dignitaries, all of whom singled out Harry for his outstanding efforts, Sally was invited to come forward to announce the final total that had been raised.

She declared it to be £536,041, although further pledges and donations had still to be counted.

The cheering went on for several minutes and Beverly finally saw Harry beam in a way that bore evidence of his delight with the outcome. The only time he lost the grin was when Liam handed over a symbolic cheque to William Wyllie, as treasurer of the Hospice Fundraising Project.

Minutes after all the photographs and media interviews had been conducted, Chris invited the audience to move the tables to one side and to get ready to boogie the night away as he set the turntables spinning. Soon the floor was filled with gyrating couples and when she peeped outside, Beverly could see people dancing around their picnic rugs.

She looked again to see if she could get to Harry but he was surrounded by people. She appreciated that what she had to say to him would have to wait until the morning. As Beverly looked on, she felt a tug at her elbow. It was Sally, accompanied by Mark.

"If you need a room for tonight, Mark can put you up," she yelled above the sound of the music booming out of the giant speakers.

"It's only a single but it has an en suite," Mark bellowed. "Will that be all right?"

Beverly simply nodded and mouthed a 'Thank you' to him.

He seemed very pleased to hear that.

CHAPTER 9

A gentle tapping woke Beverly. It took her a moment to remember where she was. The clinking of a key was followed by the entrance of a maid carrying a tray laden with breakfast things. She was conscious of a mild headache as she raised herself onto her elbows and attributed that to the many celebratory drinks she had shared with Sally, Liam, Chris and Mark. Harry, unfortunately, was unable to stay as he had an early-morning job that could not be deferred. She had so wanted to get his attention but again the opportunity had been missed. She resolved to rectify that at the first opportunity today.

The maid laid the tray into her lap and then bustled around the room opening the curtains and generally primping and tidying things.

"I didn't order breakfast," she said.

"Compliments of the management," came the reply.

"Is that normal?"

"Only for very special guests," the maid replied knowingly, winking as she did so.

Beverly smiled and suspected that her cheeks might have coloured somewhat but did not respond.

The maid gave her a long, appraising look before stating that she could understand why she had received such preferential treatment.

After she left, Beverly had to concede that Mark's attentions were not unwanted but then chided herself for indulging in such adolescent notions. She hardly knew anything about him, after all. Her thoughts returned to Harry and her overwhelming need to meet with him privately.

CHAPTER 10

While Beverly was tucking into breakfast, Harry was removing surplus items from a house vacated by an eminent psychologist. His thoughts returned to the events of the previous evening and he felt a warm glow when he thought about what had been achieved. Gran would be pleased to know they had managed to save the hospice – but at what cost? Mark had vowed he would help him get over the problem. He was good when it came to dealing with business matters although last night suggested that there might now be more pressing things on his mind. He had never seen him so focused on any woman before. Beverly was her name but who she was and where she had come from was unknown. Several times, he had seen her staring at him and wondered if Mark had noticed too. There was something about Beverly – 'call me Bev', which also resonated with Harry. What could have caused that? She seemed to be someone he might know but could not imagine how that could be.

Still deep in thought, he picked up a large cardboard box and proceeded along the upstairs landing towards the staircase. On top of the box was a portable recording device. It looked to be an expensive piece of kit that might have a good resale value and he paused to press one of the buttons. Almost at once, music began to play. It was like no music he had ever heard before. He felt completely transfixed by it. So entranced was he by what he heard, he had forgotten about the loose carpet and was suddenly falling through space from the top of a very long set of stairs. By the time he reached the bottom, his head had crashed against the metal balustrade knocking him unconscious. As he lay in a crumpled heap at the bottom, the tape continued to play but now included the soothing tones of a male voice inviting him to relax – to allow himself to concentrate fully on the messages that were being given. The voice confidently promised that he would develop a powerful memory – that he would be able to accurately remember anything he chose to recall. The tape kept repeating the suggestions on a constant loop as he lay unconscious at the foot of the staircase.

CHAPTER 11

After a refreshing shower, Beverly made her way downstairs and was met by Mark, who had been lurking in reception. After enquiring if she had been comfortable and if breakfast had been to her liking, he wondered if she was planning to do anything for the rest of the day.

Beverly told him that her only priority was to meet up with Harry.

He seemed a little crestfallen by this but asked if he could maybe drive her to his house.

She said that would be very kind of him and he seemed cheered by the news she would spend some more time with him.

When he asked if she wanted Harry to do some removal work for her, she told him it was a private matter she could only discuss with Harry.

Minutes later they were driving into the yard of Harry's croft, only to find there was no sign of him or his van. Beverly wanted to spend time looking around the smallholding and eventually, as there was no sign of Harry returning, they decided to return later, following a tour around the area in Mark's car.

He was good company and Beverly felt very comfortable in his presence. She could understand why Harry and Mark were such close friends, especially by the way Mark spoke about him.

As the day wore on, they returned to the croft several times but still there was no sign of Harry having returned. It was now late afternoon.

Mark decided to call Chris on his mobile to see if he knew where Harry might be working. Chris was able to tell him where he had been going and they decided to go there to see if he was still at the address.

The house was located some five miles from the town along a tree-lined drive that obscured it from the public road. Seeing Harry's van beside the doorway with its rear doors open caused Mark to comment that it must have been a bigger job than he had imagined.

The front door of the house was ajar and the first thing they were aware of was the sound of a voice speaking very calmly and persuasively. The source of the noise came from the bottom of a stairway that led upstairs from the large hallway. Sprawled face down at the bottom lay Harry, a small pool of blood staining the tiles on which he lay.

Beverly bent down to feel for a pulse but urged Mark to phone for an ambulance on his mobile.

CHAPTER 12

Harry was still unconscious when the ambulance arrived. Beverly offered to go with Harry to the hospital. Mark said he would lock up and follow along behind. The paramedics swiftly conveyed Harry to accident and emergency.

Mark arrived soon after with a look of concern that was shared by Beverly. After what seemed like hours, Doctor Dixon asked them to come into a waiting room, where he asked a few questions concerning what they thought had happened. He listened carefully and then enquired if any relatives needed to be informed. Mark told him that he had no one and that he was his closest friend. The doctor informed them he would need to keep Harry in overnight, as head injuries needed to be carefully monitored and assessed.

Beverly asked if they could see him but was told that what he really needed was rest. If they could look back later in the evening, he would see what he could do.

Uncharacteristically, Beverly found herself crying. She had never allowed herself to indulge in that since she had left home. Now, however, she could not help herself and started to sob uncontrollably. Mark tentatively placed an arm around her shoulder. To her surprise, Beverly found herself embracing him, as if she had known him all her life. It took him by surprise but he was happy to hold her tightly, whispering reassurances that everything would be all right.

Later in the car, Mark wanted to question Beverly about the way she had reacted in hospital. She did not seem the kind of person that would behave in that way. Beverly was aware he was speculating about her, but she asked him to be patient. There were things that she needed to discuss with Harry before she could share that information with anyone else. He decided not to press the matter and simply said that, when she was ready, he would hear what she had to say, if she ever wanted to do that.

CHAPTER 13

Harry had been drifting in and out of consciousness, unaware he was in hospital. At some point he had been sick and had heard someone saying that this was normal for someone who had been in shock. Every now and again, a soft female voice drew him back into semi awareness and shone a light in his eyes, but he felt immensely tired and took little interest in what was going on around him.

Other voices intervened from time to time, but everything was happening somewhere else, and he didn't much care about anything other than that his head ached. Eventually, he seemed to be returning to longer periods of consciousness when his head did not seem to be so sore but began to feel anxious when it became apparent that his vision had been affected. This was due to the fact that both eyes were puffed up and swollen. If Harry could have seen himself, the image would have been of a badly bruised face; covered in angry splotches around the eyes, mouth and nose, with several contusions which had been neatly stitched by an accomplished surgical hand.

Every now and again in his more lucid moments, he felt an overwhelming urge to be doing something. What that was, he could not think, but it made him feel it was very important and very urgent. Just before regaining full awareness, he heard two male voices discussing him. They were talking about his ability to memorise music and lyrics.

"What a gift," one said. "Imagine what you could achieve if you could memorise other more lucrative information?"

There was the rustle of paper and the voice of a second person saying that he wished he could memorise facts about antiques and collectibles. He would have been a rich man today, he declared.

The same voice said, "If you can hear me, Harry – that would be my advice. Forget about music and concentrate on antiques. That's where you could make your fortune."

Recognition dawned in Harry's brain. The last person to speak had been Mark.

"Mark!" he heard himself say and tried to open his eyelids to see where his friend was. The lids felt sticky as he tried to focus through the brightness of what he was later to identify as a doctor's white coat.

"Hey, he's coming round!" A female voice he did not recognise cut in.

Gradually, he could discern that there were three people looking down at him. The nearest was a doctor he recognised, then Mark and eventually the girl that was Beverly. All were staring at him fixedly, concern on their faces.

"Do you think he'll stay conscious this time?" he heard Mark enquire. "Come on, Harry, come back to us, old friend. You've been malingering there long enough now."

Then the doctor spoke. "Hello, Harry. It's Doctor Dixon here. You've had a nasty fall but you're safe in hospital now. We're looking after you and will soon get you back on your feet. Can you tell me how you're feeling?"

"Like death," Harry croaked through cracked lips.

"I'm not surprised," the doctor replied. "You had a really

nasty spill, Harry, and did quite a lot of damage when you fell. You wouldn't win any beauty contests just now but given a few days, you should be getting back to normal. Do you remember what happened?"

It took a few moments before he could gather his thoughts but then the pieces began to fall into place.

"I fell downstairs," was all he could utter.

"That's right, then Mark found you and an ambulance brought you here. Apart from some rather extensive bruising to your face, we've had to stitch up a few cuts, but they are relatively minor and shouldn't leave scars. You will probably feel quite sore all over because it wasn't just your head that was injured, although there are no broken bones. For the last eighteen hours or so, you have been drifting in and out of consciousness, but I think you may be returning to full consciousness."

"How long have I been here?"

"Since about seven o'clock on Saturday."

"The van—?"

"Don't worry about that, Harry. Chris and a few of the boys came round and finished emptying the house. They drove the van back to the yard. There's nothing to worry about there."

"Why—?"

"Why did we come looking for you?" Mark obliged. "Beverly has something she wants to discuss with you. When you never showed, we came looking for you."

Harry tried to focus on Beverly and again found himself wondering what it was about this stranger that felt so familiar and reassuring for him.

The doctor cut in at this point. "You will be feeling very tired, Harry, and you've lost a lot of blood. We're going to let you rest again and will pick up on all of this again tomorrow."

The statement was made with such emphasis that everyone understood his suggestion was not up for discussion.

Beverly advanced towards the bed and took hold of Harry's hand.

She squeezed it gently and said, "Get better soon, Harry. What I have to say will keep for now." She then bent down and kissed him lightly on the cheek.

Mark looked on in puzzlement but said nothing except that he would return to visit Harry again just as soon as possible.

Harry found himself drifting off to sleep although still wondering what it was that he felt compelled to do while also wondering who Beverly was and how she had taken such an interest in him. He was asleep in seconds and wondered no more.

CHAPTER 14

News travels fast in a small country community. When Mark and Beverly returned to the hotel, they were greeted by a group of bar regulars wanting to know how Harry was keeping.

"He's going to be all right," Mark assured them, "but he's in some mess – bruising and stitches everywhere but the doc thinks he hasn't done any lasting harm to himself."

The bar was busier than usual for a Monday night. Mark would have preferred to have shared a meal with Beverly but realised that he would have to help behind the bar because they were short-staffed. Beverly, however, wanted to go to her room, as she was feeling tired. He watched her climb the stairs, wondering, as she left, why he felt so attracted to her and also why he could feel the pangs of jealously at her apparent obsession with his best friend.

Sally interrupted his thoughts. "What do you think happened?" she asked.

It took a moment for Mark to reply, as he was still following Beverly's departure.

"He fell downstairs in a house he was emptying, Sally. Gave himself quite a wallop in the process."

"How did he seem?"

"He looked terrible, but the hospital ran checks, and they think he should recover but the concern is that he may have sustained some brain damage."

"After all he's done, too, it seems such a shame he should be suffering in a hospital bed. Do you think he'll be there for long?"

"I don't know. The doctor was a bit evasive when I questioned him."

"It's lucky you found him when you did, Mark. What made you go looking for him?"

"Bev was anxious to see him about something – otherwise he would be lying there still. Can you hang on a minute, Sally? I'll have to go and serve some of these customers at the bar. I'll get back to you."

Sally nodded agreement and took a seat at a side table. Lots seemed to be going on. Harry had not been himself the previous evening. Something was clearly upsetting him, and Mark and Chris seemed to know what that was. His visit to the bank and the way he had virtually ignored her when leaving Wyllie's office also made her wonder if his behaviour had anything to do with it. Then there was this Beverly woman, who had suddenly appeared out of nowhere. Even in the short time she had spent with Bev, she felt she was someone she would like to have as a friend, but she also wondered about her preoccupation with Harry from the many questions she had asked on the Friday night. Mark was the one that seemed besotted by her and that worried Sally. Men often fell out over a woman irrespective of how close friends they were. She hoped Beverly would not drive a wedge between them.

As she turned these thoughts over in her mind, Mark returned.

Without preamble, which was quite unusual for Sally, she

asked him directly, "Does Harry have any problems we should know about?"

Mark took a moment before replying, "Harry won't mind you knowing I guess, Sally, but your boss has called in his bank loan – says that it has to be redeemed within weeks, or he loses the farm."

Sally was unable to speak for a moment but gaped at Mark open-mouthed. "Can anything be done, Mark?" was all that she could say.

"I don't know yet, but I'll do everything I can to prevent that, Sally."

Just then, Chris walked into the bar.

"You look like you're discussing something really important," he began. "If it's private I'll go away again."

"It's about Harry and the bank," Mark informed him.

They went on to discuss the situation before Chris told them about the offer that Tristram Grant had made to Joe Burns when he had offered to buy his place.

"Do you think there is any connection?" Chris finally queried.

Sally thought for a moment and informed them that Grant and Wyllie had been spending a lot of time together recently. She had wondered why Grant had been seen entering the bank after closing time on the night of the fundraiser.

"Something is going on that we don't know about," Mark speculated.

Further discussion was interrupted by the arrival of the local football team wanting to be served.

"Let's keep our eyes and ears open," suggested Mark. "I'll have to go but we can pick up on this later."

CHAPTER 15

Harry slept fitfully, waking every so often following the ritual of having a nurse shining a torch in his eyes.

Only one thought occupied him, despite his aches and pains. It was the words that he had heard Mark say as he had been speaking to someone at his bedside: Forget about music and concentrate on antiques. That's where you could make your fortune.

This kept repeating throughout the night to the exclusion of all other thoughts. With the first light of morning, he felt compelled to find out all he could on the subject.

CHAPTER 16

The telephone rang in Tristram Grant's lounge. Ruth answered it in her normal aloof manner. She cradled the phone in her hand, before loudly informing her husband that it was the tiresome little man from the bank.

He took the receiver and listened with growing interest as Wyllie told him about Harry's mishap.

"Will he live?" was the first question.

Followed by some response that was inaudible to Ruth, he then commented it was a pity that it had not been terminal. She then heard him agree it could only help if Carey was laid up in hospital for a while, before ringing off.

Tristram looked pleased with himself, Ruth observed. He was grinning in that malicious way he had when hearing about someone else's misfortune.

"I think this merits a drink," he said. "Would you like one?"

Ruth looked back at the man she had married and knew he was up to no good but did not care. The only thing that mattered was that he started to find enough money to keep her in a manner to which she had expected but never received, despite his promises over the years.

She nodded and speculated about what could be exciting him. She knew he wasn't going to tell her but simply hoped it might bear fruit this time.

Tristram's hand shook slightly as he poured two large brandies. He was aware that Ruth was looking at him speculatively and sought to regain composure before placing the glasses on the coffee table. He was aware his wife suspected he was up to something but wasn't going to enquire what it was. Both had thought the other had money but were now resigned to living with the reality that theirs was more of a make-do relationship.

He stole a glance at the elegant woman that sat opposite him. Despite her well-groomed appearance, she lacked warmth and displayed no interest in anything that did not directly affect her own personal well-being.

She was aware that he was looking at her but pretended not to notice as she leafed through the pages of a magazine that featured designer clothes she could never hope to own. Soon she would go off to bed, preferring not to have to share any further contact with a man she had come to despise.

CHAPTER 17

Following a morning of fitting in with a busy hospital ward regime, Harry learned Mark had telephoned to enquire how he was.

"I said you were doing fine," a cheery nurse told him. "And that you would probably be up when he comes to visit this afternoon. Now it's time to give you a wash and tidy, so sit up in bed – if you can manage that, please?"

With a few grunts and groans, he propped himself into a sitting position while the nurse fussed around with a basin and sponge.

"I think shaving is out of the question today and probably for a few days to come until some of those scars heal when the stitches dissolve. My, but you made a right mess of your face," she grimaced as she dabbed gently with the sponge. "Tell me if this hurts."

It did feel very tender, but he decided not to let her know, for some foolish male reason.

"How do you comb your hair? Does it have a parting? If I give you this mirror, will you be able to do it yourself?"

The reflected image shocked Harry. Staring back was a swollen face covered in bruises and stitch marks. His nose, too, was bruised and swollen, with a scar running most of its length.

The nurse noted his reaction and was quick to reassure him that the scars and bruising would soon heal. He had been lucky he had not done any permanent damage.

"You'll be out of here quite soon I think," she went on in that cheery, reassuring manner nurses often adopt when dealing with anxious patients. "The doctor says that all the tests came back with no concerns about anything for you to worry about. How are you feeling today?"

"My ribs, arms and legs are all pretty sore as well," he replied.

"The scans show no sign of fracture – so I guess the pain will be mainly due to bruising," she speculated. "The aches will lessen in a few days too, I should think."

Her reassurances were interrupted by a beeper. She excused herself before rushing off to where an alarm had been triggered.

Harry lifted the duvet and stole a peek at the rest of his body. It was indeed covered with a lot of angry-looking bruises. Like a timid little boy, he tentatively prodded various spots, wincing as he did so.

An elderly WRVS woman, dispensing drinks, looked at him distastefully, causing Harry to swiftly remove his hand from his lower body.

"I was only—" he began.

She gave him a withering look, stating that she knew very well what he was doing and would advise him to desist from such behaviour or she would call Sister.

Harry could feel himself blushing and hoped the facial scars would mask his embarrassment.

CHAPTER 18

Sally could detect the smell of stale alcohol permeating the dingy office where William Wyllie spent most of the working day. He was clearly on edge because his left eye twitched erratically. He sat upright in the chair, rather than in the usual slovenly posture he adopted when addressing staff.

He had run out of small talk and there was a pause before he referred to the reason for calling Sally in to speak to him.

"On Friday night, just after you were leaving, Sally, you may have noticed Tristram Grant entering the branch. Why he could not wait to talk to me about some trifling Rotary Club business, I cannot imagine – but I thought I should let you know, as it is strictly against bank rules for customers to be in the bank after business hours. I trust you will be able to keep that to yourself, Sally?"

Nodding briefly, Sally noticed he was displaying another tendency that she had observed over the years she had come to know him. Whenever he was lying, he tended to tilt his head to the left. He had been doing that when he disclosed the reason for Tristram Grant being in the branch on Friday night.

Back at her desk, she went over the events which had unfolded since Friday. Was it a coincidence that Wyllie and

Grant had met shortly after Harry had been informed his loan was being called in? Probably.

Was Wyllie up to something underhand? More than likely. She had never liked the man but had kept her head down and concentrated on her duties. One thing she was sure of, however, she would do everything she could to help Harry. She looked up to see her reflection in the glass that segregated counter staff from customers. It surprised her to see her normally sunny disposition replaced with a determined expression, so unlike the friendly, mild-mannered girl who worked in the local village bank.

CHAPTER 19

Beverly asked if Mark would mind giving her a lift to the hospital, as it was coming up for visiting time.

"Give me a minute to get some stuff from my room and I'll be with you in a minute," he yelled from the top of the stairs.

He descended seconds later, carrying a box of CDs in one hand. In the other was the CD player that Harry had been listening to when he had his fall.

"I was just looking for a set of earphones for Harry," he informed her. "The hospital might not like him disturbing the other patients. I've put a collection together that might take his mind off his troubles."

Unexpectedly, Beverly slipped her arm into his as they made their way to the car park. He rather liked the feeling and didn't care that the receptionist raised her eyebrows and winked at him as they exited.

The journey to the hospital took only five minutes and soon they were standing by Harry's bed. Although Mark and Beverly were again disturbed to see the extent of his injuries, they approached with combined cheerfulness and enquired how he was feeling. Had he managed to get any sleep? Was there anything they could get him, etc.

Beverly reached inside her bag and produced a bunch of grapes.

Harry thanked her for her kindness.

Mark joked about him putting more water in his whisky and other predictable witticisms until finally producing the box of CDs.

"I thought that these might help you pass the time while you're in here – and here's your CD player. I didn't know you had one. It's been on charge, so it should be ready to go whenever you're ready, Harry. I've left the CD that was in it. Is that something new?"

Harry looked at the device with a puzzled expression before recognition kicked in.

"It's not mine, or at least it is now," he mused. "This was in a box of stuff I was removing from that house I was emptying. Thanks for bringing it in. I'm going to keep that. My own one packed up a couple of months ago, but it wasn't a patch on this one. It looks a very expensive piece of kit to be sure."

They exchanged pleasantries for some time before Beverly asked Mark if she could have some time alone with Harry. He had been expecting it but was nonetheless disappointed he had been asked to leave.

Beverly caught his arm and told him that when she had spoken with Harry, she would tell him everything.

She stood looking at the figure in the bed that had been the focus of her attention since first she laid eyes on him and smiled a rather nervous smile.

"Harry," she began but then seemed unsure of what she was going to say next. He looked back at her expectantly and invited her to go on.

"I have something very important to tell you and I hope that it will not be too much of a shock for you."

"I'm pretty tough," was his reply. "Please say what needs to be said."

She paused for a moment before reaching into her bag and extracted a wallet from which she produced a black-and-white photograph of a baby, which she handed to Harry.

"Do you know who that is?" she asked, her lip trembling.

"That looks like me when I was a baby," he responded after studying it for a moment.

"And do you know who these people are?" handing him another picture.

It was a group of three people arranged in a family portrait, typical of a sixties' posed grouping.

Harry's eyes widened as he studied the photo.

"Why, that's my grandfather and grandmother with a girl that I don't recognise," he said. "Who is she, and why is she pictured with my grandparents?"

"That's my mother," she replied.

"Your mother?"

"Yes, and your mother too, Harry. I'm your half-sister from Australia. I hope I haven't upset you by telling you that?"

He could not find the words to reply. Beverly waited anxiously; her whole attention focused on Harry. How would he react to the news? Was it too soon, considering all he had been through?

Harry looked at her in wonderment but, still not speaking, shook his head slowly from side to side.

The silence seemed to go on forever.

"I knew the moment I first set eyes on you that there was something familiar about you," he said at last.

She looked on anxiously.

"But I never knew that my mother was alive or that I even had a sister!" he marvelled.

Still, she waited and hoped.

"Come here, sister Beverly," he invited, his arms open wide.

She stumbled to his bed and threw her arms around him. They both wept as they clung together. Her embrace caused him pain, but Harry would have endured much more to experience that moment.

They did not hear the tutting noises the WRVS woman made as she gathered up the empty cups she had dispensed earlier that morning.

CHAPTER 20

Mark was alarmed to see Beverly approaching the car in a flood of tears. Her eyes were red, and she shook with emotion as she tried to speak to him.

"What's the matter, Beverly?"

"Nothing is wrong," she sobbed. "Things couldn't be better!"

"But you're crying?"

"That's right but I couldn't be happier! I'm crying because this is one of the best days of my life!"

When she had composed herself, Beverly went on to tell Mark about the journey that had led her to find her brother. Her mother had fallen pregnant with Harry as an underage teenager and the father, a holiday romance, had returned to America but did not want to have anything to do with the baby. Harry's grandparents wouldn't allow a termination. Following the baby's birth, she had suffered from post-natal depression, which wasn't widely recognised or acknowledged then. She ended up in a sanatorium where she met another resident. They formed a relationship and decided to elope, but Beverly's father would not countenance taking Harry with them. They planned to settle in Australia as immigrants in the seventies. Beverly knew nothing of this until she was sorting through her mother's effects. After the funeral, the family solicitor furnished her with a letter written by her mother. It informed Beverly that she had a brother and explained the circumstances that had led to the abandonment of her baby boy.

Mark listened with incredulity; about Beverly's childhood in Oz, her mother's state of mind and the long periods of melancholy that she suffered for months on end. Her father had been a good man, who had done his best, and for most of her mother's life they had been happy together. Now that she had found Harry, Beverly felt that she was not alone anymore and was looking forward to sharing time with him.

Mark listened sympathetically but was also relieved that her interest was in Harry as a blood relation.

"How did Harry react?" he enquired.

"He held me in his arms and we both cried," she told him. "I was so afraid he wouldn't want to have anything to do with me considering he'd been rejected as a baby, but he was absolutely fine about it. What a relief that was! I think you might now understand why I couldn't tell you anything about this until I had first spoken to Harry."

"I'm so glad that it went well for you. I must confess, I did wonder about your interest in him – and I do hope that you won't think I'm coming on too strong, but I'm so pleased you will be staying around for a bit."

"I'm going to nurse him back to health, until he's back on his feet again." She paused for a moment. "I couldn't help overhearing you all discussing his financial problems the other night. I got a business qualification at uni and would like to help him deal with his debts if he'll let me."

"It can do no harm, I'm sure," Mark replied before driving

slowly out of the car park. He was conscious that he was grinning from ear to ear as he negotiated the roundabout that led from the hospital grounds.

CHAPTER 21

His morning radio show was coming to an end. Chris signed off with his usual catchphrase, "This was Chris Collins – calling you."

Minutes later, he was driving out of the city in a car that sported the radio station's logo. He had gigs later in the day and another radio programme to work up before it went out on the Wednesday night, but at that moment, all he could think about was Harry and his troubles.

Although much younger than Harry and Mark, he was proud to be their friend. When they played together, with Sally making up the quartet, they managed to produce a reasonable sound together. Chris hero-worshipped Harry because of his knowledge of music. It was quite phenomenal the way he could capture a melody and lyrics after hearing it only once. He wished he could emulate him; even though his own memory for music was extensive, Harry's was incredible. It wasn't just popular music, but also jazz, folk, classical and operatic pieces that Chris had never even heard of.

Uppermost in his mind was how Harry could be rescued from losing the smallholding. Could he organise a gig in time with the proceeds going to pay off Harry's debts? It wouldn't be enough to clear them all, obviously, but it might give him breathing space with the bank.

On leaving the motorway, he reduced his speed to take in the full beauty of the countryside. The town he had called home for the past seven years was truly a haven of beauty and peace he adored, although his listeners might not have imagined he was a home-loving boy at heart. The short three miles from the motorway was a world away from the conurbation he had just left. It suited him just fine. He had been lucky to land the job with the station but even luckier to have found a place, friends and lifestyle that he truly treasured. *I'm getting middle-aged*, he thought ruefully, although just in his twenties. Soon he was approaching the outskirts of the village and on impulse decided to call in past Harry's place to check that everything was OK. It did have a run-down look about it, although the buildings were quite sound and would look much better with a general tidy up and lick of paint here and there.

The steading formed a 'u' shape that gave protection from the westerly winds that blew in from the Atlantic but seldom bothered locals, by also having the shelter of the hills which lay behind the house. At the other side of the farm buildings stood the house, but Harry had taken to living in the Portakabin situated alongside. The house and outbuildings had been filled to overflowing over the years, as unwanted or unclaimed auction lots had been stored there – some even from the time when Harry's grandfather had been alive. Chris knew that other lock-ups in various locations had also been used for storage until – as Harry had put it – "I'll give it a general sort out, one of these days."

On a previous visit, Harry had been looking for something that he thought his grandfather had acquired in the fifties. The barn in which he imagined it might be stored was stacked to the ceiling downstairs and the loft above was also full to bursting. The hunt was abandoned after only a cursory glance, as the futility of pursuing the search became evident after simply opening the door. It would have taken days to carry out a thorough search, such was the congestion that unfolded before their eyes.

A figure appeared from behind the Portakabin as Chris drew the car to a halt. Joe Burns strode purposely towards him in a manner that suggested he wanted to know who had entered his neighbour's yard. Despite his years, old Joe bore a dauntingly aggressive persona, which would have deterred anyone who did not know him. Chris looked at the advancing figure, a little stooped now in his gait due to advancing years. Long hours of hard physical toil had taken its toll, but for a man in his late seventies, Joe was as sharp as a pin intellectually. Not much got past him.

A look of recognition brought a smile to his face. "Hi, Chris! What brings you here today?"

The mid-morning sun illuminated a craggy-faced individual, whose broad grin beamed out from behind a salt-and-pepper beard which almost covered his entire face. Beneath the cloth cap, a pair of twinkling eyes bore evidence that he was pleased to see him.

"Just checking that everything is as it should be before I go home for a nap. With Harry in hospital, I thought it best to keep an eye on the place until he gets back on his feet."

"That was good of you. How is Harry, by the way?"

"I phoned Mark last night and he said that he's in a terrible mess to look at. He'll be sore for a long time, the doctor says, but feels confident there will be no lasting physical damage."

"He was lucky then – he could have broken his neck. It was lucky that Mark went looking for him. Why did he do that? It's not something he usually does, is it?"

Chris smiled conspiratorially. "Mark has a new interest

in life that seems to have become an obsession. Her name is Beverly and you probably saw her at the do on Friday night. She's staying at the Crown and persuaded Mark to go looking for Harry, as she wanted to talk to him about something. Mark was happy to accompany her. He seems to be quite smitten by the lovely Beverly, even if her preoccupation is with Harry."

"That makes a change for Mark," Joe observed. "It's usually the other way around, the good-looking sod. Women are always mooning around him. Mind you, she's a very striking girl and I took to her myself, what little time I spent with her on Friday night – couldn't help thinking that I should know her though. She seemed very familiar to me."

"Me too," Chris agreed. "I was teasing Mark about her on the phone, and he became quite defensive. She apparently has a past that he's going to share with me when I meet him later today. Whatever it is, it doesn't seem to have diminished his enthusiasm for her. In fact, I would say, he was even more excited than before, when he was following her around like a lovesick adolescent."

The two men laughed at the thought of Mark behaving like a loon, before Joe eventually enquired if anything could be done to solve Harry's financial problems.

"I don't know," Chris admitted. "Maybe Mark can come up with a solution. He's not short of a bob or two." Chris paused, before saying, "I was wondering if I could run a gig that could pull in some dosh, but I would need to find a venue for that to happen."

Joe thought for a moment. "How would my place do, Chris? Would that be any good?"

Chris looked at him questioningly.

Joe went on, "You know that I'm not using the old aircraft hangar. There's only a few odds and sods stored there that could easily be moved out and would give you plenty of room to hold one of your discos or whatever it is you do nowadays. There's plenty of car parking space and everything; enough for a few hundred people to attend. The only thing we'd be short of would be toilets and suchlike. I'm sure we could arrange all that if we set our minds to it."

Chris gave it a few moments' thought before replying.

"You need an entertainment licence, health and safety checks and all sorts of other restrictions come into play when you try to do something like that. I don't think we'd have a ghost of a chance of doing that in the time we have available."

A sly look came over Joe's face. "Did you know I'm still licensed to hold auctions on my site? I used to get rid of surplus plants and stuff at the end of the season and we could use that as an excuse for having a rave, I think you might call it nowadays, or a 'happening', as it used to be called in the sixties."

Chris was intrigued as Joe went on. "Could we advertise it as an event at which plants will be auctioned with music being performed?

"All that needs to happen is that we make sure that everyone knows that it is going to be a day of music, dancing and merriment. Mark could probably get a drinks licence and all we would need to make sure of is that we have enough stewards to ensure that it's properly managed. You've got the contacts, Chris. It can be a word-of-mouth thing that will be so unique and so anti-establishment that it is bound to draw in a good hundred or so punters."

Chris looked at the old man with a new sense of respect. He had always regarded him as being an astute old devil, but this was something else. "I'm up for it," he said at last. "Let's get Mark, Sally and Liam involved. If they are up for it, so am I."

Later, as Chris drove out of the yard, Joe's final words

echoed in his mind. "If I can do anything to help Harry I will – especially if it fucks up that bastard Wyllie."

Already, Chris was thinking about how the event might be staged, the people he would need to recruit, who would want to support local hero Harry Carry, probably the most popular man for miles around.

CHAPTER 22

He had a sister!

Beverly was his sister!

Tears formed in his eyes and ran down his cheeks unchecked. He did not care when a nurse asked if he was feeling all right. "I'm fine," he told her. "I've never been so happy!"

She gave an enquiring glance but decided not to press him further.

It was now Tuesday night and Beverly had spent most of the day at his bedside. They held hands as she told him more about herself and the events that led up to her coming to find him.

A steady stream of visitors interrupted their time together. Although pleased to see them, he craved hearing more about his mother and Beverly's life as she grew up so many thousands of miles away.

His head was full of thoughts concerning Beverly, his mother and grandparents. It had been a great sense of loss when Gran passed away. She had been his rock, his reason for living. Her death had left him rudderless. Gran had kept him focused on the business; had ensured that all the bills went out on time and that he lived a reasonably organised life. After her death, all that Harry could think about was the promise he had made to save the hospice from closure. He'd done that now and it gave him a great sense of satisfaction, although it had been at the expense of the business.

What would Beverly think when she discovered he was penniless and probably homeless? Would she regard him as a loser and not want to have anything further to do with him? He visualised her again as the attractive, positive young woman who so reminded him of his gran. She even moved like her and had similar mannerisms. He could see, from the photographs, that she looked like their mother. He wondered about so many things but would have to wait until the moment was right for everything to be revealed.

A firm but gentle hand on his shoulder brought him back to the present.

"You were miles away!" the doctor said. "How are you feeling, Harry?"

"Fine," was all he said.

"I think you will be able to go home tomorrow morning. I'm afraid we need your bed, as there are a few operations coming up, though I've had a chat with your sister, and she has told me that she will be looking after you. Mark will pick you up tomorrow morning at ten. I hope you make a speedy recovery."

Harry nodded and smiled. He would have Beverly to himself.

With a sigh, he leaned over to the bedside cabinet and pulled out the mini tape recorder, inserted the earphones and was immediately consumed by the music and positive messages that were being conveyed to him. A confident, soothing voice told him he could faultlessly remember anything he wanted to recall. Every now and again, Mark's words punctuated the invitation to specify the things he wanted to remember. Concentrate on antiques repeated again and again in his mind, as he slipped deeper and deeper into a trance.

Even the clamour of sirens speeding from the hospital could not detract from his total concentration. The programme continued installing the message, deeper and deeper, permeating the furthest recesses of his mind.

CHAPTER 23

Tristram had been waiting for the call. The voice on the other end simply said, "It's done," and hung up without replying.

He smiled before replacing the receiver on the handset.

"Who was that at this time of night?" Ruth enquired.

He was discomfited by her question but merely replied that it was a wrong number.

It was clear to Ruth he was lying, that there was something he was keeping from her. She had seen that look before. Somebody was likely to suffer at her husband's scheming hands.

"I'm going to have a nightcap before bed. Will I pour you one as well?" he enquired, knowing that she would suspect he was trying to deflect attention from the phone call.

She nodded and continued to observe him as he reached for the decanter. She could tell by his demeanour he was in a state of great excitement. Another telltale sign was the way he stammered while trying to engage in small talk. That was not a feature of his normal persona, as most of the time his facial expression was one of surly indifference, coupled with an air of superiority, developed since childhood.

Ruth took the proffered glass and sipped elegantly but then winced. She really deserved a better cognac than this.

CHAPTER 24

Two fire tenders were needed to extinguish the fire. The Portakabin was reduced to grey smoking ash but the house had been saved, although one gable eave bore signs of scorching.

It had been approaching midnight when Joe, closing his bedroom curtains, saw the first flicker of flames licking out of the Portakabin. Although almost a quarter of a mile away across the fields that lay between his house and Harry's place, it was clear that a fire had broken out. It was also evident it might quickly spread to the farmhouse and outbuildings, unless quickly extinguished. He lifted the receiver on the bedroom extension and dialled 999.

What next? he wondered as he threw on his clothes. Poor bugger doesn't have to look for his problems, does he?

He arrived only minutes before the first fire engine approached. The intense heat emanating from the fire meant he could not get near the Portakabin, which was now alight from end to end. Instead, Joe trailed a hose that hung on an outside wall in the yard and directed a continuous jet of water at the wooden facia boards, which overhung the gable end of the house. The fire chief praised him for his quick thinking, confirming that the farmhouse would surely have been lost as well but for his prompt action.

After it was all over, he telephoned Mark and told him what had happened. It had just turned 5am and Mark took a moment or two to digest what Joe was telling him.

"He gets out of hospital tomorrow but will be coming to stay with me in the hotel," he informed Joe.

They discussed the incident some more before hanging up. Mark decided he would keep the news to himself until breakfast.

CHAPTER 25

Harry was already dressed and waiting for them when Mark and Beverly arrived. He immediately sensed something was wrong.

When they told him what had happened, he was visibly shaken but also philosophical about the loss.

"It was an old wreck, anyway," he told them, "and needed pulling down. I guess I'll need to get all that stuff out of the house and move back in there now, but I'm not going to be fit enough to do that for a few days yet, though."

"You'll be staying with me," Mark informed him, "for as long as you need. It makes sense for you to do that anyway and Beverly will be able to look after you until you're on your feet again. C'mon, buddy, we're going to take you out of here, now."

On the way to the hotel, they broke their journey at Harry's request to visit the farmyard. Joe was standing in the yard surveying the remains of the fire. He approached the vehicle, a concerned look on his face.

"Good to see you up and about, Harry," he began. "I'm so sorry that you had to come home to this, though. Were you insured?"

"I think so, but Liam would be better able to tell you. He dealt with all those things when Gran was alive."

"We'll check. It may bring in a bit of money that you so badly need just now," Mark observed.

"I'm not sure that it would cover arson," Joe queried. "The firemen believe that it was started deliberately."

"Do you mean that someone set fire to the place intentionally?"

"It seems that way."

No one spoke for some moments as they digested the news.

"Looks like we'll have to start emptying the house sooner rather than later," Harry concluded.

Joe cleared his throat before intimating that he could store stuff in his hangar. Although he had been thinking about using it for something else, it might be to Harry's advantage but would not explain further what he meant by that.

"Let me know when you're ready to start shifting things, Harry. I'll get a squad in to help move it for you. There'll be plenty wanting to help, I'm sure."

CHAPTER 26

They were sitting in Mark's private suite where Harry would be staying until he was able to fully recover from his ordeal.

Beverly was fussing about, being cheerful, plumping cushions and generally behaving like women do when they are caring for an invalid.

Harry noticed Mark hardly took his eyes off his sister. He smiled and wondered if they might become an item. Knowing his friend as he did, it seemed entirely possible.

Was he comfortable? Could they get him anything? Did he want to rest? were the questions that assailed him as he settled down on the chaise longue. He agreed that he was a little tired, despite wanting to speak more with Beverly.

"Could I have a look through those volumes on antiques and collectibles in your bookcase, Mark?"

"Of course you can, Harry. I've always thought that you should have got into that rather than humping other people's stuff around in that van of yours."

They left reluctantly, Beverly especially, because she wanted to spend every moment she could with her sibling.

In the peace and quiet of Mark's lounge, Harry was soon transported into a realm of concentration that he had never experienced before. It was similar to the mental state that usually took over when he listened to a piece of music that was new to him – only this was much more intense and excluded all other thought. The pages were examined at a steady pace, his mind creating exact images of the pictures that unfolded on each page. The words, providing descriptions of the artefacts portrayed, burned into his brain as if they were being stored on a card-index system. Dates, descriptions, identifying marks, history and valuations were all assimilated as quickly as he could scan the information each page contained.

Despite the initial exhaustion he had experienced, Harry found himself invigorated by the information he was processing so rapidly with every page his brain devoured. When he found he could no longer read the text because daylight had turned to dusk, he realised how much time must have passed. Beverly was sitting on a fireside chair across from him, looking on with interest.

"Hello," she said. "Are you hungry yet? I've been here beside you all afternoon," she informed him.

When he looked blankly at her, she continued, "It's almost eight o'clock. We've not been able to get an answer out of you since you started reading those books."

Harry looked down to where she was pointing. Seven hefty volumes lay on the carpet beside the couch. How had they got there? He could not remember handling them.

"Yes," he conceded; he was ravenous and suddenly emotionally drained. "I could sleep for a week," he informed her.

She lifted the internal phone and spoke to Mark. He appeared minutes later with a maid. Both were bearing trays of food, which they placed on a small dining table in the corner of the room.

Harry gingerly hobbled over to take a seat and sat down

between Mark and Beverly. The food was excellent, and the two men enthused over the meal. Beverly said nothing, which caused Harry to enquire if she did not like hers. Mark enlightened him. "Your sister cooked it. How about that?"

So not only pretty but an accomplished chef as well, Harry noted.

The talk was pleasant and gentle, avoiding all references to Harry's problems but then something changed when the maid came in to remove the dinner things.

She carried a bowl of fruit and set it down on the table.

Harry was transfixed by it.

"Is something wrong?" Mark enquired.

"I'm surprised that you would use such a precious bit of porcelain like that for holding fruit. You must be wealthier than I imagined!" he joked.

His chum looked at him blankly.

Harry was surprised to hear himself saying, "It's a Chinese Kangxi blue and white, ten-inch-diameter bowl – the interior bears sixteen lotus petals – with a rim-panelled border of floral sprays – the interior shows a painted peony inside double blue rings – the exterior bears panels of peony and lotus flowers over a Kangxi Lingchi mark, identifiable by the blue double circles – value circa £2,500–£3,500."

Even Harry was surprised at what he had just said. Mark's face screwed into a frown and Beverly's mouth hung open.

"Where did all that come from?" Mark wanted to know.

"I don't know! It just came from somewhere inside of me."

"And that didn't sound like you speaking either," Beverly observed. "It was like someone else speaking."

"That wasn't your normal voice – that's for sure," Mark agreed. "Did you read that in one of the books you went through this afternoon?"

Harry was clearly perplexed at what had happened and

simply made a shrugging gesture. Beverly got up out of her chair and sifted through the books that Harry had been studying, located the page that referred to the bowl and started reading. It was literally word for word what Harry had just recited to them.

"That's incredible!" Mark exclaimed. "What made you remember that?"

They were even more astonished when they found that his memory was virtually faultless. Every entry they then selected from the volumes he had been poring over was repeated exactly as it appeared in the text.

Mark said, "I don't know how you did that, Harry, but it's clearly something that we should keep to ourselves for the present."

Beverly nodded in agreement.

CHAPTER 27

Earlier that day, Sally held a folder containing papers that needed Wyllie's signature. She paused outside his office, her hand raised to knock, when she heard him bellow at someone he was talking to on the phone.

"You bloody fool!" he bawled. "What the hell did you think you were doing? Do you want us to get locked up?"

A pause followed with another angry outburst.

"Don't tell me that you had nothing to do with it. It's just the sort of stupid thing that you would do or have someone else do for you. This will probably help him rather than turn things to our advantage."

Another silence followed.

"If there's an insurance claim, the assessors will soon deduce that there is something fishy and will want to pursue that. For Christ's sake don't do anything like that again or we'll *both* be toast!"

The sound of the telephone slamming into its cradle alerted Sally that Wyllie might soon be leaving the office because he had an appointment in just a few minutes.

She gave a tentative knock after delaying a few moments, seeking to give the impression that she had just arrived.

At Wyllie's yelled invitation to enter, she gingerly opened the door and stepped in to find him throwing on his overcoat. His demeanour and flushed facial features emphasised that he was in a filthy mood.

"Here's the papers you asked to be taken through," Sally said clutching them protectively to her chest.

"Leave them on the desk, I haven't time to deal with them now," he replied rather petulantly before bustling out of the office, leaving Sally alone in the office. She did not leave immediately but checked that Wyllie had left the bank by peering out of his office window. Satisfied that he had departed, she then checked his desk phone to ascertain the last number he had dialled. It looked familiar to her and sure enough, when she checked her files, the number he had called was none other than Tristram Grant's phone. That's not how a bank manager should be talking to a client, she mused and wondered what had made him speak to him in that way.

Only later that day did she learn that Harry's Portakabin had been burned to the ground, causing her to wonder if Wyllie's behaviour was connected. She decided to keep it to herself for the moment but would keep her eyes and ears open regarding the Grant/Wyllie relationship in future.

CHAPTER 28

Jake Butcher was chopping firewood. His muscular physique suggested long hours in the gym and bore evidence that he deserved the nickname of Butch. He was not someone locals had anything to do with because of his unpredictable nature and the likelihood of him attacking anyone he thought might be disrespectful of him. This led to many fines and the occasional provision of bed and breakfast at Her Majesty's pleasure. Every aspect of him, from his small porcine eyes to the aggressive way he addressed people, warned even the least perceptive of people that you provoked him at your peril. Deeply paranoid, suspecting someone had maligned him was enough to set him off in a flurry of flailing fists and feet.

The axe he wielded had been working well that morning until he struck a rotten log. The axe sliced through the timber but then deflected past the chopping block and struck a stone sticking out of the ground. It jarred him badly, causing him to curse roundly as his body absorbed the unexpected impact to the blow. Nearby, a hen was pecking at some seeds that had fallen from a passing cart. Butch, in his anger, bent down, picked up one of the split logs and hurled it at the chicken. He laughed when he saw it connect with the bird, raising a cloud of feathers before it fell to the ground. He watched it in its death throes and laughed even louder, unaware that someone was standing behind him.

"It might be more effective if you were to use a shotgun in future," he heard a familiar voice tell him.

Butch spun round to see Tristram Grant had been observing him from just a few feet away. He glowered at his boss, who was regarding him in a way Butch found irritating. The superior smirk started at the upturned right corner of Grant's mouth. Accompanied by the slit-eyed sneer was the impression that he was greatly superior to lesser mortals such as Butch.

"Make sure that bird is plucked and prepared for the table tonight, otherwise it will be coming out of your wages," he threatened.

Butch's fists clenched tightly but found enough resolve to prevent him from striking Tristram. As someone who was virtually unemployable and with a tied house thrown into the deal, his self-control, though stretched, held fast.

Grant produced an envelope from his inside breast pocket.

"I believe you managed the task without being observed?" he enquired.

Butch merely nodded and held out his hand to receive the envelope, quickly stuffing it inside his shirt while also looking furtively around.

"I may have another special job for you soon," Grant said, before walking back to the big house.

Butch picked up the chicken and made his way to his cottage, mouthing obscenities as he went.

From a distance away, behind a stable door, Ruth Grant observed the meeting and wondered what the exchange had been about. She would have to keep a very close watch on her spouse from here on in, she told herself.

CHAPTER 29

Liam was first to arrive at the Crown and was immediately asked to go up by the receptionist who was on duty that night. He found Mark, Beverly and Harry waiting for him in Mark's private suite. He had been offered a drink and was just raising it to his lips when Chris walked in with Joe and Sally.

Everyone knew by now that Beverly was Harry's sister. Mark had phoned around with the news when he invited each of them to come to the hotel. After everyone had enquired about Harry's health and had given their welcomes to Beverly, Mark tapped his wine glass to get their attention.

"Thanks for coming along tonight. It was Chris's idea, but he tells me that it originated with Joe. The plan is to consider ways in which we can help Harry extricate himself from this pickle he's got himself into."

Everyone shouted "Hear! Hear!" except Harry who sat on the couch looking uncomfortable.

Chris spoke next. "Joe's idea is for us to hold a dance in the hangar at his place. I would try to organise some musical entertainment and do the DJ bit."

Mark looked concerned. "You don't have a public entertainment licence, do you, Joe?"

"No," the old man growled back in his deep gravelly voice, "but I thought we'd take a chance."

"You might be fined more than you raised," Mark responded. "The authorities are very strict about these things. You need to have stewards, toilets, firefighting equipment, first aiders, risk assessments, and a whole lot of other health and safety measures in place before you can hold one legally. It's a great idea but I don't think we have time to tick all the boxes within the next three weeks. I could, of course, run an event here in the hotel. The function suite can hold a couple of hundred and there are no wedding bookings on the first Friday or the second and third Saturdays from now until the end of the month. If you can see to the entertainment bit, Chris, I can organise the other bits. Is that possible?"

Chris thought for a moment before replying that he could do that and would arrange for the station to publicise it too as a local interest feature.

"It will mean having to bring in extra staff and so on, Harry, but we can cover their wages out of the takings. You can get all the entry money and 10% of the bar sales."

"I'd be happy to work for no pay," Beverly said. "I worked part time in hotels when I was at university."

"Good for you! So will I," said Sally.

Liam said they could count on him too. Joe said he would be happy to help in any way that he could. Mark looked at Beverly with new interest.

"You've worked in the hotel and catering trade. You have a degree in business management and accounting, worked for a multinational firm in Australia. What else can you do that we don't know about?"

Harry listened intently as Beverley spoke again.

"I've done a lot of things, like everyone else, I guess, but two things occurred to me. The first is that people owe you money for work you've done, Harry. I could start to send out invoices and chase up people that haven't paid you for the work you've done for them. Do you have any paperwork that would allow me to do that, or did it all go up when the Portakabin went on fire?"

"I didn't keep any business papers in the cabin. Most of the job documentation is stashed in a compartment in the van."

"Are all your debtors in there?"

"Mostly. Jobs I did for auction houses are listed in a receipt book but were never charged. The same system was used in a separate book for solicitors who wanted houses emptied and so on."

"So, you mean that we could start issuing bills, like tomorrow?"

"I guess so," he admitted.

"What about other customers?"

"They would appear in the daily logbook with their names and addresses."

"How far back was it since you issued any invoices?"

"Probably a couple of months after Gran went into hospital. She did all that side of things."

Mark recollected it was nearly two years since she had been taken ill.

"You must have a fair bit of money to gather in?" Liam speculated.

"It must be a tidy sum that's due to you, then," Joe supposed. "You've always worked long hours even when your gran was poorly and also when you were raising money for the hospice."

The group fell silent considering this until Mark enquired what the other thing was that Beverly was going to say.

"It's about the hangar you mentioned, Joe. What do you keep in there just now?"

"Nothing much. It used to hold bags of peat, fertiliser, machinery and all sorts, but I've been winding down the garden centre using only one of the sheds – and two of the polytunnels, come to that. Why do you ask? I thought my idea about using it for some sort of performance was out of the window, after what Mark said earlier."

"Whatever happens, Harry will need to start emptying the farmhouse. I wondered if we could store it at your place and maybe try to sell some of the stuff from your garden centre if you would be agreeable to doing that. It might also bring in some more money to settle the bank loan."

"What exactly do you have stored there?" Chris asked. "Does it have any value, Harry?"

"To be honest, I forget. Some things are stuff that the auction houses wanted me to take to the tip because it hadn't sold after three attempts. The sellers would be contacted and if they did not arrange to have it removed, I would be asked to take it to landfill. As often as not, some of the stuff would have value but I never got round to sorting it out. Between visiting Gran in hospital and later, because of the fundraising, I didn't have much time to empty the van in the mornings and simply put all that stuff into the barn. Eventually, when there was no more room there, I started filling the house."

"So, it would be good to get it sorted and moved to Joe's place. Not only would you get your home back, but you might make a bit of money out of it at the same time," Sally suggested.

"What about the other places you've got stuff stored?" Chris asked.

"Do you mean the farm steading buildings?"

"Yes, but you also have stashes in other places around the country. Don't you?"

"Well, most of the rest of the stuff that's back at the farm was put there by Grandad from years back. He was a bit of a squirrel like me, I suppose. I'm not sure what he has put away over the years. It would be mostly junk, I guess, but I never really took much notice of what was in the farm sheds. I'm not even sure where the keys would be."

"What about the other places you have stuff stored, Harry?"

"I've not been near them in years."

"I think it's time we started investigating all of that," Beverly concluded, "but first we need to organise emptying the house. Is that all right with you, Joe?"

"Of course," the old man replied. "Harry has been a good neighbour and friend to me over the years. I'd be offended if you hadn't asked for my help. I'll see about getting a few blokes round to help get the house emptied at the weekend. Is that all right with you, Harry?"

"And I'll start to arrange the advertising," Chris confirmed.

Sally offered to help Beverly with the invoicing and preparation of Harry's accounts because she suspected that the Inland Revenue would be chasing him, which he grudgingly confirmed with some embarrassment.

Liam said he would pursue a claim with the insurers to find out if any money was due for the Portakabin and would do anything else that he could to help.

Beverly went over and gave Harry a hug, which made him wince, but he did not complain.

"We're going to see you all right, big brother," she declared.

CHAPTER 30

Beverly drove Harry to the farmstead the next morning in Mark's car.

Harry pointed out places of interest as they made their way through the town.

"It's only a large village, really," he informed her. "It grew up around Joe's place, which used to be a watermill where farmers took their grain to be ground into flour. That's why the town is called Millfield, as it was taken from the name of Joe's place which is still known as Millfield Farm, although most people now refer to it as Burns' Garden Centre. The population is about four thousand and has a great mix of people. They all have a sense of community, which would be hard to find in similar towns."

Beverly had only been able to give the town a cursory glance as she travelled through it on the Friday she arrived. Most of the houses were pre-war, with a sprinkling of more recent council developments on the outskirts. The main street consisted of Edwardian and Victorian buildings, with shopfronts at street level. The tidiness and lack of litter in the streets suggested that residents took a pride in maintaining their town. People they met on the journey, whether walking or in cars, waved as they passed. She was impressed by the friendliness of the people and felt she somehow belonged there.

Although still in some discomfort, Harry was able to get about more easily and was pleased to get out of the hotel, despite the fact he felt an overwhelming desire to memorise more about antiques. Having exhausted the volumes Mark held in his bookcase, he was wondering where next he could go to find out more and mentioned it to Beverly.

"Have you tried the internet? There's bound to be heaps of information on there."

"I wouldn't know how to do that," he admitted.

She looked at him incredulously but did not press the admission, promising instead to show him how to do it when they returned to the hotel.

As they left the village, Joe Burns' garden centre appeared on the right. There was one solitary vehicle in the car park.

"He's struggling a bit," Harry confided. "There doesn't seem to be the same demand for the goods he stocks. I think he may be having cash-flow problems. I wish I could help him."

It had a run-down look, Beverly noted. Competition had forced a lot of privately owned nurseries to close, Mark had told her, when he had given Beverly a rundown on Harry's friends. After they had travelled another four hundred metres along the road, they arrived at Harry's farm. A faded wooden sign hung from a post at the entrance. She could barely make out the weathered lettering which proclaimed that they had arrived at 'Woodside Farm'.

They sat for a moment at the entrance to the farm, which lay below, surveying the scene of the burned-out Portakabin and the charred woodwork on the farmhouse gable.

"It was lucky that Joe acted so decisively," Harry commented. "The whole house might have gone up in flames."

Beverly understood why it was called Woodside Farm, as

it nestled in the shelter of trees to the north and west. The southern and eastern aspects of the property led into fields of rough grazing, defined by elderly fencing in need of repair. One field bore evidence of human traffic, which suggested that both Joe and Harry would have used the route to access each other's homes by foot. Moss was heavily prevalent on the roofs of buildings, giving it a neglected appearance, although all of the agricultural buildings seemed to be windproof and watertight. A lick of paint would make a tremendous difference to the look of the place, Beverly imagined.

Eventually, they drove into the U-shaped homestead and made for Harry's van. He unlocked it and proceeded to lift the passenger seat. Underneath was a compartment full to bursting with papers.

"Those are some of the jobs I've done," he told her. "There are more in the back and some in the visor and side pockets as well."

Beverly shook her head in wonderment. "All these are worth money!" was all she said.

They gathered them up and filled three polythene bags which they took back to the car.

Before driving away, they took a walk around the steading and other outbuildings. The burned-out cabin created a depressing sight that Harry felt most keenly but did not share with Beverly.

"Can we have a peep into the house?" she enquired.

The house keys were attached to the bunch that held the van keys and Harry went over to unlock the porch door that gave entry into a vestibule. After unlocking an inner door, Beverly could see that this led into a passage which continued to stairs. She knew it was a staircase because boxes and various artefacts ascended with every step below an equally congested landing. There also appeared to be two doors on either side of the passage but progress beyond the immediate doorway was impossible, as it, too, was jam-packed full of various cardboard boxes and containers.

"Wow!" was all she could say before finally expressing her concern at how much stuff would have to be removed from the house – just to get in.

They returned to the car and drove back to the Crown in silence.

As good as her word, she showed Harry how to access various websites that dealt with antiques and collectibles. Once he got the hang of it, she proceeded to sort through the papers they had fetched from the van. Soon every flat surface, including the floor, was covered.

Not once did Harry look away from the computer screen except to request help from Beverly when he had finished with each site.

Occasionally he could be heard to mutter that prices were much lower or higher than those he had seen in Mark's books. Beverly was amazed at his powers of concentration but was equally absorbed in what she herself was doing.

Chris looked in on his way home from the morning show but got little response from Harry, who was wholly focused on the pictures and text that flickered before him on the laptop.

Beverly explained he was not being rude and that she had witnessed this behaviour before.

Sally, too, came round at lunchtime and went away with a pile of papers. When Beverly explained that Harry was in another world, Sally disclosed that he used to be much the same when listening to a new piece of music. Mark also dropped in from time to time with cups of coffee and updates on what he had been arranging. Liam had telephoned to say that Harry's insurance was up to date and that an assessor would visit that week. All of this was lost to Harry as he concentrated completely on the images being presented before him.

Over dinner that night, he surprised Beverly and Mark by disclosing that some of the articles stored in the farmhouse might be more valuable than he first imagined.

CHAPTER 31

Joe was in Harry's barn, clearing some space, when he was alerted to the glint of reflected light from the wooded hillside above.

"That'll be Grant spying on us from his estate," he mused. Like most of the locals, he held a deep dislike for the man, especially following the derisory sum he had offered to buy him out.

It was indeed Tristram Grant, accompanied by William Wyllie.

"Looks like they're getting the place ready for moving out," Grant speculated.

Down below, people were milling around, passing various objects in a human chain that led to two separate trailers. Standing in the centre was Harry, who was determining into which truck each item should be loaded. On either side of him stood two female figures who wrote something on a piece of paper, which they then attached to each object before it was conveyed to one of the trucks. A third category of goods was placed in a farm cart.

"I recognise Sally Smith," Grant went on, "but who is that rather attractive woman beside her?"

"That's Carey's sister, I'm told," Wyllie replied.

"I didn't know he had a sister."

"Neither did he, it seems. She only turned up a week ago at the 'Save the Hospice' do. Seems that they had the same mother, but she had abandoned him as a baby and moved to Australia."

"That's worrying. Do you think she has any money that might bail him out?"

Wyllie shrugged his shoulders. "Anything is possible, I suppose. I don't like the fact that so many people seem to be rallying around him. His chums will no doubt want to do all they can to help Carey out of the mess he's got himself into. People around here have a real affection for him. I'm beginning to guess that we should have waited a bit longer before trying to force him out."

Tristram did not respond but Wyllie could see that he was digesting what he had said and had adopted a look that suggested he was considering how to deal with this potential new problem.

"Don't think about doing anything else, Tristram," he warned. "There's no doubt in my mind that you were behind the fire. I would remind you that the punishment for arson is quite severe – besides which, you may have made things worse not better by your actions."

"What do you mean by that?"

"Liam Forbes called in on Wednesday to tell me that he had made an insurance claim against the loss of the Portakabin. He wanted to confirm Carey's bank details and is holding a 'Letter of Authorisation' signed by Carey entitling him to do that."

When his partner did not respond, Wyllie went on, "The cabin might fetch £10,000 he told me. That means you've actually helped him raise some funds that he might not otherwise have been able to acquire. Don't be so bloody stupid in future. You've only made things worse for us."

Tristram Grant seethed at the revelation and cursed roundly, before stomping off in a display of petulance. Wyllie watched him go and wondered why he had ever become involved with Tristram Grant. It had been desperation, of course. He acknowledged that his ill-advised stock market investments and losses at the roulette table had brought him to the desperate situation he now found himself in. Pray to God that it works out all right in the end, he found himself thinking, but a feeling of impending doom had already taken root. He continued to observe the scene below and wondered what was really going on. He would try to get Sally Smith to tell him when the bank reopened on Monday.

Down below, people scurried around, entering and leaving the house, carrying armfuls of stuff that were too far away for him to distinguish what they might be. With a deep sigh, he turned and followed the route that Tristram Grant had taken up the woodland path that led to the manor house.

CHAPTER 32

They had decided to segregate stuff being emptied from the house. After a cursory inspection, Harry would point to either the right or the left and the item would be placed on a table on which either Beverly or Sally would place a sticky label. They would write a price in code upon each ticket affixed to the item concerned. Beverly dealt with the more valuable pieces while Sally processed the goods that weren't expected to make more than £20. Liam carefully noted the total estimated value the items might realise when offered for sale.

Chris and Joe took the worthless articles to the farm cart ready for removal to the rubbish dump. Mark turned up at lunchtime with two of his kitchen workers and proceeded to dish out soup and sandwiches to Harry's helpers.

"How's it going, folks?" he enquired.

Liam looked excited, which was unusual for him, as he tried to maintain a lawyer's solemn demeanour on all occasions.

"There must be thousands here – if Harry is correct in his valuations, that is," he added quickly, having let his normally restrained persona slip momentarily.

Caught up in the moment, Sally slipped her arm into his, in an uncharacteristic show of familiarity which took

Liam equally by surprise, making him colour slightly at the unexpected physical contact.

"Really?" she queried. "I guessed it must be a large amount from what Harry was saying as we went along. How much exactly, Liam?"

He looked into her eager, smiling face and almost kissed her. In this light, at this moment, he thought her the loveliest thing he had ever seen.

He dragged his eyes away from that sweet, bespectacled face and consulted his notebook.

"The lower-valued items run to about £3,500 – but the other stuff – if Harry is right, could fetch over £12,000," he marvelled. "And the barn has still to be emptied!"

"There's not a lot left in the house now," Beverly chimed in, equally animated, "only the two upstairs bedrooms."

"That shouldn't take too long then," observed Mark. "How about the outhouses? Have you made a start on them?"

"If everyone stays on for another couple of hours, we should be able to empty some of them," Joe observed, returning from the cart with Chris in tow.

As the friends continued to discuss the possible treasures that might yet be unearthed, Beverly went over to give her sibling a hug.

"This is great, Harry," she enthused. "Now where would we find the keys for the outbuildings?"

It took him a moment or two to respond, as he appeared to be in a trance.

"They're underneath the kitchen sink," he finally replied.

"Will I get them?" she offered.

"I'll come with you, Bev. They won't be easy to find."

She looked at him questioningly.

"Come on. I'll show you what I mean."

Mark watched them go, arms around each other, and

wished that Beverly would treat him with the same affection Harry was receiving.

In the kitchen, Harry went over to the old-fashioned sink and lifted some articles from the draining board. He then slipped his fingers underneath and seemed to be feeling for something. After a few attempts, he smiled, then proceeded to lift the draining board. It was connected to a set of hinges on the side next to the wall.

"Here it is," he confided. "Grandad's secret key case."

Beverly looked on enquiringly. Attached to the underside of the wooden draining board was a compartment, only accessible when the board was upright. Harry moved a sliding catch to reveal a bunch of keys tied to a hook inside the box.

"Is that them?"

"Yes, these are the keys for some of the farm buildings along with others for lock-ups in other places."

"How many are there for here?"

"These five big old-fashioned ones are for the farm. The other seven are for other places."

"Twelve altogether?"

"Yes."

"So, there's seven other stashes?"

"In various places around the county."

"How long had he been storing things?"

"Probably since the mid-forties, I guess."

"So, the stuff in the sheds here and in the other locations would be much older than the stuff you have in the house?"

"I guess so," he surmised.

Beverly looked at him long and hard before finally saying, "Harry, if the most recent stuff is relatively valuable, the other stuff Grandfather salted away might be even more so. Do you know what's in the sheds in the farm?"

Harry thought for a moment and then gave her a rundown of what he recalled.

"The first shed is filled mainly with clocks, watches and other mechanical things. There's a lot of pottery, glass and other ceramic stuff in the second one. The third, the byre, contains furniture. The milk house has a mixture of things, bronze figurines, nautical and musical instruments, amongst other items. The final one is the shed that we used to store animal feedstuff in and it's mainly foreign stuff from all over the world…"

Beverly stood back and looked at him quizzically.

"Tell me, Harry. Who do these things belong to?"

"Granda, of course," he replied, somewhat surprised.

"But he's been dead for years, Harry."

He thought for a moment before replying. "I suppose I do," he concluded and then quickly corrected himself by saying, "I mean we do, Beverly."

Shaking her head as she spoke, Beverly told him slowly and firmly.

"You're wrong, Harry, they all belong to you. You inherited them. I don't figure in this at all. And just think about this," she went on, "the contents of these sheds might be worth a fortune. Why did you never think about selling them to realise some cash? There's maybe enough there to clear all of your debts and then some."

He contemplated the suggestion for some moments as she held his gaze.

"I guess I never thought of them as being mine. They were always Grandad's things and he was very secretive about them. He used to say that they could be a pension someday, now I come to think of it."

The silence lengthened between them, with Harry looking more and more uncomfortable as Beverly continued to stare at him, seemingly considering what she had learned. Finally, she spoke.

"I suspect that what Granda laid aside were things he thought would be worth a lot of money. I think they may have become even more valuable since he passed away. I also believe we should not open these sheds with so many people around. Let's keep this to ourselves for now and only investigate what is in there once we're on our own."

"What about Mark, Liam, Chris and Joe?"

"Yes, of course – and Sally too. I'm sure they can be trusted. Put the keys back where they were for now, Harry, and let's get back to the others before they come looking for us. I'd like to get the house emptied today. It's going to need a very thorough clean before we can move back in to live there."

After a couple of hours, the house was completely emptied except for some items of furniture and other things retained for domestic purposes. The vans transported the items to Joe's shed, and they were placed under lock and key, ready for selling at an auction to be arranged for the second Saturday following.

Inside the farmhouse, Mark had returned with two bottles of wine and the friends toasted the success of the day that had just ended. Neither Harry nor Beverly mentioned what they had been discussing in the farm kitchen.

CHAPTER 33

Sally drove back with Liam. He had haltingly invited her to ride with him. It was a lovely evening and on other occasions she might have enjoyed the walk, but this was much better. She stole a glance at the shy man that sat next to her and wished he would ask her out. Maybe she should take the initiative – ask if he would like to accompany her to the theatre or something? She had been given tickets for a performance of the local drama group. Perhaps that might be something she could suggest. Why did they both have to be so shy? As she ruminated over this, it surprised her to learn that he had said something. She had not heard him properly and had to ask him to repeat what he had said.

"It doesn't matter if you can't manage. I – I – I should never have asked you," he stammered. "It was stupid of me to think that you would want to go to that."

"Do what? I didn't hear what you said, Liam."

He cleared his throat and took a deep breath.

"I just wondered if you would like to go to the pictures tonight but if you're doing something else, I quite understand. Please forgive me if I have embarrassed you."

"No, no!" was all she could say.

"I shouldn't have asked you. It was a bit forward of me and I apologise for embarrassing you," he stumbled on before she interrupted him.

"I meant 'no', I'm not doing anything and yes, I would love to go to the pictures with you."

"You would? Are you sure? Could we go for a meal afterwards? Would you like that? When can I collect you?"

He might have babbled on, but Sally said she would like to do all of what he had suggested and would seven o'clock be OK?

Liam said it would be perfect and seemed to have difficulty not grinning from ear to ear for the rest of the journey.

She also smiled and looked ahead with growing anticipation to an evening she had longed for, ever since she had been introduced to the diffident but disarming man that was Liam Forbes.

Neither Sally nor Liam noticed Butch's battered old Land Rover parked in the lay-by adjacent to Joe's place, but Chris did. He was leaving to go home, having helped to unload Harry's last consignment and paused before accessing the main road. Butch was left in no doubt Chris had seen him. Butch cursed inwardly. He thought everyone had gone home, intending to snoop around Joe Burns' place to find out what had been going on. Now he would have to come back under cover of darkness. He slipped the vehicle into gear and roared away in a cloud of exhaust fumes.

CHAPTER 34

Chris wondered why Butch had been parked across from Joe's place. He appeared surprised to see he'd been noticed and even looked as if he was going to duck below the windscreen but managed to stop himself from doing so. He'd been up to something, sure enough, but what? He knew that Butch had done time for theft as well as a miscellany of other – usually violent – crimes. Harry's stuff was under lock and key, but he lifted his mobile and speed-dialled Joe's number once he had drawn into his own driveway and reported what he had seen.

Joe said he would keep a weather eye out for him during the night. He did not sleep much anyway, and security lighting would alert him to anyone prowling around. Chris offered to come over to keep him company, but Joe reminded him that he had a Sunday-morning show to cover and that he would be all right on his own. Butch's presence might mean nothing. What was the final figure that Liam had come up with he wondered?

Chris thought it was about £16,000 if Harry's estimations were reliable.

"It's amazing how he does that!" Joe remarked. "I hope it's accurate."

"Me too," Chris responded before ringing off.

He felt tired but decided to make a few more phone calls before making something to eat. Chris made five calls to various friends who promised to ring into his Sunday-morning show at predetermined times. This would be a feature of his weekday shows as well. He ticked off a list of names he would call later, briefing them on what he wanted them to say.

CHAPTER 35

Harry felt exhausted and decided to get off to bed early. Beverly had noticed the fatigue in him and suggested that he should get some shut-eye, as they would have an early morning at the homestead. They had spoken about what they needed to do next, with both agreeing that making the farmhouse habitable again was a priority. Mark had also asked one of the hotel cleaners to help out, after she had finished her work at the hotel.

As Harry drifted off to sleep, his final thoughts were about how foolish he had been in not realising that Grandad's store had been a conscious plan to select items which could be converted into cash. Hadn't the old man told him, time and again, that this was going to be a nest egg he could draw upon when he needed money? But all that had been on his mind, for as long as he could remember, was a preoccupation with music. It was his complete obsession and took precedence over all other interests. Now, all he could think about was antiques. How strange was that? They had replaced all interest in music, although he could still recall everything he had memorised over the years. He just didn't have any compulsion to learn anything new as far as music was concerned. His final thoughts were about Beverly. He pictured her now and smiled. She wasn't a raving beauty, but she was very attractive. He could understand why Mark was besotted with her, although he had kept this observation to himself. It was the way she tucked her chin in when she smiled that impish grin that also suggested she was someone who was fun to be with, someone that men would be attracted to.

Yes, he told himself, Bev was a breath of fresh air. She could brighten any room with her 'can do' attitude and organisational skills. How good was it that she had appeared when she did? He felt a bond with her which felt entirely natural and comfortable. She gave him a new sense of confidence and well-being that had been missing since Gran passed away. Feeling relaxed and contented, Harry slipped into a deep sleep and did not stir again until sunlight eased him awake the following morning.

CHAPTER 36

They had checked. It seemed sensible to do so, since neither Mark nor Beverly were entirely convinced that Harry's newfound powers could be relied on to be correct. She had taken snapshots of some of the more highly valued items and was comparing them to similar pieces they had identified in Mark's antiques guides and on the internet. All research confirmed that Harry had been unerringly correct in his identifications, if not always in the valuations. Some items were overpriced because they had fallen out of fashion, but others were much more than he had valued them. These were mainly oriental artefacts that had seen their value soar, probably because the guides Harry had memorised were several years old and also because of the burgeoning economic wealth of Chinese industrialists.

They enjoyed a companionable drink after that and spent some time discussing the day's events and plans for going forward.

Chris had phoned earlier and told Mark of his scheme for getting maximum interest in the forthcoming auction. His idea was simple, Mark told her. He would invite various people to phone in to his show following the daily round-up of events in the area. He would list all of them, including Harry's auction, and callers would ask questions about the event on the pretext that they wanted to know more about the items being offered for sale. It would be more subtle than that, of course, but that was the general gist of what he was planning.

An interview with Harry, concerning the hospice and his successful campaign to keep it open, would be another opportunity to lead the conversation onto the choicer articles to be offered for sale.

They had decided to offer the goods in two separate categories. The first would be the lower-priced articles, laid out in a car-boot-style fashion. These would be offered at a fixed price, with no haggling allowed. Only if a buyer wanted to spend more than £50 would a 10% discount be granted. All sales had to be in cash.

The more valuable antiques and collectible items would be sold by auction. Each would have a reserve. If that was not met, those items would be retained and sold to the trade. No telephone or internet bids would be considered.

Mark looked at Beverly and marvelled. Not only was she the most beautiful woman he had ever laid eyes on but also one of the sharpest operators he had ever known. Just now, with her legs curled up beneath her on the couch, a clipboard resting on her thighs, she scribbled ceaselessly in that animated way he had come to recognise when she became excited. He smiled wryly and wondered if she could ever care for him.

Lost in these thoughts, it took a minute for him to realise that she had said something and was awaiting a response.

"I'm sorry," he admitted, "I didn't hear what you were asking me."

"I was only asking how long you had been Harry's friend?" she obliged.

"Since we were in primary school, I guess. We've never fallen out and that is probably due to Harry's sweet nature.

He was always generous and kind, even as a child. He never sought the limelight while I was always drawing attention to myself. I was a bit of a show-off, I'm afraid. Often, I would get into fights with other kids, but Harry would step in to save me from getting thumped. He's not at all aggressive but very strong. The others would never pick a fight with him. He was just so popular with everyone because he always seemed to say or do the right thing if anyone was down or needed support. Sometimes I felt a little jealous when we were youngsters but only slightly. I was chuffed that he and I were best buddies."

"What about his absent-mindedness and apparent lack of worldliness?"

"It wasn't apparent until he was in primary seven or thereabouts. I'm not sure how it happened but it was about that time he discovered your mother had abandoned him as a baby. I don't think he learned that from your grandparents. The old man wouldn't enter into any discussion whatsoever with him over that. Grandad seems to have been particularly badly affected by your mum's departure. He was extremely fond of her and very bitter over her rejection of Harry. Neither would Gran say very much other than that your mother had not been very well when she left him behind. In those days, post-natal depression wasn't understood as it is today. It was after that, Harry seemed to become forgetful but preoccupied with music. I obviously don't know if any of what I'm telling you is true. It's just my take on things and might be completely unconnected."

Tears were streaming down Beverly's cheeks.

Without thinking, Mark rose and sat down beside her, placing an arm around her shoulders. She buried her face in his chest while sobbing uncontrollably. He held her tightly as he heard her mumble expressions of pity for Harry, because their mother had been unable to cope.

"I knew she wasn't well," she finally confided. "Mum spent long spells in various sanatoriums in Oz. I think she was suffering from manic depression. When she was OK, she was the most wonderful person you could possibly imagine but in her darker periods, she just withdrew from the world and cried a lot. She took her life when I was only ten."

Mark felt her cling to him more closely. He held her tenderly and listened attentively as she went on to tell him about her life in Australia.

Her dad had tried to make up for her mother's inability to care for Beverly and for this, she was grateful. He worked hard and had always been able to put bread on the table but obviously lacked the parenting skills a mother would have given naturally. Beverly had been a studious child, immersing herself in learning, possibly as a means of distracting herself from the unhappiness she felt whenever her mother was going through spells of depression or absence in the asylum. Her death left Beverly exposed and vulnerable. It was only because of the attentions of a childless female neighbour that got her through a very unhappy time in her life. This became even more crucial when Beverly's dad died in a road traffic accident. She was approaching her eighteenth birthday when it happened. The neighbour had taken her into her home and cared for Beverly during her time at university. It was only when she reached twenty-one that she learned about her mother's origins and the possibility of her having a brother back in the UK.

There hadn't been much money but the house they owned had been leased by the trustees of her father's estate, which had accrued a considerable sum over the years.

On attaining majority, the lawyer who handled her parents' affairs, met with Beverly to discuss the various options she now had and finally to pass over a letter that her mother had written for the day when she reached her twenty-first birthday. That was when she first discovered she had a brother. It had taken her some effort to come looking for him. All sorts of anxieties went through her mind before she plucked up enough courage to book a flight to the UK.

Not once did Mark interrupt as she continued to speak.

Coming to Britain, finding Harry and the fear of rejection had been an intolerable strain. Now, however, she could not be happier, since she had been accepted unreservedly by both Harry and his friends. She was going to do everything she could to make him happy, to get him back on his feet, to care for him. Confidentially, she told Mark that she had been instructing her solicitors to raise the money to clear Harry's debts and hoped to be able to do that with the house back in Australia offered as security.

When she stopped speaking, Mark realised she had fallen asleep. She must be drained, he thought, and had simply talked herself out. As she lay in his arms, he vowed that he would do everything in his power to keep her there. He wanted to have this woman as his lifelong partner but now might be too soon for him to make that known. He could not imagine how bad he would feel if she rejected him.

CHAPTER 37

She could feel William Wyllie's eyes upon her as she made her way to her desk. It was unusual for him to be in the bank before opening time as Sally had the task of opening the branch each morning. She could detect a movement at the window as he hurriedly closed the slats of the blind through which he was observing her approach. His welcome when she entered was equally unexpected.

"Hello, Sally. How are you today?"

She said that she was fine and hoped that he was too.

After some more inconsequential chatter that was totally alien to his normal behaviour, he finally got round to asking if she had been doing anything special at the weekend.

Indeed, she had, she thought to herself. Liam had taken her to the cinema and dinner afterwards. They also went for a picnic on Sunday. She felt a warm glow and might even have coloured slightly as she thought of it but was certainly not going to share that with Wyllie.

"Nothing special," she eventually responded, "just this and that."

"Only I thought I saw you at Harry Carey's place on Saturday?"

So that was what was on his mind, she deduced.

"Yes, that's right, Mr Wyllie. Along with some others, we were helping him to flit some stuff from his house so that he could move back in following the loss of his Portakabin in the fire."

"It's probably a bit late in the day for that. I think he should be looking for other accommodation considering his current position. Do you think he has found somewhere else to live?"

Sally said that she did not know if he had or had not.

"Let's hope he does find something soon, for his sake," Wyllie went on. "The bank will want him out as soon as possible. You'll know, of course, that he is unable to settle his overdraft and has only days before he will need to vacate the premises?"

She said that she had not realised that Harry's situation was as desperate as that, to see if Wyllie might inadvertently reveal some information that might be useful to know.

"When exactly does he have to vacate?"

"He has to redeem the loan before the end of the month. That's in just over three weeks from now, Sally. I know that you have been friends with him for many years now. I think it would be good if you would remind him of his obligations and ensure that the process is completed as smoothly as possible. It is always regrettable when something like this happens, especially to someone like Harold Carey but matters must take their course in such affairs, as you well know. My own position is, of course, under scrutiny with our superiors, so anything you can do to move things along would be appreciated."

Sally merely nodded and said that she understood.

Wyllie looked uncomfortable and clearly wanted to probe some more but instead told her that he would be going out to see a client later that morning, leaving her to speculate over, what had been for her, a most unusual conversation.

CHAPTER 38

They were holding hands when he entered the dining room. Upon his appearance, they parted like a pair of embarrassed adolescents.

Harry smiled knowingly. He wasn't the most observant man in the world but knew that his sister and best friend had developed an affection that had gone beyond mere friendship.

Mark got to his feet and began to stammer that he had something Harry should know. Beverly looked down at her cereal bowl and seemed uncomfortable.

"We have decided to go out together, Harry. For goodness' sake, what am I saying?" he went on. "What I mean is that Beverly and I... would like you to know that... we are very fond of each other and..."

"You would like to be an item, I think is what you are trying to say," Harry cut in. "That's marvellous. I think that everyone, even I, could see you were well suited – and you know how unobservant I am, Mark. I'm very happy for you both. Why wouldn't I be? My best friend and my only sister sharing affection for each other is something I heartily approve of!"

Beverly got up out of her chair and hugged her brother.

Mark, with a look of relief, shook Harry's hand, vowing he would take good care of Beverly for as long as he might live.

They were interrupted by a waitress, who, by her expression, was fully aware that Beverly's bed had not been slept in the previous evening. News travels fast in a country hotel, Beverly thought but did not care who knew.

Last night had been very special. Not only had she unburdened herself to Mark but had also come to realise that he cared about her as much as she had been attracted to him. He was someone that she felt safe and secure with. Someone she could rely on. They exchanged glances every now and again throughout breakfast, hoping that they were not causing Harry any embarrassment, but Harry reacted as if it was entirely natural and expected.

With breakfast over, the three of them, along with one of the hotel cleaners, who also had a knowing smile, made their way out to Mark's car. Armed with a stock of cleaning things, the quartet set off for the farmhouse.

The car radio was tuned to Chris's programme, and they hummed along to 'Flowers in the Rain'.

It had just finished playing as they entered the farmyard. Chris's familiar tones filled the car as he gave a rundown of the coming local events slot.

He gave a generous amount of time extolling the special auction and car boot sale that would be taking place in 'Joe Burns' Garden Centre'.

"What a great day out!" he prattled on. "All the items on sale will be selected from stock that Harry Carry has accumulated over the years. If you are looking for a bargain, that's the place to be a week on Sunday. You won't believe the variety of stuff on offer at bargain basement prices. You can also browse the plants and garden accessories on special offer in the garden centre. Take along the teenagers – there will be a disco for them – and for the younger ones, a bouncy castle will also be onsite. Never mind making lunch, mums – a barbecue will cater for both meat eaters and vegetarians. You don't want to miss this special day as it might not come around again for a very long time!"

They listened in some amazement in the car as Chris went on to repeat the time and place, the uniqueness of the event, stressing there would be plenty of parking at a very modest fee, etc., etc.

"Wow!" said Mark. "Chris has really pulled out all the stops on this one!"

They were to discover later that Chris had only started to whet the listeners' appetites. Half an hour later, a caller to the programme asked if this was the same Harry that had saved the hospice. The caller had, of course, been put up to this by Chris, who expertly steered the conversation onto the nature of the event and how stock had accumulated as Harry had unselfishly devoted his time to the cause.

"The items he will be selling should have been disposed of months ago. He needs the room and is offering items at bargain prices to give himself some space."

Once again, for those who had not heard it before, the date, time and attractions were repeated.

Another caller, some thirty minutes later, enquired about the antiques that might be on offer. He had borrowed Liam's list and rattled off a few items that he felt sure would whet the listeners' interest. Someone else wanted to know about the car boot sale and if they could take along their stuff to sell. Chris said that maybe in future they could arrange that with Joe Burns – but on this occasion, the goods on offer would be supplied exclusively by Harry Carry.

"And by the way, every separate article sold will have a unique number that might win the purchaser one of four £50 prizes to be drawn at the end of the sale day."

As the girls occupied themselves cleaning the house, the radio brought the news to them. Beverly could not stop herself from laughing as Chris persisted with his hard sell. To her, it was clear it was being stage-managed by Chris. She wondered if others would see through his strategy.

Mark had reluctantly returned to the hotel but was going to return in the afternoon with spare mattresses and some hotel bedding they could use if able to get the bedrooms ready that day.

Beverly thought of him now and felt a warm glow course through her body. It must have been a couple of hours after she fell asleep that she woke to find herself cradled gently in his arms. He had simply smiled at her in that tender way he had and suddenly they were kissing. He asked if she could ever care for him. She replied by suggesting that they might answer the question in another place. When he looked confused at this, she took his hand and led him to his bedroom. She felt it was the natural thing to do but surprised herself at even suggesting such a thing.

CHAPTER 39

When Wyllie left the branch, Sally decided to take the opportunity to do a little digging into Harry's bank account. What she discovered made her refer to other bank entries. Every time that Harry increased his borrowing, a similar sum of money was taken from another account in the name of 'Wiltris Enterprises'. This intrigued her, not just because of the coincidence in money movements, but also because she had never heard of the company that echoed Harry's borrowing patterns.

Things began to make more sense when she discovered who were Wiltris signatories.

So now she knew parts of the puzzle; who were involved but not why, when, where or how this affected Harry. She would keep digging and hope to unearth the other factors that might explain things. Maybe Liam could fathom it out?

CHAPTER 40

She had kept a discreet distance and continued past the café into which he had just entered. She was confident he had not seen her tailing him, but Ruth swung into a car park a few hundred yards along the road and followed the path that led back to the café on foot.

Tristram was up to something he did not want her to know about. She wondered if this might be an assignation with a woman. Treading carefully when she neared the café building, Ruth took care to ensure her approach could not be observed from any of the windows. A builder's truck parked nearby would give her some cover, so she made for it, finally peeping through the windows of the cab in order to scan the interior of the eating area, without showing too much of herself.

She quickly located Tristram sitting at a window table. He was leaning forward on his elbows looking earnestly at the person on the table across from him. Every now and again he would lean back, gesticulate dismissively and say something in that supercilious way she found so irritating. Who was he talking to? Now he was pounding the table, displaying the inherent aggression that seethed within him and was always simmering just under the surface.

A suited arm reached out across the table and grabbed his wrist. It belonged to William Wyllie, who had lunged towards Tristram. Wyllie was red-faced and glaring menacingly at Tristram. The two held each other's stare for a few seconds before Tristram visibly relaxed and leaned back in his chair. Wyllie also disappeared out of view and slowly retracted his arm. Tristram forced himself to relax. Ruth could see he was listening attentively, although still seething about having been treated like that by a mere bank manager. How could that be? Her husband would not have allowed someone like Wyllie to treat him in that way unless he had some hold over him. What could that be she wondered?

It was clear that she wasn't going to learn much from where she was but decided not to attempt getting closer to the building for fear of being discovered. She decided to return to her car and continue her surveillance of Tristram as unobtrusively as she could manage.

That it had not been another woman was a disappointment. She would have been overjoyed to have grounds for divorcing him. Tristram had some money that was paid to him as an allowance, which was not enough for either Tristram or herself to pursue the lifestyles they both believed to be their right. It was a loveless marriage which, less frequently now, involved sadomasochistic rituals. There was no affection in their couplings, but both exulted in giving and receiving pain. These encounters could be quite brutal and sometimes disfiguring but both were careful to ensure that the violence was inflicted where no one would see.

Lost in her thoughts, Ruth made her way back to the estate house, unaware that she had also been followed.

CHAPTER 41

Had she not been so preoccupied, Ruth might have noticed that Butch had been following her.

She might also have witnessed Harry jumping around in a state of excitement as she drove past the end of the road that led into the farmyard close.

Her tail did notice, however, and Butch decided to pull over to see if he could discern what had caused him to behave in that way. From his vantage point from the lay-by, he could identify three male figures congregated around the door of one of the outhouses. One was clearly Harry, and the others appeared to be the disc jockey Chris Collins along with that old duffer Joe Burns.

He had reason to dislike Burns for several reasons but the most recent was that he had detected him last night as he had been checking out the sheds in the garden centre. The old boy must have seen the security lights being triggered by his movements, had given a warning and then discharged a double-barrelled shotgun, shouting that another salvo would be following that if he found anyone skulking about his property. Butch assumed that the gun had been fired merely as a warning, but did not want to risk being peppered by lead shot and made a hasty escape across the fields to where he had parked the Land Rover in a thicket, just off a farm track. It was more important not to be linked to the trespass if he was not going to be associated with any past or future actions.

Back at the garden centre, Joe had scouted around the grounds and began to doubt that there had been any human intruder, thinking it might have been a fox or a badger that had triggered the security lights. A few seconds later, just as he was about to return to the house, he'd heard the distinctive cough of a beaten-up Land Rover that could only belong to one person.

Your suspicions about Jake Butcher were well founded, Chris, he thought to himself as he closed and bolted his kitchen door.

CHAPTER 42

It had taken a while to ease off the lock on the first shed. The others seemed to be equally stuck with disuse and the inevitable rust which had accumulated during the decades they had remained closed. A spray can of penetrating oil was applied, and the first door eventually opened.

"When were you last in here?" Joe enquired.

"Probably twenty years ago," Harry replied. "It was Grandad's place, and he was always very insistent that I should never go into any of the sheds unless he was with me."

"I remember wondering when he stopped keeping livestock and thought that it was a waste to have all this storage without anything to put into them," Joe remarked. "I could have done with the space at busy times as an overflow for some of the garden centre stuff, but he was quite insistent that he wouldn't have any space available for that. I didn't press it at the time but often wondered what he could be keeping in them. Looks like we're going to find out now."

The door finally yielded after some effort, squealing on protesting hinges as they forced it open. Cobwebs hung from the roof and a general covering of dust lay upon the canvas sheets, which covered various indistinguishable objects.

Hesitantly, they took tentative steps into the shed, brushing stray cobwebs before them as they went.

Harry found a switch that produced a weak light, only marginally better than the daylight which permeated from outside.

He stood in the only floor space available and marvelled at the amount of stuff stored in the shed. Joe could feel his indecisiveness but urged him to remove the canvas sheets to discover what they concealed, remarking that, whatever it was, great care had been taken to ensure a leaking roof would not damage the contents.

They decided to lift a large wooden chest outside. It would be easier to inspect in daylight while also providing more floor space when examining the other containers that filled the shed. It wasn't as heavy as they might have imagined. Once the chest was placed on the cobbled forecourt, Joe produced a knife to sever the baler twine that held the canvas covering in place.

The lid opened easily to reveal more waterproof coverings in the form of old oilcloth table coverings and waterproof clothing. When all were removed, a pile of boxes, neatly stacked to gain maximum storage, was revealed.

Harry gingerly removed one of the boxes and carefully lifted the lid. A layer of cotton wool concealed what lay beneath. Harry again removed the packing and passed it to Joe, who was bending over, intent on finding out what was inside the container.

It held a series of smaller boxes. Laying them on the lid of the chest, Harry carefully uncovered a pocket barometer inside.

Joe gaped as Harry went into memory mode.

"Late 19th-century gilt-brass aneroid pocket barometer, with an altimeter scale thermometer. Housed in a watch case with small mother-of-pearl compass – value about £450 – £550."

The next item was even more impressive. Once again, Joe was intrigued by the way in which Harry seemed to go into a trance before speaking in a tone he had never heard before.

"Early 19th-century mahogany cased two-day marine chronometer. Gimbal-mounted silver dial. McLachlan London – value £2,000 – £3,000."

With every new find, Harry behaved in exactly the same way until all the boxes were removed from the chest. Only when empty did he return to his normal speaking voice, Joe noted.

He waited some moments before addressing him.

"I'm amazed, Harry! How can you remember all that?"

Harry said it just seemed to come from within him without even trying.

"Have you any idea how much you valued all this stuff at?"

Harry shook his head.

"I stopped counting after you got to £25,000!" the old man informed him, a look of incredulity on his weather-beaten face. "If those other containers are as valuable as this one, you are sitting on a fortune here in this run-down old farmyard of yours. Your grandfather must have had a very good eye to have laid those aside for a rainy day. He must have been expecting a monsoon if this is anything to go by!"

The sound of a vehicle entering the yard halted further discussion. Chris was returning home from the morning show and was getting out of his car. He had a large grin on his face.

"What did you think of the plugs I got for your sale, Harry?"

When neither man spoke, he looked concerned until finally Joe told him about the contents of the chests.

On hearing the news, Chris grabbed Harry and then proceeded to prance around the farmyard with him in a jubilant dance of triumph.

Joe looked on, a wide grin lighting his grisly features and speculated about what else might lie behind the doors of the other sheds.

Beverly came out to see what the fuss was about.

When Mark drove into the close several moments later, they hardly noticed him arriving. He looked on enquiringly when they shared their news with him.

From the lay-by, Butch looked on with interest. What could be exciting them so much he wondered? What a pity Mark Brown might have seen him as he had driven past.

What the heck, he thought. *It's a free world. I have every right to be here. He probably didn't even notice me. His only interest these days seems to be in that Beverly woman, who has just arrived in the village.*

CHAPTER 43

Liam was waiting for Sally when she left work that night. She felt a surge of pleasure to see him parked across from the bank. He waved to her in that shy way he had and beckoned her to join him in the car.

As she made to enter at the passenger side, she saw Wyllie looking over in her direction but pretended not to notice. She leaned towards Liam and placed a kiss on his cheek. He smiled roundly at that but then became very grave as he stammered that, if she didn't mind too much, he would like to cancel their date for tonight – not because he wanted to he quickly added – but because Beverly had called an urgent meeting and hoped they could both attend. He would like to go out with her the following night if she wasn't doing anything else, though. Sally was relieved he wasn't shying off and immediately agreed to both propositions.

He would run her home, he said, and collect her again about seven o'clock, if that was OK with Sally.

She readily agreed and asked if he knew what it was about, with the request coming at such short notice.

"I don't know," he admitted, "but I was asked to take along the last will and testaments of Harry's grandparents."

Intrigued, they travelled on to Sally's house. She wondered if she should share the information unearthed at the bank but resolved to leave off doing so until later.

She was pleased to note that several of the neighbours observed her getting out of Liam's motor. That would give them something to wonder about, she thought, as she walked up the path to the front door of her parents' bungalow.

CHAPTER 44

So mousey little Sally Smith was dating Liam Forbes, Wyllie mused.

Good luck to them, he thought, as he reached for his mobile phone. There had been a text from Tristram Grant asking him to call back when he was sure any conversation would not be overheard.

Tristram answered on the third ring.

"What the hell took you so long to get back to me?" the angry voice enquired without preamble. "I texted you more than two hours ago!"

Wyllie struggled to ignore the petulance in Tristram Grant's tone, replying that unless he had forgotten, he still had the job of running a bank.

"What's the matter now?"

"Something important happened at Carey's place today. I don't know what it was, but they all seemed to be celebrating over something that happened in the yard."

"How do you know this?"

"Never mind about that. It doesn't seem the kind of behaviour you would expect from someone who was due to be made bankrupt."

Wyllie was quiet for a moment while he thought.

Tristram continued angrily, "That chum of his – the one that has the programme on local radio and has been bleating on about an auction they are going to hold on Sunday week in the garden centre – says that Carey will be offering stuff he's wanting to sell. They're clearly trying to raise as much cash as they can. Maybe they will be able to settle the debt before you can call it in. What the hell do we do then?"

Wyllie's head was reeling with everything he was hearing.

"I doubt that anything Harry Carey owns would fetch much," he cut in.

"How can you be sure? What about this group of friends he seems to be surrounded by? Would they come up with the readies if they are so chummy with him? Come on, Wyllie, you are supposed to be the financial brains behind this caper. You're not doing very well, are you? Isn't it time you got your finger out and got this thing settled once and for all? Don't forget how much we both have to lose if this thing goes belly up."

A plan that had been hatching in Wyllie's mind had now begun to crystallise.

"I think desperate times need desperate measures," he told him. "But that does not include you letting that Neanderthal you employ anywhere near Carey or his gang. I think I have a solution that will not just put paid to any moves Carey might make but also ensure he will not be around for very much longer."

"You don't mean to bump him off, surely? Even I would baulk at that, Wyllie!"

"Not extermination so much as becoming a guest in one of Her Majesty's prisons," he replied cryptically.

CHAPTER 45

The farmhouse kitchen was warm and welcoming. Harry could not remember feeling so comfortable and so much at home for ages.

The girls had done a marvellous job in bringing it up to scratch. The fresh smell of cleaning materials and the aroma of an evening meal still lingered throughout the house. A stale, musty smell issued from some of the rooms, but another couple of days of elbow grease would have it pristine throughout, he had been assured. Tonight, he would sleep in his own room in his own home and that made him smile even more broadly than before, when he realised that his grandfather's heritage might put an end to all of his money troubles. His reverie was interrupted by the arrival of Chris and Joe. Beverly had already greeted Mark, Liam and Sally and was showing them around the house. After the customary small talk, Beverly got down to business.

"Thanks for coming," she began. "Today has been a bit of a revelation. We haven't explored all the areas where Grandpa Carey stored his many acquisitions, but Harry has already identified that there are tens of thousands of pounds' worth of stuff in the first shed he and Joe opened this afternoon."

Liam and Sally gasped in unison. Unlike the others, this was news to them.

Following some questions and answers, mainly directed at Harry, Beverly steered the conversation back to why she had called the meeting.

"If, as we might reasonably expect, the antiques and collectibles that remain to be assessed are anything like the value that Harry has unearthed, we need to consider the following points. Liam, with Harry's agreement, I asked you to bring along the wills to establish – beyond all doubt – that Harry is the rightful owner of the artefacts that are stored here and in other places around the countryside. Is Harry the rightful owner?"

Liam confirmed that he was.

"Secondly, we should be aware that the value of these items will be above and beyond what local people will be prepared to spend on some of the more expensive articles. They will only be of interest to serious collectors with deep pockets."

Everyone agreed.

"Thirdly, your suspicions that the Portakabin was torched is of concern. It seems that someone was trying to break into Joe's hangar last night, where Harry's sale goods are stored."

Chris, Joe and Mark all nodded in agreement at this last revelation.

When Sally looked enquiringly, Joe voiced his suspicion that Jake Butcher might be involved.

"The fourth and final point is that we need to get everything moved to a place of safety just as soon as we possibly can. Somewhere that will provide safe storage if the remaining items are deemed to be as valuable as those we have already unearthed."

Liam was the first to speak and reaffirmed that all the heritable property of his grandparents' estate was legally

Harry's beyond any shadow of a doubt, providing he could provide proof of purchase.

"Show him the papers that you unearthed when you were rummaging through the stuff in the shed, Harry," Joe prompted.

He got up and handed an inventory that listed the goods stored in the first shed. Attached to the stock sheet was a bundle of receipts that corresponded with the entries, which Liam immediately recognised to be in Harry's grandfather's upright style. Although a little faded, the writing was quite legible.

Why, Mark wondered, had Harry never known about this?

Maybe it was because in those days, Harry could only think in terms of music. It occupied his every waking moment and obsessed him so much that most things simply passed him by unnoticed. It had led to him being chastised by the village headmaster on many an occasion for inattention in class. At other times, he would forget things within minutes of hearing or doing something. It was a source of amusement that he would cycle to the shops, but then walk home, leaving his bike outside the grocery store for several days, until someone reminded him he had left it there.

He was brought back to the present by Liam suggesting a secure storage facility that could fit the bill. Many firms, including his own, used them for storing confidential and legal documents. Liam would ask them if they could accommodate Harry's stuff.

Mark also felt that they would have to go further afield to sell some of the items and maybe the internet might be another means they could employ to access a wider spread of clients and specialist collectors.

Of greatest concern was the threat Jake Butcher posed.

"He's that creep Tristram Grant's gopher, isn't he?" Mark observed. "He's banned from every pub around because of his violent behaviour. We don't allow him into the Crown because of that."

Uncharacteristically, Sally found herself blurting out that she suspected Butch was merely a pawn, being used by Grant and Wyllie to drive Harry out of his home, then wished she had not been so indiscreet.

They all looked at her questioningly, but she would not say more, she told them, until she was able to confirm what she suspected.

The firm set of her jaw deterred anyone from pressing her further.

At ten o'clock, the meeting broke up. Beverly and Harry waved them goodbye from the kitchen door.

In the same clearing that Wyllie and Grant had observed the house clearance on Saturday, Tristram Grant watched with interest as he trained his binoculars on the scene below.

CHAPTER 46

Beverly was already out of bed. The smell of bacon reminded Harry of Sunday breakfasts, when Gran was still able to get about.

She looked up on hearing him enter the kitchen.

"How did you sleep?" she enquired.

"Like a top," Harry replied.

"Me too. There's something about this place that makes me feel I belong here."

"You do now," he said earnestly. "And I hope you will never leave, unless, of course, you want to. I don't want to lose you ever."

She smiled in a way that so reminded him of their grandmother. He wanted to hug her, but Harry, who wasn't the kind that displayed his emotions too openly, hesitated. Beverly, however, had no such inhibitions. Realising he wanted a cuddle, she threw her arms around him in a bear hug that made him gasp.

"You won't get rid of me ever," she promised him. "I'm going to be here forever, if you'll let me."

A movement at the window caught her eye. Old Joe waved as he made his way to the kitchen door. He entered breezily, declaring that he could easily manage a bacon sandwich if there was one available.

Talk centred around the previous evening's discussions as they drank coffee and ate breakfast.

"I was thinking," Joe began, "that we really need to get on with finding out what else you've got in those sheds. Seems to me there's a lot more to find, unless the rest is filled with rubbish – but I'll bet a penny to a pound, there's more valuable stuff there and I'm dying to know what else you've got. Besides, if there are valuables, others might want to pinch them. They should really be under lock and key in a more secure place than here."

Further discussion was interrupted by Mark's arrival with the cleaner.

When they came into the kitchen, he went straight over to Beverly and gave her a cuddle. The cleaner smiled knowingly but said nothing.

"I think it's time we got on with our chores," Joe remarked, winking conspiratorially to Harry as he did so. "Our two lovebirds might like to have some time on their own. It's almost ten hours since they last saw each other, after all," he observed sarcastically, with a cheeky smile on his face.

The cleaner tittered quietly before scuttling away to fill a bucket with water.

"I'll see you outside, Harry," Mark told him as he got up to leave. It was clear, however, that his chum's sister would receive more of his attention than his best friend of thirty years was likely to get today – or in the future.

Once in the yard, Harry and Joe selected the key that would unlock the third door and were pleased to discover that it was a lot freer than the first they had entered. Shed door two was still firmly stuck. Penetrating oil had been liberally applied to shed one the previous day and had been effective in releasing the decades of rust that had accumulated in the lock mechanism but shed two defied all attempts and remained locked.

Shed three revealed a similar scene to what they had confronted in the first shed. This time, however, Joe had equipped himself with a broom which he used to dispel the cobwebs that hung in great profusion.

This was a much larger area compared to the first shed. Once again, everything was covered in waterproof protective coverings. Some were made of canvas tarpaulins, while others were bits of old sou'westers, yachting sailcloth and the like. This time, the shapes they covered were not as regular in shape as the previous shed but vaguely resembled the outline of chairs and other bits of furniture.

"Let's get going then," Joe urged.

They began by removing the item nearest the door. It was quite light in weight and when the covers were removed, a brown wood table was revealed.

Harry went into memory mode on seeing it.

"A Regency rosewood- and satinwood-banded Pembroke pedestal table – circa 1820, value £1,500–£2,000," Harry informed Joe, in the tone he had come to expect from the previous day's valuations.

"I just knew that there would be more to find," Joe repeated. "Don't do another thing until I come back!"

He left Harry examining the table and made his way to where he had parked his truck, returning moments later with a long length of cabling attached to an inspection lamp.

"No need to hump all this stuff outside if we can get some light on the subject," he explained.

It took some time to unwrap the furniture in the shed. Great care had been taken to ensure that the passing years would not cause deterioration to the items which had been stored. Each discovery evoked the same reaction from Harry.

Joe looked on in astonishment as, without hesitation, his neighbour identified and put a price on whatever they revealed.

A rather grand mid-18th-century George II walnut- and feather-banded chest-on-chest, on bracket feet, estimated at between £6,000 and £8,000, contained an oilskin pouch. Once again, the contents of the pouch provided proof of ownership.

"To think that some of this stuff has been lying undisturbed since as early as the 1920s!" Joe exclaimed, pointing to an entry on the stock sheets. "I guess that a lot of this stuff became unfashionable and was bought for a song," he speculated. "This chest cost your grandad two pounds ten shillings according to this receipt. That's £2.50 at today's decimal conversion! Mind you, that was a week's wages back then – so I suppose it was a fair bit of money at the time! But you think it might be worth more than £6,000 now, Harry. I wish I'd had the old man's eye for a bargain. I wouldn't be stuck with a declining garden centre and a few acres that nobody wants."

"More goodies?"

Mark and Beverly were silhouetted in the door frame and Joe was first to respond.

"There's nothing in here that Harry has priced below £500. Some are several thousand! I kept a rough tally, and it amounts to well over £80,000 if my arithmetic is correct."

Mark emitted a long, low whistle at the news.

"You can almost clear all your debts from this shed alone, Harry."

"We will have to sell them first, though," Beverly observed.

"But that should be easy!" Mark replied.

"I wouldn't count on it! These items will have to be offered to a much wider market than just locally. I think we need a good quality digital camera and a website to attract the kind of buyers who would be willing to pay that kind of money."

Mark's mobile phone began to ring.

It was Liam with a message that he had located a secure warehouse that could take Harry's stock and proceeded to give details of charges.

"Book space in my name, Liam," he responded. "I'll cover the rental until Harry gets some money in, if that is necessary."

Liam replied that he had given his own firm's details, as they already held an account with the storage company.

"Listen, Liam, we need to move this stuff fairly quickly. Everything that Harry turns up is worth a lot of money – much more than we could ever have imagined – if he's right that is, but as you know he's been unerringly 'on the nail' with everything we've been able to check."

He listened carefully before ending the call, telling the others that Liam would arrange for everything to be uplifted and transported to the storage centre within the next forty-eight hours.

Beverly, clearly excited by the news, was also dying to tell Harry something.

"This might seem like small beer now," she began, "but the postman has just delivered some mail that suggests a few cheques have been sent back from the accounts that Sally and I sent out. I know that because they are the stamped addressed envelopes we sent out with the invoices. Would you like to open them now or later?"

"Later would be better," Harry replied. It was clear that he wanted to get on with finding out what the other locked doors concealed.

CHAPTER 47

Liam ended the call to Mark and contacted a removal firm. They would be able to move the stuff on Thursday, they confirmed.

He paused for a moment to review things.

Harry was clearly on his way to settling his debts but possibly stood to become a very rich man once all the artefacts had found buyers. What a piece of luck! There was no doubt he deserved it after all he had done to save the hospice and all he had been through since then.

Something wasn't right though, especially following what Sally had confided in him on their way home from the meeting.

Wyllie clearly had some ulterior motive in allowing Harry to rack up all that debt before suddenly insisting on its redemption at such short notice. Had his superiors noticed the level of borrowing and compelled him to call in the loan?

Who was behind this mysterious firm 'Wiltris' that seemed to have been mirroring Harry's borrowing? Was that a coincidence? His legal mind suggested otherwise.

Sally had been able to identify money movements out of the Wiltris account, which matched Harry's borrowing – but why?

Something Harry owned was worth a lot of money, he deduced, and must be tied up somehow with the farmstead.

Joe Burns, whose property adjoined Harry's land, had been trying to offload his place for about two years now, with no offers coming in from anyone, except for the derisory amount that Tristram Grant had offered.

Then it clicked! Wiltris was a name made up of the forenames of William Wyllie and Tristram Grant.

It was so obvious now that he thought of it, but could they really be that unsubtle? Perhaps, yes, as the chances of being detected would be very unlikely.

Were they a limited company? If so, the directors would have to be registered in Companies House.

The intercom on his desk buzzed and a female voice informed him that his clients were on their way up to see him. He would carry out some more investigations once he had dealt with them.

CHAPTER 48

Wyllie was getting annoyed. Where in hell had all the payphones disappeared to? He'd been driving around for ages and couldn't find any wherever he looked.

He needed to make the call where it could not be traced, so the bank phone was useless, as was his own landline or mobile phone. Payphones that took credit or debit cards were also best avoided.

The golf club! Why hadn't he thought of that before? They still had a payphone that accepted coins. It would also be relatively private at this time on a Tuesday and the phone was inside an antiquated booth that was virtually soundproof. Within minutes, he had driven to the clubhouse and entered the booth. No one was within earshot. Furtively, with trembling hands, he dialled the number scribbled in his address book.

A male voice answered on the third ring. "Her Majesty's Revenue and Customs," it informed him in what he took to be a Welsh accent.

"Put me through to the inspector's office, please," Wyllie requested.

Seconds later he was telling an inspector that he believed one Harold Carey – trading as 'Harry Carry Deliveries' had been involved in tax evasion. Wyllie then proceeded to give details of Harry's address but hung up immediately after the inspector asked him to identify himself.

Sweat stood out on his forehead. He dabbed his brow with the handkerchief he had used to cover the mouthpiece. A passing female golfer on her way to the ladies' room looked at him quizzically but carried on past without remark.

The phone did not take incoming calls, so Wyllie was not concerned about the tax office ringing back to enquire who had just been using the phone.

Although he wanted to distance himself as quickly as possible from the scene, Wyllie forced himself to drive slowly out of the car park.

CHAPTER 49

Cheques had been mailed by return of post, others delivered by hand, as Harry's financial problems had been widely discussed in the community. Some carried little messages of congratulations concerning Harry's efforts in saving the hospice from closure. Others apologised for the delay in settling the bill but pointed out that they had been reminding Harry to issue accounts for some time.

Beverly was touched by things some had written, and by the promptness of their response. Her brother was clearly highly respected and even loved by many of the local residents.

The biggest cheque by far was from the local auction house. Every load that Harry removed avoided them having to pay landfill charges. They had provided an itemised list of dates and times he had provided the service, which was much more than had been invoiced.

Meanwhile, Harry and Joe were joined by Chris, who was helping to list and price the items in sheds four and five. Every now and again, Chris could be heard to shout "How much?" followed by a John McEnroe impersonation of "You cannot be serious!"

Looking out of the scullery window, Beverly watched

them unwrapping and inspecting bronze figures, pewter and other metal items. There was also an occasional sword and other military artefact.

Sometime later, when they were going through the contents of the fifth shed, she could discern ceramic and other oriental items being handled with extreme care.

While this was going on, nobody, except Joe, was paying any attention to what was going on outwith the farmyard close. He absented himself, having first armed himself with a brass telescope and made for the house. Once inside, he asked Beverly if it would be all right to go upstairs to one of the bedrooms to give a better view of the woods that belonged to Tristram Grant. She came with him, curious to know what he wanted to discover from the vantage point.

Once more, the glint of glass from a clearing amongst the trees gave evidence of someone observing the scene in the farmyard through a pair of binoculars. Jake Butcher was the person that he picked out through the lens and as chance would have it, two other figures were seen approaching from behind. These turned out to be Tristram Grant and William Wyllie.

All three men engaged in animated conversation. Grant seemed to be the most excited of the three. He was waving his arms around, pointing at the farm and then wagging a finger in an aggressive manner at Wyllie. The latter appeared to take umbrage at this and made to grab Grant, but Butcher stepped between them and held Wyllie by the lapels. It looked like things might escalate into a fight, but Wyllie grabbed Butch's wrists and turned to walk away, mouthing something as he did so. Tristram went after him, with Butch in pursuit. They apprehended Wyllie between them, and an animated discussion ensued.

Joe was so engrossed by events he was observing that Beverly's request to have a look through the telescope went unheeded at first.

"Have a good look at those three faces, Beverly," he advised. "It may be entirely innocent, but I'd bet a pound to a penny that they are behind Harry's current problems."

"Who are these men?"

"That big dollop of lard in the business suit is William Wyllie, the bank manager that called in Harry's loan. The one that looks like a thug is Jake Butcher, who I think was the one skulking about my place on Sunday night. He's a violent, unpredictable character that's been in and out of jail for several cases of assault and some burglary as well. The third, weedy-guy, that looks like something out of a Boris Karloff film, is Tristram Grant. He owns the estate that lies across the road from Harry's farm and my place."

"What do you think they are arguing about?"

"I don't know but just before I gave you the telescope, Butch had been watching what Harry, Chris and I had been up to down below."

"Could there be something about your two places that would be interesting them?"

"It seems very likely," Joe conceded, "but what? Let me have another look."

He was just in time to see the trio departing, Grant still gesticulating and Wyllie shaking his head emphatically as they made their way out of the clearing, with Jake Butcher following behind.

"I think the sooner we can move the stuff in the sheds, the better," Joe advised. "I think the others should be told about this as soon as possible."

The opportunity arose sooner than they might have imagined, as first Mark arrived to take the cleaner home and then Liam, who had Sally riding beside him in his car.

Before they could get downstairs, Chris had already launched into a long and loud account of what they had uncovered in the sheds. He finished with the possible value of the things they had uncovered which he had totalled up to well in excess of £100,000.

They all gasped in astonishment except for Harry, who seemed to be trying to get his head back from wherever it had been.

"Let me tote up what we've uncovered so far," he intervened. "Sheds four and five, the ones we've just finished, hold about £105,000' worth. Shed one is around £35k and shed three is about £82k – that's £222,000 by my reckoning!"

"And we haven't been able to get into shed two yet!" Joe observed.

They all speculated as to what it might hold but grew silent at the arrival of the cleaner, struggling into her coat as she came towards them.

"Sorry," she said to Mark. "I didn't mean to keep you waiting – only I was waiting for a load to finish in the washing machine. What a racket that old thing makes when it's going through the spin cycle. I never heard you arrive." They all looked relieved at this admission and individually resolved not to be so indiscreet with their discussions in future.

Mark seemed reluctant to leave but bundled the cleaner into his car, saying he would return just as soon as he had driven her home. The others waved him away, then made for the house, with Joe making sure that all the shed doors had been locked, before also following them into the kitchen.

Harry, he noticed when he got there, seemed to be more his old self. The memorising phase and almost trancelike state he went into when identifying and valuing the artefacts seemed to drain him. He sat in what had been his grandmother's chair, listening absent-mindedly to the babble the others were making around him. Cups of tea and coffee were consumed as they continued to discuss the implications of what had been discovered regarding the valuations.

Joe decided to wait until Mark returned before sharing what Beverly and he had witnessed through the telescope.

CHAPTER 50

Wyllie was shaking with anger as he drove from the Grant estate.

A trail of gravel and dust flew out behind as he sped along the driveway. He almost ran in front of a passing lorry as he made to join the main road.

It was enough to make him realise he needed to be more in control of his faculties, and drew into the side for a moment to compose himself. He glanced in the rear-view mirror and was alarmed to see that the nervous twitch, which always accompanied periods of anxiety, was very rapid and pronounced. *That's why I lost so much at poker,* he realised. *Everyone can tell when I'm uptight.*

Wyllie had been severely provoked by Tristram. The characteristic sneer that always adorned the latter's face, suggesting that everything around him had an unpleasant smell, was symptomatic of the man. Always immaculately dressed but in a way that smacked of Beau Brummell, he nevertheless gave the impression of a creature of the night. Perhaps the jet-black mane, plastered with oil to ensure that not a hair was out of place, added to the illusion. The suspicion that it regularly received the application of hair dye suggested a preoccupation with being completely in control as to how he should be perceived by lesser mortals. And those dark eyes that bore into you only served to emphasise the impression that this was someone who would stop at nothing to get what he wanted. He was clearly unhinged and completely unpredictable. Despite having attended 'quality' public schools, he did not possess much intelligence. That could be due to centuries of inbreeding, Wyllie speculated.

If it had not been for Jake Butcher, he might have strangled him.

What was he thinking? Grant had that effect on him, especially when he criticised what he had been doing with regard to the tax authorities. His impatience was bound to lead to their downfall but how could he stop him from doing something reckless and ill-thought-out? As long as that Neanderthal Butcher was protecting him, anything might happen. He would try to hurry HMRC along and once again drove off in the direction of the golf club to access the public phone to make another call before returning home.

CHAPTER 51

The room went quiet as Mark entered the kitchen.

"So, tell me what has been happening," he invited.

Beverly indicated that he should sit next to her on the couch.

Chris was first to speak.

"We've been adding up the valuations Harry has done so far, and it looks like he's sitting on almost £250,000 if he's correct with his valuations. Mind you we've checked out a few on the internet and it seems that some are undervalued – particularly the Chinese stuff. It's gone through the roof in the last decade. I think the prices that Harry memorised were taken mainly from your reference books, Mark, and they date from around 1980."

Beverly cut in at this point. "Some of the stuff is too specialised and pricey for local collectors. They will need to be placed with specialist auction houses and dealers. Only some of the items we've unearthed might find a buyer locally."

"There's still the second shed to investigate," Chris reminded them. "And what about the other places that your grandad stashed stuff? How many of them are there?"

"I can think of another seven stores," Harry informed

them. "Four are garages just off the council housing estate and the other three are on local farms."

"Can you remember what's in any of them?"

"The garages are mainly leftovers from local sales that he stored there until he had had an opportunity to sort through them. It's mainly cardboard boxes, filled with stuff people had put up for auction, but nobody wanted. If stuff like that was not sold after three consecutive sales, we were paid to take them away, to prevent them going to the rubbish dump. Granda didn't like to throw anything away until he had checked the contents of the bags and boxes but there never seemed to be a time when that actually happened."

"Do you think they might contain any valuables?" Chris enquired.

"I have no way of knowing," Harry admitted. "Around that time, I was only interested in music. Nothing else seemed to matter. Now all I can think about is learning as much as I can about antiques."

"Don't you remember anything?" asked Mark.

"Well, it mainly happened after the car accident. You remember more than I do about that, Mark."

Everyone waited to hear what Mark had to say.

"I don't think I'm saying anything Harry would not want me to tell you," he began, "but up until the time that your grandfather rolled the van with you in it, you were, how can I put it, quite normal?"

Beverly looked at him enquiringly.

"What I mean," he went on, "was that Harry was just like you or me. He didn't have the ability to memorise music or anything else, for that matter. The accident happened on a frosty morning. Harry was knocked unconscious, and it was several hours before he came to again.

"He was clearly shaken up and for days seemed to be

walking about in some sort of stupor. All he was interested in was music. Old Doctor Smith assumed it was down to the trauma caused by the accident. Whatever it was, Harry's personality changed, and he was never the same person I had known since we were children. I don't mean he wasn't the same considerate, generous person he had always been, only that he was less aware of things going on around him. I sometimes noticed that he was unaware of people's moods or reactions to things that were said. I often wondered if that was due to that bang on the head, Harry. It seems too much of a coincidence that you are now obsessed with antiques rather than music, especially since suffering another head knock."

Beverly listened with interest and then asked if Harry could remember any of what Mark had just told them.

"Not much," he admitted. "I do remember hearing Mark suggesting that I should be getting into antiques when I was lying in hospital. Ever since then, I've felt compelled to find out all I can about them."

"What about the recording you are always listening to when you go to bed?" she enquired. "Have you always had it?"

"No, that was something that came from the house I was emptying when I fell down the stairs."

"I thought it was music that you were listening to but the other night I looked into your room to say goodnight and you had fallen asleep. All I could hear was a man's voice speaking in a creepy way that made me think it was a hypnosis programme you were listening to."

"Maybe it is," Chris suggested. "Where is it now, Harry?"

"Upstairs in my bedroom. It calms me and helps me sleep."

Beverly asked if she could get it down for them all to hear what was on the recording and went to get it. The disc was played on the CD player of Mark's radio, which he had taken with him when they went to clean the farmhouse. After a few minutes, the trancelike monotone, accompanied by a variety of subliminal sound effects, provided answers to Harry's newfound powers. The recording was full of suggestions that he would develop a powerful memory on any subject he cared to recall.

Mark looked at his friend and noted that Harry had already slipped into what seemed to be a trancelike state. Should he switch the recording off and if he did so, how would it affect him? His indecision was interrupted by Chris who immediately pressed the pause button, which drew an almost immediate response from Harry. He simply opened his eyes and looked about questioningly.

"Did I fall asleep?" he asked self-consciously as everyone was staring at him.

"Sort of," Beverly told him in wonderment. "I believe you were hypnotised, Harry. That tape seems to be the reason why you are preoccupied with antiques."

A lot of discussion ensued while they debated what this might mean and whether they should seek medical advice. It was agreed they should contact the family of the man who had lived in the house Harry had emptied.

Further thought was interrupted by Joe.

"Beverly and I saw something you should know about," he informed them. "When you were emptying the sheds, I took the telescope you found, and we looked at the wooded area across the main road that forms part of the Grant estate. Who was keeping a watch on the place but Tristram Grant, Wily Willie and Jake Butcher. They had a set of binoculars trained on the yard below and seemed very interested in what you were doing," he said, looking at Chris and Harry.

"What's more," he went on, "they seemed to fall out. Wyllie made for Grant, but Butcher grabbed him and shook him up a bit. They left soon after, but it was clear they had fallen out over something. Butcher stayed behind for a while and kept surveillance on the farmyard, until Mark arrived. We came downstairs then. I don't know how long he remained there."

"They are clearly interested in what we are doing," Chris concluded.

"But why?" Mark queried.

"I don't like any interest that those two might have in our places," Joe responded. "Ever since Tristram Grant offered to buy me out, I have had the feeling that there's more to it than just the garden centre he's interested in. Now Wyllie's calling in Harry's loan. His place is no better than mine. What have we got that could be worth much of anything? Between us, we might have some three hundred acres of poor agricultural land that's only fit for light grazing. It's a mystery to me!" he concluded.

Liam was next to speak.

"Maybe not so valueless as you might imagine, Joe." He looked at Sally before continuing. "I've been doing some digging, following some things Sally discovered."

Sally looked flustered at this and coloured as she said, "I hope you don't think that I'm being indiscreet, but when I discovered that Grant and Wyllie were in cahoots and trying to keep that secret, I decided to see if I could find out why."

"And what did you discover?" asked Mark.

"I'm not sure," she replied, "but Liam will tell you more."

"It seems that Harry's loan was underwritten by a company called Wiltris. Every time Harry drew out money, Wiltris lodged a similar amount in their account."

"Who are Wiltris?" Mark enquired. "I've never heard of them before."

"That's because they would not want to advertise their presence," Liam told them. "If you care to think about the name, you might be able to deduce who the two main shareholders are?"

As recognition dawned on their faces, only Harry seemed confused.

"Wiltris is a combination of William and Tristram," Liam explained.

They all grew silent as each absorbed what Liam had told them.

"So, they are after Harry's place as well as mine," Joe concluded. "But why?"

"I'm not sure yet but I think it may have to do with the fact that a planning application has been submitted for the land on which your two properties are situated. I could not get access when I called the council to enquire about it. They tell me it will be available upon my return from London."

"Is it made in the name of Wiltris?" asked Mark.

"No, it's a property development firm which has made an application to develop the area your farms occupy. It's a mix of industrial and commercial units and includes shopping malls as well."

"Who would want to do that here in our little village?" Chris queried. "It's got nothing going for it in that respect."

"Just consider this for a moment, Chris. How far are we from the motorway here? Maybe five miles by second-class roads but if you think of it as the crow flies, it is less than half a mile. Joe's and Harry's fields stretch three quarters of the way there and the land between your fields and the motorway belongs to—"

"The Grant estate?" Mark offered.

"Correct!" Liam confirmed.

"If he could acquire your land, he would be able to develop the whole area," Joe voiced, although everyone had come to the same conclusion.

"But how can you apply for planning permission if you don't own the land?" Mark wanted to know.

"It is an area specified as being suitable for commercial development in the 'Local Area Plan'," Liam obliged. "You do not have to own it to put in for planning permission. Not many people know that but clearly Wiltris does, and I suspect that this is the reason why they have lured you into this situation, Harry."

"Tell me again," Beverly insisted. "Why would anyone want to build an industrial complex here?"

This time, Mark obliged. "With a connecting road to the motorway, this would be an ideal site for any firm wanting to service the conurbations, all of which are virtually within twenty miles of where we are sitting. There would be little or no opposition from the village residents because your places are sufficiently far enough out of the town to discount any objections by local people. Am I correct in thinking that, Liam?"

He nodded before Mark continued. "Knowing how desperate the council is to encourage investment, I believe it would be voted through on the nod. It would be the end of the town as we know and would inevitably lead to a spate of house building to accommodate the personnel that would be required to work in the industrial park. Good business for you, I guess, Mark, but probably the death knell to the local shops and businesses that eke out a modest living here."

A silence fell over the room as each pondered the implications of what Liam had told them.

"Well, they won't get my place as long as I have breath in my body," Joe vowed.

"Nor mine, if I can help it," Harry affirmed. "This place is special to me and if I can, I'd like to keep it that way."

Everyone cheered at hearing this. Harry looked a little

discomfited at having said what he did, unaccustomed as he was to expressing emotion in such a public way.

Once again, a hush fell over the room until Chris addressed Liam.

"What can we do to prevent this happening?"

"We need to raise the money to clear Harry's loan. With a bit of luck, we might just make it. Sally tells me that there is already a large amount of money coming in from the bills that she issued."

Beverly, who had been checking her emails, got to her feet and said, "I have some news for you all. Mark knows a little bit about it, but it has just been confirmed. I've transferred some money from Australia which has been deposited in a bank in the next town. It's not Wyllie's bank, I made sure of that. Anyway, there will be a banker's draft made out to an account in the name of Harold Carey for the sum of £150,000, which, along with Harry, I intend to deposit on Monday morning, Sally. I've also taken the liberty of opening an account with the other bank in your name, Harry, and will be inviting you to transfer all your future earnings there. I hope that is OK with you?"

Once again, emotion overcame him, and Harry found that tears had filled his eyes. He couldn't find the words to thank her but instead got to his feet and clasped her to him. The others looked on with smiles on their faces.

"I'll repay you just as soon as my money comes in," Harry vowed.

"I think things might be sorted," Joe remarked.

CHAPTER 52

The following morning, Mark and Beverly set off to collect the banker's draft that would settle Harry's account. Armed with the cheques that had arrived, the new account that Beverly arranged would see a healthy inflow of almost £7,000.

Minutes after they had left, two men in business suits drove into the yard but finding nobody there, looked around the farmyard before departing again in their car.

The necessary procedures completed at the new bank, brother and sister returned with the banker's draft.

"I don't know how to thank you for this, Beverly," Harry began. "Mark tells me I'm not very good at expressing my feelings, but I hope you understand how grateful I am that you have done this for me. I'll pay you back, of course – every penny and then some more!"

"Of course, you will, Harry, but I'm not looking to make anything out of this. It's the least I could do. You would have done the same for me, I'm sure."

"I would," was all he could say.

Sally was on duty and had just finished dealing with a customer when they arrived. She seemed a little nervous but immediately set about processing the banker's draft. As soon as the transaction had been completed, she set about closing Harry's account. When satisfied that she had dealt with everything correctly, she asked them to wait for a moment while she called the manager. She lifted the desk phone and was heard to say, "Mr Wyllie, I have Mr Carey at the counter. Could you please come through? I need your signature to confirm that I have processed some transactions correctly."

Wyllie appeared within seconds, a look of apprehension on his face.

"What transactions are these?" he enquired.

"Mr Carey is closing his account with us," she informed him.

"But he can't do that," he blustered. "What are you thinking of? He owes the bank in excess of £150,000."

"That's right," Sally replied, "but his sister has just settled the debt with this banker's draft and Harry has paid the outstanding interest with Miss Smart's debit card."

"What banker's draft and what debit card payment?" he demanded.

"Why, this one, Mr Wyllie," she replied politely, pointing to the relevant transactions. "I just needed you to confirm that my calculations of the interest owing on the account are correct."

Colour drained from Wyllie's florid features, while the nervous twitch beneath his eye went into overdrive.

When he did not reply, Sally spoke again.

"I take it that you are in agreement then, Mr Wyllie. Please countersign here," she requested.

He could barely manage to scrawl his name on the proffered documents but did so in what seemed to Beverly a state of shock.

When he had finished signing, she looked him squarely in the face and said, "I take it that this transaction now finalises matters, Mr Wyllie? I would not like to think that we will be hearing from you again, especially since you seem to have broken several banking codes by allowing my brother to become so indebted. We do expect to receive written confirmation of these transactions by registered post. Please do not ignore this request."

Wyllie did not reply but simply returned her stare, fully aware that this was not a request he had received but an ultimatum.

Beverly and Harry left the bank without looking back as Wyllie stood dumbfounded by what had just occurred.

If they had looked back, it would have been to see Sally Smith pretending to shuffle some papers at another desk, her face wreathed in smiles. She did not hear Wyllie departing until a slamming door bore evidence he had left the retail area and had returned to his lair.

CHAPTER 53

It took all of half an hour for Wyllie to regain enough composure to telephone Tristram Grant.

"Something's happened," he informed him. "We need to talk, and urgently."

"Good news, I hope?" came the query from the other end.

"No, quite the opposite, Tristram. I'm afraid we're scuppered!"

Grant's fury was palpable.

"What do you mean by that?"

"Nothing I can talk about here. Only know that Carey's loan has been redeemed in full. Where and when can we meet?"

"I'm out of town just now," came the reply. "Tonight, seven o'clock at the golf club."

Grant rang off before Wyllie could continue the call.

CHAPTER 54

"I would have loved to have seen his face!" Mark said when he heard about their encounter with Wyllie. They were having coffee in the Crown. Beverly looked at her brother fondly as she went on to explain the new banking arrangements and their plans for the rest of the day.

"We have a locksmith coming to see if he can help us gain entry to shed two – the one we haven't been able to access yet. He should be with us in half an hour. I guess we should be making tracks," she said with some reluctance.

They hadn't been alone together since the first night they had shared Mark's bed, and she longed to feel his arms around her once more. Mark, it seemed, felt the same as he held her for much longer than was customary for a goodbye kiss.

"Let's go out somewhere, just the two of us tonight," he suggested.

She replied that she would like that and asked him to call when he managed to get free from the hotel.

The locksmith arrived early and had parked in the yard, awaiting their arrival. He quickly set to work and soon opened the reluctant locks. There were two keyholes on the door.

"There must be something very important in here," he

mused as the door squealed in protest when pulled open. "Just look at the thickness of the door and the reinforcements that have been added on the inside! What do you keep in here to make it such a secure area?"

Beverly thanked him but did not respond to his question. She instead asked how it could be locked again once they had looked inside.

"I'll have to dismantle the locks to service them and maybe make a couple of new keys for that to happen," he informed them. "I'll do that now. I've got the tools in the van. It'll cost extra, of course."

Beverly said that would be fine and to please go ahead.

When she turned around, Harry had already made his way into the shed and was looking around for a light switch.

Every wall was clad in cement rendering, she noticed. The walls and roof had also been finished that way, probably to make it wind, fire and waterproof.

"Let's wait until we're alone before having a proper look," she suggested to Harry.

He nodded reluctantly and made to leave. Anything that Beverly suggested was clearly the right thing to do. He trusted her implicitly.

As they went outside, Joe Burns arrived. He had walked through the fields.

"I see you've managed to gain entry then?" he observed.

CHAPTER 55

Chris arrived just as the locksmith was leaving. Beverly, Joe and Harry were standing by the door to shed two as he brought the car to a halt.

"Wait for me," he cried as he leapt from the car.

Joe held the keys, as he had stayed with the locksmith while he worked on the locks and serviced the mechanisms.

Gingerly, they followed behind Harry, who led the way into the concrete cell. He was itching, as they all were, to find out what the space contained.

Beverly fetched an inspection lamp that they connected to the power supply in shed number three, as there was no electric light in shed two.

The walls had slotted angle shelving of the type that would be found in a warehouse. The shelves were packed with pottery and glass items, some of which twinkled back at them from the reflected beam of the lamp. Almost immediately, Harry went into memory mode.

Chris started recording Harry's assessments on a clipboard as he went along the rows. None of the items were valued at more than £500, with the majority being in the £60 to £80 bracket. It seemed a bit of an anticlimax, and Chris said so.

After about half an hour, Harry had covered every item in the lock-up except for the contents of a chest that occupied the centre of the floor.

Could it contain the main item of value, they wondered but dared not say so. The chest, when opened, was lead-lined and 'weighed a ton' according to Joe, who had tried to move it.

The interior only yielded another smaller container about the size of a jewellery box. Beverly reached inside and handed it to Harry. It did not weigh much and the contents could not be inspected because it was also locked. While the others speculated what it might contain, a faraway look came into Harry's expression.

Chris noticed first and asked Harry what he was thinking.

"I think I know where the key might be," he told Chris, and with that, left the shed with the others in tow, the casket under his arm.

They followed him into the house and upstairs to the bedroom, which Beverly occupied. Harry handed her the box, before going over to the brass bedstead where he removed the right-hand finial.

It came away from the bedhead. A series of keys were attached on a long brass chain. Intrigued, the others looked on as he selected a key from the bunch and inserted it in the lock of the casket. It opened easily.

The only thing the box contained was a thick envelope, addressed to Harry.

CHAPTER 56

Chris was first to speak, suggesting that they should leave Harry alone to open the package. Harry, however, asked Beverly to stay.

With shaking hands, he passed the envelope to her and she held it for a moment wondering what to do.

"That's Grandad's writing," he said at last. "Will you open it for me?"

She looked at him searchingly before nodding and finally breaking the seal.

She offered it back to him, but Harry declined.

"Please read what's in it."

Moments passed before Beverly emptied the contents on the bedcover.

Some photographs tied in a pink ribbon along with a baby bangle and strand of blonde hair lay alongside a couple of pages of blue writing paper. They did not have time to examine the contents further, however, as a shout came from Chris, calling for them to come downstairs, as they had visitors.

Reluctantly, they made towards the door, but Beverly first placed the contents of the package in a drawer in the bedside cabinet.

Standing in the kitchen were two dark-suited men.

They immediately announced that they were from Her Majesty's Revenue and Customs, investigating allegations that Harold Carey had been evading paying taxes. As usual, Harry was unable to respond. Beverly was first to speak.

"I am Harry's sister," she began. "I'm sure there has been some mistake…?"

The taller of the two officials told her that they could only discuss their business with Harold Carey and enquired where he could be found.

"I'm here," Harry told him, "and my sister Beverly is now handling all of my financial affairs."

Joe and Chris, who had been looking on, made to leave but Harry invited them to stay.

The tax inspectors exchanged glances before the taller one spoke.

"I must warn you that tax evasion is a serious offence, Mr Carey. We will be requiring to examine all the financial records relating to your business activities. Are you sure that you want others to know about such matters?"

Harry nodded.

"I'll be happy to provide you with everything you need, gentlemen," Beverly informed them. "Please tell me what you require, and we can deal with your queries right away. I only arrived here a couple of weeks ago but have started to bring my brother's financial affairs up to date. What makes you think that Harry has been cheating on his taxes?"

The smaller of the two men said they had received an anonymous telephone call and were obliged to investigate any allegations as a matter of procedure.

"Please come with me," she invited and led them to the dining room, where various papers were lying in folders on the dining table and other surfaces throughout the room.

"What do you need to see first?" she enquired.

Harry had followed her through but then asked if he could be excused as both men sat down to examine the folders they had requested. As he left, he heard Beverly explaining why his affairs had become so disordered. Both Chris and Joe were waiting expectantly outside.

"I'll bet Grant and Wyllie are behind this," Joe speculated.

Chris nodded in agreement.

"It's lucky for you Beverly turned up when she did," he added.

Further discussion was interrupted by the sound of a furniture van arriving in the yard. Three men got out of the cab and asked where they could collect the goods that had been ordered by a Mr Forbes.

Harry asked them to wait while he went to collect the keys from beneath the draining board and returned in seconds with them jangling by his side. The arrival of the van had alerted the inspectors that something was happening outside, and both came out to investigate.

"What is happening here?" the taller one wanted to know.

Once again, Beverly intervened.

"The contents of these sheds are going into a store. We have just come to realise that they are quite valuable and need to be in a secure place until we decide what we are going to do with them."

"And who do these goods belong to?" queried the smaller of the two inspectors.

"They belong to my brother. They were left to him in our grandfather's estate."

"Do you have proof of this?"

"As a matter of fact, we do," she replied with some emphasis. "There is a copy of the wills of both grandparents, which we accessed quite recently. Our solicitor, Liam Forbes, located them only last week."

"Are these items specifically mentioned in the wills?"

Beverly hesitated for a few seconds before replying.

"No, not in the wills but each item is listed on stock sheets, along with receipts, specifying the dates, prices paid and the sellers' names and addresses."

"Could you show me these, please?"

Harry indicated that they should follow them and proceeded to open the first shed. He produced the wallet that held the information they required and handed it to them.

"The other sheds hold similar records," Beverly put in.

The inspectors exchanged glances and asked to see them also.

When they had finally inspected each area, the two men asked that the removal firm should provide them with details of what would be uplifted and the destination of the items. They also telephoned Liam's office to make an appointment to see him, following confirmation that he had arranged for the goods to be moved. They also asked that he provide them with sight of the original wills, which he kept on file in his archives. Another call confirmed that the items would be stored in a lock-fast area in the repository where the antiques were to be taken.

Having satisfied themselves that no items were being unlawfully removed, the inspectors returned to the farmhouse, with Beverly offering a cup of tea or coffee.

They left later that afternoon, stating they might have to return but gave a cautious opinion that no intentional attempt to defraud HMRC had been detected. The value of the artefacts being stored might be subject to estate duty, however, they stated before departing.

Joe, Chris and Harry oversaw the packing and loading of the contents of the sheds. The removal men had come prepared.

Items were carefully packed into containers, with their contents listed on the outside of each storage box.

While this was going on, Harry seemed distracted. A worried frown beset his normally unemotional expression. Both Chris and Joe noticed and wondered what information the box found inside the chest contained.

After the inspectors left, Beverly beckoned for Harry to return to the farmhouse. Joe and Chris waited outside, pretending to be busy tidying the yard, although both were intrigued to know what was about to unfold.

CHAPTER 57

She had already retrieved the package and its contents when Harry entered the kitchen.

"Thanks for dealing with that for me," Harry began. "Are they satisfied that I wasn't trying to diddle them?"

"I think so," she replied. "But tax inspectors are a very distrusting breed, and they will no doubt want to pick up on something we've overlooked. You know how they are. They need to justify their existence."

Another silence ensued before Beverly suggested they should examine the packages' contents.

First, she spread some pictures out on the table. They were photographs of their mother, taken at various times from childhood up to adolescence. Some were group pictures, which appeared to be taken at various events like school picnics and other social gatherings. Several photos featured her with their grandfather and grandmother.

Beverly was fascinated. These were photographs of her mother at different stages in her life, along with the grandparents she had never known. She stole a glance at Harry to see how he was reacting to the images. Tears streamed down his cheeks. She felt her stomach contract with the emotions both were experiencing as they looked upon their forbears, captured in a different time and in different circumstances. She noticed, too, how her mother was always clinging to her father. There seemed, Beverly imagined, a strong affection between the proud father and his young daughter.

"Shall I read the letter, Harry?" she enquired, at last.

He merely nodded.

My dear Harry,

I have never been able to tell you just how much you mean to me. I realise now that it was because I loved your mother too much. She was everything to me and it all turned sour when she became pregnant. I had such high hopes for her. It was as if my heart had been ripped out of me when we learned you were expected, with no father to give you a name.

Later, after you were born, when she could not take any more of my recriminations and left you with us, a defenceless suckling child, it was more than I could bear. My heart hardened against her, and I resolved (foolishly, I now realise) never to allow myself to love anyone as much again. Following the hurt that your mother caused with her departure and abandonment of you, I could not bring myself to forgive her. Now, of course, I would welcome her back if ever she returned.

Granny told me it was a medical condition called 'post-natal depression' that afflicted her and that she could not help being the way she was. I understood all that but still could not allow myself to extend the love to you that had been so freely bestowed on your mother. It is a failing, I know. Please never think I did not love you, Harry. I just couldn't bring myself to tell you. I was always very proud of you, although you may not have known that from the way I behaved.

When you read this, it will be because you will have come across the stuff I have acquired over the years. They were items I purchased with a view to them appreciating by the time you discovered them. No one knows what I have been doing – not even Gran. I wanted it to be something to make up for all the misery and hurt that had gone before.

The doctors tell me that I may not have long to live, which is why I am writing this letter. I have been a very obstinate old fool and earnestly hope you can find it in your heart to make allowances for my behaviour towards you. I very much regret that I did not unburden myself sooner. It already feels better to know that I have tried, in some part, to let you know how things were.

If you have any need of help or advice, consult Joe Burns, our good friend and neighbour. I always relied upon him when I needed guidance. He is very fond of you and will be pleased to aid you in any way he can.

Finally, please do not think too badly of me. I earnestly wish that things could have been different between us. Only know that, like your mother before you, I loved you both very dearly, probably too much for me to deal with.

Have a good life, Harry.
Granda

When Beverly finished reading, she found her eyes were stinging with tears. The words had blurred on the page as she struggled to read in as unemotional a manner as possible. Harry, however, was sobbing uncontrollably.

"I always longed to hear him say he cared for me," Harry admitted when the tears subsided.

CHAPTER 58

Earlier that morning, after Wyllie had telephoned, Tristram Grant picked up a mobile phone he kept secreted in the Range Rover.

He pressed the speed dial and waited.

"What is it?" a rasping, irritated voice asked without preamble.

"Wyllie has screwed up again."

"Tell me how."

"I've just had him on the phone. Carey has had his loan redeemed. It seems his sister has settled his debts in full, this very morning."

There was a long pause before Tristram heard the voice speak again. He had begun to wonder if the line had been lost.

"You'd better get it sorted then cos you know the consequences if you don't."

"But how—?"

"I don't really care how you do it – but that's up to you, Grant. If you want to keep your good name – such as it is – you'll find a way. If you can't sort it out, you might find you need the services of an orthopaedic surgeon, when you end up with a couple of broken legs.

"My boys aren't too fussy when they get to work. I'm sure you'll understand how painful failure can be for people who let me down. Get on with it!"

Tristram tried to continue the conversation but realised that the call had ended. Should he phone back? No, he decided, that might just annoy him even more.

His thoughts were interrupted as the Bluetooth reverted back to radio function. As he reached over to switch off, the voice of Chris Collins filled the car. Ruth had left the radio on the local station frequency. Collins was prattling on about the extravaganza, as he put it, which would be held this coming Sunday, at Burns' Garden Centre.

As he listened, Tristram suddenly had a thought. Maybe he couldn't do anything about the loan now, but he could take his spite out on Carey and his little band of helpers. His eyes narrowed as he thought it through. "Bastards!" he muttered. "I'll teach you to get in my way."

With the radio silenced, he drove out of the parking lot with a determined look on his face. A casual observer might have concluded that this was the expression of a seriously maladjusted individual.

While Tristram hurtled back towards the big house, Ruth had also received a call. She replaced the receiver in its cradle and peered out into the darkening night. The call she had just received left her angry and concerned. Although her view from the window would have gladdened the heart of anyone witnessing roe deer crossing their expansive lawn, she was hardly aware of their presence. Things were unravelling due to the inept way Tristram and Wyllie had been handling things. Perhaps she now needed to take some corrective action to redeem the situation and wondered what that might be.

The bumbling fools had mishandled things 'big time' she realised, but it was too soon for her to show her hand just yet.

CHAPTER 59

As Sally exited the bank, she found herself in bright sunshine. It reflected her mood. A parked car flashed its lights from a few yards along the road. Liam had made a date to join her after work. She self-consciously ran her fingers through her hair and adjusted her spectacles as she made her way along the pavement to join him.

Despite all that had happened recently, the fact they had finally started dating and seemed to be comfortable in each other's company had lifted her spirits tremendously.

Liam bent over and gave her a peck on the cheek as she sat beside him. That was also new and gave her the confidence to kiss him back, even though it was daylight in a very public place.

They moved off and proceeded along the high street in the direction of Harry's farmstead.

"I thought we should look in to see Harry before we go on for a meal," he suggested.

"That would be good," she said.

"There have been a few developments today."

Sally looked at him expectantly.

"I had a visit from tax inspectors. They wanted to know about Harry's financial affairs."

"What did they want?"

"Basically, proof that he had legally inherited the farm and its contents. I was able to provide them with that and also confirmed that the various antiques his grandfather had left were purchased for him and were not part of his inheritance – so they could not be considered for inheritance tax. They were interested in the valuation of the stock acquired by Harry's grandfather, which would not have been eligible for taxation, as they were not inherited but gifted to Harry from the day they were acquired. I missed that point originally but noticed later that all of the purchases were receipted in Harry's name – not his grandfather's."

"So," Sally mused, "Grandad Carey paid for the goods but receipted them in Harry's name?"

"Yes, they were personally owned by Harry from day one – no estate tax is due."

He paused for a moment to negotiate a farm tractor pulling a cart.

"I told them he had allowed himself to fall behind with his business affairs, following his grandmother's death and subsequent efforts to save the hospice. I also told them that Beverly and you had started to put things in order. They seemed to accept that."

"But why would they come along just now?"

"I think that someone must have told them that he was fiddling his tax. They are obliged to follow up on whistle-blower allegations. It would be routine practice for that to happen."

"Do you think Wyllie is behind that?"

"Who knows but it gave me an idea. If things are being mismanaged at the bank, as you suspect, an anonymous call to head office might give him a taste of his own medicine?" he concluded, as they arrived in the farmyard.

CHAPTER 60

Harry clung to Beverly for several minutes. She rubbed his back and hoped it was comforting him. At length he pulled away from her and apologised, saying that it was no way for a grown man to behave.

She responded by telling him that it was good that he had let his emotions surface and also that he had probably been holding too much in for far too long.

They sat down and again sifted through the photos, discussing each as they examined them.

"Grandad wasn't unkind," he said after a pause. "Only very remote. He never showed me any affection. I don't suppose he knew how much I craved that. Granny was different altogether. She was always giving me a hug but almost never when he was around. I'm beginning to understand more about him now."

"Can you imagine how badly he must have felt, too?" Beverly observed. "Just think how much Mum's leaving must have affected him; why he would never allow himself to go through that anguish again. His only concern was to ensure you were provided for. I wonder if Gran had any inkling about the stuff he acquired?"

"I do remember him saying that banks were not a good

way to make money. They are only interested in making our money make money for them."

"In your case, that certainly seems true."

"I do vaguely remember the day we crashed. I had finally plucked up the courage to ask him about my parents. It angered him and he drove too fast round a bend. I don't remember much else, other than that I ended up in hospital. It's funny how these memories are coming back to me now. Mark was right when he said it was then I began to be obsessed with music. It seems the most recent head knock has had the same effect on me but now regarding antiques. I don't seem to care so much about music now."

They sat companionably discussing their previous lives, until the sound of a vehicle entering the farmyard prompted Beverly to check the time on the bedside clock. It was almost six o'clock.

From the window, she could see Liam and Sally walking hand in hand towards the house. Beverly smiled, thinking how happy and well suited they appeared together.

Liam said hello and Sally smiled as she entered the kitchen. She had picked up the day's mail from the porch and was looking for a knife to open the brown 'reply-paid' envelopes they had sent out only a few days before.

"There are fifteen of them," Sally announced with a smile.

"I've not had time to open them yet," Beverly confessed. "With all that's been happening today, there was never a moment to deal with them."

"We know that you had a visit from the Inland Revenue," Liam told her. "They came to see me this afternoon."

"How did you get on with them?"

"OK. I think they were convinced no tax evasion had taken place, but I would urge you both to be extremely careful in any financial matters from now on. Even if there is nothing to hide, they will, more than likely, return unannounced, just to satisfy themselves that nothing fishy is going on."

"Where's Harry?" Sally enquired.

"He went upstairs to compose himself. He just received some news from the past and it has affected him emotionally. Me too, for that matter," Beverly added. "I don't think we can talk about it yet but it's not bad news – only things that we were both glad to learn about our grandparents. Right, let's open the mail. We can share our news while we're doing it."

Fourteen of the letters contained cheques amounting to over £1,200. The fifteenth was from an estate agent advising them that the house's occupant had moved away from the area and that the bill should be sent to a solicitor in London. The name and address were supplied.

"Isn't that the house address where Harry had his fall?" enquired Sally.

Liam confirmed that it was, and this prompted more discussion. If they could contact the previous occupant's family, they might be able to explain Harry's condition.

"Could I follow up on that for you?" Liam enquired.

Both nodded agreement.

CHAPTER 61

A buff-coloured envelope was lying on the mat when Harry came down for breakfast the following morning. There was no postmark. The note was from someone that lived in the next town and although an address was clearly typed, the signature was illegible.

Harry wondered who might have sent it but supposed it might have been from a previous client. It read:

> *Dear Harry,*
>
> *I have some items of light furniture that need to be taken to the auction rooms for this week's sale. Could you please call in tomorrow about 3pm to collect them?*
>
> *As I am confined to a wheelchair, I would be grateful if you could enter the house from the rear garden and uplift all the articles in the room. They can be accessed via the French doors. The doors are a bit stiff, so you should give them a good tug when gaining entry.*
>
> *We can discuss your fee when you get here.*
>
> *Thanks, in anticipation.*
>
> *Signature*
>
> *16 Queen's Road, Johnstown*

Harry stuffed the note into his shirt pocket just as Beverly was coming down the stairs.

"I'll be out tomorrow on a job," he told her.

"Are you sure you're up to it so soon?" she enquired.

"Of course I am," he replied.

CHAPTER 62

About the same time Harry was sitting down to breakfast, Liam was motoring south to attend a conference in London. He liked driving. The weather was ideal for travelling and the traffic relatively light at that time in the morning. There was another reason for going but he had not told anyone what it was, until he knew that it would bear fruit.

Last night had been one of the most enjoyable times he could remember. The restaurant had been an ideal setting for a romantic meal. He smiled fondly as he thought of Sally and the time they had spent together. It was more than he could have ever hoped. The petite, unassuming girl he had longed to get to know ever since arriving in town was interested in him. Although he was aware that people regarded him as a dull and rather reticent lawyer, Sally, bless her, seemed pleased to spend time with him. He caught a glance of his face in the rear-view mirror and was surprised to see that, uncharacteristically, he was grinning broadly.

As the miles slipped by, his thoughts turned to Harry and the remarkable events that had led up to the present. Harry was quite amazing. Not only had he achieved the seemingly impossible task of saving the hospice but had also succeeded in wiping out his debts at one fell swoop, albeit through the unselfish intervention of his hitherto unknown half-sister. Beverly, too, was something else. He knew that Sally and Beverly had struck up a warm friendship and their good chum Mark had clearly fallen for her big time. Like he had for Sally, he mused, but it had taken a lot longer to pluck up the courage to even speak to her.

His mind strayed to the behaviour of William Wyllie. His lawyer's instincts suggested that 'Wily Willie' and Tristram Grant were not the only individuals involved in seeking to acquire Harry's and Joe's farms.

With planning permission, the entire development land might fetch around £70 million. The more he thought about it, the more likely it was that the relatively worthless farmland could command premium prices if planning permission was granted.

A furniture van pulled out in front of him as he drove along, causing his thoughts to turn again to Harry. What had happened to make him how he now was? The obsession with antiques had replaced the interest he once had for music. It all seemed to tie into the time he had fallen downstairs. Maybe the house's previous occupant could shed light on what had caused him to behave the way he did?

CHAPTER 63

Mark arrived just as ten was striking on the town clock. Harry was pleased to see him but understood that the real reason for his visit was to be with Beverly. Harry had arranged to visit Joe to check on the progress of the auction but mainly to give Mark and his sister some time alone together.

"Hi, buddy, how are you today?" Mark enquired.

"Fine. How about you?"

"I'm good too. Where are you off to just now?"

"Joe and Chris are waiting for me over at the nursery. We're just going to check on the arrangements for the weekend. Are you all geared up yourself?"

"Yeah. The tea tent and bar are going to be set up on the Friday afternoon and we'll stay overnight at Joe's, for added security. Is everything all right your end?"

"I think so but that's why I'm meeting up with Chris and Joe today to go over things."

"See you then," Mark said, as he was clearly impatient to be with Beverly, who was waiting for him just inside the back door entrance.

Harry smiled as he watched his friend bound across the yard to the house. He looked like a teenager again.

Mounting the gate of the field that led to Joe's place, he could not help but feel that things were changing. Grandfather's letter had affected him greatly. The revelations it contained released a flood of emotions that for years he had refused to contemplate. He now realised that diverting all of his thoughts to music, whenever painful memories threatened, was how he had coped with the hurt that was always with him. The hospice appeal had been another coping mechanism. He was pleased it had also been a means of honouring Grandma's dying wish.

Unburdening himself to Beverly had been a cathartic experience. He felt that maybe now, with her help, he could return to a normal way of life, so long denied him, following the traumas he had experienced since his childhood. He hoped she would stay and that maybe Mark and Beverly would make their relationship permanent.

All at once, he realised that he had crossed both fields and was now about to enter Joe's property. Chris and Joe were standing in the yard examining a clipboard and did not notice his approach. When he drew abreast, it was to hear them discussing the parking arrangements.

"I think we'll need to open up a field to accommodate all the vehicles that are likely to turn up on Saturday," he heard Joe remark.

"We'll need to get a couple of people to direct the cars then," Chris observed.

"How many are you expecting?" Harry enquired as he drew level.

After both acknowledged his arrival and enquired how he was keeping, Chris suggested it might be as many as three hundred in the morning for the car boot sale.

"Probably as many again in the afternoon for the auction," he speculated. "There's been a lot of interest coming in from listeners and the station manager is delighted but also annoyed at the number of queries we've had to field recently. Our advertising reps are also reporting an upsurge in bookings – so all in all, he's very happy with what has been happening, since news of the event was first broadcast."

"Let's hope it helps you shift some gardening stuff as well, Joe," Harry remarked. "That would be a win-win situation for everyone. We will, of course, donate 10% of our sales to the garden centre for the use of your facilities."

Joe observed him for a moment before responding. "Chris, would it be possible for you to include a message to your listeners that we will be offering all of our stock at half price on the day? I've been thinking about the future and come to a decision. I'm packing it in. My part-timers are not as young as they used to be either and competing with the large garden centres is becoming more difficult with every passing season. It's time I took things a bit easier at my time of life."

Chris and Harry looked at him with surprise.

"I know, it's not been an easy decision, considering how long I've been here but I need to face facts. It won't get any easier. Like you, Harry, I've also got debts that need to be settled – so the only way that I can meet my creditors will be by selling up. It will be a wrench, considering my father, grandfather and his father before him all lived and worked the land. One thing I will never do is sell to that scumbag Grant or his sidekick Wyllie. I'd rather die than do that!"

Chris was first to speak. "I had no idea that things were so bad, Joe."

"It's been in a steady decline now for years," Joe responded. "I guess that I've been in denial for a long time now but have to concede there is no future for me here. I guess it's sheltered housing or an old folks' home for me. Let's not dwell on it just now. We have work to do, to make sure that the weekend is a success."

With that, Joe turned and walked towards the outbuildings.

Chris and Harry exchanged worried glances, before following in behind. Harry, who had been feeling elated prior to Joe's news, was saddened by what he had just heard and wondered what could be done to prevent Joe having to sell up.

CHAPTER 64

Mark listened attentively while Beverly updated him on recent events.

"He seems a lot happier now since I read him Grandfather's letter," she confided, "as I am too. Poor Harry, it must have been awful for him, never receiving the love he craved, from an old man who could not bring himself to display affection for the grandson he clearly adored."

"He was never the same after the accident, that's for sure," Mark replied. "Harry went from being an outgoing, fun-loving rascal to someone who became very introverted and private. Apart from his obsession with music, he never got excited about anything, apart from saving the hospice. His gran's death affected him badly too, as you can imagine. Apart from his chums, and we did our best to help him snap out of it, he was always a lonely, brooding figure who bore no resemblance to the Harry we had grown up with. Only his concern and impeccable manners towards others remained unaltered. That's why so many people love and admire him. He once told me that as far as he was concerned you should always strive to leave people and places better than you found them."

Beverly considered this before going on. "You'll know

that Liam dealt with the tax inspectors, but did you know that he is going to a conference in London today and will be meeting with the owner of the house where Harry had his fall? Maybe we can get to the bottom of why he is so obsessed with antiques and how he has developed this almost encyclopaedic knowledge. I've listened to that recording but it does nothing for me, I'm afraid. Let's hope they can shed some light on it."

"Yes, let's hope so. I must confess that, like Liam, I'm also concerned about Wyllie's involvement in trying to get hold of Harry's croft. There's something going on that we should know about. I'm also sure that Tristram Grant is involved. He tried to get Joe to sell his place at a ridiculous price."

"Liam says he will be doing some digging when he returns," Beverly remembered. "I think he will be giving us an update after he returns from London."

CHAPTER 65

It was a detached Georgian manor house bordering Hampstead Heath where Liam arrived later that evening. The owner, Amelia Hart, clearly wasn't short of a bob or two, he speculated, after checking that the address he held was correct. A maid answered the door, and on production of his business card, invited him into a tastefully decorated room in which an elegant woman of late middle age was seated at a writing table.

She got up and crossed to where Liam stood, offering her hand in welcome.

"Thank you for allowing me to visit you at this late hour," he began.

"Think nothing of it," she replied. "I was intrigued by your enquiry."

Liam looked around to see if anyone else was in the room before enquiring if her legal representative would be attending.

She smiled and informed Liam that she herself was a lawyer and had acted for her late father.

"Can you now tell me what all this concerns? I understand it's not just about non-payment of a house clearance bill?"

"It's difficult to explain," Liam began, "and I was hoping that you could shed some light on the matter."

"Come and sit down," she invited. "I'll see what I can do."

Liam summarised what had happened since Harry's fall and how he seemed to have been affected by the recording. She was thoughtful for a while before replying.

"My father, Professor William Hart, was a psychiatrist. He retired about twelve years ago and went to live in the house where your friend had his accident. He died some three years ago and although I loved escaping to the house whenever I could, it became obvious that it needed to be disposed of following his demise. I simply could not afford the time to spend holidays or weekends there because of commitments both here in the UK and abroad. I have no children living in Britain – they settled in Canada and America. I saw no point in holding on to a property that was simply going to go into decline with no one living there. It went on the market last year and sold within weeks."

Liam noted that the way she spoke was in the style of someone addressing a jury.

She paused for a moment and enquired if Liam had listened to the recording.

"Only briefly," he replied. "It had no effect on me whatsoever, as far as I can tell."

She was quiet for a few moments, thinking about what she was going to say next.

"My father was a brilliant man who, although a trifle eccentric, was always looking for ways of influencing human behaviour in a positive way. He had worked for years, following his retirement, on developing a series of suggestions (you might call them hypnotic messages) that could be contained on a recording others could use to help them in achieving their undeveloped capabilities. The therapy was intended for subjects who were introverted, or too preoccupied with other life issues to achieve their inherent abilities in a positive, effective manner. The intention was to devise a programme that would help underachievers identify and develop their inherent skills in a positive and successful way. He had even given it a name – The Hart Start Continuum System."

Liam leaned forward in his chair and waited for her to continue. After a lengthy pause, she told him that she had always wondered what progress he had made but following a severe stroke, the work had been abandoned and forgotten about, as far as she was concerned.

"I'm afraid I cannot be of further help to you in the clinical respect, Mr Forbes, but I know someone who might be able to explain what has occurred. Alex Green was his student and then assistant for a couple of years before taking up a post in Edinburgh. They were as thick as thieves and would have shared a lot of information about the techniques he was attempting to develop. If you will allow me to pass on the details on your business card, I'll see if there is anything Alex can shed light on regarding your friend's condition."

After some polite conversation, Liam thanked her for her offer of help before returning to his car for the long drive north.

CHAPTER 66

"So – all of the car boot items have been ticketed for people to pick up and pay for as they exit from the hangar we are standing in," Chris informed them.

Joe scratched his chin and suggested that some of the shopping baskets in the garden centre could be made available, to encourage shoppers to load up with as many items as possible.

"What value have you placed on the car boot items, Harry?"

Chris looked at a list he was carrying, before replying, "If everything was sold at the prices quoted, the total might amount to £5,000 or thereabouts."

Harry was already moving towards the large barn that had previously been used to store hay and agricultural machinery. Four rows of items arranged on tables stretched from the entrance to the auctioneer's pedestal.

Chris continued his running commentary.

"Everyone has to enter the barn through the doorway we have just entered, having been first issued with a bidding ticket at the kiosk. No ticket – no entry. The payment desk is also in the kiosk where the tickets are issued. No auctioned items can leave the barn without receiving a receipt that authorises their release," Chris continued.

"How many lots are there?" Joe interrupted.

"Three hundred and forty-two," he replied.

"If we manage an average of £30 per item, that will gross over £10,000 wouldn't it?" Joe calculated. "But you valued some of those items in the hundreds, didn't you, Harry?"

"Yes, but who can say what they will make on the day? Has there been much pre-sale interest?"

"I've been amazed at how many people have been viewing all week," Joe responded. "It's actually been great for the garden centre too. My sales have never been so good! Many of the pre-sale viewers have gone off with all sorts of stuff that would normally be sticking at this time of year. It just shows you, doesn't it? Get the punters over the door and sales will follow."

"Maybe you shouldn't cut your prices too soon then," Chris suggested.

Joe agreed to hold off on the half-price offer until during the auction.

While not wishing to seem disinterested, Harry had been distracted by the news that Joe was considering selling up. He had not taken much interest in what was being discussed but had instead been forming a plan as they traversed the site. He wanted to discuss it first with Beverly, before sharing his thoughts with the others, however. Despite everything, he smiled when he thought of his go-ahead sibling and acknowledged how much he had come to depend upon her.

CHAPTER 67

William Wyllie was looking at the bottom of his fourth glass of whisky and soda when Tristram Grant burst into the conservatory at the golf club.

He could tell immediately that something was exciting Tristram by the maniacal look on his face and hyperactive movements.

"What are you doing tomorrow afternoon?" he demanded without preamble.

"Why do you want to know?" came the guarded response.

"I need you to make a phone call to the police."

"Why would I do that?"

"You are going to report a crime on this mobile phone," Tristram informed him.

"What are you talking about? What crime is going to be committed tomorrow?"

"You will be reporting a theft."

"How do you know that will happen?"

"Trust me it will – that's all you need to know."

"Why me?"

"Because you will be in your car, on the other side of town, miles away from the scene of the crime."

"Don't you know that mobile phones can be traced, and the police are able to identify the location from where a call has been made?"

"This is a pay-as-you-go phone. It would be untraceable to you."

"So why don't you make the call yourself, if it's your idea and is as foolproof as you claim?"

"I have to be somewhere else, or I wouldn't need to ask you to do it for me."

"What about that thug Butcher you usually use to do your dirty work?"

"He's also going to be busy, but I wouldn't trust him to do the job right. It needs someone with more than a couple of brain cells for this to work."

Wyllie searched for a reason not to get involved but Tristram was persistent.

"I have a plan to get even with Carey. It might also scupper his plans and give us another chance to get our hands on the farm. I take it that you are aware of the consequences for both of us, if we fail to do that?"

After some deliberation, Wyllie reluctantly agreed, resigned to doing Tristram Grant's bidding.

"Tell me how that thing works then and exactly what you want me to say," he conceded.

CHAPTER 68

Liam woke to the chirping sound of his mobile. He screwed up his eyes and stared at the screen. It was an email. Through bleary eyes, he saw the message was from Alex Green.

That was quick, he thought and raised himself to read the text.

Dear Mr Forbes,

Amelia Hart has told me about your friend Harry and the remarkable changes that have occurred since listening to Professor Hart's recording. I would be grateful if you could call me to discuss how I might get in touch with Mr Carey.

My contact details follow.

Yours sincerely,

Alex Green.

Liam reread the message before jumping out of bed and heading for the shower. He would contact Harry later in the day, after clearing his morning appointments.

CHAPTER 69

Mark was saying his goodbyes when Harry returned home.

"Everything going to plan?" he enquired as he got behind the wheel of the car.

"Pretty much," Harry replied.

"I'll see you tonight then when I pick up Beverly. We're going out for a meal. Must run or I'll be late for lunch. We've got the Rotary Club in today."

Harry waved as his friend drove away.

Beverly called him into the house and gave him a hug when he entered.

"How are you, Harry? You're looking very thoughtful. Is anything wrong? Are you thinking about Grandad's letter?"

He looked at her for a while, wondering what to say but eventually found the words.

"No, I'm not thinking about that, Beverly. It's something else."

She looked at him steadily, waiting for Harry to speak.

"It's Joe," he finally blurted out. "He just told me that he has lots of debts and the only way he can clear them is to sell up."

She waited to hear what else he had to say.

"I'd like to help him if I could, and I'd like you to tell me if an idea I have could solve his problems."

Beverly nodded encouragement for Harry to tell her more.

"I was wondering, maybe it's not possible, but if I was to sell some of the stuff that has been left us, we could maybe buy Joe out? Do you think that would work?"

"It could well do, considering how financially solvent you are now, Harry, but we could explore this further with Liam when we see him. He's asked if he can come over to have a word with you about his trip to London. It appears that an Alex Green, an associate of the gentleman whose stairs you fell down, wants to meet you. He'll be coming over after five and Sally will be with him, so she might also be able to give some advice."

"I thought that maybe if we owned both farms, there would be more opportunities open to us, Beverly. The other thought was that if the garden centre incorporated an antique showroom, more people would want to come there. It's just an idea but I think it could work if you were up for it."

"You said if *we* owned it, Harry."

"That's right. I appreciate that you might not fancy tying yourself down to staying here but if you did, it would be great to have you as a business partner. I wouldn't expect you to invest any money. I am quite determined that we should both share the inheritance. We are of the same bloodline and I'm confident that, if our grandparents were still alive, it is what they would have wanted. I planned to share with you anyway and will not take no for an answer. Whether you stay or leave, I would still do the same. You are the only living relative I have. You have brought nothing but good since you came here. I would much rather you stayed, of course, but that is entirely up to you. I hope Mark might also help you to decide that you should stay."

"Harry! I didn't come all this way for what I could get out of you. I've told you that before. That was never in my thoughts. I'm just so relieved to have found you and want to assure you I'm very happy to have you as my brother, even if you didn't have two pennies to rub together. Yes, I plan to stay around for however long you want me to be here. You can be sure of that."

Harry looked relieved and, uncharacteristically, smiled. Beverly had seldom seen him display facial emotion before and was surprised but said nothing. Maybe Harry's emotional state was reverting to how he had been as a youth, prior to the accident. She decided to wait to see how things might evolve. Could he be returning to his former self, she wondered?

She returned his smile and held his hand. "Let's discuss this later. Would you like a cup of tea?"

CHAPTER 70

Liam had been busy all morning but finally got around to checking on any planning applications lodged for Joe's and Harry's land. What he discovered made him gasp. There had been an application placed just six months ago. He now suspected collusion with council officials, in hiding the application from public scrutiny. Poring over the plans confirmed his suspicions that the farms were the subject of a scheme to turn the two crofts and part of the Grant estate into a business park.

It made perfect sense if you were a speculator. The properties skirted the motorway on the eastern boundaries and would be readily accessible to conurbations within a ten-mile radius. All that was required would be an access road on Joe's land with egress being achieved further north on another property that did not belong to either Joe or Harry. The land adjoining the farms was, he knew, part of the Grant estate. That was why Tristram and Wyllie were involved. The prospect saddened him as he envisaged the impact it would have on the locality. The applicant, he noted, was a property development company based in the south. It would be standard practice to make the application through a third party if the principal investor didn't want to be identified. So, who, he wondered,

198

might that be? He didn't believe that either Wyllie or Grant would have the resources to develop anything on this scale, but maybe they had been able to secure loans against the Grant estate. How could he find out?

He reached for the desk phone and placed a call to the developers. When the telephonist at the other end answered, he asked to be put through to Wiltris but was told that the company did not occupy the premises he was calling. She did, however, refer him to a telephone number he recognised as being local to the Johnstown area. He rang off and dialled the number, on the pretence that he was trying to contact a client. He was intrigued to learn who resided at that address. It wasn't Tristram Grant or William Wyllie.

Forewarned is forearmed, he thought, as he returned the handset to its cradle.

CHAPTER 71

The friends gathered in Harry's kitchen, eagerly awaiting Liam's news.

He arrived with Sally, keen on sharing what he had learned since the London trip.

Joe had already enjoyed a couple of beers and was considering having another at Beverly's invitation.

Harry was engrossed in a new antiques catalogue Mark had given him and could barely take his eyes off it long enough to acknowledge Liam and Sally's presence.

Chris was on his mobile phone, talking to someone about an upcoming gig but ended the call as Liam and Sally entered the room.

They listened attentively while Liam recounted his meeting with Amelia Hart and the subsequent email from Alex Green.

"It seems Amelia Hart's father and Alex Green – his sometime assistant – had been working on creating a programme of hypnotic suggestions that would enable subjects to develop super memory skills. This might explain why Harry is how he is now. Would you be willing to meet Alex Green, Harry?"

"Of course I would," he replied.

"Maybe we'll get to the bottom of this fascination you have with antiques?" Mark speculated.

Harry just nodded, eager to return to the magazine he had felt obliged to put to one side.

"Will I make the arrangements for Alex Green's visit?" Liam offered.

"That would be good. Any time but tomorrow, though, because I've got an afternoon job in Johnstown."

"I doubt if it will be as soon as that because Amelia Hart told me that Alex is based in Edinburgh. Will you be available the weekend of the auction, Harry?"

"That would be good, I think," he replied, looking to Beverly for confirmation.

Beverly nodded and then asked how long Alex Green might be visiting.

Liam didn't know, as he had wanted to fix definite dates with Harry before responding.

"I'll get onto that tonight, after I've shared the rest of my news," he continued.

Everyone waited expectantly as Liam decided where to begin.

Sally looked on adoringly.

"From the investigations I carried out this afternoon, it seems that someone wants to turn Joe's and Harry's farms into a business park."

"I knew there was something big and underhand about the whole business," Joe erupted. "And I'll bet that Wyllie and Grant are behind it too – unless I'm very much mistaken!"

"You're right to a point," Liam conceded. He looked around the room before continuing.

"Yes, they are clearly involved but they're not the driving force behind the scheme. A company they set up called Wiltris led me to offices of a very well-known organisation that you may have heard of. The company concerned operates several bookmaker shops, casinos, lap-dancing clubs, men-only saunas, car dealerships and payday loan shops, to name just a few of their interests."

"Let me guess," Mark interrupted. "I'm thinking that you are talking about Dalrymple Developments, owned by Donald Dalrymple, that well-known crook who always seems to avoid prosecution."

"Correct! I am of the opinion that he is behind the application but is using Wiltris as a means of concealing his involvement in the enterprise."

Beverly looked quizzically at Mark who obliged by telling her what he knew of Donald Dalrymple. It was a litany of shady dealings, allegedly supported by protection rackets in the early days, evolving into vice and drug dealing but always at arm's length, so that any prosecutions had come to nothing. It was also commonly believed that previous attempts to bring him to justice had failed because those that could have provided testimony against him either suffered acute amnesia or simply ceased to exist; falling victim as they sometimes did to car accidents, house fires or walking too close to the edge of high buildings or clifftops. In every instance, 'Dodgy Donald' as Mark referred to him, always had a cast-iron alibi and earned the reputation of being untouchable.

Joe was first to speak. "I guess we're done for, lad, if that's who we're up against," he said, looking steadily at Harry.

Harry did not respond but looked again at Beverly who began to speak.

"This Dalrymple individual sounds like a really heavy-duty threat. Is he as dangerous as you are making out, Mark?"

Mark looked at Liam, who confirmed he was someone he wouldn't want to have dealings with at any cost. The man was a law unto himself. He was even beginning to feel sorry for

Grant and Wyllie. Liam imagined that Dalrymple must have some hold over the two men, which would bode ill for them if they did not succeed in acquiring Harry's and Joe's properties.

There was a lengthy silence as everyone digested Liam's news.

Eventually Sally enquired if they had any option now but to sell up and move on before something terrible happened to either Joe or Harry.

Joe became animated and rose to his feet, thumping his fist in the palm of his hand. "I will never sell to that crook!" he thundered. "I would hope that you would feel the same, Harry, but I could understand if you chose not to tough it out. I'm an old man, staring death in the face, while you still have most of your life ahead of you and then, of course, there's Beverly to consider. I wouldn't like to think what he might resort to."

All eyes fell on Harry who looked first to Beverly and then Mark for a reaction. Sally noted that Harry had raised his head and was looking decidedly determined by the set of his jaw. Liam, too, noticed Harry's face was flushed, his eyes glittering and fiery. Uncharacteristically, Harry looked at each in turn before speaking.

"Joe, it will be the last thing I will ever do as long as I am able to draw breath. I'm going to fight for what we have here as long as it is possible for me to do that. I realise that it might put everyone in danger if any of you are thought to be helping me. I won't be disappointed or angry if you decide to distance yourself from all of this, Beverly. You should consider getting as far away as possible, although it pains me to see you leave. I couldn't bear to think that you could be drawn into the sort of danger this might develop into."

Silence reigned again, mainly because Harry's behaviour was so unexpected. To begin with, he had made direct eye contact with everyone in the room. Before, he would simply look in the general direction of the person he was addressing, avoiding direct engagement. It was also surprising to hear him string so many words together and to be said with such determination. Harry's normally unemotional style had changed.

Mark was the first to react. He got up from where he was sitting and hauled Harry to his feet. "Welcome back, buddy," he enthused as he enveloped Harry in a bear hug. "You're beginning to look like the Harry I used to know. You can be sure I'll be here for you, every step of the way. We'll fight this together and see off these crooks, if I have anything to do with it!"

"Me too!" vowed Chris, who had been noticeably subdued during the last few minutes. "The pen is mightier than the sword, although that might be the wrong analogy here. I'm sure that we can rally support through the radio station to prevent that happening," he asserted. "And I won't be leaving either, Harry, so put that out of your thoughts."

Sally and Joe also voiced their support, and everyone stopped to listen when Liam cleared his throat.

"I think that there may be several legal ways we can frustrate Dalrymple, Grant and Wyllie," he informed them, "but it will need us to act fairly secretly in the meantime. I have the feeling that things will turn nasty before we see an end to this problem."

Liam wouldn't be drawn on what he was thinking, despite entreaties from the friends but simply said he would have to be sure of his ground, before sharing his thoughts with them.

They talked on into the night, considering all the implications of what a business park development would mean, before Chris reminded them they should concentrate on maximising sales at the auction, which was now only nine days away.

CHAPTER 72

About the same time that the friends were returning home from Harry's place, Ruth Grant was slipping out of a casino by the rear entrance. Her departure did not go unnoticed, however. Jake Butcher had tailed her and was hunched behind the wheel of a 'borrowed' car. He smiled as he watched her slink furtively away, her head darting from side to side as she made for her own vehicle, which was parked in the casino's lock-up garage.

Even Butch could put two and two together, although he wasn't the sharpest tool in the box. It had been purely by chance he had seen her leaving home and decided to follow to see where that led. That was one bit of insurance he might need to call upon, if things became difficult. She treated him like dirt and belittled him at every opportunity. *Well, my fine lady,* he thought to himself, *I think I know something about you that you wouldn't want that little shit, Tristram Grant to know about, when he's not around.*

He waited for a few minutes after Ruth had left, before driving away, unaware that he himself had been under surveillance. A burly figure was studying the casino's security cameras and had made a mental note of who it was that had been parked in the compound adjacent to the rear entrance.

As the car turned onto the street, the driver's face was illuminated by the streetlight adjacent to the car park.

CHAPTER 73

Chris and Harry were over at Joe's place, deep in conversation with the auctioneer. Joe was also engaged with a man viewing articles in the auction hall. No one paid any attention to the stout woman examining the car boot items, nor did they see her place several items on the tables that she had removed from inside her coat. It was her third visit to the preview, and she had been careful to ensure that each of the articles she added to the trestles was priced with the same type of ticketing applied by Harry's helpers. Having achieved her task, she moved quickly away to where she had parked. Once in the car she sent a text that simply said, 'It's done', before driving swiftly away.

In the auction hall, a flamboyantly attired man approached Harry. Ralph Fortescue, a local antiques dealer, was someone Harry liked and trusted.

"I'm amazed at what you've got for sale here, Harry. Where did all this stuff come from? It's a veritable Aladdin's cave you've got here."

"Oh, just here and there over the years," he replied guardedly.

"There are, of course, some items that are clearly way

below their potential value, while others are quite overpriced, I would suggest."

Ralph really knew his onions when it came to antiques and collectibles, and this troubled Harry.

"What lots do you mean, Ralph?"

They wandered round the rows, listening to Ralph's assessment of the various items he considered were too high or too low in their estimates.

Chris asked the auctioneer to note the lots that needed to be changed on his sale list.

"Although you have mainly undervalued most items on the price guide, especially the Chinese, Oriental and African artefacts, the overpriced items tend to be in the minority. I would be inclined to increase your reserve prices on the ones that we have been identifying just now. I'll give you a steer on that, if you care to take some notes," he offered.

Harry thanked him for his advice and asked if he would do that, but as time was getting on, could he leave that task with the auctioneer, as he had to be in Johnstown for a pick-up.

"As an expression of my gratitude, please tell me if there are any items that you were planning on bidding for yourself, Ralph."

Ralph identified three lots that he had wanted. Harry said he could have them at a reduced price for advising him on their potential value.

The dealer was delighted at Harry's offer, saying that he would be happy to add 10%, as he wanted to contribute something to the hospice's coffers.

After shaking hands on the deal, Chris jumped into the van with Harry as they left to collect the furniture in Johnstown.

CHAPTER 74

"It was good of Ralph to let you know about the prices," Chris observed as they made their way along the dual carriageway.

"He's a decent bloke," Harry agreed, "and probably unique in the antiques world in that he is as honest as they come. I've done him a few favours in the past, but he didn't need to do that. It restores your faith in people, doesn't it?"

"Your assessment of antiques is not infallible then, Harry?"

"No, and that is probably because the sources I've used have been from catalogues that are years, maybe even decades, old. I must get a hold of more up-to-date reference books and probably spend more time on the internet to get current values."

The conversation soon turned to the revelations of the previous night before they arrived at their destination. Chris checked the left side of the road while Harry looked at the right as they sought to locate number 16 Queen's Road.

Eventually they found it, and Harry drove the van through the gateway and parked the van at the rear of the building.

He laid the note he had received on the dashboard and reread the message to Chris.

Dear Harry,

I have some items of light furniture that need to be taken to the auction rooms for this week's sale. Could you please call in tomorrow about 3pm to collect them?

As I am confined to a wheelchair, I would be grateful if you could enter the house from the rear garden and uplift all the articles in the room. They can be accessed via the French doors. The doors are a bit stiff, so you should give them a good tug when gaining entry.

We can discuss your fee when you get here.

Thanks, in anticipation.

Signature

16 Queen's Road, Johnstown

For some reason he could not later explain, Chris picked up the note and put it in his shirt pocket, before dismounting from the van.

The French windows were open and a glass pane beside the door handle was broken. Beside it, a taped piece of paper fluttered in the breeze. The note informed them that the householder had needed to visit the doctor but to go ahead with the uplift. Two £50 notes were taped to a drawer on one of the occasional tables in the room, which the author hoped would be sufficient to cover the cost of transportation. The signature was again illegible.

When the room was emptied and they made to set off to Johnstown's salerooms, Harry paused and returned to the house. It was an afterthought that made him write a receipt for the hire, along with a summary of what had been removed, then posted it through the letter box at the front of the house.

Just as they were turning out of the street, the sound of a police car's siren could be heard approaching at speed.

"Sounds urgent!" Chris commented. "I wonder who's been breaking the law?"

Later Harry cursed gently as they approached the salerooms only to find they were closed for the day.

"I guess we'll just have to come back on Monday as they won't take stuff in on a Thursday," he told Chris.

Only when entering the farm road did they become aware of a police car parked in the yard.

CHAPTER 75

The first Liam learned of Chris's and Harry's arrest was when he received a call from Beverly on his car phone.

"In custody?" he repeated when he heard what Beverly had just said. "…But why?"

"The police were waiting for Chris and Harry when they returned from a job in Johnstown. They'd had a call from someone saying that the boys had broken into a house and had emptied the lounge of some valuable furniture."

"You're making this up," Liam retorted.

"I wish I was! They've been taken into custody. I thought you could maybe go down there and sort things out, Liam?"

"Of course, I will. I'm heading there now."

Ten minutes later, he was at the front desk in the police station, asking to see his clients, demanding to know exactly what they had been charged with.

The senior officer, DCI Jones, who was dealing with the case, summarised the substance of the allegations received from an unidentified source and said that Harold Carey and Chris Collins had been in possession of articles believed to have been removed from the property where a theft had allegedly been perpetrated.

When Liam stated he felt sure there must be a rational explanation for the incident, the police officer continued.

"We also received an allegation that several stolen items are being offered for sale in a car boot sale to be held at Burns' Nursery. My officers are investigating as we speak."

"I'm sure that must also be a mistake," was all that Liam could offer. "Can I please talk to my clients now?"

The chief inspector led Liam to an interview room and told him that both men would join him shortly. "I can hardly believe that someone like Harry would be involved in any dishonesty, but I've learned never to be surprised at what people can get up to," he confided, as he left the interview room.

Harry and Chris appeared visibly shaken, but showed signs of relief when they saw Liam enter the room.

Before either could speak, he advised them to say nothing until he had established the circumstances surrounding their arrest.

The anonymous note was mentioned and Chris, remembering that he had pocketed it, passed it for Liam to inspect. With no one at home when they arrived at the house, they went along with the note that instructed them to remove the furniture and take the payment of £100 taped upon the drawer.

No, they did not have a copy of the note which had been taped to the French windows, but Harry had written a receipt; a carbon copy recorded in his receipt book.

Harry said nothing as Chris responded to Liam's questions.

"Where is the receipt book, Harry?"

"It's in the glove compartment. The van is parked outside the police station," he went on. "They insisted that it be taken in as evidence."

"And where is the money – the two £50 notes that you received as payment?"

Harry reached inside his wallet and passed the bills to Liam. He did not touch them but left them on the table which separated them.

Minutes later, the door opened, and DCI Jones entered, carrying five evidence bags.

"These are the items which were identified as being stolen," he stated. "Can you explain how they came to be in the car boot sales area?"

Harry examined them individually before declaring he had never seen them before and that they were not on the list of items that had been taken to Burns' Garden Centre.

Liam interrupted before Jones could continue.

"I was present at the listing of the items selected for the car boot sale and antiques auction, Chief Inspector. I can swear to the fact that lists of both lots were created and witnessed by several others. I presume the alleged items will be fingerprinted to check whether or not they have been handled by Harry, or any persons present at the time? Also, the lists were printed for dissemination to prospective buyers, and I think you will discover there is no mention of the items which have turned up at the garden centre."

"We will be carrying out all relevant forensic checks," Jones assured him.

"Referring back to the house-breaking allegations, I would like to offer the two £50 notes, on the table in front of me, as evidence that payment was offered for Mr Carey's services. Apart from any forensic traces on the notes, I think you will agree that £50 notes are unusual and if withdrawn recently from a local source, might lead to the identification of the person or persons who left them in the house. I would also ask that you retrieve the receipt book from Mr Carey's van, which carries an entry that records acknowledgement of the payment of £100, along with the items that were uplifted. It seems highly illogical for a thief to write a receipt for stolen goods – don't you think – or to list items that had been stolen? It seems that Mr Carey and Mr Collins have been victims of an elaborate plan to implicate them in a crime they did not commit."

Harry marvelled at the speed at which Liam had grasped the essential details of the situation and appreciated he was thinking several stages further ahead than either he or Chris had been able to progress.

"We will, of course, take all of these factors into consideration," Jones responded.

"Detective Chief Inspector – are you charging Mr Collins and Mr Carey, or are they merely helping you with your enquiries? I feel sure that they will do all that they can to answer your questions as fully and honestly as possible."

DCI Jones paused before answering.

"At present they are helping us with our enquiries. I will be seeking to obtain statements from everyone concerned, including Mr Burns whose premises are being used to sell the goods to be sold or auctioned on the Saturday following this one. I must also advise you that the sale will have to be deferred until we have conducted an inventory of all the items offered for sale. They will then have to be checked to confirm that they are not recorded on a stolen items list."

"You can't do that!" Chris blurted. "The event has been publicised for weeks and thousands of people are likely to turn up!"

"I'm afraid I can, and am obliged to do so, Mr Collins, unless Mr Carey can provide evidence that he came upon the items legitimately. Are you able to do that, Harry?"

Reluctantly, Harry shook his head. "The stuff that I'm offering in the car boot section is largely stuff that I was asked to remove from auction houses because they had not been sold.

They are just some items that I retained rather than taking them to the dump."

"The stuff being offered for sale in the auction is a different matter," Liam offered. "You have receipts for everything in the barn, don't you?"

Harry agreed that he could produce receipts for most but not all of the auction room items.

"Then I'm afraid you may have to cancel unless it can be established that these items were honestly acquired," Jones stated, with such finality that no one, not even Liam, sought to contradict him.

Mark, Beverly, Joe and Sally were waiting in the reception area of the police station as Chris and Harry were released to return home.

Watching from a discreet distance, Jake Butcher dialled a number on his mobile phone and pressed it to his ear. "Carey and crew have just been released," he informed the person at the other end. "Should I go ahead with the rest of the plan?"

He listened intently, nodding at what the person on the other end of the line was saying. When the call ended, he made his way to an agricultural merchant's yard, a couple of miles from town. So preoccupied with thoughts of what he was about to do, Butch was completely unaware that he was being followed.

CHAPTER 76

Having satisfied himself there was no one in the yard, Butch pulled a ski mask over his head, donned a pair of rubber gloves and made his way to a second-hand tractor parked in the outdoor sales area. He quickly hot-wired it and drove out of the yard, proceeding along the road that led to Burns' Garden Centre.

After a few minutes, just a few hundred yards short of the garden centre, he drove into a field. Fifty yards along, hidden by a hedge, he reversed the tractor up to a tanker he knew to be full of pig slurry. Swiftly he coupled the tractor to the tanker, then waited until he heard the town clock strike midnight, before returning to the road, heading in the direction of Burns' Garden Centre.

Butch stopped fifty yards before the entrance to Joe's site. He then opened the valve that sprayed slurry, gagging as he did so when the contents began to discharge. Back in the tractor cab, he gunned the throttle and proceeded towards the garden centre, noting with some satisfaction that a deluge of slurry, reflected in his tail-lights, was gushing out from behind the tanker. Apart from leaving the road with a coating of obnoxious effluent, the discharge also drenched the verge and hedges bordering both sides of the road.

Upon reaching the garden centre car park, he swung the tractor inside the parking area, stood hard on the brakes, pulled on the hand brake and killed the engine. He was instantly out of the cab and running towards the opposite field as lights started coming on in Joe's house. The cover of another hedge ensured he would be well out of sight before reaching the mountain bike he had placed a couple of hundred yards along the edge of the field. He now needed to recover the Land Rover he had secreted behind a derelict building, close to the merchant's yard.

It had gone very well, he told himself, as he pedalled furiously across the fields to where he had left the vehicle. It was only when he got to the Land Rover that he become aware of a large figure stepping out from its shadow to meet him.

"What the...?" was all he managed to utter before the pain of something heavy being driven hard against his left leg made him scream in agony. He had barely hit the ground when his body was pummelled by a series of blows, which he was sure were breaking every bone in his body. Although he did not know it then, he had indeed suffered two broken legs and multiple bruising to his arms and ribs. As Jake fought to maintain consciousness, he was aware of one of his assailants warning not to take too keen an interest in Donald Dalrymple's affairs. He might not get off so lightly next time, he was informed.

CHAPTER 77

The local radio station was sending out repeated messages on the morning show that due to unforeseen circumstances, the auction and car boot sale had been deferred.

Another item of news informed listeners that a man had been discovered, badly injured near an agricultural merchant's yard. Anyone who could provide any information concerning the incident should contact the police at the following number, etc.

There was also a road traffic warning. The road leading past Burns' Garden Centre had become dangerous through spillage from a slurry tanker. Drivers were advised to avoid the area. Clean-up operations were expected to carry on for the rest of the week and maybe even into Sunday.

DCI Jones was mulling over the events which had occurred over the past twenty-four hours in what was, after all, one of the lowest crime incident areas in the country. He decided he should speak to Liam Forbes and placed a call on his desk phone. When Liam answered on his mobile, he was meeting with the others in the Crown Hotel, discussing what to do next following what had happened the previous evening. The stench from the slurry had made both Joe's and Harry's places uninhabitable.

Jones came quickly to the point of his call.

"Liam, I think that you may have suspicions as to why all these incidents have occurred. I'm of a mind they are connected somehow. Can you tell me if you have any suspicions which might help me understand what is going on here?"

Liam excused himself and continued the call in the empty dining room.

"It's only a hunch," he said, "and you must understand that I may be completely wrong in these assumptions, but several facts have emerged over the last week," he began.

When he finished speaking, the policeman thanked him and said that his request for confidentiality would be respected. He was left wondering about what he had learned, then reached for his jacket before phoning reception to say he was meeting with DS Black at the hospital.

The friends were in a downcast mood as they sat down to breakfast in the Crown. Sally and Beverly were dishing up the food, while the others discussed what had occurred the previous day.

"That's really screwed things up," Joe complained. "What a bugger!"

Mark was less concerned about the cancellation. "At least no one is injured. Has anyone heard who the accident victim was?"

Liam was able to inform him that Jake Butcher had been badly beaten. "It was no accident," he continued. "I understand he was smelling very badly of pig slurry when they found him."

Joe remarked that he wasn't at all surprised to hear that Butch was a suspect but would also bet that Tristram Grant would be involved, somehow.

Mark said that he would like to have a few minutes alone with Wyllie, Grant and Butcher, but Beverly advised they remain calm.

"The best way to deal with these schemers is to beat them at their own game. It sounds like they may have fallen out, if what we have heard about Butcher was down to them."

"I don't think it was Wyllie or Grant that beat him up," Liam suggested. "I think that the beating he received was done by professionals. To my mind, it could be Dalrymple who's behind the beating. At present I can't work out why, if Grant, Wyllie and Dalrymple are in cahoots?"

"Could Butch be working for someone else?" Joe wondered.

"It seems unlikely," Liam responded. "He's definitely Grant's pet poodle, unless they've had a falling-out. DCI Jones is off to interview him at the hospital. That could yield some information that might explain things."

Mark wanted to know if Sally had noticed any changes in Wyllie's behaviour. She thought for a moment before replying.

"He's a queer fish at the best of times, but I did notice he was particularly agitated yesterday. He cancelled all of his afternoon appointments but did not seem to be doing anything other than fiddling with a mobile phone when I went into his office to get his signature. He then told me that he was going out and that I should lock up, as he did not intend returning to the bank."

"About what time did he leave the office?" Liam enquired.

"It must have been about 2.30," she remembered.

"What are you thinking, Liam?"

"The police received an anonymous call from an untraceable mobile phone at about 2.45. That's just fifteen minutes short of when Chris and Harry left the Johnstown address."

"Do you think Wyllie sent the message?"

"It seems pretty likely, don't you think? I also wonder if the stolen items that appeared in the car boot section, was an attempt to get the auction stopped. Did you see anyone acting suspiciously when viewers were visiting, Joe?"

"Now you come to mention it, there was a stout woman who looked a bit out of place. I remember thinking that at the time but was talking to someone else when she was wandering around the tables, and just assumed she might be a bit eccentric."

"What made her stand out?" Mark queried.

"Well, yesterday was very warm – a veritable heatwave and I could see sweat running down her face, but she was wearing a heavy woollen coat all the time that she was in the car boot area."

"So… do you think she might have planted the stolen articles?"

"I never saw her do that but it's possible."

"Don't you have CCTV on site, Joe?"

"Yes, but not in the car boot section."

"Would it cover the car parking area? I guess you might be able to pick her out from there, as she would have had to go through the car park, either driving or walking, to view the goods on sale."

"That's possible," he acknowledged. "But we won't be able to go back to the garden centre until they've reopened the road."

"We might get an identification which might lead somewhere," Liam concluded. "I think the police may want to check that out, Joe, so make sure it doesn't get wiped."

"I think I'm beginning to see a plan," said Beverly. "Someone was hell-bent on preventing the auction going ahead; implicating Chris and Harry in a bogus burglary, planting stolen goods at the car boot section, and the runaway slurry tanker were all attempts to prevent the sale going ahead. I think that could only lead back to 'Wily Willie' and the 'Treacherous Tristram' Grant," she concluded.

Everyone laughed at the alliteration, although it was clear

to the friends they were up against formidable adversaries who could take things much further if the current diversions proved unsuccessful.

"I'm more concerned about the fate that befell Butch," Mark stated. "I wonder if the Dastardly Donald Dalrymple was behind his beating? That would really worry me."

The room went silent as everyone considered his remarks.

Joe again was first to speak. "I'm not going to let that hoodlum deter me."

"Nor me!" they all chorused, although each had their own private reservations, despite the show of bravado.

CHAPTER 78

Jake Butcher was not in a talkative mood. Any questions put to him were answered with a 'Don't know' when questioned about his injuries.

"Can you tell us then what prompted you to steal a tractor and slurry tanker and drive it to the garden centre? And before you deny it was you, Butch, there is enough forensic evidence to convict you of the crime – so don't deny it," DCI Jones warned him.

Although he knew that the police had him 'bang to rights', Jake wasn't going to admit anything and said so.

"Are you charging me? Because if you are, I demand to have a solicitor present."

Jones tried a different tack. "We are pretty sure you were put up to it and who was behind it," he stated. "We also believe we know who ordered your beating."

The latter statement had a noticeable effect on Butcher, and Jones imagined that he detected a flash of terror cross his face.

"No comment," was all that he would say to that and any subsequent questions.

DS Black read him his rights and then proceeded to list

the charges, which included stealing an agricultural tractor and slurry tanker and wilfully discharging the contents of the vehicle upon the public highway to the endangerment of road users, the health of the general public, etc.

Butch acknowledged he understood the charges but would say nothing else beyond that. Frustrated, the two officers left the hospital ward and sought the doctor who had treated Butch. As expected, he believed the injuries his patient had received were consistent with being beaten, by persons unknown. He believed the injuries were consistent with having been struck repeatedly by blunt objects such as clubs or baseball bats. The patient insisted he had been the victim of a hit-and-run car accident but the doctor attending him dismissed this as being extremely improbable.

As the two detectives drove back to the station, DS Black looked at his boss who he suggested knew more about the case than he was letting on.

"I have some theories," Jones replied, "but they are little more than that at present. I need to do some digging before I can arrive at any conclusion."

Black knew not to press his boss further. He would be told in good time. DCI Jones was nothing if not thorough.

CHAPTER 79

Beads of sweat stood out on William Wyllie's forehead. He was waiting in a lay-by for Tristram Grant to meet with him.

What had he got himself into? He looked wistfully at the family group sharing a meal at a distant picnic table. He longed to feel as relaxed and carefree as they appeared to be. A rap on the passenger's window interrupted his thoughts. Tristram climbed into the car, seemingly appearing from nowhere. He had been hiding behind a bush for some minutes, deciding not to reveal his presence, until sure that Wyllie had not been followed.

"Where the hell did you come from?"

Grant glared at Wyllie and told him to settle down. He was here now. How he had arrived was of less importance than why he had come.

Wyllie was almost hysterical.

"Look here!" he babbled. "Things are getting severely out of hand. I've just learned that your gorilla, Butch, is at death's door in hospital. How did that happen? Is it in any way connected to us?"

"Get a hold of yourself, you fat tub of lard. Don't draw attention to yourself."

"How do you expect me to behave? What has Butch done to receive such a going over? Don't you feel you're also in danger of being beaten up? And by association, am I in danger of being attacked?"

"I don't think Butch's beating had anything to do with you or me – unless of course Carey and his crowd got wind of what he had done and decided to teach him a lesson."

"What makes you think they would do that?"

"Well, the slurry spillage was down to Butch. Maybe they found out and went after him to exact revenge?"

Wyllie paused for a moment to digest what he had just heard.

"Butcher did that? Did you tell him to spread the slurry?"

When Tristram did not reply, Wyllie understood his partner wasn't going to admit to anything openly.

Tristram then told Wyllie that some stolen items had been found at the car boot sale and the police were investigating as he spoke. Wyllie knew better than to ask how he knew.

"I'm worried, Tristram. This whole thing seems to be getting out of hand. I don't know what you or Butch have been up to but I'm not putting up with it any longer."

"You don't have any choice in the matter, I'm afraid. You're already in up to your neck. All it requires is a call to your head office to query what has been going on at your branch, for you never to work in the banking sector again. So don't force me into doing that. Besides which, any worries you might have about being attacked will be realised – not by me personally but A.N. Other, who you definitely don't want to upset."

Tristram realised that he had said too much. Wyllie was not aware that anyone else was involved in the scheme. Tristram cursed himself for the indiscretion and watched with concern as Wyllie digested what he had just heard.

Wyllie was feeling foolish. He now realised how naïve he

had been to imagine that Tristram Grant was the only other person involved. He knew, better than anyone, the desperate state of his finances, also brought about by heavy losses at the gaming tables. It wasn't a huge leap of imagination for even Wyllie to suspect that the person to whom he referred was Donald Dalrymple – the man who had let him extend his credit to an eye-watering amount.

Tristram flew into a rage, having lost all self-control and grabbed Wyllie by the throat. "Forget all you've just heard and for Christ's sake, don't go around repeating what I've told you to anyone. The people we're involved with are very unforgiving, especially when they think they have been crossed. You're stuck with this, my fat friend, and you'd better get used to the idea. There's no way out. The sooner you realise that the better!"

Wyllie was shocked by what he had just heard but even more so by Tristram's aggression. He was actually foaming at the mouth as he delivered the warning. Wyllie now recognised that Grant was more than just a little unhinged. He could imagine him resorting to all sorts of measures against anyone who might frustrate him. With what appeared to be a great deal of effort, Tristram sought to regain composure before uttering a final threat and jumping out of the car. He stamped off into the undergrowth, leaving Wyllie regretting ever having agreed to become involved in the scheme to acquire Harry's and Joe's land.

As he disappeared into the undergrowth, Wyllie realised he hadn't returned the phone that Tristram had supplied him for reporting the Johnstown burglary. It would have to remain in the glove box for now. There was no way he would want to be in Tristram's company any longer than he could help.

CHAPTER 80

Liam decided to take Sally for lunch at the Crown and invited Beverly and Harry to join them. Having commiserated over the cancellation of the auction, Liam then informed them he was also there to book a room for Alex Green, who was hoping to stay the following weekend, if that was acceptable to Harry?

He said it would be fine and looked forward to meeting him.

"I'm glad to have a chance to speak to you, Liam. It's about Joe's place. I don't know if you are aware he is thinking about selling up. I don't suppose he'll mind you knowing he's got money problems and needs to sell the farmstead to settle his debts."

Liam looked at Sally, but she looked away. Even though he banked at her branch, and she knew of Joe's financial problems, it would have been unethical for her to divulge that, even to Liam.

"Do you know how much that might be?"

"No, but I was wondering if it would be possible for me to buy him out, Liam?"

This time he looked at Beverly, who explained the strategy.

"Harry was wondering if we could do that, not just to help

Joe but also to protect Harry's farm from a hostile offer from developers. If we owned both places, that would help to see them off, wouldn't it?"

Liam paused for a moment to digest what he had just heard. "You could certainly afford to buy Joe out," he confirmed, "but I'm not sure how it would benefit you by doing that."

Harry smiled before replying. "No one in our town would want a giant business park built here. I would be planning to turn a large portion of the farms into a woodland park. We would also turn the rest of the arable land into a plant nursery and extend the garden centre to house a restaurant with an adventure play park for children. In addition to that, an antiques and collectibles emporium would be established."

"That's very ambitious," Liam replied.

"Don't you think we could do that?" Harry queried.

"Of course you could. Does Joe know what you are proposing?"

"No, we wanted to run the idea past you first," Beverly informed him.

"I'd also want Joe to remain in the farmhouse for as long as he wants to stay there – rent free," Harry added.

Discussion followed throughout lunch. When the meal was over, they made their way through to the bar where Joe, Chris and Mark were enjoying a drink. On seeing Beverly, Mark came out from behind the bar and kissed her on the cheek.

"How was lunch?" he enquired.

"It was fine," she replied.

"Can I get you all a drink?" Joe offered.

"Not for me," Harry replied, "but I would like to talk to you about something private if you'd care to come through to the dining room for a moment."

Joe looked questioningly at him but slipped off the bar stool and followed Harry and Liam into the adjoining room.

"This looks serious, Harry," Joe began.

"Serious, but nothing to worry about – in fact, quite the opposite," Liam informed him.

"No – nothing to be anxious over," Harry reassured him. "It's just that I was wondering if you would consider selling your farm to me – or at least Beverly and me, I should say. If you did, it would mean that we could more easily frustrate Grant, Wyllie and whoever is behind them if the farms have one owner."

"Buy me out, Harry?"

"Yes, but you wouldn't have to move out of the house, Joe. It would be a condition of the sale that you would continue to live there rent free."

"Rent free?"

Liam nodded to confirm what Harry had said.

Joe's next question was to ask if Harry was sure. Could he afford to do that?

Liam confirmed that he could and still have a large sum remaining from the estimated value of Harry's legacy, still waiting to be liquidated.

And so, the deal was concluded in less than five minutes. Liam would draft a contract stating that Harry would purchase Joe's farm at a fair market valuation. The contract would stipulate that £20,000 would be given as a deposit to enable Joe to clear some of his creditors and the balance would be payable following the sale of some of Harry's antiques. Harry and Joe shook hands before returning to the bar, where Joe announced what had been discussed.

"Harry is now the owner of my farm," he beamed, "and we'll have that drink now – thank you, Mark!"

After all of the congratulations had been received, Harry held his hands up for silence, before telling everyone that the title deeds would name two owners – Beverly and him.

Everyone cheered. Beverly blushed, declaring she didn't want Harry to do that.

Sally noted that the news was well received, especially by Mark.

CHAPTER 81

DCI Jones sat staring at the blank grey wall beyond his desk, trying to make sense of recent events.

The alleged theft of furniture and money from the Johnstown address by Harry Carey and Chris Collins was clearly an attempt to frame them.

The two £50 notes they were alleged to have stolen had not been traced to any withdrawals from local banks, but he was not surprised by that.

The call, which had alerted the police to the alleged theft, had been phoned in from a pay-as-you-go mobile, which was untraceable. Further investigation placed the call near the local golf club. He was also aware that William Wyllie was a member there. DS Black had been despatched to establish if he had been in the vicinity at the time the call was made.

CCTV footage from the garden centre placed a serial shoplifter in the premises on the day Harry and Chris had visited the Johnstown address. She denied any involvement. The items deposited did appear on a stolen goods list from a charity shop in a nearby town but had little value.

Then there was the Jake Butcher affair. It was clear he had removed the tractor and slurry spreader, releasing the contents at Burns' Nursery. All three incidents seemed designed to prevent the auction going ahead – but why?

The assault on Butcher had left him terrified and uncooperative. While it was true that Butcher was as bent as they came, and also a thug and bully – he was also, basically, a coward. Previous dealings with him had yielded information that the force had been able to use to secure convictions; especially if Butch thought that it would help him evade prosecution, or to get even with anyone he considered to be a threat to his own interests. Jones speculated that either he did not know his attackers or was afraid to reveal their identities. The latter supposition seemed more likely, he concluded.

His thoughts went back to what Liam Forbes had told him about Harry's problems with the bank and William Wyllie's apparent involvement with Tristram Grant in seeking to acquire Joe's and Harry's homesteads.

Most interesting of all was the trail that led back to Wiltris and the registered office being in Donald Dalrymple's premises. Dalrymple was someone that Jones would dearly love to put away. It hadn't been for the lack of trying. Every time he thought he might feel his collar, there were cast-iron alibis, which frustrated every instance he had tried to bring the swine to court. How, he wondered, were these three men connected?

Tristram Grant was also someone Jones deeply disliked. Everyone did.

Another thought crossed his mind. Grant's property bounded Harry's and Joe's fields. Liam Forbes' investigations had discovered that the outline planning application had included the Grant estate. Maybe this was why the additional land would be required? The scheme could not go ahead without access through Burns' and Carey's land.

His thoughts were interrupted by an incoming call. DS Black was reporting back.

"Hi, Chief, we've established that William Wyllie was at the golf course when the call about the house breaking was transmitted. The golf club steward said he arrived around that time and spent some minutes in his car before making a call on a mobile phone. He is sure about this because he was speaking to a member who kept him in conversation for some minutes outside the club adjacent to the car park. He knows it was at 3.15 because the man he was talking to asked him to check the time. He was due to have a round of golf with someone at 3.30. It was unlike the other golfer to be late he added."

"Anything else?" Jones enquired.

"Yes, there was. The steward was concerned that Wyllie appeared to be sweating profusely but had not opened any of the car's windows, although it was a very warm afternoon, as you may recall. Concerned that he might not be well, he approached the car and asked if he was feeling all right. Wyllie assured him that he was fine but didn't encourage further discussion. The steward didn't pursue the matter but decided to keep an eye on him from inside the clubhouse. He saw Wyllie speak into a mobile phone, which he tossed into the glove compartment before driving off at speed."

"How interesting!" Jones observed. "I think we need to pay Mr Wyllie a visit, DS Black."

CHAPTER 82

Around the time DCI Jones was speaking to DS Black, Harry was talking things through with Beverly. She was aware that something had changed in his demeanour. She asked how he was feeling.

"It's strange that you should ask," he replied. "I feel different, somehow."

She waited for him to continue.

"My preoccupation with memorising seems to be diminishing. When it was music that occupied my thoughts, almost to the exclusion of everything else, along with the campaign to save the hospice, I didn't think about much else. It was much the same with antiques. It is an obsession, I realise now. But there are so many other things clamouring for attention that it seems to be getting edged out from my thoughts, although I still have the urge to learn all that I can about them."

Beverly encouraged him to go on. "Are you feeling anxious because of it?"

"No! I can honestly say it is becoming less important as time goes by. So many new things have been competing for my attention. It all started with your arrival, Beverly, along with everything that has happened since then."

"Does that worry you?"

"Quite the opposite, I'm beginning to feel more like I used to be before the accident with Grandad. I'm starting to realise that immersing myself in memorising music was something that helped me cope with what happened that day. Then, when Granny passed away, the hospice had the same effect of completely occupying every waking moment. It was difficult to give any thought to the business. I just seemed to be going through the motions on a daily basis. I think it's called a coping mechanism which often follows a traumatic experience."

Beverly nodded, encouraging him to continue.

"I'm only guessing, of course, but it seems that I may have been avoiding facing up to what Grandad told me as it was something I did not want to hear or accept."

"What did he say?"

"It's strange but I cannot recall what he said. Maybe it's too painful for me to remember and my mind won't allow me to deal with it."

A silence ensued, finally broken by Beverly.

"But you *are* feeling OK?"

"I think so. All that has been happening lately has forced its way into my consciousness like never before. I'm very pleased because I know I wasn't happy before. Every day since the car accident, I merely existed – aimlessly muddling through the days, without ever feeling happy or fulfilled. I simply existed to memorise music, raise funds and move stuff around in the van."

Beverly put her arms around him and said she was pleased to know that he was beginning to regain his old self.

"Who knows, maybe this Alex Green psychologist that's coming tomorrow might be able to help you regain your true identity?"

"I would like that," he confided.

CHAPTER 83

Despite the best efforts of the fire brigade and council workers tasked with clearing up the effluent, the air was still heavy with the stench of pig slurry. Even though the road surface was washed clean, slurry still clung to the vegetation at the roadside and down the access road that constituted the driveway into Burns' Garden Centre. Unlike the public road, the driveway and car park were made of gravel. It would probably take weeks for the smell to disappear completely, Joe acknowledged ruefully.

Chris returned with him to see if there was anything that he might be able to do to help Joe. Other than supplying him with a nose plug, Joe said he would just have to make the best of it, and hope for rain. The two men went inside where Joe offered Chris a cup of tea.

"I would offer you something stronger, but I guess you can't do that if you're driving, Chris?"

"I'd like to have a snifter to celebrate your sale, Joe, but it's not worth losing my licence over. There will be other times, I'm sure."

Joe shook his head in wonderment. "Harry's offer came out of the blue. I had no idea that he would think of doing such a thing! And he's letting me stay here rent free as well! I'm really all choked up about it. He's been so generous. I've no doubt that with Beverly in tow, they'll make a go of things here. Best of all, it's going to frustrate that conniving pair of swindlers and that pleases me almost as much."

Chris looked thoughtful before responding. "Liam seems to think that Dalrymple may be behind them. He's a pretty heavy-duty baddie, if all I've heard about him is true."

"That rather concerns me too, Chris. If Dalrymple is behind it, you can be sure he will not take this lying down. Harry, in fact all of us, need to watch our backs. He's a pretty ruthless individual who doesn't take kindly to being thwarted."

"Do you think Butch, Grant's gopher, was beaten up on Dalrymple's orders?"

Joe looked puzzled. "Why do you wonder about that?"

"Well, if Butch was carrying out Grant and Wyllie's instructions and Dalrymple wasn't happy about that, he may have used that as a warning for the terrible twins to back off."

"That seems a bit far-fetched. Why would he not just rough them up a bit? Why take it out on Butch?"

"There's maybe another reason altogether that's totally unconnected, I agree, but what could that be?" Chris wondered.

"Perhaps we'll never know and quite frankly I don't care. That Butch deserves everything he gets. He's long overdue a good hiding, I would say!"

Chris was examining a photograph on Joe's mantelpiece. It was a picture of Harry as a toddler cradled in his grandmother's arms. Harry's grandfather looked on, rather sternly, Chris observed.

"He thought the world of Harry, you know, but could never show it," Joe informed him. "When Harry's mother became pregnant, he was utterly devastated. I've never seen anyone take anything so badly. It was such a surprise to everyone how he behaved because she was the apple of his eye. He was besotted by her. I think he loved her too much. So, when Harry came along, he was unable or unwilling to afford him the affection that the child deserved – afraid, I believe, it might cause him another broken heart."

"Did he treat Harry badly?"

"He always made sure that Harry was treated well, fed and clothed but never showed him any affection in a physical sense. Anytime when Harry was a tot and held out his arms for a cuddle, he would quickly pass him to his granny. She gave him all the loving she could, but it was often heart-wrenching for me to see the way that Harry craved his grandfather's affection and would do everything he could to get his attention and approval."

"Didn't you say anything?"

"I did once and was told that if we were to stay friends, I would never raise the subject again. I chose not to, in the hope that things might improve as time went by. It didn't, of course, as you know, even though the two of them spent a lot of time together in the van. I wish I had done more to bring them together – but I didn't. It has been a great regret that I didn't push things further."

"What caused Harry to change? Mark and Sally believe it was due to the accident."

"They're probably right. I know that heated words were exchanged just before the accident occurred. The old man admitted that to me when we were sitting by Harry's bed in hospital. I think that may have had a bearing on Harry's behaviour following his recovery. What was said, I don't know, but I have my suspicions it was why he became so introverted. The strange thing was that the roles seemed to reverse after that. Old Carey tried to build bridges with Harry, but he was having none of it and gave him no encouragement. It was heartbreaking to witness. I once came across the old man crying, and Harry's gran told me it was because he was full of remorse about what had happened and how he desperately wanted to make amends."

"Was that when he started buying stuff for Harry's inheritance?"

"Oh no, he'd been doing that for years. He always intended to provide for Harry. He just couldn't allow himself to show any sort of open affection to the lad."

"Well, he seems to have done that rather well, don't you think, Joe?"

"You haven't seen the half of it yet, Chris. There's stuff stored all over the place that hasn't been looked at yet. I know where some of it might be found, and no doubt Harry will get round to accessing it one of these days. Whether it is as valuable as what has already been unearthed, we will only know in the fullness of time."

Chris pursed his lips and blew a long, low whistle. "Well, we can only hope it's a sizeable sum. God knows he deserves it after all he's been through."

CHAPTER 84

Heads turned as Ruth Grant strode imperiously down the ward towards Jake Butcher's bed. Barely affording a nod to the nursing staff attending to other patients, she might have been walking on a catwalk in Milan. Dressed entirely in black, she epitomised the type of character you might expect to see in a horror movie.

Jake had not seen her arrive but was instantly aware something had caused the ward to go quiet. His heart sank as he saw her approach his bed. She was attempting to smile sympathetically at him, as a concerned employer might, but her token attempt at empathy was clearly artificial and forced. She was carrying a bunch of supermarket flowers, which she handed to a nearby nurse, requesting that she should find a vase for them. As the nurse departed, and still attempting to look concerned and reassuring to anyone observing her interaction with Butch, she had no words of comfort for him – only threats – delivered in a low, menacing tone.

"Well, look at what happened to you, you stupid little turd. Be under no illusion what else will befall you if you ever interfere in my business again."

Jake did not reply but stared mutely back at the woman who frightened him even more than her deranged husband.

"I understand the police have been to see you and would like to know what caused your injuries. Let me make it clear so that there are no misunderstandings on your part. If either Dalrymple, or I, are implicated in any way regarding your current condition, you will be subjected to a long, very painful experience. You will pray for death to bring relief."

"I've told them nothing," he whined. "I don't know nothing."

Her eyes narrowed as she leaned forward over his bed. "Remember too, that you will not be safe, even in prison, where we can assume you'll be going as soon as they're able to move you from here. What have they charged you with?"

Butch haltingly listed the crimes of which he had been accused, insisting that none of them could be connected to Dalrymple or Ruth.

"See that it stays that way, if you know what's good for you, then."

"I was only carrying out Tristram's orders," he mumbled.

"More fool you, then! Only a fool would have anything to do with my idiot husband. You clearly fall into that category."

"Will Tristram help me with lawyers?"

"I very much doubt it. He won't come anywhere near you now for fear of being implicated. You must be aware that anything you say will simply be a case of him denying he was involved. It's simply his word against yours. That's why I'm here, as there's no chance he will ever risk being seen in your company again."

"Does he know you're here just now?"

"Of course not and you'd better be sure he never finds out or it will be the worse for you."

She let her threat sink in before continuing.

"By the way, I'm having all your stuff moved out of the cottage and taken to the dump. You won't be needing it now,

243

as you'll be spending quite a few months, maybe years, in jail. So don't imagine you will ever be able to return there. The letting agents have already been instructed to find a new tenant for the property. Tristram has already written you off as expendable and will shed no tears over your demise."

All of the ward's occupants had been looking on, intrigued by the elegant woman leaning over Butch's cot, apparently placing a comforting hand on his chest. They would have misinterpreted her actions, however. She had noticed that Butch had been periodically massaging his rib cage, grimacing as he did so. She was now leaning on the exact spot at the centre of his discomfort, gradually increasing pressure as she whispered to him.

"This is just a reminder how painful things can get for you if you ever think to cross me again."

It took a huge effort for Butch not to cry out in agony. Ruth smiled triumphantly; her sadistic proclivities aroused by the act of administering pain on a defenceless victim. When Butch finally did cry out, she slowly relieved the pressure. Anyone watching saw her other hand stroke his brow, as if comforting him in his distress.

"Remember," she threatened through clenched teeth, "things can only get worse if you ever upset me again!"

As she stepped back from the cot, the sympathetic expression returned as she looked around at the ward's occupants. It was the look of a woman exhibiting heartfelt pity for the invalid she had been comforting. For added effect, she pulled a handkerchief from her bag, placing it over her mouth, as she raised her other hand in farewell, before making for the exit, her eyes glued to the floor. She almost collided with two suited men who were approaching. DCI Jones and DS Black noted her departure. Jones commented that she was well named. Black looked at him quizzically.

"Ruth as in Ruthless," his boss explained.

"I believe she's also known as Cruella de Vil," his colleague replied.

At the nurses' station they were met by the ward sister who told them that Mr Butcher was in some distress, and she did not want him disturbed any more today. The officers exchanged glances before informing her that they would return tomorrow.

Butch sighed with relief as he saw them depart but realised it would only be for a few hours before they returned to question him again.

CHAPTER 85

Jones and Black decided to visit Wyllie's bank but were again frustrated to learn that he had phoned in sick. They decided to go to his house. He lived alone following his wife's departure with a pharmaceutical salesman. They found him in the conservatory at the rear of the house in an advanced state of inebriation although it was not yet eleven o'clock.

Wyllie attempted to get out of the chair in which he was lolling with the appearance of someone attempting to flee from the scene. Such was the extent of his drunkenness that he flopped back, unable to achieve a standing position. His florid complexion was wreathed in sweat; his hair tousled in a way that suggested he had just got out of bed. The whites of his piggy eyes were deeply veined and red, a sign that he had been crying. Snot dripped from his nose, ending just above his lips, which were caked at the corners with what the officers imagined to be dried vomit. He looked up at them with an air of foreboding, which also implied he had much to fear by their intrusion.

Neither policeman spoke but stared at Wyllie, waiting for him to talk. It was a ploy that generally worked, eliciting more information than might have been obtained by straight questioning.

Wyllie blustered and babbled a lot of inanities before seeming to get a grip on himself, enquiring what they were doing in his house.

"We believe that you can help us in our enquiries relating to a case we are investigating," Jones informed him.

"But I've done nothing, it was Tristram Grant that got me involved in this," he stammered.

"Involved in what?" Jones enquired.

DS Black kept quiet, fixing his whole attention on Wyllie to unnerve him further. It seemed to be working.

"What illegal activity did Mr Grant involve you in?"

"Nothing! I swear it."

Wyllie was struggling to sober up, but it was clear his thoughts were befuddled. He set his lips tightly, like a stubborn little boy not wanting to admit he had done anything wrong. His right hand came up to cover his mouth in an attempt to stop him making any additional indiscretions.

"We understand that you were seen by witnesses at your golf club on the day a house was allegedly burgled in Johnstown," Jones continued.

"What of it?" Wyllie retorted.

"You were seen to make a phone call that alerted the police to the alleged break-in. We also believe that it was from a stolen phone which you were seen to place in the dashboard of your car. I must ask you now to provide me with your car keys in order for us to confirm or discount the device from our enquiries."

Wyllie looked blankly at them before asserting that the car keys were lost.

Black then asked if the key fob that lay on the wicker table beside the empty bottle were the keys he said had been misplaced?

"If you don't mind, I'll just test them to make sure that

they are the right ones and check the contents of your car at the same time."

Wyllie clearly did mind but realised there was nothing he could do about it.

Black quickly took the keys and made for Wyllie's car, parked haphazardly on the driveway. He soon returned with a mobile phone in his hand.

"Look what I've found!" he announced.

DCI Jones nodded approvingly before telling William Wyllie that he would now be required to accompany them to the station, to assist them with their enquiries.

CHAPTER 86

The rain teemed down as Liam dashed from the car to his office. It was very welcome, he reasoned, because it would help cleanse the remaining slurry that still clung tenaciously to the vegetation around Joe's place.

On entering reception, he was informed that a gentleman from Wyllie's head office was wanting to speak with him. The receptionist had asked him to wait in Liam's office.

The bank inspector introduced himself as Edward Smith and gave his business card to Liam explaining that he was a little earlier than they had arranged due to the fact that he had first gone to the local branch to see Wyllie, only to discover he had reported sick. Having had a brief discussion with the accountant concerning certain matters, he decided to make his way over to see Liam, although he knew that he was more than an hour early for their meeting.

Liam wondered how Sally had reacted to Smith's arrival, which would not be expected, as investigators of banking irregularities did not announce their visits when investigating possible malpractice. He did not inform Smith of his involvement with Sally, wondering if she had said anything about their relationship when being interviewed by the inspector.

After the usual protocols that needed to be observed when professional people meet, Liam enquired if his visit to the bank had yielded any information to support his suspicions Wyllie had been behaving inappropriately in relation to his client Harold Carey.

It was a guarded reply, in language people engaged in banking employ when wanting to give a non-committal response to a tricky question. Although his responses were non-specific, Liam's training as a lawyer deciphered that Edward Smith was inclined to believe that Wyllie had not been following banking procedures and that the integrity of his actions could be called into question. Following a few minutes of probing, Smith finally got round to enquiring what Liam was proposing to do in relation to his client. It was evident he wanted to deal with the matter as discreetly as possible, avoiding any bad press or embarrassment that the affair might cause his employers.

"If it is a matter of compensation, we would be minded to reimburse Mr Carey for any losses or inconvenience he might have suffered," he offered.

So, the bank had already identified that something irregular had happened, Liam concluded. When he did not respond immediately, Smith pressed on with another question.

"How do you propose to deal with this, Mr Forbes? Has Mr Carey instructed you how he wishes the situation to be resolved? Our bank would prefer to bring the matter to a speedy conclusion, to ensure that your client is recompensed for any distress he has suffered as a result of this unfortunate affair."

"I'm afraid that the matter may be out of our hands, Mr Smith," Liam replied. "Since I last notified your bank about our concerns, there have been associated developments that have involved other criminal enquiries. I am not in a position to discuss them with you because the case is at a very delicate stage, involving other parties. I can only refer you to DCI Jones for further information. He is the senior officer, investigating the other crimes that appear to be associated with my client's problems. He may be able to furnish you with answers I am unable to provide."

The inspector appeared deflated. What he imagined might have been an expensive but private solution to the problem had now slipped beyond his grasp.

Smith listened with a sense of dread as Liam lifted the telephone. Jones answered on the third ring and said that he would be grateful if Mr Smith would come to the station without delay. He finished by telling Liam there had been some important developments he would like to discuss with him later.

CHAPTER 87

Wyllie had been taken to an interview room. He was being given time to consider his position before making a statement concerning his role in reporting the break-in at Johnstown.

He had rallied but was still very muddle-headed and wondered how he could extricate himself from the situation. What did they have on him, anyway? Yes, he had reported the crime on a stolen mobile phone, but the break-in could have been a message that someone else had witnessed and relayed to him to report. The police had already told him they knew he had made the call from the golf club car park. What a fool he had been not to destroy the phone the moment he'd used it! So, what did they have? Not much, he reasoned. The phone might have been stolen but maybe he could say that he had found it – that he was intending to hand it in to lost property at the station. Yes, that was it. That's what he would say. They couldn't prove otherwise. All the other problems Tristram had inveigled him in were not at issue here, or so he thought until the interview room door opened and DCI Jones, along with DS Black, entered the room, accompanied by Edward Smith.

The look of resignation on Wyllie's face on seeing the bank inspector spoke volumes.

Jones spoke first. "We will resume our enquiries following a brief conversation with Mr Smith who I am sure is known to you."

Smith came forward self-consciously and spoke directly to Wyllie.

"The bank has been alerted to various anomalies and allegations concerning your conduct, Mr Wyllie. As a consequence, your employment is suspended until a thorough audit of the branch's transactions have been completed. You will receive a formal letter to that effect following my return to head office."

Wyllie groaned and held his head in his hands. He did not witness Smith's departure.

Jones paused for several minutes before speaking.

"We have had a long chat with your employer," he began. "It seems that you have an awful lot of explaining to do, Mr Wyllie."

Wyllie raised his hands and simply nodded, accepting that the situation was now beyond redemption.

Two hours later, the officers had returned to Jones's office to compare notes. Wyllie had sung like a canary. They now had confirmation of his collaboration with Tristram Grant in seeking to acquire Joe's and Harry's homesteads and of Jake Butcher's alleged role in the slurry tanker affair – but would not admit to anything concerning Wiltris or any links to Donald Dalrymple, although they had pressed him hard on that point. They charged him with attempting to pervert the course of justice as a starting point and told him that more charges would be added following ongoing enquiries. He was being held in detention overnight and would be interviewed again in the morning.

Black looked at his boss and thought he knew the signs. He was almost euphoric but holding himself in check. He had suffered embarrassing disappointments in the past when he had unsuccessfully attempted to secure a conviction against Donald Dalrymple.

"Do you think we might nab him this time, boss?" he enquired.

"If you mean Tristram Grant, perhaps. Dalrymple will be much more difficult, I suspect."

"What about Ruth Grant? We didn't get anything from Wyllie that incriminated her, but she was visiting Butcher in hospital."

"Maybe she was there at Tristram's request, delivering a message to Butcher? I cannot imagine she would dance to his tune – but who knows? There are rumours that they go their own ways when it comes to carnal pursuits, I've heard."

"I can't imagine anyone wanting to share body fluids with either of those two. There's no accounting for taste," Black observed.

Both men laughed.

"What are we going to do now, sir?"

Jones thought for a moment before speaking. "We have no reason to arrest Grant as we have nothing to charge him with, yet. It's unlikely he'll know that Wyllie's in custody, but these things have a habit of getting out with time, so we can't wait too long before feeling his collar."

"What could we charge him with, anyway? Apart from what Wyllie has told us about granting unsecured loans on the basis of a forged signature, we don't have a lot to go with."

"The auditors can help us put Wyllie away when they identify the scam they have collaborated on – so it might be a case of conspiring to defraud Wyllie's bank, I'm thinking. I'd love to get him for more."

"Me too!" Black agreed.

Jones looked at his watch. "It's almost five o'clock," he observed. "I'd better give Liam Forbes a ring."

Liam was not in the office, however. His secretary informed Jones that he had gone to keep another appointment but could be contacted on his mobile if it was urgent. He decided that it could wait until morning and headed home.

CHAPTER 88

Liam was waiting for Sally, a discreet distance away from the bank entrance. She looked about her as she exited and looked worried for a moment until he flashed his headlights to attract her attention.

She flopped in beside him and proceeded to give him her news about Edward Smith's visit. He told her he'd had a visit too. Slightly disappointed that her news was not as sensational as she had hoped, Sally asked him what they had discussed.

He gave her a quick résumé, along with Jones's request for him to report to the police station.

"What happened when he visited the bank?"

Sally was bursting to tell him all but said she had been told not to discuss his presence with anyone. She said that on this occasion, she could not help herself from sharing the news with Liam – as long as he promised to keep it to himself.

"When he came into the bank, he asked to see Mr Wyllie and was quite annoyed when I told him he had called in sick. After introducing himself, he enquired if I could help with some enquiries he needed to make. It was all about Harry's account to begin with but then he wanted to know who had stood guarantor for his borrowing and you'll never guess who that was, Liam?"

"Could it have been Tristram Grant?"

"No, not Tristram but you're close."

She paused for effect before revealing that it was Tristram's father.

"But he died about two years ago, didn't he?"

"That's right and the papers were only signed fifteen months ago!"

"Did the inspector know that, Sally?"

"He did when I told him," she replied, her eyes twinkling with excitement.

"How did he respond to that?"

"He was quiet for a few minutes but then asked me if I had any knowledge as to how this might have occurred. I said that I had no knowledge of the transaction but maybe Mr Wyllie, or Tristram Grant, might be able to shed light on the matter."

"That was rather clever of you, Sally," Liam observed. "How did he respond to that?"

He thought for a moment or two before asking if Tristram had an account with the bank.

"Could he see Mr Grant Junior's banking history, he wondered? After he had pored over the account for a while, he looked at me in a way that said I could maybe tell him more about the situation than could be gleaned from simply looking at bank records. Would I be so kind as to share my thoughts with him? It would be off the record he assured me."

"And did you?"

Sally smiled conspiratorially. Liam loved the coy look that spread across her features, resulting in an impish appearance he had not witnessed before.

"First he wanted to know about Tristram's financial standing. He's mortgaged up to the hilt, although he likes to portray himself as the wealthy Lord of the Manor – as we all know. So – I told him he had problems servicing his debt with the bank. He had noticed that himself and wondered why such an unsustainable debt had been permitted for so long."

Liam listened attentively.

"I said I could not comment on that, as he was one of Mr Wyllie's friends and tended to deal with Mr Grant's affairs himself. He asked lots of questions after that, particularly about Harry, how his debt had been cleared and all that sort of stuff. When I'd finished, he told me that he had another appointment, which I now realise must have been with you. His final words were that he was very grateful for my input and that I must not discuss the matter with anyone."

Liam smiled.

"I believe we might be making progress," he said, before driving away towards the Crown.

CHAPTER 89

A yellow Volkswagen Beetle was parked near the entrance to the hotel. Liam pulled in beside it. Seconds later, Harry and Beverly drew up alongside them in the van.

"Are we meeting tonight?" Sally asked.

Liam reminded her that Alex Green was arriving today and that they were going to meet him along with Harry, Beverly and Mark. "I've booked dinner for all of us, did you forget?"

Sally said she had but was looking forward to meeting the 'trick cyclist'.

"He's a psychologist," he corrected her, "not a psychiatrist, as far as I remember."

Before they could even say hello, Mark emerged from the hotel grinning broadly. He seemed to have been lurking inside, awaiting their arrival. It was clear he was very excited about something.

"You're looking very animated!" Liam observed as he got out of the car.

Mark nodded vigorously, beaming one of his most radiant smiles. "Come on in," he beckoned. "Have I got a surprise for you, Harry."

Intrigued, they followed Mark into the hotel.

"Alex is waiting for us in the dining room," he informed them. "Don't stare, if you can help it."

Mark grabbed Harry by the arm and led him towards the restaurant. Expecting to see some bookish academic, Harry was surprised to discover that there was only one person in the room. The fair-haired woman, sitting at a table, smiled and rose to her feet as the rest of the party entered.

"I'd like to introduce Alexis, also known as Alex Green!" Mark announced with relish.

Everyone laughed, except for Harry, whose eyes were transfixed on the attractive woman sitting there.

"Hello, Harry," she said, "I'm so pleased to meet you. Thank you for agreeing to see me."

"Me too," Harry stammered as he took her hand in his. "But how did you know I was Harry?"

"Mark showed me a group photograph of the gala concert," she informed him. "I think I know who you all are except for this lady," she said after correctly identifying Liam and Sally, before looking enquiringly at Beverly.

"I'm Harry's sister," she informed her, holding out her hand, but Harry had not released his hold on Alex. Beverly withdrew her own hand, smiling knowingly. Everyone had witnessed how fascinated Harry was in the newcomer. They were also aware that Alex's throat had reddened. Beverly wondered if it was because everyone was staring at her, or if there might be another reason for the reaction.

Alex was the first to recover her composure and enquired where Chris might be, as he had been in the group photo that Mark had shown her. Mark informed her he would be coming along later and that Joe Burns, Harry's neighbour, was also expected to join them. "But let's get everyone a drink," he suggested. "What can I get for you, Alex?"

She turned to face him and asked if she could have a glass

of red wine. She was still holding Harry's hand, which he eventually and seemingly reluctantly let go without taking his eyes from her.

Sally, too, had witnessed the interaction between them. She caught Beverly's eye and both women nodded conspiratorially.

Mark had arranged the table seating so that Harry and Alex sat alongside each other. During the meal, they hardly spoke to anyone else. It was clear they were enjoying each other's company and had more or less exchanged information about their lives and personal likes and dislikes in a variety of contexts. The women also noticed how Alex tended to lean closer to Harry while periodically stroking her hair.

Harry had even touched her lightly on the shoulder. He was clearly transfixed by the vivacious woman at his side. Beverly also noticed he had established full eye contact. That was something he found almost impossible to do, except with very close friends and Beverly herself. He was smiling a lot and even laughing at some shared confidences.

Now, even Mark had cottoned on to what was happening. His best friend seemed completely infatuated by Alex. What was not to like? he thought to himself. She was lovely to look at with the kind of charisma that would light up a room.

He wondered how Beverly might be feeling. She was fiercely protective of her brother and might be concerned, maybe even a trifle jealous, that someone else was receiving Harry's attention. He looked at her enquiringly, only to see she appeared to be very pleased with the way things were unfolding.

When the meal was over, they moved to Mark's suite for coffee and liqueurs.

Alex and Harry claimed the couch and seemed completely oblivious to anyone else in the room. Sally noted that they were sitting with their legs crossed towards each other. She seemed to remember that this meant they were unconsciously creating a barrier preventing anyone else invading that space. Although feeling slightly excluded, the others made polite conversation, until a light knock at the door alerted everyone that Chris and Joe had arrived.

Before anyone could say anything, Harry had sprung to his feet and was informing the two men that he would like to introduce them to Alex Green.

Mark again noted how Harry's behaviour had changed. This indicated a complete change in Harry's demeanour, which once more gave him hope. Perhaps his chum was beginning to recapture the unique character that had endeared him to everyone.

Joe, being Joe, once the introductions had been completed, went straight to the heart of the matter.

"Do you think you know how Harry might have developed this phenomenal memory, Alex?"

The room went quiet as she decided how to respond.

"I'm not sure," she hedged. "Harry's case is quite unique. I've never known anything like it. Since given the news, I've trawled through countless journals and psychiatric papers but am unable to come up with anything that really explains what has happened here."

She leaned forward before continuing.

"I suppose it is all right to tell you a little bit about the work I was engaged in with Professor Hart. It was very hypothetical and based upon the belief that anyone could memorise facts through NLP. Sorry for using an acronym that might not mean anything to you – NLP stands for Neuro-Linguistic Programming."

"I've heard of that," Chris interrupted. "It's basically hypnotic suggestion, isn't it?"

"That's correct, up to a point," Alex conceded, "but what seems to have happened in Harry's case has gone way beyond what William Hart had dared believe was possible – although that was what he was ultimately seeking to achieve."

"How so?" Liam enquired.

"Well, NLP is usually programmed through sleep learning, for want of a better description. What seems to have happened here is that Harry appears to have been deeply motivated to learn and memorise facts while in an unconscious state. This could be a tremendous breakthrough in our understanding of the human mind and what it is capable of achieving."

"So let me get this straight," Beverly persisted. "The abilities that Harry has acquired are above and beyond what you were trying to achieve."

"Well, yes and no. William always believed it might be possible that the effect might go beyond just hypnotic-induced learning while the subject was in a very deep trance. His contemporaries dismissed the proposition as being fanciful. It made him something of a laughing stock in academic circles. Knowing him as I did, my feeling was that he might just have something worth investigating."

"So, what progress did you make, Alex?"

"Not as much as we would have liked, I'm afraid. William was quite elderly when he started the research and subsequent trials. I helped when I could but then I landed a job in Edinburgh and only managed to liaise with him at the weekends. He felt he was getting close to some kind of breakthrough, but I was seconded overseas for a three-month spell and although we kept in touch by email, he suffered a massive stroke which rendered him incapable of carrying on with the project. He died on the day I returned to the UK."

Chris had another question. "So, you do not know what sort of progress he made, if any?" he probed.

"As I said, we kept in touch while I was abroad and he did seem to indicate he had developed a means of programming an individual to learn and memorise extensive, detailed information. He also said he was working on a series of suggestions that might achieve those objectives, but I never discovered what those entailed. It now seems that Harry, while in a comatose state, was subjected to the programme. Perhaps this explains why he has developed the skills he now has."

"Harry once was unconscious for a couple of weeks before, when he was younger," Mark informed her. "When he came out of it, all he was interested in was learning all he could about contemporary music. His knowledge is encyclopaedic, as I told you earlier, before the others arrived. Could that have happened again – only this time with antiques?"

Alex looked thoughtful but did not speak.

"I'm sure Harry won't mind me saying this, but the previous time he came out of the coma, his personality had changed. Before then, he was the life and soul of the party, the most charismatic individual you could hope to meet. After the accident, he became introverted and, dare I say it, uncommunicative – except when it came to dealing with people in his business affairs, or in other social contexts. He was always politeness personified."

"Go on," Alex prompted.

Mark looked at Harry before continuing. He received a nod, encouraging him to continue.

"Well, months later, when first his grandfather died and his grandmother was diagnosed with cancer, he seemed to sink further into a depression he couldn't shake off. Later, when his granny was nearing her final hours, she told him she'd heard that the hospice was under threat of closure and hoped he could do something to prevent that."

Everyone was hanging on to what Mark was recalling. Tears rolled down Harry's face.

"Would you like me to stop, Harry? Maybe I've said too much?"

Harry shook his head. "No, please go on, Mark. I'm just being a bit emotional."

"If you're sure, I'll go on, then." He paused again, before continuing in an effort to gather his thoughts.

"That became his other preoccupation. The 'Save the Hospice' campaign was an overwhelming success, raising far more than was actually needed. I began to worry about him again, especially when we discovered that the bank wanted to foreclose on Harry after allowing him to rack up massive debts. Although he still had his music to distract him, my fear was that he would simply cave in and give up."

Joe had been quiet for most of the time since entering the room but then voiced his own view of how things had developed.

"Like Mark, I also feared for Harry's state of mind but something remarkable happened. Beverly turned up 'out of the blue'. It seemed to have an almost miraculous effect upon him. He began to resemble the old Harry we knew before the head knocks. It was marvellous what Sally and Beverly achieved in getting him back on a commercial footing. More than that, though, he now seems to have rediscovered the empathy for others that had deserted him, following the accidents. Oh yes, I know what he did in saving the hospice was a charitable act but that was more because it was a promise he made to his grandmother. He seemed to be devoid or disinterested in any human interaction – except with close friends, that is – of which I am proud to count myself one."

Beverly had reached over and held Harry's hand while Mark sought the other one.

"Harry's was not the only life that Beverly brightened," Chris observed.

The laughter, which followed, eased the tension that had been building. Alex looked around the faces which had belonged to strangers and acknowledged that Harry's friends were people she was comfortable with. She would like to become their friend also.

Eventually, Harry spoke because everyone was looking at him to see how he was reacting to what had been said.

"I'm so lucky to have such great support from you all," he mumbled. "And do you know something, I've already said this to Beverly, but I feel different. You're right. I was avoiding getting involved with anyone or anything that might cause grief. I'd just had so much of it before that I didn't think I could stand any more. Thanks for sticking by me. I really appreciate how supportive you've been over the years."

Another silence ensued before Liam directed another question to Alex.

"I fully appreciate you may not be able to help Harry fully resolve his issues but I'm getting the impression he seems to be overcoming them somewhat, from what the others are saying. I guess time will tell. There is, however, another question concerning Professor Hart's work, that Amelia Hart hinted at, which I'd like you to respond to, if you can?"

Liam saw Alex look over apprehensively. His lawyer's training had taught him to focus on every detail that might have a relevance to any situation.

"Amelia told me that her father had regular visits from one or more of the security services. What was their interest in Professor Hart's work?"

Alex looked round the room at the expectant faces before finally coming to a decision.

"I was on the outside looking in," she began, "and not supposed to know about his connections with Thames House.

He hinted that if I were to continue supporting him, it would be necessary to sign the Official Secrets Act."

Liam nodded knowingly. "For those of you who don't know, Alex is referring to counter-intelligence," he revealed. "Is that correct, Alex?"

"Yes," she replied. "MI5 or something like that was what I thought he meant."

"Did you ever meet with any of them?"

"No, they never visited when I was there."

"What would they want with Professor Hart?" Sally enquired.

"I'm only speculating, and no doubt Alex has considered this also. If the mind-programming system William Hart was seeking to develop could be achieved, it would provide a massive advantage for counter-intelligence."

Alex nodded in agreement.

Another silence ensued before Chris suggested that things were getting a bit serious, and they all needed to lighten up a bit, especially with Alex having just arrived after what must have been a long and tiring journey.

She thanked him for that and agreed that she was rather exhausted but also stimulated by what she had learned. "I'm really looking forward to continuing this, Harry. Will it be all right for me to come to your place at, say, ten tomorrow?"

Harry said that it would, without the now regular habit of referring to Beverly to seek her approval. His sister smiled as she saw him walk Alex to the door and thought, *I'll bet he can't wait for morning to come.*

CHAPTER 90

Harry found sleep impossible. Usually, when he went to bed, the nightly routine of switching on the tape had him drifting into a deep slumber. After the first few words, he was never actually aware of the suggestions that issued from the disembodied voice, so deeply did it permeate the deepest recesses of his brain.

Tonight, however, something strange happened. When the tape ended, he was suddenly awake, his thoughts racing as he visualised, in sharp focus, the face of Alex Green. Try as he might, sleep evaded him as he visualised the woman who had so completely entranced him from the first moment he had seen her. It was an extremely pleasant sensation that made him smile at the thought of being with her again, yet also unsettling. He recalled her movements and mannerisms, the sweet sound of her voice, and most of all, the dazzling smile which produced a warm glow within him. He was acutely aware of feelings he'd never experienced before and was excited by the emotions she had ignited in his otherwise insular existence.

Alex was also finding sleep elusive. "I'm behaving like a lovesick teenager," she kept telling herself. Despite the rational thoughts of an intelligent, thirty-something woman, she was finding it impossible to erase Harry from her thoughts. Seeing his photograph had sparked feelings she found unsettling. When they did finally meet, the experience was quite unexpected. She found herself wanting to hold him in her arms, to feel his body next to hers. She tried to understand why this had happened. Was it because he looked so apprehensive, so in need of affection? She wondered how things would develop between them, anticipating the morning liaison might be both awkward and exciting.

CHAPTER 91

Ruth awoke to the sound of a vehicle arriving at the manor house. Intrigued, as they received few visitors, she went to the window and was alarmed at discovering a police car at the front entrance. She heard the front doorbell ringing loud and shrill, followed by the sound of muffled footsteps in the parquet hallway below.

The creaking sound of the heavy oak door being opened was followed by a voice enquiring if Mr Grant could spare them a few moments to assist them with their investigations. There was no reply as she pictured a sour-faced Tristram indicating that they should come into the house. Seconds later, she heard the sound of the study door clicking shut.

She slipped into a nightgown and tiptoed barefoot down the creaking staircase, before proceeding to the study and pressing her ear to the door. Although she could not hear everything as clearly as she would have liked, it was easy to distinguish who was speaking. Tristram, in his normal petulant tone, was complaining about "the intrusion at this unearthly hour."

Ruth noted that the hall clock showed the time to be 5.30am. What could this be about? she wondered. Was it something that might affect her?

Inside the room Tristram was feeling decidedly uncomfortable and had tried to dismiss the policeman's questions in a blustering fashion, when he asked him if he knew William Wyllie.

"Of course I do, what's that got to do with me?"

"And have you been in touch with him recently?"

"He's my bank manager. I perhaps spoke last with him a fortnight ago."

"You haven't spoken since?" queried the officer who had introduced himself as DS Black.

"No, I just told you so. Are you deaf?"

"Not even on the telephone?" he persisted.

"Absolutely not!"

"No communication whatsoever then, personally or otherwise?"

"How many times do I need to tell you? Are you stupid as well as deaf?"

DS Black then enquired if the mobile phone lying on the coffee table belonged to Tristram. When he received confirmation that it was, he then asked if it was switched on. Again, Tristram confirmed that it was.

The other officer, DCI Jones, took another mobile phone from his pocket and pressed speed dial. Seconds later, Tristram Grant's phone started ringing.

Tristram looked at the phone in dismay. He now realised that the phone the chief inspector was holding was the one he'd given to Wyllie.

"I'm afraid we'll have to ask you to accompany us to the station," Ruth heard one of the officers say. She did not wait to hear more but scuttled away to the dining room opposite, gently closing the door as she heard her protesting husband wanting to know why he was being taken into custody.

"You are not being arrested," she heard one of them say.

"You are merely helping us with our enquiries at this time. Do you need to inform anyone where you are going?"

Tristram responded swiftly, saying that there was no one that needed to be notified, except his solicitor.

The house became very still and quiet following the closure of the outer door, followed by the unmistakable sound of displaced gravel being scattered by the rapid departure of a motor vehicle.

I wonder what Tristram's been doing to warrant a visit from the police? she wondered.

Without waiting another moment, she picked up the landline and telephoned an ex-directory number. Although very early for most people to be awake, she knew that Donald Dalrymple would just be thinking about going to bed. Such were the hours casino owners kept.

"What the hell do you want at this time of day, Ruth?" was how he responded to her call.

CHAPTER 92

Sally felt clumsy and awkward as she fumbled with the locks. She imagined the three auditors waiting to gain access to the bank's archives were becoming impatient with her. It was only 8.30. She was early, as the bank wasn't due to open until 9.30. They were clearly anxious to get started.

Eventually, she made the correct choices and hurried in to switch off the alarm. Without preamble, they requested access to various records, but she informed them that some documents could not be produced, because the manager held the only set of keys. When asked if she could contact the police to retrieve them, Sally agreed to do that. She lifted the phone to contact the police station and was put through to DS Black. He said he would get back to her. The telephone rang several minutes later. Black told her that they had not been on Wyllie's person, so they had asked him where they were.

"They're in a bureau drawer in his lounge," Black informed her. "I'm sending over a car with an officer who has a key to gain entry. She'll collect you shortly and accompany you during the search. Incidentally, my boss is wondering if the auditors have arrived?"

Sally replied that they had. "Did you want to speak to them?"

"We'll both take a walk over to the bank in about an hour. There have been developments, and we are in the middle of an interrogation that could prove relevant to their investigations. Please stress we will want to speak to them before they leave."

Without removing the handset from her ear, Sally informed them of DS Black's request. "Was there anything else?" she enquired. Black told her he would get back to her if other queries arose.

The arrival of the other bank staff necessitated that, as the senior member, she needed to inform them about the presence of the inspectors, stating that they should co-operate with any requests they received in her absence.

When the police car arrived at the bank entrance, she strode out into the sunlight to access the passenger door. As she did so, a yellow convertible Volkswagen Beetle tooted as it approached from the direction of the Crown Hotel. Alex Green waved as she passed on her way to meet Harry. Sally waved back, and despite the seriousness of the situation at work, she smiled and wondered if she was going to discover how Harry had developed the phenomenal skills he now possessed.

She did not notice Liam who was also waving from his office window. He had observed all the comings and goings as he pored over the sale documents that would transfer ownership of Joe's farm. Seeing her getting into a police car caused him to wonder if Sally had become implicated in Wyllie's shenanigans but felt relief as the car took off in the opposite direction from the police station.

Returning to the documents he had been working on, Liam paused for a few moments to consider recent events. Alex Green had been a revelation. Not the nerdy academic he had imagined but a stunningly attractive female who would turn heads in any company. His training had taught him to study people's behaviour, and he believed Harry had been bowled over by her arrival. He got the impression she had been similarly affected. He hoped they would get on well and maybe develop an effective working relationship. One thing did concern him, however. It was the implied involvement of the security, or counter-intelligence, agencies, whoever they might be. Professor Hart's work was too important for them not to maintain an interest in any developments that might assist them in their fight against the forces that threatened the country. Perhaps he was suffering from an overactive imagination but also realised that, if Harry's powers could be harnessed, the advantages such powers might achieve were inestimable.

Dragging his thoughts back to the present, he lifted the phone and dialled Joe's number.

When he answered, Liam invited him to come into the office to discuss the details of the sale of the nursery.

CHAPTER 93

Like Wyllie before him, Tristram didn't take long to cave in to police questioning and owned up to the banking fraud he had tried to perpetrate to acquire Harry's property. He also admitted, when pressed, that he had arranged to incriminate Harry and Chris in the burglary he had staged with Wyllie's assistance. When accused of arranging for stolen goods to be planted at the car boot sale, he owned up to that as well. Yes, he had paid Jake Butcher to steal the farm equipment that disgorged the slurry at Burns' Nursery in an attempt to prevent the auction going ahead. When pressed, he agreed it had simply been an act of spite. He wanted to get even for having been frustrated in acquiring the two properties.

When pressed to explain where he obtained the planted stolen items, or how the mobile phone had been acquired, he was less forthcoming. He was equally uncooperative concerning the beating that Butch had received. No matter how hard they pressed him, Tristram would not say another word.

After they had told him about the charges he was facing, DCI Jones informed him the bank was undergoing an inspection and that additional charges might arise following the auditors' findings.

He was then locked in a cell at the opposite end to which Wyllie was incarcerated. The swaggering disdainful persona he once displayed was now of a man that realised his ability to dominate and manipulate those he believed his inferiors had come to an abrupt conclusion. Despite the affront to his ego, his greatest worry was how Donald Dalrymple might react. He had been careful to avoid implicating him throughout the grilling the detectives had subjected him to, but Dalrymple, he realised, would want to make sure it remained that way. He was well aware of the punishments that could be meted out to people who might be a danger to him and that extended into prison, where it was now quite clear both he and Wyllie would be heading for months or even years.

He sank onto the bed with his head in his hands and wept uncontrollably; partly through anger but mainly through the sense that his life was in grave danger, irrespective as to where he might end up.

CHAPTER 94

Alex was enjoying the drive to Harry's place. Like Beverly before her, the small market town, relatively unchanged over the years, was everything she loved. The welcome she had received was also very gratifying and encouraging. Harry had such good friends. She wished she could become part of the group to experience the undoubted support and affection they shared.

As she left the built-up area of shops and houses, Burns' Nursery appeared. It was about four hundred yards from the town boundary, and she was now looking for Harry's place, which Mark had told her was only a quarter of a mile further ahead. Knowing that she was too early for a ten o'clock appointment, she slowed down and, on seeing a lay-by ahead, decided to pull in to review what she had planned doing when she got to the farmstead. Her shared notes on the work with Professor Hart were incomplete. On returning to Edinburgh following her time abroad, they had disappeared from the locked filing cabinet where they had been placed. A break-in during her absence had resulted in other data being stolen, along with a laptop she had left behind. Being a resourceful type, Alex determined to access the internet site she had used to share information with Professor Hart.

The access code was easy to remember but probably sufficient to prevent entry by anyone stumbling across the portal.

She recalled the password as she reviewed her notes.

W.H *^!)"(="^%A.G.

Decoded, it was easy to remember as it stood for 'W.H861029+265A.G'.

Minutes later, she released the handbrake and drove out of the lay-by heading for the farm. Despite herself, she could not help feeling excited but also a little apprehensive about seeing Harry again. As she drove into the yard, the farmhouse door opened as both Harry and Beverly came out to meet her. She hoped that the warm flush she had just experienced wasn't showing on her face.

Beverly greeted her with an embrace and said she was pleased to see her again. Harry merely shook her hand and stood aside as the two women linked arms as they headed inside.

Alex would have preferred that it was Beverly who shook her hand, and that Harry had given her a hug, but immediately scolded herself for thinking such a thing.

Over a cup of coffee, Alex enquired if they were connected to the internet and could she use it to access some notes she needed, in connection with her investigations?

Beverly gave her the code which she immediately entered on her laptop.

"Sorry about this," she said, "but my office was burgled, and a lot of stuff was stolen, including the data Professor Hart and I had been sharing. I really need to retrieve it if we are to try and make sense of what has been happening here."

The information came back within seconds. Alex could not have been aware that the contact she made alerted a civil servant in south-west London. He noted the co-ordinates from which the request had been transmitted and within seconds emailed a senior officer with the information he had just acquired.

Within minutes, two agents were tasked with investigating what Alex Green was doing in the area. They were to adopt a watching brief to ascertain what lay behind her renewed interest in the 'Hart Continuum System'. Accommodation had been reserved at the Crown Hotel, Millfield.

CHAPTER 95

Jones and Black were reviewing what they had achieved over a cup of coffee in the police canteen.

"It wasn't as difficult as I thought it would be," Jones confided.

"It was far too easy, I agree. Both of them held their hands up to virtually everything except how the mobile phone and the stolen goods were acquired," Black replied.

"Neither could explain how Butcher received his injuries, though. It seems pretty likely a third party is involved and that, I believe, could be Donald Dalrymple."

"Why would they have got involved with Dalrymple? We know there is a connection through Wiltris being registered to one of Dalrymple's premises but more than that, we have nothing else to connect them with him."

"That's true but it does not take a great deal of imagination to surmise that Dalrymple is the means of them funding this business park Liam Forbes has unearthed from planning applications. Grant is virtually penniless and would be unable to fund a venture of that magnitude, but someone like Dalrymple could easily acquire the wherewithal to do that. Grant would, of course, benefit if the plan got approval, as it would include the land which his estate occupies."

"How did Wyllie get involved?" Black wondered.

"Who knows? Both Grant and Wyllie will be indebted to Dalrymple in some way. It might be gambling debts they cannot honour. I've also heard that Wyllie seems to have an unhealthy interest in little girls. Grant, too, is rumoured to have a proclivity for deviant sexual practices. Perhaps it's none of those things but I get the feeling that Dalrymple is behind it all. I would dearly love to nab him for anything that would put him away for a very long stretch."

"I also wonder if Ruth Grant has a role in the affair?" Black said. "She never came across as someone that would consider comforting the sick, especially when it's a lowlife like Jake Butcher. Do you think we should pull her in too, boss?"

Jones thought for a moment, and then said, "I believe it might be more revealing to simply visit her and observe how she reacts to the news that Tristram is in custody. We can treat her relatively politely – simply enquiring if she had any knowledge of her husband's financial affairs."

"I'd like to be with you when you do that," Black offered.

"Let's wait a bit yet and see what else we might learn. The bank investigators might uncover information that could be useful before confronting the 'ruthless' one."

CHAPTER 96

Alex was explaining what she was hoping to explore during her visit.

"There are several things I'd like to do today, if you can spare the time, Harry?" she began. "I've got some equipment in the car that will help me assess your condition but be assured none of it is painful or too stressful."

Harry said he was happy to comply with anything that she asked him to do.

Some fleeting, unexpected thoughts flashed through her mind as she pondered some of the requests that she would have liked to have suggested. She continued, relieved that his exceptional skills were memorising facts, not reading people's minds.

"First of all, I would like to copy the tape you found, which seems to influence your current behaviour. Following that, I'd like to wire you up and induce you into a hypnotic state. Thirdly, when I've taken those readings and returned you to wakefulness, I would like to carry out the same test after you have listened to your own tape."

"I guess you'll need a quiet place to do that?" Beverly observed. "Why don't you take Alex through to the sitting room? You can use the couch and easy chairs. I'll keep out of your way while you are doing it."

Alex thanked her before retrieving her equipment from the car with Harry in tow. When they returned, Beverly asked if she would like to join them for dinner that night.

"I'm cooking for Mark, if he can manage to get away from the hotel for a while. It would be great if you could join us for a bite to eat."

"That would be great, if it's not too much trouble?" Alex confirmed.

Harry smiled, happy at the prospect and noticed that Beverly winked at him mischievously when she caught his eye. He felt his face redden. Were his feelings for Alex so transparent?

By the time the tests were completed, the clock had crept round to 2.30 in the afternoon. They returned to the kitchen to find a light lunch had been prepared for them.

"How's it going?" Beverly asked as they entered.

"Quite remarkable," Alex enthused.

"How do you feel, Harry?"

"Great!" he replied, looking like he meant it.

"What have you discovered, then?" Beverly addressed Alex.

"Quite a lot, really. I took copies of the tape and listened carefully, but it had no effect upon me, as far as I could tell. It seems there is something missing when anyone else but Harry hears it."

"We've all had a go, but like you, nothing seemed to happen to any of us like it did to Harry."

Alex looked thoughtful before responding.

"When I induced Harry into a trance, my equipment showed the sort of blood pressure readings, heart rate and brain activity that one would normally expect. Following that, I did the same test after he put on the headphones and listened to

284

Professor Hart's tape. It was astonishing how quickly and deeply Harry responded. I've never seen readings like that before and I've tested thousands of subjects over the years. There's clearly something else that's missing from my understanding of the process, which affects him in such an extreme way."

"What do you think that might be?"

"I've come to the belief there must have been something different that allowed him to achieve such intense receptivity. How long were you in a coma, Harry?"

He looked blankly at Beverly, who then told Alex he had been unconscious from Sunday morning to Thursday evening.

Alex gave the information some thought before enquiring if Harry would mind her examining his hospital records for the time he had been in hospital.

"That's fine, if they will allow us access to them, I guess."

Alex said that with Harry's blessing she would write a formal request to the hospital to examine his files. Could they maybe do that following the tests she would like to carry out, and after they'd eaten?

Half an hour later they returned to the sitting room. Alex took out her laptop and accessed a website that carried catalogues of American antiques and collectibles.

"Have you ever seen this before, Harry?"

"No," he replied. It was new to him.

"It just came online last week," she said. "There are over five hundred entries on it. How long do you think it would take you to memorise all of the information it contains?"

"I don't know. How long have I got?"

"Just take your time and tackle it like you normally would and let me know when you've finished. Would it be helpful if I left you alone when you're doing it?"

"No, it will not be necessary for you to leave. I'm not conscious of anyone or anything when I'm memorising things."

Alex observed him as he went into memorising mode, noting how completely absorbed he became in what he was doing. Apart from clicking the mouse to change pages, his concentration appeared to be absolute. Twenty minutes later, he sat back and seemed to return to his normal state of awareness. It was clear to Alex he had slipped into another cerebral dimension while processing the information presented on her laptop.

"How did you get on?"

"OK, I think. Are you going to ask me questions about the items I was looking at?"

"Yes, but how do you feel? Are you tired? Do you need a rest?"

"No, I'm feeling fine."

She turned the laptop to face her and began to ask him to tell her what he had memorised about random items she called up on the screen.

Unerringly, Harry repeated the information that appeared against each item exactly as it was written.

She could hardly believe what she had just witnessed but was forced to accept the evidence of her own eyes.

"You are truly an amazing person, Harry," she finally conceded. "If I had been told such a thing was possible, I wouldn't have believed it!"

He smiled, knowing that he had been able to impress the beautiful woman who was looking on at him in wonder.

CHAPTER 97

They'd agreed to meet at an out-of-town inn that was one of the legitimate businesses Dalrymple owned. He was already there, although the car park was empty. Ruth knew that his vehicle would be parked inside the hotel garage out of sight. He was always careful not to broadcast his movements to the world at large. Dalrymple waved to her from a side door, beckoning her to join him in the garage and quickly disappeared inside.

She hurried into the building, checking that no one was watching. He was sitting in the driver's seat waiting for her to join him. As she made to get in, a figure emerged from the rear of the car and stood next to the side-door entrance. Ruth recognised the man as one of the many so-called door stewards that accompanied him everywhere he travelled.

"What the hell is going on, Ruth?" he demanded. "What has your stupid sod of a husband got himself into with the police?"

"I don't know," she replied nervously, acutely aware of the aggression in Dalrymple's body language.

"You were supposed to keep an eye on him! I trusted you to do that one little thing for me but now things are developing in a way that is getting out of hand." He glared at her with unconcealed hostility, waiting for her to speak.

"All I know is what I heard from outside the room when the police came to see him. There was something about a stolen mobile phone, obtained from Wyllie. From what I could gather, Wyllie used it to report some sort of crime which led back to Tristram, somehow."

"The trouble with that idiot of a husband of yours is that he thinks he's smart but we both know better. I'll bet he's tried to up the ante, somehow, to pressure Harry Carry and it's backfired. I guess they might also be suspicious of the stunt he got Jake Butcher to pull with the slurry tanker."

"I went and visited him as you asked me to, Donald, and left him in no doubt what would happen if he poked his nose into your affairs again."

"How did he react to that?"

"He was wetting himself. I don't think he'll spill anything to the police."

"It would be impossible for them to connect that to me, anyway. They came down from Newcastle, did the job and returned home before daybreak."

"What are we going to do?"

Dalrymple was quiet for a while. Ruth knew better than to interrupt his train of thought and remained silent. An emphatic nod suggested he had worked something out in his head.

He lifted his mobile phone and speed-dialled a number, which was answered on the second ring. It was on loudspeaker so that Ruth could hear what was being discussed. She recognised the voice as belonging to his solicitor, Isaac Lipman. There was no preamble. Dalrymple simply delivered instructions into the mouthpiece.

"Ruth Grant is with me and is listening in. She'll meet you shortly at the police station where Grant is being held on some sort of charge. Find out what that is and get him out of there as quickly as possible. Ruth will stand bail. The local bank manager is also in chokey and I imagine that has something to do with the charges Tristram Grant is facing. If you make that connection, get him released too. Phone me when you know they will be released. I'll have a taxi waiting to take them home."

He rang off and turned to Ruth. "You heard what I just said. Don't say anything other than that you have heard that your husband is being detained at the police station and that your solicitor is acting on Tristram's behalf. Leave Lipman to do the talking."

As Ruth made to leave, Dalrymple extracted a jiffy bag from his inside pocket and handed it to her.

"There's £7,000 in used notes in there," he informed her. "Five is for you to bank against future legal costs. I can't be seen to be funding your fool of a husband's legal expenses. Keep £2,000 back for contingencies. Don't spend it until I say so."

Ruth nodded and leaned over to kiss him, but he pushed her away, telling her there was no time to waste.

Fifteen minutes later, she arrived outside the police station where Isaac Lipman was already waiting in his car.

Jones noted her arrival and called Black on the internal phone. "Things are beginning to happen," he informed him. "If you care to look at the security monitor, you'll observe Mrs Tristram Grant and Slippery Isaac Lipman approaching the front desk. I'll come to your office to agree how we are going to play this one. I'm going to phone the front desk, to keep them waiting in reception until we're ready to see them."

The wall clock in his office showed it was almost 3.30pm. He decided to phone the bank to see what progress had been made, before joining Black in his office.

CHAPTER 98

Sally answered DCI Jones's call and immediately transferred it to Edward Smith, the bank inspector, who had returned after lunch and was ensconced in Wyllie's office. Jones came quickly to the point after establishing who he was speaking to.

"I need to know quickly, in plain language, if you have discovered any further criminal acts that your employee William Wyllie has committed, along with any charges that the bank will be intending to prosecute him with."

Smith decided that any attempt at circumspection would be futile. "Yes," he confirmed. "We have found evidence of false accounting and fraud. Do you want the details now, or can you wait until I come over to the station?"

Jones told him that would be fine but then went on to ask if they had examined Wyllie's personal accounts and whether there was anything they might need to investigate.

The distaste in Smith's response was evident from the halting way in which he spoke.

"Our auditors have identified a large portion of Wyllie's income being paid into what we now understand to be an account in the name of Tristram Grant. That may mean nothing illegal, but it is paid on a monthly standing order and has been for three and a half years."

"Do you imagine that it might be blackmail?"

"How can one tell?" Smith responded. "It's the other payments that concern me."

"What other payments are you referring to?"

"We may be wrong, but we suspect that they go to a website on the dark web. Your own people will no doubt be able to ascertain if our suspicions are correct."

Jones pursed his lips and thanked Smith for the information, assuring him that he would be as discreet as possible but also that he needed to consult with him as soon as he could get over to the station.

CHAPTER 99

Mark was conversing with a member of staff when two men in green boiler suits approached the reception desk.

"We're booked in for a couple of nights," they informed the receptionist. They identified themselves as Charles Whyte and James Melville. She confirmed the booking.

She asked them to sign the register and enquired if they had a vehicle in the car park.

Whyte gave her the registration of the van they had arrived in and proceeded to make the entries for his partner and himself. An entry in the name of Alex Green caught his eye and he exchanged a glance with Melville, inviting him to look at the register, surreptitiously pointing at Alex's entry as the receptionist consulted her monitor.

Melville's eyes widened in recognition of the name, thinking that this was very fortuitous but was even more interested to hear the conversation that Mark was having with someone called Beverly, who had just telephoned.

"Yes," he was saying, "I'll be over for dinner about seven, once the hotel's evening meals have been organised. I'm looking forward to having some time with you and Harry. What's that you're saying? You've invited Alex Green? She's going to be there as well? That's great, it'll maybe give us a chance to find out more about Harry's condition. Or are you just getting involved in a little matchmaking there?"

The men listened intently, while not wanting to appear to be eavesdropping. They heard laughter at the other end of the line, followed by undecipherable words that sounded like a denial.

"I like her too," Mark confided. "I think she would be very good for Harry. In fact, I think they would be good for each other. I've never seen him so absorbed in another living person, ever!" he exclaimed before ringing off.

Returning the phone to its cradle, he then enquired if the men would be dining in tonight, to which they replied in the negative.

"You probably heard," he told the receptionist, "I'll not be here for dinner tonight and Alex Green will also be having dinner at Harry's place. You have my mobile number if you need to get in touch about anything. And yes, before you ask, I will be returning to the hotel tonight. Could you book a taxi for 6.45pm? I'll arrange for the driver to come back for us when I know when we'll be returning."

She smiled at him coyly. "I guess you will want me to lock up just in case you're delayed," she teased.

"Don't be cheeky," he warned as he strode jauntily through to the kitchen.

Whyte stole another glance at the register and noted that Alex Green was in the room next to the one he and Melville were allocated.

"Sometimes things just fall into place," he mused as the pair made their way upstairs.

CHAPTER 100

Beverly had not been idle during Alex and Harry's time in the sitting room. Apart from preparing the evening meal, she had also taken the liberty of contacting the doctor who had treated Harry following his fall. She discovered he was on duty until eight that night and could find time to see Harry and Alex, providing that there were no emergencies to deal with.

She informed them what she had done and suggested that if they were finished for the day, they might like to go to see the doctor before dinner, as there was plenty of time to do that.

"Why don't you take Alex for a tour of the area, if there is time, after you've been to the hospital, Harry?"

The look of gratitude was obvious. He would never have thought of suggesting that himself.

Alex, too, seemed pleased at the suggestion and wondered if they could also return to the hotel, to freshen up and get a change of clothes.

Beverly had taken to Alex the moment they met and believed she felt the same way.

Sometimes you just know when you are going to get on with someone, she thought.

As they were about to leave, a van with two men in green

boiler suits drove into the farmyard. Harry met them at the door. They were carrying out water-sample testing of properties that had their own private water supply, they informed him.

"Would it be all right to take the samples now? It will only take moments," they assured him.

Harry said it would be fine. They asked to be shown to the kitchen where they needed to take samples.

Alex and Beverly squeezed past the men and stood chatting as Harry led them into the house.

"Were you just leaving?" the taller of the two enquired.

Harry told them his sister would be remaining but that he and the other lady were on their way to a meeting.

"Don't let us hold you back. We can manage fine on our own," the other man replied.

Beverly waited to wave Alex and Harry away. As she did so, the two agents were already in the process of leaving.

"Thanks," they both chorused as they exited the house. "We'll get back to you if there is anything to report."

Once out of earshot, Melville turned to Whyte. "It's going well so far," he enthused.

Whyte agreed. Within an hour of reaching the hotel, they had secreted video and listening devices in the farmhouse kitchen and sitting room.

"All we have to do now is to wait for them to tell us what's going on when they meet for dinner tonight."

"I guess we should be checking in with Control for an update," Melville reminded him, as they drove out of the farmyard and headed back to the hotel.

CHAPTER 101

Isaac Lipman and Ruth Grant were showing increasing signs of annoyance at the delay in accessing DCI Jones. On the third occasion that Lipman approached the desk sergeant, the phone beside him rang. He picked it up and listened for a few moments before addressing Lipman. "PC Allan will conduct you to DCI Jones's office," he informed him, "following an interview with another gentleman who is about to arrive in the next few minutes."

"This is intolerable!" Lipman complained. "Mrs Grant and I have been waiting here for more than an hour. In the meantime, my client is being held in custody without my having access to him. I must protest at the treatment we have been subjected to and will certainly pursue this further if there is no progress within the next fifteen minutes."

His rant was interrupted with the arrival of DS Black.

"I'm so sorry to keep you hanging around," he began, "but we are waiting for information from another party concerning Mr Grant's case. He is on his way here now and should be with us shortly."

"What are the charges?" Lipman demanded.

"To date, Mr Grant, your client has admitted to several

misdemeanours relating to fraud, conspiring with others to pervert the course of justice and being in possession of stolen goods. He has voluntarily signed a statement to that effect."

"If he did that without a lawyer being present, you might find that his statement doesn't stand up in court," Lipman informed him.

"I'm afraid it will. We gave Mr Grant three opportunities to have a solicitor present, but he declined. The tape will verify that and will be available to you at the appropriate time. Right now, we are considering other charges, which are being lodged by a third party and will advise you of those when we have examined the evidence concerning the alleged crimes. We will, of course, notify Mr Grant that you are here offering to represent him, and will respect his wishes, whatever they might be."

Ruth then interjected. "Mr Lipman is also here to represent my husband's friend, who I believe is also being held in custody."

"Did you mean William Wyllie, the bank manager? I did not know that they were such close friends but having discovered the charges against them, I can now see that their complicity in the alleged crimes that have been committed is connected."

Lipman cautioned Ruth not to say any more by placing a finger over his lips out of Black's vision. It was obvious she regretted the outburst, turning sharply on her heel and returning to the plastic seat on which she had been waiting since entering the station.

Further conversation ended with the arrival of Edward Smith.

Black smiled at him as he entered, mainly for effect, but also to unsettle Lipman.

"I'd like to introduce you to Mr Edward Smith," he

announced. "Mr Smith is a bank inspector who, with a team of auditors, has been uncovering evidence of more financial crimes connected to both Mr Wyllie and Mr Grant. This is Mr Lipman, a solicitor, and the lady sitting over there is Ruth Grant, Tristram Grant's wife," he informed Edward Smith. "Mr Lipman has offered to represent both of the accused despite Mr Grant's reluctance to have a solicitor act for him," he continued. "Your employee William Wyllie may now decide to engage Mr Lipman's services following the information you are about to furnish us with, but to date, he has also declined any legal representation."

Lipman said nothing but scowled at Black, who once again smiled pleasantly, if somewhat triumphantly, at the lawyer.

"We will return to you just as soon as we have had an opportunity to assess the reliability of the information Mr Smith is going to present us with," Black concluded.

He gestured for Smith to follow but stopped midway to the door. He returned to speak to the desk sergeant. "Could you please inform Mr Wyllie and Mr Grant that Mr Dalrymple's solicitor is offering to represent them in their current difficulties? Sorry," he corrected. "Don't mention Mr Dalrymple, that was a foolish mistake on my part. Just tell them that Isaac Lipman is waiting for them in reception. It's just a slip of the tongue," he said to Lipman, who was about to object to what Black had just said. "It's just impossible to think of your firm without making a connection with Mr Dalrymple, who you have been working for so conscientiously over so many years – my apologies for that. Oh, and please let Mr Grant and his good friend Mr Wyllie know that Mr Grant's wife is also waiting in reception."

Jones found it hard not to laugh. He had positioned himself, just out of view, behind the desk sergeant's area and had heard the conversations between Black, Lipman and

Grant. Black was very good at causing uncertainty by some of the things he came up with. It seemed as if he had been able to do so again with Lipman. From the window next to where he had been eavesdropping, he smiled as Lipman scurried out of the station, a mobile phone pressed to his ear. He was no doubt reporting back to a certain Mr Donald Dalrymple.

CHAPTER 102

"I have to confess there were times when I wondered if you would ever come out of that coma, Harry. But here you now are, as large as life and looking different somehow to how you were before," Doctor Dixon revealed as he sat across from Harry and Alex, a thick file of notes encased in a manila folder on his desk.

"How have you been keeping?"

"OK," was all that Harry offered, in his usual non-committal fashion.

"I must press you," Dixon persisted. "What have you been doing? What has been responsible for this exceptional change in you? I'm hearing that so much has been going on in your life – the auction and everything else that seems to be happening around you just now."

"I've been very lucky. My long-lost sister, Beverly, turned up out of the blue and that made a terrific difference to my life. She has been so good at helping me get back on my feet – that, and the great support I've had from my friends and, of course, you," he added hastily.

"Well, it certainly seems to be working, whatever brought about the change. I'm so happy to see you looking so well."

300

He paused for a moment before continuing. "But you haven't introduced me to your companion yet."

"Forgive me for that, please. This is Alex Green – sorry, Doctor Alex Green, I should have said. Alex is interested in my condition and would like to know more about the fall and my time in hospital."

Harry marvelled at how many words he had strung together when replying to Doctor Dixon. Where did this new eloquence come from, he wondered? It was certainly out of character.

Alex stepped in, after treating the doctor to a dazzling smile that made him wish that he knew this elegant woman more intimately.

"Harry has invited me to carry out tests on some behaviours that have evolved since his time in hospital. I suspect that it may have had something to do with the vegetative state he was in at the time and other external influences that have developed since he regained consciousness."

Alex continued in medical speak that Harry was unable to follow. He was in fact completely focused on Alex and the manner in which she charmed the doctor when explaining what she was seeking to discover.

Dixon nodded every now and again, before eventually turning to Harry and asking if it was all right for Alex to have sight of his medical records.

Harry gave his permission and the doctor left them in the office, somewhat reluctantly, Harry felt, because it seemed he had also been charmed by being in the company of the woman who sat beside him. Uncharacteristically, Harry felt a short burst of resentment. That was another emotion he had not felt for many years.

With the doctor gone, Alex set about examining Harry's notes. He watched her as she ploughed through the data in front of her, completely absorbed in what she was doing, muttering to herself now and again and regularly scribbling notes in a pad she had taken with her. Eventually, she sat back and looked at him with a look of incredulity.

"Do you know you were virtually at death's door for most of the time you were here, Harry?"

When he didn't respond, she shook her head and told him that she would have been very sorry if that had happened. He thought he saw her eyes moisten but looked away as she turned her head in apparent embarrassment.

She finally suggested that, as time was getting on, she would like to return to examine the notes more thoroughly with Harry's permission. He found Dixon talking to some nurses in the ward and told him of Alex's request. The doctor said that he would keep them in his desk for easy access for when she returned.

CHAPTER 103

On the journey to the Crown, they did not talk much, other than when Harry pointed out points of interest. Alex parked next to the van which had conveyed the two men who had visited Harry's homestead on the pretext of carrying out a water-sample analysis. One of the men, James Melville, was sitting in reception, reading a newspaper, as Alex and Harry entered the foyer. He gave a brief "Hello again" as they entered, which Harry acknowledged with a nod before approaching him to enquire how he had got on with the tests.

Melville replied that everything was fine and that there were no problems with the water quality.

They were interrupted by Mark, who had seen them arriving and came out to greet them.

As Harry's attention was diverted, Melville pressed a phone to his ear and said, "The package has arrived."

Charles Whyte understood that the message was a warning Alex Green had returned and would soon be making her way upstairs.

"Copy," he replied, before collecting his equipment and exiting from Alex's room.

Downstairs, Alex asked to be excused, as she was going

back to her room to freshen up before dinner. Before she left, Mark told her he had ordered a taxi and that they could all return to Harry's place together if she was OK with that. She agreed that it would be good for them all to share a cab, before ascending the stairs.

All three men watched approvingly as she disappeared upstairs.

"What a pity she's so bandy-legged!" Mark observed.

"She is not. She's got perfect legs," Harry retorted much more vehemently than he intended.

Mark collapsed into fits of laughter at his friend's angry response.

"Only teasing, Harry. I suspected you were rather keen on her!"

Harry laughed as well. Mark had caught him out and he felt embarrassed that his feelings should have been so obvious.

"Do you think she's noticed?" he asked self-consciously.

"I think Alex is very well aware of your interest in her, as are the rest of the gang. From where we were sitting, I got the impression that she feels the same way about you."

"Do you think so? I couldn't imagine she could ever be interested in someone like me."

"I'm sure that there is no accounting for taste, old buddy, but Beverly also thinks that Alex is rather smitten with you, too. Don't sell yourself short, and make the best of things tonight, since your sister has contrived to play Cupid at dinner."

A look of realisation crossed Harry's face as he suddenly understood what Beverly had been doing. That everyone else was aware of his infatuation with Alex was also disconcerting yet pleasing at the same time. He never thought his feelings would have been so transparent.

Mark slipped an arm across his shoulders, directing him

to the bar for a drink. "Tell me. How did you get on with the tests?"

Melville would have liked to have followed to hear what Harry had to say but contented himself knowing he would not only hear but also be able to record all of the conversations in Harry's kitchen later that night.

CHAPTER 104

It was almost 5.30 before Jones entered Liam's office. Sally was with him and had just been giving an update of the events that had unfolded during banking hours.

He seemed a little taken aback to discover Sally was there with Liam and looked questioningly at Liam who, rather bashfully, informed him that Sally and he were going 'out together' – that they were an item. He cursed himself for using such archaic language but then acknowledged that legal speak was deeply ingrained in the way he spoke. He glanced at Sally and hoped that he hadn't been too presumptuous but saw she was smiling, looking even pleased, if he was reading the signs correctly.

Sally dropped her gaze and stared at the floor. She felt thrilled to hear how Liam regarded their relationship. Jones smiled and said he understood, before talking about his reasons for wanting to speak to Liam.

"I guess you know what this is all about, Miss Smith, but I must ask you not to discuss what I have to say with anyone else at this time," he began.

Sally nodded agreement.

Jones then went on to give a summary of what he'd

discovered concerning Grant and Wyllie's scheming and how they had been very quick to admit what they had been up to.

"We suspect, as Liam has suggested, others – who shall remain nameless at present – are involved. If you can uncover anything else that will secure a conviction, I would be most grateful, Liam?"

Liam assured him that he would do that if anything materialised from his current enquiries regarding Wiltris and the planning application.

Jones bade them good day and left the office, a wide grin covering his florid features.

CHAPTER 105

Beverly had excelled herself. The meal was superb, and she had succeeded in creating an intimate atmosphere with the introduction of some candles in the sparse but functional kitchen.

After a few glasses of wine, however, Beverly observed that Alex would place her hand on Harry's arm or shoulder as she emphasised a point or laughed at some joke someone had made. Mark noticed that Harry had not looked as animated or happy for years. He was clearly enjoying being in Alex's company.

Talk eventually turned to previous lives. Mark recounted some of the more memorable adventures Harry and he had experienced as boys. A lot of banter ensued, which Harry participated in, somewhat to Mark's surprise. The women were intrigued to learn about the scrapes they had got into and wanted to hear more, until Mark asked Beverly what sort of childhood experiences she'd had in Australia. It was the story of a tomboy who enjoyed all sorts of sporting activities.

"So, tell us a bit about yourself, Alex," Beverly invited.

"What's to tell?" she replied. "I grew up in a fairly typical lower middle-class home in the suburbs. My parents were very loving and supportive. I had a very happy childhood with lots of good friends. I did reasonably well at school and made it to university but with no clear thoughts about what I was going to study there. Having always been interested in people's behaviour, it was suggested I might major in psychology – and that's what I did."

"Did you meet Professor Hart at uni?" Mark enquired.

"Yes. We seemed to hit it off from the start. He encouraged me to do my doctorate. I have a lot to thank him for, not just as a teacher, but also as a very dear friend."

"Speaking of Professor Hart, I understand he wanted you to work with him and that it was his sudden illness and later demise, which prevented that happening."

"Yes, I was really looking forward to doing that, but it was not to be. Still, I'm here now and absolutely fascinated to be able to have access to Harry, to see if I can discover what happened."

"So, you only see me as a guinea pig?" Harry cut in, feeling almost at once that he shouldn't have framed the question quite so bluntly. It had been in jest but had sounded resentful.

Alex could not hide her dismay at what Harry had just said. "Oh, please don't think that, Harry. I would have been delighted to have known you, without any of this happening," taking his hand in hers as she spoke. Almost at once she withdrew it as if it was a red-hot iron, placing both hands firmly in her lap, looking first at Beverly, then Mark and finally Harry.

Harry then did something that surprised even him. He reached out and took the hand that had previously held his and clasped it firmly with both of his.

"I'm sorry that came out the way it did, Alex. I was merely teasing. Even if you were only interested in me and my condition, I would still have been pleased to know you and share time with you tonight."

It was now evident to Mark that this was exceptional behaviour on Harry's part. Concealing his emotions had been an entrenched characteristic since the accident.

Alex looked relieved. The silence, which ensued, was broken by Beverly, who began to giggle. They all began to laugh so loudly that they almost missed Liam and Sally's arrival. Beverly was first to react and invited everyone through to the sitting room for drinks. The women set about clearing the dishes and shooed the men away, despite half-hearted offers of help.

Beverly looked at Sally and enquired, "So – what have you been up to today?"

Sally touched her nose with her index finger and said, "Lots and lots, Beverly, but I think that we should wait until we join the boys. Liam knows much more than I do. I think he's just dying to share his news with everyone!"

Less than a quarter of a mile from Harry's house, Whyte and Melville were sitting in their van. Both wore earphones.

CHAPTER 106

Liam was full of the day's events. Sally, too, was able to add to what she had witnessed as the auditors examined the bank's records.

After he finished updating them on the situation, it was clear that Alex was looking puzzled. Mark suggested she should be brought up to date. The others agreed.

She listened attentively as Liam summarised how Grant and Wyllie had conspired to acquire Joe's and Harry's properties. He went on to air his suspicions that the fire, alleged burglary in Johnstown, the planting of stolen goods at the car boot sale and the tax inspectors' visit were down to them. He also believed that the slurry tanker incident had been planned by Grant and Wyllie but probably executed by Jake Butcher, now languishing in hospital. That Wyllie and Grant were now in police custody awaiting further charges and declining all offers of legal representation from Isaac Lipman, Dalrymple's solicitor, puzzled Liam.

"Who," Alex enquired, "is this Dalrymple person?"

"A very nasty individual," Liam responded. "He has the reputation of being an untouchable. Although the police have tried to nail him on several occasions, he's always managed to evade prosecution. There is a suspicion that he is in league with Wyllie and Grant, but nothing can be attributed to him at present, other than that a company called Wiltris has its registered office at one of his properties."

"Isn't that enough to incriminate him?"

"What would it prove? It would only confirm he is a shareholder in the company. Any misdemeanours could have been carried out without his knowledge – he could claim."

"Why do they want the homesteads?"

Liam looked around the room before answering. "The motorway skirts Joe's and Harry's land. It would enable a slip road to be created, which would also enable access to Grant's estate. Its potential as a commercial industrial site would run to hundreds of millions of pounds. Given its proximity to the conurbations within half an hour's drive in practically every direction, the farms would make the proposition feasible."

"But that would completely destroy the character of the town and surrounding area," Alex declared. The others nodded in agreement.

"I will do everything I can to prevent that," Harry told her. "That's why Beverly and I have bought Joe's place."

"Was Joe intending to sell?" she enquired.

"No, but he was finding things tough, financially. If it hadn't been for our grandfather's legacy, we would also have had problems raising the cash."

The conversation turned to the discovery of the various artefacts, which had been discovered and placed in secure storage.

"I'm not sure that I've been able to value them accurately, though," Harry admitted. "Some of the estimates I made were based upon information taken from older catalogues. I've since come to appreciate that newer antique price guides are different from the ones I first consulted. Some are valued too high while others are way too low. I really need to get them expertly valued."

Although Liam was known for his caution in matters that could not be corroborated, he believed that Harry's pricing was probably understated overall. He had greater worries with regard to Harry's safety, he revealed.

"DCI Jones and I had a long discussion about what might happen next. Dalrymple is not someone who will give up acquiring the farms, especially when there is so much money at stake. Jones believes he will come after you, Harry, perhaps not personally but through others to get what he wants. I'm afraid he might include you in that, Beverly."

"Over my dead body," vowed Mark.

"I wouldn't try to frighten you needlessly, but Jones is very concerned for your safety and has warned me that you need to be ultra careful from here on in. I'm afraid that all of us associated with Harry and Beverly could be a target."

"In what way could he do that?" Sally asked Liam.

"He wouldn't do it himself, you understand. It would be hirelings of some sort or another, paid to put the frighteners upon someone, so that Harry might be compelled to sell up in return for their safety."

"I've heard about this," Mark informed them. "There was a case some years back where a bookmaker was forced to sell a chain of gambling shops and casinos at a knock-down price. Following the sale, he complained to the police he'd been forced to sell because his daughter's life had been threatened, unless he sold to Dalrymple. The police tried to make a case of it, but it went nowhere. Three years later, the bookie and all his family were found in the smouldering remains of a villa, where they had sought to hide from Dalrymple and his thugs. It coincided with Dalrymple's photograph in the national press attending a dinner in London. The bookie warned the police that Dalrymple had threatened to get even. As there was no corroborating evidence to support the allegations, the Crown decided it could not provide protection. He tried to hide his family abroad but it is believed Dalrymple located them in northern Spain. It must have been a terrible existence knowing that Dalrymple was out to get them."

"There have been other instances of Dalrymple's barbaric deeds but I'm not going to list them here tonight," Liam added. "Only be aware that we may all be in some danger, and also for the need to be vigilant. The police cannot provide any protection. They have budgetary and other constraints that prevent them from allocating staff, especially since no tangible threats have been made."

Harry was alarmed. "What have I got you into, Beverly? I never meant to put you in any danger."

"It's not a problem, Harry," she responded with as much bravado as she could muster. "They'd better not mess with my brother or me or they'll be sorry, I can tell you!"

"What about Chris and Joe?" Sally queried. "They don't know any of this. Shouldn't we warn them about what you've just told us, Liam?"

He agreed that he would brief them the next day, as it was getting late, and Chris would already be in bed because of his early-morning radio programme.

CHAPTER 107

Even before they returned to the hotel, Control had requested a callback.

"Does he never sleep?" Melville queried.

Whyte guessed he might be an insomniac.

Both men were impressed by the way their boss was able to rapidly summarise the substance of the conversation they had recorded only minutes ago.

"Harold Carey – aka Harry Carry – appears to be capable of memorising information in a way that seems superhuman," he began. "Alex Green, a former colleague of Professor Hart, is investigating how he can do this but seems uncertain as to whether or not it is something that can be replicated or repeated. Carey also seems to be in some danger, as he stands to frustrate a lucrative property deal involving a criminal known as Donald Dalrymple."

Melville nodded to Whyte but said nothing as Control continued.

"There are several tasks I want you to carry out from first light tomorrow. I'll be arranging support for you from within the department. I was a bit cynical about Carey's ability to memorise things, but it seems he is the real deal and needs protecting. If his life or any of his acquaintances are threatened, you are authorised to employ actions to prevent that happening. I'll get back to you with precise instructions tomorrow."

The line went dead, leaving the two agents to ponder what was expected of them, as both recognised the situation was far more important than they had first imagined.

CHAPTER 108

DCI Jones received a call at 6am informing him that he should expect a visit from the chief constable at ten o'clock.

Ruth Grant was visited by two men in green boiler suits at 8am, requiring access to her water supply.

Isaac Lipman was called to his offices at 7.45am following the triggering of a burglar alarm.

A power outage at Donald Dalrymple's casino was attended by three electricity workers at 9am, who needed access to the building.

DCI Jones sat across from the chief constable and another man who did not give his name. It was apparent, however, that he was of higher rank than the chief constable. He came straight to the point.

"You are holding two men by the names of Grant and Wyllie," he began. "We consider them to be a threat to national security and will be holding them indefinitely on charges of espionage. As a consequence, they are to be transferred to me and transported to another place for further questioning."

Jones looked at his superior, who was giving nothing away.

"Furthermore, you are requested not to pursue any interest in Donald Dalrymple, who I believe you have suspicions of being in league with Grant and Wyllie. Do I make myself clear, DCI Jones?"

Jones could only nod an acknowledgement.

"I appreciate that you would dearly like to bring Dalrymple to book but that will have to wait, I'm afraid. There are matters of great national importance involved. Your investigations might compromise ours, which is why I have come to impress upon you the gravity of the situation. It may be possible, following the conclusion of this operation, that Dalrymple will be delivered into your hands. The prospect of his entire empire being closed down, following a successful prosecution in court, is anticipated. It may also be necessary for you to act as a go-between, Chief Inspector, but more of that later. If anything occurs that gives you cause to believe there is anything I need to be aware of – or if you think anyone's life may be threatened – then get in touch right away. Here's my contact details."

He waited to hear if the DCI had any questions before continuing.

"Thank you for your co-operation, Chief Constable, DCI Jones. I'll see myself out."

He left without shaking hands.

Jones got up to look out of the window at the rear car park, just in time to see Grant and Wyllie being bundled into a minibus, handcuffed to two men in grey suits. A third got out of the driver's door and held the passenger's door open for the man who had just left Jones's office. He was clearly a person of importance, judging by the way in which the driver deferred to him.

The chief constable joined Jones at the window to observe the departure, sighed, and said, "Sorry, but I'm not able to tell you anything about this. Please be sure to impress upon DS Black that you follow his instructions to the letter."

Jones knew better than to pursue the matter and could only

speculate about what was happening. The alarm at Lipman's offices suddenly ceased, creating a silence, which was somehow louder and more sinister than before.

CHAPTER 109

Very few car boot items were left unsold following the 10am opening.

It was clear that many were undervalued but Harry was unconcerned. They had been acquired for pennies over the years and some had simply been lots the salerooms wanted taken away, having remained unsold for more than three auctions. How times had changed! Yesterday's junk was now desirable and collectible, he mused.

The auction had commenced at noon and a large crowd had gathered in the salesroom. Bidding was brisk, with most items achieving higher prices than Harry had estimated. With Alex and Beverly by his side, his main concern, however, was that they were not in any danger. He looked around continuously, a worried look on his face.

Such was his preoccupation that he almost missed Ralph Fortescue approaching.

"It's going very well, Harry," he observed. "You must be making a fortune here today. And who is this you've got in tow? I know your sister, Beverly, but surely this fair lady can't be another sister you haven't told us about."

"No, this is Alexis, a family friend," Beverly cut in, as she could see that Harry was having difficulty knowing how to introduce Alex.

"How do you do?" Ralph greeted her, offering his hand. "I'm an old friend of Harry's who dabbles in antiques."

Alex shook hands and made small talk before Ralph got round to addressing Harry.

"Thanks so much for the last deal we did, Harry. I made a bundle out of those things you knocked out to me so generously."

"Thanks to you too, Ralph. I was very grateful to you for keeping me right on the items you thought were undervalued. It made a difference to the guide prices in the sale catalogue."

"Glad to help, old boy! I don't suppose you have anything else I might be interested in acquiring. I'm particularly keen to source old timepieces for one collector and also ceramics for another client."

"I might have one or two things that could be of interest, Ralph. What precisely would you be looking for?"

Beverly hooked her arm into Alex's, suggesting that they leave the men to carry out their conversation in private and made their way to Mark's mobile bar for a glass of wine.

Their departure alerted a man and woman who exchanged glances, before the female looked meaningfully at her partner in the direction that Alex and Beverly had taken. He nodded as she followed them towards the drinks area. Seemingly concentrating on the auction, the man was never more than three feet from Harry and Ralph. Only his eye movements betrayed the fact that he was monitoring anyone that came near them, as the crowd moved around the salesroom. He was intrigued to overhear that Harry was meeting Ralph on Monday to view items stored in a high-security warehouse.

CHAPTER 110

Chris, Liam and Harry were counting the takings in Joe's kitchen. Beverly, Alex and Sally arrived soon after the final tally was completed.

"Where did all those buyers come from?" Chris marvelled. "Without knowing how much you've taken, I'd guess that it's a lot more than you imagined, Harry."

"In my professional capacity as a banking executive, I estimate you will be well over the initial valuation," Sally joked. "Some of the prices achieved were way above what you thought they'd make, Harry. And yet I heard some of the dealers who'd been bidding declaring they had been able to get good deals."

"I heard that, too," Liam agreed. "Like Chris, I was astounded by the numbers that turned up today. It seems that you may be onto something with your idea to turn part of Joe's farm into an antiques emporium."

"It doesn't always work as well as it did today," Harry responded. "If it hadn't been for Chris promoting it on the radio and the fact that a percentage of takings will be donated to the hospice, we might not have done so well. But I'm absolutely delighted with the result, I have to confess. How much do you think we've made, Sally?"

"The gross takings appear to be about £83,000, which means that after expenses and minus the contribution to the hospice, you should clear about £68,000."

"That's a great result!" Beverly enthused as everyone came together in a group hug.

CHAPTER 111

It had taken more than four hours to have the window boarded up and the alarm reset. Isaac Lipman consoled himself, satisfied that nothing seemed to be missing but worried that an appointment to meet Donald Dalrymple had been delayed. Dalrymple didn't like to be kept waiting, and from the sound of his voice when he telephoned about the break-in, his ill humour was evident from the way he spoke. It would not improve waiting for Lipman to get back to him.

He decided to check the security camera recordings while the engineers tried to reset the alarm system. Every time they tried to reinstate it, a fault appeared to be located inside the building and was taking time to rectify. Eventually, one of the men left to collect a component that needed replacing. Lipman decided to phone Dalrymple to provide an update.

Two men in green boiler suits, sitting in a parked water services van just one street away, gave a 'thumbs-up' gesture. Their colleagues had successfully established the camera and audio device in Lipman's office.

"I'm hoping to get away in about an hour," Lipman informed Dalrymple. "There's been a delay while they fetch a part that needs replacing. Do you still want to see me?"

"Of course I bloody well want to see you!" came the angry reply. "Things are out of control. What the hell is happening? Why are Grant and Wyllie refusing your offer to represent them? Have they been released yet? What other crimes are they being charged with?"

Lipman was unable to shed light on any of Dalrymple's questions and sought to placate him as best he could by saying he felt sure he'd get to the bottom of it soon enough.

"I'm not concerned about Wyllie, as I've not had any contact with him, but Grant is another matter. He can implicate me and probably will if the police exert pressure on him."

"What can he tell them that would incriminate you, Donald? You are merely business partners. Your hands are clean as far as that goes. You had nothing to do with torching Carey's Portakabin, setting up the burglary sting in Johnstown, planting stolen merchandise at the car boot sale or spreading the slurry at Burns' Garden Centre. That was almost certainly down to Grant and probably Wyllie, unless of course you gave any instructions for that to happen, which I feel sure you did not. No, you made a bad choice in your selection of business partners is all that can be levelled at you. You know nothing of the incidents that occurred. You now realise, if asked, that Grant had been showing signs of mental instability for some time. If pressed, you might speculate that it's quite possible he was involved in the various things that were perpetrated against Burns and Carey."

"OK, but what about the development? What can we do about that?"

Lipman thought for a moment before replying.

"You could approach Carey and Burns again through an intermediary. The approach could be that Wiltris was not aware of Grant's or Wyllie's behaviour in trying to force a sale. Your line should be that Wiltris would never have been a party to such a strategy, and for this, the company is offering a sincere apology for any difficulties experienced."

"Do you think they'll buy that?"

"Who knows, but at least you could try that first. You will appreciate that the prices offered by Grant and Wyllie will have to be greatly increased. I think that Burns was offered something in the region of £120,000 while Carey's was nearer £150,000 to clear his bank borrowing."

"How much are you suggesting?"

"I think you might need to quadruple that if you want to persuade them to sell."

"That's over a million if they both accept!"

"I don't think even that might be enough but might just do the trick. I know that Burns is being pressed by his creditors and doesn't have too many options but to sell. Carey, as I understand it, has settled his overdraft with the bank and he's also got that auction going on today – so he might be less willing to accept an offer but I've no doubt that if push comes to shove, you'll find a way to make him see sense."

"There's still the business of Tristram Grant's acres. Through his gambling debts, I virtually own the estate, as he put it up for security. Wyllie won't be a problem. According to Grant, he has a liking for young girls, which was how Grant got him to co-operate so readily, as he threatened to expose him to the police."

"What about Ruth Grant? Doesn't she jointly own the property?"

"Ruth won't be a problem. She's already agreed to sell, though her weasel-faced husband doesn't know that yet."

"Do you mean that Mrs Grant is complicit in the scheme?"

"It was her idea. Tristram was only being used, along with Wyllie, to try to expedite matters, without anyone becoming aware of what we were planning."

"I see. You never shared that with me, Donald. It would have been helpful to know that."

"What you don't know won't trouble you, Isaac. I don't tell you everything."

The sound of a door opening in Lipman's downstairs office announced that someone was entering the building. Dalrymple heard it also and was quick to question if Lipman was alone.

"It's only the burglar alarm people returning to finish the job. There's no one else here except me," Lipman assured him. "It's been a pest having to wait for them to fix things."

"Tell me about it. We had a power failure this morning. The whole street was out. The electricity company guys left just before you rang. They've been swarming all over the place. They believed it was caused by something inside our building, but it turned out to be a transformer in the yard next door."

"So, do you still want me to come to you, Donald?"

"I guess there's no point now after what you've told me. Let's get together once the weekend is over to give me a chance to think things through. In the meantime, find out all you can about Harold Carey. I think he's going to be the fly in the ointment. See if you can find out what his weak spot is. He may need to be persuaded it will be in his best interests to sell."

CHAPTER 112

Mark joined them in the farm kitchen with two bottles of champagne to toast the success of the auction. Liam was quick to notice that something was troubling him.

"Is something wrong, Mark?"

"I'm not sure. After what you told us last night, I couldn't help but look about for possible attackers. Maybe I'm being a bit paranoid, but I got the distinct impression that Alex and Beverly were being shadowed by a woman in a tweed jacket. Every time I looked, she was within touching distance of Beverly or Alex. What made her stand out even more was she seemed to be continuously placing herself between them and anyone approaching where they were standing."

"Would you be able to pick her out from the CCTV?" Joe asked. "We could look at it now if you have time. Everyone was filmed as they came in to register."

The champagne forgotten for the moment, they decided to check out the video recordings.

Joe locked the takings in a safe before inviting everyone to join him in the garden centre office where the monitors were located. It didn't take long for the friends to pinpoint the man and woman who had been tailing Alex, Beverly and

Harry. Further scrutiny of the external cameras picked out the presence of three others, who the couple met up with in the car park at the conclusion of the auction.

"I know two of those guys!" Mark exclaimed. "They're the two water testers staying in the hotel!"

"I've seen them too!" Beverly confirmed. "They were at Harry's place yesterday."

"I thought they looked familiar," Joe added. "They were here yesterday as well. It must have been after they'd been to your place, Harry."

A silence followed as everyone considered what they had learned and was finally broken by Sally, suggesting that Liam should notify DCI Jones.

Liam agreed and requested that Joe removed the tapes for police examination.

"I think we should all stay close together from now on, until we know what these people are up to," Liam continued. "Where's the phone, Joe?"

When Liam's call came through, DCI Jones was polishing his shoes. He found it had a calming effect when confronted by situations he did not understand. What Liam had to say got his undivided attention, however. All thoughts of shoe polishing were abandoned.

"I'll be with you in minutes," he told Liam. "Are you all still at Burns' Nursery?"

His journey was delayed by the realisation that he was still wearing carpet slippers. It became evident after stepping into a large puddle where he had washed his car that afternoon – another therapeutic activity he indulged in when feeling frustrated. Other colleagues would have opened a bottle of Scotch, but not him. Alcohol didn't agree with him or the ulcer that had evolved over twenty years of shift work combined with a diet of junk food that had seen his weight rocket from a healthy eleven stone to something approaching seventeen. Cursing, he returned indoors to change into outdoor shoes.

Calm down, he kept telling himself as he fumbled with the laces. Simply get over there and assess the situation.

This was something he had to do on his own, Jones realised. He could not involve DS Black, even as backup. Until it could be established that lives were in danger, he had to keep his involvement at arm's length, having been warned in no uncertain terms, just six short hours ago.

Driving faster than was legal, his attention was focused on the road and was only barely aware of the water services van parked in the lay-by just along from the nursery. Although noting its presence, he did not think too much about it, other than that it was unusual to see a works vehicle with a London registration number in the area.

Inside, Whyte and Melville were cursing themselves for not planting a bug in the sales area, where the friends were viewing the video footage.

"I don't like it!" Whyte said.

"I've a feeling we've been rumbled," his partner agreed.

"Who's that in the car that just drove into the car park? It looks a bit like one of the plods Control went to meet this morning if I'm not mistaken."

"Do you think we should call Control?"

Melville was quiet for a moment before responding.

"Let's wait until they return to the farmhouse and see if we can learn anything when they get there," he suggested.

They later discovered that Control would tell them exactly what had been discussed, following a telephone conversation with DCI Jones.

CHAPTER 113

Having established who Alex was and after being reassured she should be present, he listened to what the friends had to say. The footage, the video revealed, left Jones uncertain as to how he should respond. Liam noticed he was suffering some inner turmoil and asked if he would prefer to talk to him privately.

The chief inspector thanked him, and the two men stepped outside to converse.

"Look, I'm fairly confident you are not in any danger from the individuals that you have identified," he began, "but I'm not able to tell you more than that just now. Please treat this in confidence until I'm in a position to reveal more."

Liam studied Jones's face and concluded from the set of his jaw it would be pointless to pursue the matter further.

"When will you be able to do that?"

"I'm not sure – but soon – I hope. Just keep acting as normally as possible until I get back to you."

"You don't think this has anything to do with Dalrymple, then?" Liam persisted.

"I can't say that categorically," he conceded, "but I'm fairly sure it's not directly connected."

Liam noted that Jones seemed anxious to move away. He

was studying a business card in his left hand while keying a number into his mobile phone.

For such a large man, Jones could move quite rapidly, Liam observed, as he watched him sprint across the park to his car. Within seconds, he was conversing animatedly with the person he had just dialled.

What should I make of that? Liam wondered as he returned to the others.

CHAPTER 114

Jones could not help but feel a little triumphant to share his news with Control.

"I'm afraid you've been rumbled," he began. "Your two spooks, the water services guys and, of course, you yourself, were recorded on CCTV this afternoon at the auction. Two others that you sent as protection were also identified."

There was a lengthy silence from the other end before Control asked him to continue.

"Tell me what you know and also, what if anything they think they know," he demanded sharply.

Minutes later, Control conceded he might need to collaborate more fully with Jones.

"I think that would be helpful," he agreed. "These are pretty smart people you're dealing with. They know about Dalrymple and suspect that he might try to come after them to force Harold Carey into selling. Your people aroused the suspicion that you are working for Dalrymple. That's why they called me in – and don't worry – I've not told them anything, other than that they are in no present danger."

The silence, which again lengthened, caused Jones to wonder if the line had been lost, but eventually Control told him, somewhat reluctantly, that there was some likelihood Dalrymple might be considering making an approach to buy the farms.

"How can you be so sure?"

"Let's not go into that. Let's just say we are monitoring the situation."

"What do I tell them in the meantime?"

After another pause, he suggested that Harry should be briefed as to what was going on but that he, Control, would do that along with DCI Jones in attendance.

"That's fine with me but I feel that we should also include Liam Forbes in that. He's someone who should be involved, especially if Dalrymple makes a move to acquire the farms."

"Can he be trusted to keep his mouth shut?"

"Absolutely," Jones confirmed.

Again, following a lengthy silence, he asked if Jones could go back to the group and reassure them not to worry unnecessarily.

"Can I tell them that your people are there for their protection?" Jones persisted.

There was a grudging acknowledgement that he should do that but also that they must not share this information with anyone else.

"What about my sergeant?"

"If you can guarantee his absolute discretion – then do that. I'll be back in touch shortly."

From the garden centre shop, Chris observed DCI Jones leave his car to cross the yard, pocketing his phone as he did so. *He looks a lot more confident than he did a few minutes ago,* he thought, as the chief inspector breezed into the shop.

"Right," he said. "I've been reassured that the people who you identified will be no threat to any of you. They are indeed keeping a watchful eye to ensure that you are in no danger –

more than that I cannot say, at present. I do need to speak to both Harry and Liam in private, however, so if you would not mind leaving us for a moment, I'd be obliged."

CHAPTER 115

Dalrymple hated inaction. Things were spiralling out of control.

He had just learned that Grant and Wyllie had been moved to another location, to answer additional unknown charges.

What had the stupid sods been getting up to?

Lipman usually gave good advice – God knows he paid him enough – but all that he could suggest was that he would have to dig deeper to get his hands on the farms. There was only one way to go, he reasoned. That was to pressure Carey and Burns into selling, and that needed to be done sooner rather than later. How could he do that? Maybe the way to achieve that would be through Ruth. He reached for the phone and pressed the speed dial.

"Hi, Donald, have you any news?" she enquired on answering.

"No, nothing," he admitted rather petulantly. "What about you?"

"Ditto!"

"Look, I've been thinking. Maybe Burns might accept an increased offer if you were to approach him, Ruth."

"I'm not sure that he would, Donald, after knowing how much he detested Tristram."

"Tell him that you have just learned of Tristram's approach and how annoyed you were at the derisory sum he had offered. Tell him that you are prepared to double – no – treble the offer he made."

"Do you think that will work?"

"Who knows? I do know that he has money problems and will have to sell out soon."

"But by association, would he ever consider selling to Tristram Grant's wife?"

"I don't think it will make any difference if he is that pressed for funds. You could also tell him that because of Tristram's dishonest dealings, you are starting divorce proceedings. Maybe that might be enough to persuade the old goat to do a deal."

"Divorcing Tristram will be a pleasure. God knows I've waited long enough for that to happen, but won't that complicate the issue concerning the development?"

"I don't think that Tristram Grant will have long to live following his release from prison," Dalrymple growled. "You can be sure there will be a very unpleasant accident scheduled for him in the not-too-distant future."

"Just make sure that it happens before the divorce proceedings commence," she enthused. "OK, what do I have to do?"

CHAPTER 116

Although relieved by Jones's assurances that they were in no immediate danger, Harry could not help but feel events were having a worrying effect upon Alex. She was trying to appear unconcerned, but he was aware she was less than comfortable with the way things were turning out.

After the policeman left, the friends decided to deposit the takings in the bank's night safe before going on for a planned celebratory meal at Mark's hotel. Harry asked if he could get a lift there with Alex, as she had driven them to the auction. They set off together before the others were ready to leave.

"I know you are due to go back home tomorrow," Harry began once they were on the road, "but I would be happier if you decided to return tonight."

She did not reply but shot him an enquiring glance that barely concealed the disappointment she clearly felt.

"You must have regretted getting into this," Harry stumbled on. "Please understand that I had no idea you would be exposed to any danger by coming here. I'm as confused as anybody about what's happening. I'm really sorry, Alex. If I could change things, I would. It's been wonderful having you here and I don't want you to leave, but I would hate for anything to happen to you, just by being associated with me."

Alex did not respond but stared fixedly ahead.

"Maybe I could come to you? Would that be acceptable?"

Alex was clearly giving some thought to how she was going to respond as the silence between them lengthened.

"I am concerned about how things have turned out," she admitted, "but not for my own safety. There's someone else I need to think about," she confided.

"I'm sorry," Harry stammered. "It never occurred to me that you would have other commitments. Someone as attractive as you is bound to be in a relationship. I don't know why I never thought of that."

She sneaked a glance at him again as she manoeuvred the car into a parking space.

"Forgive me," Harry went on, "I'm afraid I'm a bit naïve when it comes to other people's lives. I've been so preoccupied with my own, it never occurred to me you might be spoken for."

Alex looked at him in amusement, then started laughing, adding to Harry's embarrassment.

She switched off the engine before repeating his words, "'Spoken for'. I've not heard anyone use that term for many years, Harry."

Alex's laughter only served to intensify the discomfort he felt. He could feel his face colour and looked away. What a fool he had made of himself!

Alex took pity on him; she gently turned his face towards her.

"I'm not in a relationship or 'spoken for' as you put it, you silly man. I was referring to my father, who is housebound and depends on me to care for him. It's only because a friend is staying over this weekend I was able to come here to meet you."

"You mean you're not... attached to anyone on a... romantic basis?"

No sooner than he had spoken the words than he regretted having uttered them. How inept and cheesy could he get?

Alex's smile widened and a fondness came into her expression.

"There's no one like that in my life, Harry."

He only just managed to stop himself asking her if she was sure about that.

"I would very much like to spend more time with you, Harry, apart from in a professional context."

"Me too!" he replied earnestly, causing her to smile even more widely

"Since you've been here, my life has changed in ways that I couldn't have imagined. I'm beginning to have feelings that I never thought I'd experience. I—"

He never managed to find the words he was searching for because Alex sought his lips in a gentle caress. All at once they were embracing, albeit awkwardly, because the car gearstick got in the way. As they clung together, neither was aware of the others arriving or saw the smiles and winks the friends exchanged as they made their way into the hotel.

"I won't be leaving until tomorrow, Harry," Alex said with such finality that he knew better than to contradict her. "I'm not afraid for myself, only for you. We'll see this thing through, I'm sure."

"If you're sure," was all he could say in reply.

CHAPTER 117

Joe was in the sales area when Ruth Grant arrived at the garden centre. Her demeanour bore the appearance of a woman who was less than pleased about being in such a downmarket environment. Her smile, as she approached him, was forced and artificial, although intended to appear warm and friendly.

"Good morning, Mr Burns," she began, "I was hoping to find you here today."

"I'm always here," Joe responded, "and not likely to be leaving until they carry me out feet first."

"My, that is rather dramatic. You must like the place very much."

"I've lived here all my life and I've no desire to be anywhere else."

Ruth forced a sympathetic but transparently insincere smile before speaking.

"I quite understand that you are very attached to the place, Mr Burns, and I would like to talk to you about that, if you could just spare me a few minutes of your time."

Joe held her steadily in his gaze. She could sense his hostility and quickly moved the conversation along.

"I'm here to apologise," she began, searching his face for a reaction, but Joe showed no emotion.

"I believe my husband offered to buy your garden centre for a derisory sum and issued various threats if you declined his offer. It was without my knowledge or approval. I was very angry to learn about what he had done and can only offer my sincere apologies for his behaviour."

Joe did not respond. The silence lengthened, making her feel obliged to fill the vacuum. This was not how Ruth had intended to conduct the conversation and felt wrong-footed by Joe's reluctance to speak.

"Please understand that Tristram's actions were in no way known or authorised by me," she lied.

She paused to see if what she said was having any effect but was met with the same intense stare that was now beginning to unnerve her.

"That's why I came here to see you personally, to apologise," she continued. "It isn't common knowledge," she went on, "but I have started divorce proceedings."

Joe finally spoke. "Thank you for telling me that," he said but offered nothing more.

"I would still be interested in acquiring your property, however, and would be prepared to offer a realistic sum if you would consider selling to me. I was thinking of offering around £300,000, Mr Burns. How would you feel about that?"

Joe finally smiled.

Sensing that she might have persuaded him he should take up her offer, she continued.

"It would be a quick settlement. The money could be in your bank account by lunchtime tomorrow if you are agreeable to my offer."

He was chuckling now and nodding. Ruth thought she

had swung the deal and was holding out her hand for Joe to shake on it.

"I'm very sorry," he informed her with some relish, "but you are too late. I've already done a deal with my neighbour. Harold Carey now owns this property. It is unlikely he would consider selling to you or anyone else, even if you were to offer ten times what you just offered me."

Ruth felt her jaw drop. The bonhomie she had struggled to project deserted her. She was unable to respond coherently and could only listen dumbfounded as Joe continued.

"Yes," he was saying. "Harry has great plans for the properties. They're being drawn up as we speak. It will be a great thing for the town and the area. What's more, I'm going to be able to stay here in the house until I don't need it anymore."

Ruth's anger was palpable. Joe watched as she struggled to keep her feelings in check, aware that if she could, she would have attacked him. Her body became rigid, fists clenched by her side, her eyes glinting with hostility.

It might have only been a mini-second that she allowed her true feelings to surface, but Joe was left in no doubt he was confronting someone who was intrinsically spiteful and vindictive.

"Thanks for coming to apologise in person but as far as buying me out is concerned, I'm afraid it's been a wasted journey," he told her as a parting shot.

Eventually, with what appeared to be a huge effort of self-control, she blurted out that she was sorry to have wasted his time and stamped out of the shop, her black ankle-length coat flapping behind her in the storm that had threatened all morning.

Joe reached for the desk phone as he watched Ruth speed out of the car park.

When Beverly answered his call, he asked if he could speak to Harry.

"Sorry," she informed him. "I think he might still be at the Crown. He didn't come home last night."

CHAPTER 118

That morning, at Harry's insistence, Alex had reluctantly agreed it would be best if she returned home earlier than planned. She had packed her things and was settling in behind the steering wheel when Mark emerged from the hotel calling for Harry to come to the phone.

"It's Beverly," he shouted from the doorway. "She has a message from Joe that she wants to pass on to you."

"Tell her I'll be with her in minutes," Harry replied. "Alex is going to drop me off on her way home."

Mark gave the thumbs-up sign and wished Alex a safe journey, before returning inside.

Alex blushed. "Do you think that they'll know you spent the night here, with me?"

"I think that goes without saying," he responded with only a slight hint of embarrassment. "It seems we were expected to get together, although it wasn't something I could have ever imagined in my wildest dreams," he confided.

"It's very unprofessional of me," Alex observed impishly.

"Hey, I'm not a patient and you're not my doctor, although I have to say that your therapies have been exceptionally beneficial, as far as I'm concerned."

They both laughed conspiratorially as Harry climbed into the passenger seat.

Mark watched intrigued as he saw them embrace before eventually driving off, still apparently giggling like a pair of adolescents.

"Harry will be with you shortly," he told Beverly, "and it looks like your matchmaking has borne results."

He held the phone away from his ear as Beverly hooted approval. She was clearly delighted they had got together and said so. Mark, too, was pleased that his chum had finally allowed himself to form an emotional relationship with another person. For too long, he mused, Harry had avoided all human involvement, other than with those who constituted his oldest and closest friends. Things were really changing for the better, he told himself and shared that thought with Beverly.

"Did they share a room?" she wanted to know.

"Harry slept in one of the guest rooms," he told her. "But the maid didn't make up the bed in Alex's room this morning, as it hadn't been slept in," he revealed.

Another whoop again caused him to hold the receiver at arm's length.

"I think she'll be great for him," Beverly confided. "And have you noticed, he's hardly looked at a catalogue or antiques website since she arrived?"

Having discussed the various possibilities regarding how things might develop, Mark wondered if he should enquire how their own relationship might progress but decided to put that off for a little while yet. Changing the subject, he then asked if Beverly knew what Joe had wanted to speak to Harry about.

She recounted what Joe had told her about Ruth's visit but cut the conversation short as Alex and Harry arrived in the yard.

There was no need for her to hurry because the couple were talking animatedly in the car and hardly noticed as she approached the vehicle. A tap at the driver's window finally got their attention.

"Are you coming in for a coffee or something?" she enquired, a knowing smile on her face.

"No, Beverly. Thanks all the same but Harry's insisted that I take off now, rather than wait until tonight."

Recognising that the news had deflated Beverly somewhat, Harry was quick to tell her he would be travelling up to Edinburgh on Friday, "To continue the investigations," he added hastily.

At this last statement, Alex began to giggle. Beverly, too, started to laugh – leaving Harry to look confused and uncomfortable – until he, too, saw the unintended humour of what he'd just said.

When the laughter subsided, Beverly leaned into the car and gave Alex a hug. "I'm so sorry that you won't be staying longer but surely you'll be back with us?" she pleaded.

"You can count on that," Alex confirmed, sneaking a glance at Harry, who responded with a grin.

Beverly looked on tenderly as Harry bent over to plant a kiss on Alex's lips before getting out of the car. Without looking left or right, she raised her hand in goodbye, accelerating out of the yard and onto the main road.

Harry felt a part of him was leaving and suddenly felt a deep sense of loss, the kind of which he had not experienced since his grandmother passed away. Beverly looked at her brother fondly before offering him her arm as they sauntered back to the farmhouse.

"Joe has some interesting news for you, Harry. He's waiting for your call."

CHAPTER 119

If there was one thing Donald Dalrymple hated, it was feeling he was not in control. Harold Carey he now identified as the reason for frustration and subsequently the focus of his malevolence. When Ruth asked how he planned to proceed, he was at a loss to know how to tackle the problem. Isaac Lipman had been no help, either. His advice was to let things settle for a few days until this latest development could be properly understood and assessed. Dalrymple hated inactivity almost as much as the loss of control. Grudgingly, he agreed to wait, although his instinctive reaction was to resort to violence, which was his preferred method of gaining compliance with those that sought to frustrate him.

He was no fool, however, and decided to telephone a number he held in memory. It was never written down anywhere, not even on the pay-as-you-go mobile phone he kept in a locked desk drawer.

The gruff voice that answered recognised Dalrymple's number and greeted him by name. "Hello, Donald. What can I do for you today?"

"I may have a job for you shortly," he told him. "It might require a few personnel for what I have in mind, and it could also involve a demolition contract."

"Will demolition also require disposal? That would be extra."

"Probably; but it might not be necessary. Just be ready to respond quickly if I get back to you."

Dalrymple rang off without another word. If Carey did not agree to sell, he would soon learn that anyone close to him would be in extreme danger. A warning was usually enough to persuade anyone just how serious that could be. He wouldn't make threats himself, of course, that would be the work of the third party he had just spoken to. All he needed now was to discover how best to apply that pressure.

Having locked the phone away, he pressed a buzzer that summoned one of his minders. When he entered the room, the lackey was ordered to find Slack Alice and bring her to him. Too old now for doing tricks, she was nevertheless very good at ferreting out information. He would get her to find out what she could about Harold Carey and his associates. His next call was to Isaac Lipman, who told him that he was with a client and would phone back in a few minutes.

As he waited for Lipman's call, Dalrymple pondered what steps he could take to remedy the problem that entailed getting Harold Carey to capitulate and sell the farms. Not to him directly, obviously, and Wiltris was clearly out of the game now with Grant and Wyllie under lock and key somewhere. Would they squawk, he wondered? Grant certainly understood what would happen if he was implicated in any way. That the Wiltris Company was registered as having its head office on his premises was worrying. Lipman would be instructed to wind it up as soon as possible but that could not be achieved without both Grant and Wyllie authorising it.

His thoughts moved to Jake Butcher, who was still apparently in hospital. Would he talk if pressurised by the police? He thought not, but determined to have one of Lipman's employees pay him a visit to ensure his silence. An incentive to keep his mouth shut might not only include a warning that more of the same or even worse might be administered should suffice. Perhaps a brown envelope with some money, delivered personally by Ruth, on condition that he relocated somewhere else when able to be moved from hospital, would be the best solution? This was costing more money than he had been prepared to invest in the affair. Although he could well afford it, the prospect rankled even more.

How much would it take to buy Carey out? Would a million be enough? If he could find a way of threatening Carey or someone close to him, it would be a lot less. The fact that the police were now looking over his shoulder meant he would have to be ultra careful and would probably have to offer a realistic market valuation. Could Ruth be the person to channel the money through? He'd raise that with Lipman when he called back.

Further speculation was interrupted by the desk phone, which rang three times before he answered it. The caller display showed that Isaac Lipman was on the line.

Dalrymple lifted the handset and told him what was on his mind.

CHAPTER 120

Sally and Liam arrived just after Harry had spoken to Joe. They were on their way to have lunch at a country pub but had learned of Ruth's visit.

Clearly, Ruth was acting on behalf of someone else, Liam observed. That person was more than likely to be Donald Dalrymple, he deduced. If that were the case, Harry needed to be aware of how dangerous that could be – not only for Harry but anyone closely connected to him, he warned.

Liam was quick to add that the people who had been shadowing them should not be regarded as a threat. DCI Jones had assured him that they were there as a protection. More than that, he could not divulge at present.

After some discussion, Liam phoned Harry.

"Listen, Harry," he began, "Jones has asked that we meet him, along with some other individuals tomorrow, to brief you and me on what we might need to do going forward. It is quite sensitive, and I cannot tell you more at present because I simply don't know what that entails. I've simply been asked to set the meeting up. I am also invited to attend. Jones has indicated that it is with your safety in mind the request is made."

Harry nodded and waited for Liam to continue.

"We've to report to the police station at 9am tomorrow. We will be taken to another location, where a meeting, involving the police and another party, will take place. Are you OK with that?"

Harry confirmed that he was. "What do you think this is all about, Liam?"

"I don't know, Harry, but I suspect it has something to do with Dalrymple. Whatever it turns out to be, you are clearly at the centre of things."

CHAPTER 121

Alex was barely aware of the journey home. During the first few miles, she had difficulty focussing on the road as her eyes were constantly filling with tears. What was happening to her? She wasn't a lovesick adolescent anymore, and swore out loud, because she had always considered herself to be a practical, unemotional individual. Harry somehow touched her in a way nobody else had done. She smiled despite the tears as she recalled the previous evening's events.

After dinner, Mark invited Harry to stay over. He accepted immediately, grateful that he could be close to Alex, he'd admitted, considering all that had occurred on Saturday.

She was disappointed to learn he would be sleeping in the room next to hers, but after everyone had gone to bed, she had gone to say goodnight and things had developed from there. She smiled again, a deeper, longer smile as she recalled the tenderness of their embraces. She had never felt so cherished or fulfilled. It took all her resolve not to turn around at each slip road she passed but continued onward in the knowledge they would be together again in a few days.

She reflected on the events that led her to investigate Harry's amazing powers. The initial reaction was one of scepticism and then intrigue. Although Professor Hart had been convinced a super-powered memory could be achieved, her training and personal experience told her that it could only be possible up to a point. What Harry had achieved was unbelievable. How had that happened?

The suggestions contained on the audio tape did not affect others as it had Harry. She had listened to it herself and although aware of some of the techniques Professor Hart had employed, she was unaffected by the recording. It must be the depth of unconsciousness Harry had fallen into that was the key to his ability to absorb and be so completely affected by the hypnotic programming.

Poor Harry. He had been through so much. Beverly had filled her in on the events of his life, with Mark providing additional insight into the circumstances which had affected him in the way that it had. She pictured him now, the gentle, unassuming man who had won her affection, saw his lopsided smile and earnest expression as he struggled to engage with her.

But what was it about him that attracted so much unwelcome attention?

That there appeared to be a move to acquire his property through dishonest means was one thing. But others were also taking an interest and that was something else she wondered about. It had to be something to do with the security services, she reasoned. If Harry's powers could be created in others, the advantage that would give secret agents would be immense. Yes, she concluded, that must be the reason for all that had occurred. If they decided Harry's powers would be an asset to them, his life could become insufferable. He would be subjected to all sorts of tests and assessments if they thought his skills could be created in others. She wondered how she could protect him if it ever came to that.

CHAPTER 122

Chris was delighted with the newspaper coverage of the auction and car boot sale. He had already informed his listeners that £7,000 had been donated to the hospice from the proceeds and that Harry Carry wanted to extend his thanks to everyone that had supported the event. He reread the front page of the local paper and felt sure Harry would be pleased at the way the reporter had covered the story. A photo of Harry, Alex and Beverly accompanied the article. The photographer must have been pleased to have captured such a good-looking group of people. That's what sells newspapers, he acknowledged, as he got ready to deliver the road and weather report.

It was also of great interest to Donald Dalrymple, who was briefing Slack Alice about what he wanted her to do. She had discovered that one of the women was Harry's sister and the other his love interest. This information was easily obtained from one of the chambermaids at Mark's hotel. The maid was an acquaintance Alice had got to know in her previous line of work. She had served in a burger bar in the red-light district when Alice was still operating as a working girl.

Dalrymple was pleased to learn that Harry was very close to his sister, who, she understood, had recently arrived in the area. He was, she had learned, besotted by the blonde woman who appeared alongside him in the newspaper picture. It was also current gossip amongst hotel staff that the owner, Mark, who was Harry's best friend, was also emotionally involved with Carey's sister. They imagined a wedding might not be too far away.

Could this be the leverage he craved that would force Carey to sell? After Alice left, he reached for the phone and telephoned Ruth.

"I think we might be able to put a bit of pressure on Carey," he told her.

CHAPTER 123

Jones was waiting in the rear car park when Liam and Harry arrived. He indicated they should go into an anonymous-looking grey van, driven by a man neither Liam nor Harry recognised. He took them to a deserted farmhouse about five miles away. The driver parked the van inside a Dutch barn and killed the engine. He indicated they should follow him into the farmhouse. As they made their way there, Harry noted several other vehicles parked at the rear of the building, out of sight from the road. One of the vehicles was the one the water testers had used when they visited his farm.

Jones led the way into the farmhouse, followed by Liam and Harry. The driver did not follow but remained outside, seemingly acting as a sentry. In the entrance hall, they were met by Charles Whyte and James Melville, who, although he did not know their names, Harry recognised as the two water testers. They invited the three men to follow them to an upstairs room.

Two men and a woman were waiting for them. Liam and Harry recognised one of the men and the woman from the garden centre video. The third man, seated by a fire, was clearly in charge because of the way the others deferred to him. He

357

got up from his seat and crossed the room, ignoring Jones and Liam to shake Harry's hand.

"Thank you so much for coming," he began, before inviting everyone to take a seat.

After much scraping of chairs on the bare wooden floor, he then addressed the gathering.

"First of all, let me put your minds at rest," he paused, looking at each in turn. "You are not in any danger here, as DCI Jones will confirm. It is precisely because we believe your life is in danger, Mr Carey, that we have invited you here. I cannot tell you too much about who we are at present – only be assured that we are all in the service of Her Majesty's government and have been tasked with ensuring that you, your relatives and friends receive our protection."

He directed his glance at Jones, who confirmed the statement with a nod of his head.

"You will have already recognised four of our operatives from previous instances, when two visited your home and were captured on CCTV at Saturday's auction, along with the two agents who were tasked with shadowing you at the sale. That was unprofessional and will certainly not happen again."

Liam noticed the female of the group wince at her leader's remarks.

A lengthy pause ensued while he sought to find the words to carry on.

"It seems," he continued, "that an individual known as Donald Dalrymple, an alleged crime baron, has designs on your property and also that of Mr Joe Burns who, I now believe, has sold his property to you. Am I correct in that assumption, Mr Forbes?"

"Almost," Liam replied. "Mr Burns' property has been purchased by Mr Carey and his sister, Beverly Smart."

"I see. I was not aware of that. Who else would have that information?"

"Only Harry, Beverly, Mark Brown, Sally Smith, Chris Collins, Alex Green and Joe Burns himself would know that – and Ruth Grant, who tried to persuade Joe to sell to her, at a greatly increased price."

Control already knew that, from his surveillance people monitoring Dalrymple's and Ruth's telephones, but wanted to be sure that no information was being held back by Harry and Liam.

"From now on, you will be shadowed day and night by our people, less conspicuously than before," he added wryly. "This will also apply to Miss Smart and Doctor Green," he continued.

"Shouldn't we warn them that they might be in danger?" Harry queried.

"I think they already have such suspicions," was the reply.

"But Alex lives in Edinburgh! How will you protect her when she doesn't even live here?"

"Miss Green was followed by car on her journey home yesterday and arrived safely at 17.10 hours. Three of our agents were deployed to provide surveillance and protection around the clock. You should have no fears about that."

Another silence followed. Harry exchanged glances with Liam and Jones before speaking.

"What danger are we in, exactly?"

This time DCI Jones spoke.

"We have reason to believe Dalrymple will seek to put pressure on you to sell. This is likely to be through a third party, employed to carry out his dirty work. He'll make threats, like he has done in the past, but they will be unattributable to him personally, as you can appreciate. The threats, when made, will have an ultimatum that unless he gets what he wants, the person – his immediate family or loved ones – will be threatened, tortured or exterminated."

"We understand he has arranged this in previous instances," Control continued. "You may have heard a whole family were killed because they would not sell a betting shop chain to him some years ago. They went into hiding in Spain, but he was able to track them down two years later and took revenge. In the intervening period, the betting shops were subject to all sorts of problems like arson attacks, gas explosions and water flooding incidents. Several employees were beaten up for no apparent reason, other than that they worked for the company. It got to be that nobody would work for the group, and it eventually folded. You can guess who then acquired the organisation for a pittance."

Jones interrupted. "We believe he will attempt to do the same to you, Harry. That is why we are talking to you today and why these measures to protect you and yours have been put in place."

"Not very successfully," Liam observed. "Your methods do not give us much confidence, Mr—"

Control did not respond to Liam's invitation to reveal his name but continued to give reassurances.

"I have to confess to being extremely embarrassed at the previous lack of professionalism," he conceded. "We should have been more aware of the situation but felt that speed was of the essence in getting feet on the ground, as it was not clear how imminent any potential threat against Mr Carey's person might have been. Now it appears, from intelligence gathered over the last couple of hours, any moves on Dalrymple's part will be some days away – but we are prepared for any situation in which we may need to intervene should matters come to a head."

Liam was far from convinced and queried how they could be so sure.

Harry interrupted before anyone could answer.

"I'm not concerned for myself," he said, "but the thought of my friends and particularly my sister, Beverly, or Alex Green being in danger is extremely worrying."

"I fully understand," Control acknowledged. "Be assured, however, that we have taken care to ensure both ladies will be closely monitored twenty-four hours a day. Other agents are currently deployed to ensure they are protected. There is a team of more than twenty operatives engaged in ensuring that neither you nor the women will come to harm."

Ever practical, Liam enquired how that was to be achieved.

"First of all, a long-lost cousin, in reality one of our operatives, will be coming to live with Harry and will be stationed there until the situation is resolved. It will be necessary for your sister to be briefed in that strategy, Harry. They will never leave the farmhouse and will act as a communication link to our other agents. When either you or your sister leaves the premises, you will be shadowed by other agents until you return home."

Harry and Liam exchanged glances before Harry spoke.

"I'm supposed to be going up north on Friday to be with Doctor Green to carry out some tests. Will that still be possible, and how can I feel confident that Beverly, my sister, will be safe in my absence?"

"Perhaps she could stay with your friend Mark Brown, while you are away?" he replied.

Liam was quick to realise that Control, whoever he was, knew a great deal about Harry, his relatives and friends.

"We are also aware of your own situation and your relationship with Sally Smith," he responded. "Ms Smith, as well as your good self, will also be receiving our protection, Mr Forbes."

For once, Liam was at a loss for words and struggled for something to say in reply.

"You must surely realise that we need to know everything about you all if we are to provide effective protection to your group?" he continued.

Before Liam could speak again, Harry wanted to know what safeguards had been put into place for Joe and Chris.

"They have been allocated the same level of surveillance and protection," he assured him.

After a few moments of silence, DCI Jones began to speak.

"It is vital that you all behave as normally as possible. We want not just to protect you from harm but also to ensure that Dalrymple is arrested and put away for a very long time. I'm sure you can appreciate how important that is, Harry. With the support of my colleagues here, it should also be possible to identify and dismantle the web of crime he controls, not only in his own sphere of operations but also with other associated criminals he engages with to carry out his operations."

Both Harry and Liam conceded that it was the only way to proceed and said so.

"What we now need to know," Control continued, "is what your daily plans will be going forward. What appointments are you committed to this week apart from the Edinburgh journey?"

"Well, there are various deliveries that need to be made following the auction and I'm due to meet with Ralph Fortescue this afternoon for a viewing and valuation of some antiques he's interested in buying."

"Who is this Fortescue person and where and when will you be going to carry out the valuation?" Control enquired, a pen poised as he prepared to scribble the details on a notepad resting on his lap.

Both Liam and Harry spent the rest of the morning providing Control and his colleagues with information to ensure that the intelligence services were fully briefed on their movements and, as far as they could, the movements of Joe, Mark, Chris and Sally.

It was also agreed that an agent would accompany Harry in the van whenever he was making deliveries. His cover would be he had been hired by Harry as an occasional porter to assist with removals and suchlike.

The questions were both searching and thorough, so much so that both men felt mildly exhausted by the time that they were able to return home.

CHAPTER 124

Wyllie and Grant were suffering different levels of anxiety. In Wyllie's case, it was the lack of alcohol that troubled him most. Despite acknowledging his career and, therefore, his life were in ruins, it did not bother him nearly as badly as the prospect that he could not get a drink to settle his nerves. Remembering Tristram's threat to expose him as a paedophile played heavily on his mind. He'd heard what happened to people like him in prison if other inmates got wind of what he'd been up to. He shuddered at the prospect of what that might entail. It would be a lot worse than the incessant craving he was suffering from the lack of alcohol, he concluded.

A few cell doors away, Tristram was even more anxious. He could see no possible escape from what awaited him. Even if released from prison, Dalrymple's thugs would make sure he would never be able to testify against him. Why had he been so stupid to rack up all that gambling debt, a sum he could never hope to repay? The only possible solution had been to acquire the Burns and Carey farms, thereby enabling access to his own land, creating sufficient space for the commercial park development. Even if he received a lengthy custodial sentence, Dalrymple's influence was not limited to the outside world.

It would be easy for him to call in a few favours from some very violent inmates to silence Tristram for ever. The more he thought about what could happen, the more he realised he had no future, however things turned out. The nagging pain that throbbed in his head was driving him to distraction. He could not think clearly and experienced a rising sense of panic which eventually climaxed in a blinding pain behind his eyes, causing him to cry out in agony, then worry no more having suffered a massive brain haemorrhage.

Wyllie heard the scream of his onetime collaborator and the sound of something hitting the floor but was too wrapped up in his own worries to wonder what had caused the disturbance. Had he known that one of his greatest worries had just been negated, it might have brought some comfort, but it would be another hour before Tristram Grant's lifeless body was discovered.

If Ruth had known of her husband's sudden demise, she might also have concluded that one of her major problems had also been resolved. At that moment, she was otherwise engaged, sharing a line of cocaine with Donald Dalrymple.

While Ruth and Dalrymple were getting high, Isaac Lipman was drafting an offer to purchase the farms and had already arranged for one million pounds to be placed in Ruth Grant's number two account. He smiled wryly as he reread the contract. Even if Carey and his sister accepted the offer, they couldn't expect to enjoy a long and carefree life. Dalrymple would seek revenge. He was sure of that.

CHAPTER 125

Nobody spoke on the return journey. All were preoccupied with their own thoughts, Harry especially.

As arranged, a man called Peter met them in the police car park and introduced himself as Harry's van boy. One could hardly describe him as a boy, however. Standing over six feet tall and probably seventeen stone in weight, he was the epitome of a boxer whose features had suffered as a result of his involvement in the sport.

Liam's parting advice to Harry was to be extra vigilant and aware of what was going on around him. He assured them he would as Peter (call me Pete) jumped into Harry's van, before heading off to meet Ralph Fortescue at the storage facility.

Pete didn't say much other than if there was any trouble, Harry should defer to him, especially if any violence should occur.

"Keep behind me if that happens!" he stressed, then said nothing more for a few miles. Eventually, he enquired whether he should address Harry as Mr Carey or by his first name.

"Harry will be fine," he replied.

Having got that out of the way, Pete then asked where they were going and what they would be doing for the rest of the day.

"I'm meeting a dealer who's interested in some items I have stored in a warehouse," Harry informed him. "Following that, there are several items people purchased at the Saturday sale that need to be delivered. I'm glad you'll be able to help me with that, Pete."

Pete nodded and went on to say that it would be necessary for Harry to brief him on every day's schedule. He also needed to know what was planned on a weekly basis but warned it would have to be reviewed daily, to ensure that Control was aware of their movements. Little more was said after that, until they drove into the repository. Pete opted to stay in the van, while Harry went to meet Ralph, who was patiently waiting at the entrance of the warehouse. Having showed his security pass and signed Ralph into the building, they made their way to the racks where Harry's goods were stored, accompanied by a staff member driving a forklift. Ralph was impressed, especially when Harry indicated the packing case he needed to access.

"How many cases of stuff do you have here, Harry?" he enquired.

"I think there are nineteen, if my memory serves correctly," Harry replied, producing a stock list from his inside pocket. "Yes, there are nineteen all told and the one we want is number five," he told the forklift driver.

With the packing case lowered to the ground, Harry selected a key and opened the locks. Ralph looked on in amazement.

"It must be costing a lot for storage," he observed.

"Yes, but the items I have here are too valuable to store anywhere else."

"Where did you get all this stuff, Harry?"

"It was acquired over many years when my grandfather was still alive and now I'm wondering how best to market it. Maybe you could advise me on that score, Ralph?"

"Didn't you think of entering them in the auction?" was his next question.

"Some of them would be best placed with dealers or in specialist auctions, I suspect – but as you know, my valuations are probably well out – and I'm not always sure of their authenticity. There could be fakes in here, Ralph. Right, let's see what we've got."

The contents were laid on a table, with Ralph examining each piece as it was removed. Harry referred to the list of items, ticking them off as Ralph estimated what each artefact might be worth.

During an hour of careful scrutiny, Ralph's eyes grew wider with each item produced. He eventually stood back and exhaled loudly.

"Some of these items are worth thousands! How do your estimates compare with my valuations?"

"Yours are a lot higher than what I imagined, Ralph."

"And you have all these other boxes, too! What else do you have besides the ceramics we've just inspected?"

Harry consulted his stock sheets before replying.

"Well, there's pottery and glass in two more boxes, clocks and watches in another one, bronze figurines, metalware and militaria in four containers. There are also five cases of foreign and oriental pieces, and the six larger cases have items of assorted furniture."

"Tell me, Harry, what value did you place on the items I have just valued?"

"I estimated £13,000 by my reckoning, Ralph, but I was working from old price guides."

"I'll say," he replied, "this one box we've just opened is worth about £10,000 more than your valuation . You're sitting on a fortune here, Harry! I'm completely astounded by what you've shown me."

Harry, too, was astonished at what Ralph had told him. Both men were silent for some moments before Harry enquired if the items Ralph had been seeking were what he had inspected.

"Yes – and more besides them. I would like to make an offer for the Moorcroft Wisteria pattern vase and the pair of Hazeldene patterned vases as well. Those should fetch at least £7,000 from serious collectors. I'm sure there would be no problem in shifting them. I can find a buyer for the Doulton Lambeth vases by Eliza Simmance at around the £2,500 mark and the Martin Brothers stoneware tobacco jar should make £1,000 easily."

"That's £10,500 at retail prices, if my calculations are correct," Harry observed. "What were you going to offer for them, Ralph?"

There was a long pause before he answered. "There's several ways we can do this and I'm going to lay it on the line for you.

"You can sell them off to people like me at trade prices, which eliminates the problem of finding buyers for them, but that might only give you a fraction of what they are worth if you were to sell them direct to collectors. The second option is to enter them in specialist auctions around the country or even abroad, but the carriage and insurance costs, along with the auction house's commission charges, would eat into your profits. Thirdly, you could offer them online, but the problems of delivery would also need to be considered. A fourth option is to engage someone like me to sell them for you on a commission basis. Those are the routes I would suggest you might consider."

Harry smiled. "There is a fifth way. I'm planning on opening up my own auction house. Joe Burns has agreed to sell me his farm and I intend creating an antiques market there, along with some other attractions. What I've told you is very confidential just now, Ralph, so please don't mention what I've said to anyone else."

Ralph stood staring at Harry open-mouthed for some moments before nodding his understanding.

"You say the pieces you've mentioned would give you a quick sale, Ralph?"

When he nodded again, Harry told him that he could have all four pieces for £6,000, provided he could call on him again for advice but also for Ralph's guaranteed silence regarding his future plans.

Ralph readily agreed and shook hands to seal the deal.

With Harry's permission, Ralph photographed several items as they returned them to the packing case, suggesting that he might find buyers for some of the ceramics that might be of interest to collectors he knew.

Repacking complete, Harry and Ralph signed out through security and agreed to meet later to discuss progress.

Harry was aware that Pete had photographed Ralph as they parted.

"Who was that?" he enquired.

A battery of questions followed which Pete typed into his iPad before transmitting, for Control to investigate, Harry presumed.

CHAPTER 126

They collected another agent on the drive back to Harry's farm. His name was John. He was smaller than Pete but powerfully built. Back at the farmhouse, he introduced them both to Beverly and explained what their individual roles would be. John and Pete repeated the dos and don'ts they needed Beverly and Harry to conform to in order to provide effective protection.

For the remainder of the day, Harry and Pete continued with deliveries, the latter being ever vigilant in monitoring movement around them as they drove from place to place. He also insisted on being first to enter any premises they visited. He was certainly thorough, Harry acknowledged.

There had been so much to absorb since meeting with the other agents, Harry reflected. He wondered how effective the measures to safeguard Alex would be, and longed to be with her once again. Control had reluctantly agreed he should join her in Edinburgh at the weekend, but Harry was now wondering if that was something he should reconsider. Would it expose Alex to any danger if he went north? Might Dalrymple's foot soldiers follow and discover where Alex lived? As he ruminated over that and other concerns, which included Beverly and the others being placed in jeopardy, he suddenly became aware that a silver car had been following them and mentioned it to Pete.

"That's backup, Harry," he informed him. "We have personnel deployed around you. It's good that you spotted it and shows you are taking things seriously. Well done for noticing that!"

Harry merely nodded and concentrated on steering the van into the farmyard, less troubled now than before but also acutely aware that the situation was much more serious than he had first imagined. If the level of protection was this intense, the threat must be very real and perhaps imminent. What, he wondered, should he do about his trip to Edinburgh?

CHAPTER 127

It was late afternoon before DCI Jones located Ruth Grant. She had just returned from her tryst with Dalrymple when the house phone rang. Jones said he needed to speak to her urgently and would come to the house. Ruth's initial reaction was one of concern that he might have uncovered something through interrogating Tristram but agreed he should come right away. After he rang off, she phoned Dalrymple to say what had happened. He in turn telephoned Isaac Lipman, instructing him to get over to the Grant house, just as fast as he could.

Jones came quickly to the point. "I'm afraid I have some bad news for you, Mrs Grant. I'm afraid your husband suffered a stroke while in custody and despite attempts to revive him, was pronounced dead at 15.00 hours today."

It was not what Ruth had expected to hear. Despite her desire to be rid of Tristram, the news left her unable to speak.

Jones watched closely for a reaction and the female police officer accompanying him took a step forward, but Ruth held up her hand, warning that she did not want to be approached. The doorbell interrupted further discussion, as Lipman, not waiting to be invited in, barged into the study where they were assembled.

"What's happening here?" he demanded.

"Tristram is dead," Ruth informed him.

"How did that happen?"

Jones supplied the details, and Lipman, true to his instincts, was quick to query the circumstances.

"There will be an inquest," Jones informed him.

"Too true!" Lipman responded. "If there has been any evidence of police brutality, you can be sure that Mrs Grant will bring an action against the police."

"He was on his own in his cell when the incident occurred," Jones informed him, "and the first medical assessment suggests he died almost instantaneously from suffering a stroke. We will, of course, know more following an autopsy report."

Lipman would have continued to query Jones had it not been for Ruth, again holding up her hand, requesting that he be silent.

Jones then enquired if there was anyone she needed to contact and could his colleague provide any support.

"Isaac will attend to things," she replied.

"We'll get back to you regarding any further developments," Jones informed her, as both officers made to leave.

Having watched the police car depart, Ruth turned to Lipman and held both thumbs in the air. "At last!" she cried exultantly. "I'm free at last, Isaac."

Donald would also be delighted one of the loose ends would also be resolved, Lipman remarked.

Whether it was relief that there were no unwanted questions to answer or just the sheer joy of having become a widow, Ruth began to laugh, gently at first but then with a shrillness that surprised even her. Lipman looked on intrigued, realising that Tristram had not been the only one in the relationship with mental issues.

Eventually, when her hysteria subsided, he suggested they should let Dalrymple know what had occurred.

CHAPTER 128

Mark was with Beverly when Harry returned to the farm.

Agent John had taken up residence in the kitchen because it gave him a clear view of the approaches to the house, so they all went into the lounge to confab.

"This is beginning to look very serious, Harry," Mark observed.

Harry merely nodded before apologising for the way things had turned out.

"It's not your fault," Beverly rebuked him. "You've done nothing wrong."

"Maybe so, but I can't help feeling responsible. It's just too terrible to think what might happen to any of you because of this business with the farms."

Further discussion was interrupted by the telephone ringing. Beverly answered it before passing the receiver to Harry.

Jones was on the line. After enquiring how things were progressing with the bodyguards, he then informed him that Tristram Grant had died in custody.

"It might not have any effect upon things, but I think you should be aware of the situation. Be doubly careful in every respect," he warned.

When he rang off, Harry shared the news with Mark and Beverly.

"I had planned to be with Alex over the weekend but now I'm not so sure if I should leave you here alone, Beverly – or even if I might be endangering Alex by going there."

Mark was first to speak. "Bev can come and stay with me at the hotel or I can come here," he offered. "You do have trained bodyguards in place after all, Harry. You being here would make no difference, I feel."

Beverly agreed. "I'm sure I'll be fine," she insisted. "You should go to Edinburgh."

"Perhaps you might both like to come with me and make a weekend of it?" Harry suggested.

Mark said he couldn't go because of a couple of wedding functions at the weekend and Beverly told him she had no wish to be a gooseberry.

Everyone laughed at that, relieving the tension they all felt.

Next door in the kitchen, John adjusted his earphone and smiled. He hadn't been to Edinburgh in years and wondered if Pete or he would be accompanying Harry there.

CHAPTER 129

So Tristram Grant was dead. In one respect it was welcome news, Donald Dalrymple decided, but what, if anything, had Grant revealed to the police? He eventually decided that if the plods had discovered anything, they would have been accosting him by now. No, he reasoned, Grant had kept schtum, knowing that anything he might have said to implicate him would have been to his personal detriment. Wyllie, even if he had any suspicions about the relationship between Grant and himself, would have been unable to provide any reliable evidence that would stand up in court.

His thoughts went back to the discussion he had just had with Lipman.

"Let's cool things for the moment," he advised. "Give it a few days, Donald. Let's see how things pan out. I've got the papers ready for the farms acquisition, but Tristram's death has altered things a bit. Rather than having Ruth approach Carey, I think it would be more appropriate for another firm of solicitors to do that on her behalf."

"Why not your firm?"

"I believe that anything connecting me and therefore you, might be a disincentive for Carey to sign on the dotted line. No one knows of your relationship with Ruth, except for a chosen few that can be relied on to keep their traps shut. An approach from another solicitor might just do the trick, if you follow my reasoning?"

Dalrymple did understand and said that it would be something they should do.

"Right, set it up for next Wednesday. Give them seventy-two hours to accept before the offer is withdrawn."

"What if they decline or demand a higher offer?"

"Don't worry on that score," Dalrymple growled. "I'm going to make sure they play ball."

Lipman didn't ask how that might be achieved but pitied Harold Carey if he had the temerity to refuse the offer.

CHAPTER 130

He decided to phone Alex from his van. She answered on the third ring.

"Are you all right?" was the first thing she said.

"Yes, I'm fine except that I'm missing you very badly," he confessed.

"Me too," she admitted.

There was a long pause before the conversation resumed.

"Look," Harry began, "an awful lot has been happening here. I'm surrounded by bodyguards, and I believe you are also being shadowed by government agents up in Edinburgh."

"What? Do you mean they are keeping an eye on me, too?"

"Yes, they're worried that this Dalrymple guy might try to get to me through you. That's why I called. I just wanted to let you know that you are protected. I'm so sorry that you've been drawn into this – all because someone wants to own the farms."

"I think it is much more than that, Harry. I have a theory I'll explain when I see you. You are coming up on Friday, aren't you?"

"Do you really want me to come?"

"Of course I do."

"Are you sure? I wouldn't want to put you in any danger."

"Yes, I'd like you to come if you can get away."

He was relieved to hear that Alex wanted him to visit, although he realised it might not be the smartest thing to do. They chatted some more before ending the call. He returned to the house with an added spring in his step.

In Edinburgh, Alex smiled fondly at a group photograph Beverly had emailed of the last meal they had shared. She planted a kiss on the image of Harold Carey, who she now realised she adored beyond all reason.

CHAPTER 131

Although alarmed by Harry's earlier revelations, Alex decided she would not allow herself to become paranoid. Nevertheless, anything different from the everyday routine caused her to wonder if she might be in danger. More importantly, she became more concerned for her elderly father. While he had carers who visited regularly while she was away, it was a constant worry he would be exposed should anyone want to get at her through him. The solution was to have him moved out of the home until the situation could be resolved. But where could that be? The answer came in a manner that she could not have anticipated.

A call from Harry alerted her that a minder would be calling at 7.30pm. He had been asked to announce her arrival by Control. She would be accompanied by another agent, who had also been deployed to provide cover for Alex, but instead of shadowing her when she left home, this individual would remain in the flat with her father twenty-four hours a day. She wanted to ask questions about the arrangement, but Harry warned that the call might be monitored and that he would catch up on her news when next they met. After enquiring if she was all right and also saying that he was fine, he ended the call.

Minutes later, a text came through telling her he was longing to see her again. She planned to text him back, but the doorbell rang as she was considering what to write.

The woman standing on the doormat looked familiar, but it took her a few moments to recognise where she had seen her before.

"I'm the woman you saw on CCTV," she said by way of introduction before squeezing past Alex into the hallway. She was carrying an overnight bag. Another woman, stationed at the foot of the stairs leading from the pavement to the house, turned and went into a car that was idling at the kerbside. It reversed about fifty yards along the street before its lights were extinguished and the engine switched off.

"That's a colleague," she informed Alex. "She will be keeping an eye on you wherever you go when you leave the house. She's on watch just now until ten o'clock, when she'll be relieved by someone else."

"I only just heard that you were coming," Alex answered by way of conversation. "What are you going to be doing here? What am I supposed to be doing?"

"To the last question, the answer is nothing, Doctor Green. Please try to act as normally as possible. You will be under surveillance at all times. My colleagues and I are tasked with ensuring that you and your father are kept safe 24/7 over the coming days or weeks."

When Alex did not query any of the information that had just been imparted, the woman decided to carry on.

"My name is Wilma and as far as anyone else is concerned, I'm a colleague who will be staying with you for a few days. My purpose is to provide protection for your father, who I understand is not able to leave the house without assistance."

Alex nodded. "If you are going to be staying here, I think you should call me by my first name, Wilma."

"Thank you, Doctor Green. I mean, Alex."

She paused for a moment before continuing. In her hand, she held a scale drawing which she proceeded to unfold in front of Alex.

"There are a few things I need to check with you about the house," she began and then proceeded to confirm the room layout, the rear entrance, fire escape, the intruder alarm and any other security measures that were in place. She then went on to record the names of the care staff that visited Alex's father, when grocery deliveries were scheduled, and so on.

She's certainly very thorough, Alex had to admit and felt greatly relieved that the woman would be with her father while she was at work.

"I guess I should revise our grocery list, then. What kind of things do you like to eat, Wilma?"

CHAPTER 132

Sally let herself into Liam's office, announcing her arrival with a gentle tap on the inner office door. She found him poring over some charts.

"Is this what Harry is planning on doing with the land?" she enquired.

Liam embraced her before replying. "Yes, these are his ideas committed to paper, although goodness knows how it is all going to end up."

She moved closer to inspect the drawings and whistled softly.

"Wow! That looks very ambitious."

Liam was clearly impressed by what Harry had envisioned and proceeded to explain the various elements of the project.

"First of all, Joe's property will retain the garden centre facility, but the watermill will be extended and converted into an antiques-cum-vintage-collectibles emporium. Space will be rented out to dealers and the site will also incorporate a restaurant. One of the other two barns will be used for periodic auctions. The other building will provide accommodation for arts and crafts workshops and retail areas."

"Is that a playground?" Sally wondered.

"Yes, there will be a children's play area alongside the restaurant. These other areas surrounding the car park, occupying about ten acres, are to be screened by evergreen hedges and populated with polytunnels to grow strawberries and other soft fruits. Seasonal vegetables will also be raised, and another area will concentrate on growing plants that can be marketed through the garden centre and by mail order."

Sally's eyes widened as she took in the extent of the development. "What's all this here, Liam?" she asked, pointing at a green area populated by symbols of trees.

"Oh, that's the orchard in the first block, but this one here," he said pointing beyond it, "will be for growing field herbs, the next for dried flowers and the other one beyond it will be for plants like lavender, bergamot and other species that will produce essential oils."

"What will he do with that?"

"The dried flowers can be sold as finished bouquets or for flower arrangers to work with. The essential oils will be used to produce scents and perfumes, I believe."

"So, if I'm correct, Harry will not be able to do all this on his own, even with Beverly and Joe to support him," she reasoned.

"No, he plans to provide the facilities in most cases for craftworkers and others to develop and manage. The idea is to encourage people to set up businesses, which will be relatively unique and appealing to a wide spectrum of customers. When this bit is fully operational, it will provide an income, through self-employment, to maybe thirty individuals. The bits he'll manage himself will probably add another twenty to thirty workers, probably more in the summer months."

"But that's not all that I'm looking at here, Liam. What about the other bit that extends across Joe's farm and into Harry's place?"

"That will be turned into a small woodland of native broad-leaf trees, where it bounds the eight fields that skirt the motorway. Apart from providing a green barrier between the fields and the roadway, it will also act as a nature walk to support and encourage wildlife."

"And these little boxes at the edge of the forested bit. What are they?"

"That's wooden holiday chalets," Liam informed her.

"He still seems to have retained some fields, though," she observed.

"Yes, those might be rented out to horse owners for equestrian purposes. He has an idea that a 'Riding for the Disabled' scheme might be encouraged there."

They stood quietly for some minutes, trying to absorb all that lay before them, until Sally finally spoke.

"Who would have thought it? I would never have believed Harry was capable of such a scheme, having witnessed him becoming increasingly introverted over the years. He clearly has a lot going on in his head that I never credited him with. Once upon a time, he was completely immersed in his music and raising money for the hospice. It's all he ever seemed to think about, apart from the van delivery business. So – Harry Carry is well named. He didn't just cart stuff around in his van. It's now clear to me that lots of other things were going on in his mind."

"I'm not so sure about that, Sally. I rather think that it was the arrival of Beverly and now more recently Alex that has dragged him back to becoming engaged with the present day. That head knock may have also been instrumental in helping him become the person he used to be."

"You could be right," she conceded. "He was a very intelligent and capable child. It was only after the accident he became so repressed and uncommunicative. I suspect we haven't yet witnessed all the changes he's going to undergo with the passage of time. Incidentally, how did you both get on today with DCI Jones?"

Liam's face became solemn. He reached out to take Sally's hand.

"Sit down for a moment while I tell you what happened. We're sworn to secrecy, but I feel sure I can rely on you not to speak about this to anyone."

When he had finished, Sally could not hide her concern.

"It's good to know that they're taking this seriously, but I can't help but worry about what this Donald Dalrymple hoodlum might do."

"I'm not just concerned for Harry, Beverly or Alex," Liam confessed. "He might try to bring pressure to bear on any of us, including you, Sally. You've been a close friend of his since childhood, after all."

"Do you really think he might try to get at Harry through us?"

"Who knows? I believe he's capable of anything. The police must be very concerned, by the way they've reacted. You need to be very careful, Sally. I'd be devastated if anything happened to you."

"Don't worry. I can look after myself. I didn't get a third dan in karate for nothing," she joked.

It made Liam smile, but his face grew serious as he remembered he hadn't told her about Tristram Grant.

That could also be connected, he speculated, although Jones insisted it was entirely due to natural causes.

They talked for several more minutes before deciding to go for an evening meal.

CHAPTER 133

On Tuesday morning, a phone call from Smith-Paterson Solicitors was received, enquiring if a meeting could be arranged with Mr Carey and his sister on Wednesday. Beverly took the call and asked what it was about. The caller, who sounded elderly, said he could only discuss that in person, and could they arrange for their own legal representative to be with them when he visited. He would prefer to hold the meeting at 3pm. Was that convenient, or would another time be more appropriate?

Intrigued, she agreed to check with her brother and Liam.

The caller thanked her and requested that she call back to confirm. His name was Rowland Smith, she learned, and he could be contacted on his direct line, which was…

Harry did not pick up on her first attempt, so she left a voice message. Liam himself answered when she called his office.

"Yes," he confirmed. He knew the firm and Rowland Smith in particular. He regarded Smith as being a man of integrity who ran a reputable long-established practice. "I'll be there at three if it's all right with Harry. I wonder what it's about. It can't be anything to do with Dalrymple. He always uses that Lipman creep to do all his dirty work."

Harry phoned back to confirm that it would be fine with him and wondered if Beverly or Liam had any idea what the visit was about.

"Liam doesn't think it has anything to do with Dalrymple but isn't ruling anything out," she told him. "How are you getting on with Pete there to help you?"

"Great, but he's hyper-cautious and doesn't like me being out of eye or earshot for a moment. I can't even go for a pee on my own!"

Beverly laughed as she returned the phone to its cradle. She had been standing at the kitchen window and was just about to return to the pantry when she saw Chris and Joe drive into the farmyard.

She giggled again when minder John rushed to her side to see who was approaching.

"It's all right," she told him. "They're friends, not foes!"

She thought he looked a bit disappointed, imagining that this sort of job was a bit lacking in excitement for him.

"I'll introduce you when they get inside," she told him. "You're our second cousin twice removed, aren't you?"

He merely nodded and shrugged resignedly.

CHAPTER 134

Chris and Joe were the first to arrive, followed by Mark, Liam and then Harry himself.

They had arranged to inspect the rough plans Liam had shown Sally the previous evening.

With the papers laid out on the kitchen table, Liam invited Harry to explain the various features depicted on the plan.

Everyone was impressed at the extent of the project. They were also aware that Harry was enthusing over the various elements it contained. His usually reserved demeanour was delivered in a manner that was exciting, confident and practical.

It was evident from the way he fielded questions that he had thought things through.

"Yes," he conceded. "The project will be developed in stages. I plan to open the emporium and restaurant first, while establishing the nursery areas. These latter actions will not only provide supplies for the restaurant but also stock which will be sold through the garden centre at much better margins than present. Introducing some soft-fruit areas, to generate income in the early years, will also be a priority. Tree planting can be supported with grants and subsidies from various sources, but the holiday lets will not be tackled for at least three years."

Joe, too, was uncharacteristically effusive. "You've got a great plan there, Harry!" he enthused.

Chris peppered Harry with questions. Although everyone thought of him as the local radio DJ, he had qualified as an accountant before electing to follow a career in radio.

Mark just nodded as Harry presented or explained each aspect of the plan. He felt pride in the way his chum was dealing with things. Beverly was also showing that she was wholly in approval and squeezed his hand every time that Harry dealt with a query.

As ever, Liam had been standing slightly apart from the others, observing their faces to gauge reactions. Eventually, when all the questions had been answered, he spoke.

"Something nobody has queried is how you are going to finance the scheme, Harry. Would you like to tell them about that now, or would you like me to tell them?"

Harry invited Liam to explain how the venture would be funded.

"It's still just an idea at present but he plans to set the enterprise up as a limited liability company. The initial capital investment will be £500,000.

"Beverly and Harry will own 60% of the initial share allocation between them. Twenty-five per cent of the stock (£125,000) will be offered to Joe, Chris, Mark, Liam and Sally so that each can own 5% of the company. An additional 10% (£50,000) will be offered to 100 local investors and will be capped at £500 per individual shareholding. The final 5% (£25,000) will be owned exclusively by Harry, the profits of which will be donated to the hospice from annual profits."

When no one queried this, Liam went on to say Harry expected everyone to be directors of the organisation, to ensure the effective management of the scheme. Agent John, who had taken himself outside while the friends were discussing the proposal, listened with growing interest to what he'd heard through his earpiece. He also nodded to himself on hearing what had been discussed but this time with an air of approval.

Everyone was clearly impressed and said so, Beverly especially.

"Sally doesn't know about this yet. Is it all right for me to tell her now?" Liam enquired.

"Of course," Harry replied.

Liam spoke again. "Everyone should understand that, although there is clearly an opportunity for everyone to make money out of the scheme, it is not the only reason for Harry's desire to set the company up this way. Having multiple owners, especially those who have been his loyal friends over so many years, was the principal reason for doing it this way. The other was that the 10% allocated to local people would ensure the community would benefit while also knowing they have an interest in how the town could prosper in the years ahead."

"It should also see off any hostile approaches from Dalrymple," Chris observed. "He might be able to pick off just one or two of us to get his hands on the farms but not when there will be so many shareholders, as I imagine you envisage having."

"That was a key consideration in coming to that decision, Chris," Harry confirmed.

Agent John, who had been raised in the city and harboured a belief that country dwellers were perhaps a trifle unworldly and naïve, felt forced to concede he had been misguided in that assumption. Once again, he nodded approvingly at the strategy the bumpkins had devised. *Yes,* he thought, *country but cute.*

Elsewhere, Control had also been eavesdropping. He, too, was impressed by this latest development.

CHAPTER 135

Tristram's demise had been a game changer. As far as the police were concerned, it created lots of problems. The death of anyone held in custody opened up all sorts of unwelcome investigations Jones could have done without. He would have liked to place that responsibility at Control's door, but the chief constable told him it was something the police – namely DCI Jones – would have to deal with.

Wyllie, he understood, was to be released on bail but had been unwilling to return to the outside world. He requested, instead, admittance to a rehabilitation unit insisting that his whereabouts was kept secret from the outside world. There had been a marked deterioration in his personal condition without a regular intake of alcohol. His hands shook and black circles around jaundiced eyes bore evidence of the withdrawal agonies he was suffering.

He'd admitted to all the charges brought against him by the bank and also of conspiring to procure Harold Carey's farm by fraudulent means in association with Tristram Grant, but beyond that, he would not go.

As Jones pondered the situation, his thoughts turned to Jake Butcher. He was convinced Butcher was involved in the scheme to pressurise both Joe and Harry to sell. According to the hospital, he was very lucky to still be alive, considering the beating he had suffered. It would be weeks before he would be able to walk unaided, they told him, but just that day, a couple of porters arrived at around 5am and bundled him away in an unmarked white vehicle resembling an ambulance. There was no record of him being admitted to another hospital anywhere in the county, following enquiries DS Black carried out that morning.

It would later become known that the bogus porters had been hired by Dalrymple. They'd told Butch he would be spending the rest of his convalescence in a safe house in the country. When able to be moved, he would be conveyed on a fishing trawler to a secluded port on the east coast of Scotland. Dalrymple had also promised he would receive £10,000 for his continued silence. That was what Jake Butcher was told and had forced himself to believe, but the North Sea is a very large and deep expanse of water where things can be disposed of without much chance of them ever being rediscovered. From Dalrymple's point of view, it was a neat and less expensive way of tying up a loose end. A mere £3,000 would rid him of Jake Butcher forever.

Although Jones had no knowledge of what lay in store for Butcher, he assumed Dalrymple had decided to eliminate him from his investigations. He suspected it was something he'd done countless times before but had never been brought to justice.

Grant, Wyllie and Butcher were dead ends now, he concluded. Maybe the intelligence services personnel held the information that could secure convictions, but they were not minded sharing that with him at present. Control had promised they would seek to provide evidence that would secure the convictions Jones craved – or maybe not – he added cryptically. He was confident, however, that Dalrymple and his whole corrupt empire would rot in prison. Then again, a different outcome might result in a considerable saving for taxpayers, he mused, a faraway look in his eyes.

Jones's in tray had reduced considerably over the last forty-eight hours, following an order from the chief constable not to leave the station until the affair with the security services was concluded.

He was aware that DS Black was wondering about his reticence to share information, but never queried why he was being excluded from something he sensed was very important. Black had a sharp questioning mind that often introduced ideas Jones might never have considered in a month of Sundays. He wished he could talk to him now but realised that it was out of the question.

This was clearly a major incident, which must be of great importance, he reasoned, considering how many personnel had been assigned to the case. Why? he asked himself, for the umpteenth time. The security services didn't concern themselves with domestic crime unless it involved insurgents or enemy agents. Could it be that Dalrymple was involved in terrorism in some way? No, he could not envisage that. He was no supporter of causes that did not result in his own personal benefit. So, what was the connection?

He had to acknowledge their main focus had been directed at Harold Carey; likeable Harry Carry, everyone's friend but unlikely to be of great importance to the country's intelligence service. Not only Harry, of course, but also his sister and close friends. Control had deployed such a large number of operatives around them, Jones was forced to conclude that Harry and company were the reason for their interest, but what could that possibly be?

CHAPTER 136

Ralph Fortescue was sitting on a scruffy reproduction chair in the lock-up he referred to as his showroom. It was nothing more than three rented garages connected by two internal doorways on the fringe of a council house estate.

He had been able to sell all the items Harry had supplied him with at such generous terms. There were other interested customers for some of the other items he'd photographed at the repository. How could it be that all of a sudden Harry Carry had all these treasures, he wondered? And there were eighteen more unopened crates!

Clearly, the value of the remaining items could be worth substantially more than Harry had estimated. He did say that most of his valuations had been based on guides, some of which were decades old. Prices fluctuated; it was true. What commanded big prices in previous years would fall out of fashion, but some items, like Chinese antiques, were going through the roof! He also wondered about the gold and silver items Harry had referred to in passing. Didn't he also say there were bronze figurines? There was no question in his mind that the total value must be worth hundreds of thousands of pounds and maybe – just maybe, there could be some items that might be worth that much in their own right. They must be worth a lot, he reasoned, if Harry had seen fit to pay the high costs of storing the collection in a high-security warehouse.

Despite his flamboyant, some might say eccentric, appearance, Ralph realised that working with Harry could be very lucrative. The photographed items he had shown to established clients were snapped up, practically immediately. It amounted to thousands of pounds in commission for Ralph alone if Harry accepted their offers. All his life, he'd just managed to scrape along, barely managing to eke out a living, buying and selling. At fifty-six, he hadn't made a fortune, though, and with no pension to look forward to, this might be his best chance of setting something aside for his old age.

He stared into space, imagining what might be possible, before lifting the wall phone and dialling Harry's mobile.

Harry answered on the van's hands-free system.

After the usual exchange of pleasantries, Ralph got on to the reason for his call.

"Look, Harry," he began, "I've got firm offers for nearly all the items I photographed when we were in the repository. They are way above your valuations, and I was wondering if we could meet soon to discuss whether or not you want to sell them for the prices I've agreed with potential buyers."

"I'm sure you've been able to get a good price for them, Ralph, and I'll be happy to sell through you, but it will be next week before I can access them. I'm going to visit someone over the weekend. Tomorrow, Thursday and Friday morning are all booked up with other commitments. Will next Monday afternoon be OK?"

Ralph said that was fine with him and enquired if there was anything else he might be able to sell on Harry's behalf.

"I'm sure there is, Ralph, but let's discuss it in more detail once we get together at the repository on Monday afternoon.

I have a proposition that you might be interested in. It should be to your financial advantage if it appeals to you. By the way, I'm expecting you will be happy with an agent's fee of 15%?"

"Delighted, Harry! That's very generous of you. I'll be glad to find buyers for you forever, at those rates," he enthused.

Pete, who had been listening into the conversation as he rode in the van, looked at Harry and commented that he must have been speaking to the dealer he'd photographed at the storage warehouse.

"Do you trust him?" he enquired.

"More than most," Harry replied.

CHAPTER 137

On Dalrymple's instructions, Slack Alice had been doing more digging and was in the process of reporting back. They were meeting in the inner office of his casino, which also comprised a suite of rooms he generally considered his home.

She had learned through indiscreet gossiping with a domestic worker in Mark's hotel that Harry had a close circle of friends, who were very protective of him. Her boss, she confided, was not only Harry's best friend but also a potential brother-in-law, as he and Harry's sister had become an item.

When he asked if there was anyone else he might be close to, Alice went on to give a brief history of the rest of the friends.

"Is that it?" Dalrymple growled.

"No, there is someone else more recent. It seems from the gossip I picked up that he's fallen for a Doctor Green that stayed with him recently."

"Is the guy a faggot?"

"No, the doctor is a woman, Donald. Why does everyone think doctors must be men?"

"Where does she practise?" was his next question.

"She's not a medical doctor, or at least I don't think so.

I do know, however, that she lives in Scotland and that he's going to visit her this weekend."

"Scotland's a big place! I should know. I've been there often enough! Where in Scotland, Alice?"

"She didn't know, but it should be easy enough to find out. He's going to be with her this weekend. I'm told he will be driving up there on Friday. All you need to do is follow him to discover where he's going, surely?"

Dalrymple did not like that response but chose to ignore it for the moment until he had wrung every last bit of information out of her. When he was quite sure that she had nothing more to give, he threw six £50 notes on the table. She moved to pick them up but cried out in pain when he grabbed her wrist.

"Just in case you forget, what we just discussed is between you and me, Alice. If I hear that you were foolish enough to mention this to anybody else, your life will not be worth living – and when I want your advice, I'll ask for it. So, keep your trap shut in future," he growled.

Dalrymple gave her arm a final wrench, causing her to cry out. When he finally released his grip, she massaged her arm before tentatively reaching for the notes he had strewn before her.

"Remember, Alice, when you do as I ask, things can go well for you so if you hear of anything you think I should know about, get that information to me soonest. You'll always be well paid but never presume to tell me what to think or do. That really irritates me, and you wouldn't want to make me angry, now. Would you?"

Alice nodded anxiously as she took her leave, clutching her wrist where the red marks of Dalrymple's fingers had left scarlet streaks on her otherwise pasty skin.

Seconds after she left, an adjoining door swung open as Ruth emerged from the room beyond.

"Did you hear that?"

"Yes. It sounds like we might have a bit of leverage on Mr Carey after all," she replied. "How do you plan to do that, Donald?"

"I'm not sure yet," he confessed, "but there seems to be plenty of possibilities. I'll need to see who's available first."

CHAPTER 138

Rowland Smith was met by Liam, who ushered him into the farmhouse. Beverly and Harry were waiting in the sitting room. The solicitor declined the coffee Beverly offered, preferring to proceed immediately to the reason for his visit.

"Thank you for seeing me at such short notice," he began. "I have been instructed to make an offer for both of the farms that you own, Mr Carey, Ms Smart. The offer of one million pounds sterling is made by your neighbour Mrs Ruth Grant. The funds to finance this sale have been deposited in one of my firm's accounts but will only be held there until 5pm on Friday of this week. If the offer is not accepted within that time, my client will withdraw and not contemplate any higher or subsequent offers. I have been asked to stress that condition," he concluded.

Liam exchanged glances with Harry and Beverly, noting that both, although surprised at the identity of the prospective buyer and size of the offer, were both shaking their heads emphatically.

"I'm afraid you've had a wasted journey, Rowland. My clients jointly own the farms and have only recently proposed plans for a major development of both properties. The project goes before the council for outline planning permission next month."

Smith was quiet for a few moments before continuing. "A million pounds is a very considerable sum of money. Are you both absolutely sure that you want to decline Mrs Grant's offer?"

Beverly responded first. "We have our own plans that will be much more lucrative than the sum Mrs Grant is tabling."

"We also feel that our plans for the two sites will be more in keeping with the community's wishes, Mr Smith," Harry added.

"How so?" he enquired.

"We are aware of an existing outline planning permission request, lodged by Wiltris Ltd, which seeks to develop the two farms and part of Mrs Grant's estate as a commercial and industrial park," Liam informed him. "As the farms are the only means of providing access to the development from the motorway, Mrs Grant's offer is clearly made with this objective in mind, but we recognise that if it was ever given the go-ahead, our local community would be completely overwhelmed by such a venture."

Smith digested the information. "I have no knowledge of any of these factors," he admitted. "My role is simply to make Mrs Grant's proposal known to you and I am obliged to leave a written copy of the offer, whatever the outcome of this meeting."

He placed the papers on the coffee table in front of him and prepared to leave. Before he could make any progress, however, Harry reached across from where he was sitting and tore them in half.

"Please take these with you, Mr Smith, and return them to Mrs Grant, with a message that we will never consider accepting any financial overtures that would alter the natural environment and beauty we enjoy here."

Smith nodded his understanding and thanked everyone for their time. Liam escorted him back to his car. When he returned, Beverly and Mark waited for his reaction to what had transpired.

"You did the right thing, Harry, but I wonder what repercussions it will produce? We can assume Dalrymple is behind Ruth Grant's offer. I don't think she has access to money of that magnitude."

Pete and John, along with another listener in Control headquarters, also wondered where she had accessed the funds. The phone tap in Ruth's lounge provided clues when she relayed a message to Dalrymple following Rowland Smith's report. What Dalrymple then proceeded to do was far more revealing. When Ruth hung up, he placed another call to a Manchester number. When the person at the other end answered, he simply told him the job was on and that they should meet in his garage on Thursday at noon.

CHAPTER 139

They had agreed to meet with Control on Thursday afternoon, to discuss the arrangements relating to Harry's trip to Edinburgh. Pete was going to accompany him on the journey, which they would make in Harry's van. It was to be made known that the two men were going on a buying trip to Scotland. Harry was intrigued by the instructions given by Control but agreed to comply with them to the letter.

CHAPTER 140

Pete and Harry wore identical red boiler suits and Yankee baseball caps as they drove in the van towards Edinburgh. Pete spent most of his time checking the rear-view mirror. He occasionally spoke into a device inside his boiler suit and seemed to be getting a response from the recipient in the headset he was wearing. This had seemed to be nothing more than an iPod, but which Harry now realised was a mobile communication device. After a hundred and twenty miles, he took a slip road that led to a motorway service station and drove into the parking area for commercial vehicles. Once stationary, the two men got out of the cab and entered the concourse.

Four pairs of eyes followed their progress from the area reserved for cars. Ten minutes later, two men in red boiler suits came out of the service station, got into the van and returned to the motorway. Two men in a black BMW followed closely behind. Two other men in a Subaru trailed the BMW.

At the first junction following the service station, Harry's van proceeded towards the Glasgow turn-off, with both the BMW and Subaru in pursuit.

Back at the service station, Pete and Harry, having divested themselves of the boiler suits and hats, were now driving northwards to Edinburgh in a grey Ford Escort.

CHAPTER 141

It was a street of terraced Edwardian houses, typical of Edinburgh.

Pete asked Harry to pull into the side while he phoned ahead. Satisfied it was safe to approach, they proceeded to a parking space outside Alex's front door.

The door to the street opened but it was a stocky-built woman of medium height dressed in jeans and a sweatshirt that greeted them. She looked carefully about her before urging them into the house. No sooner had they crossed the threshold than they heard the door swish to a close, followed by the sound of bolts being clicked into place.

"Are you being watched?" Pete enquired.

"Not that we're aware of," came the reply, "but we'd heard that you were followed on your journey here."

"I'm pretty sure that we lost them at a service station we stopped at," he informed her. "They are now on their way to Glasgow with two of our guys tailing them."

Harry was anxious to see Alex and interrupted the agents to ask where she was.

"She's waiting for you in the lounge," the female agent informed him. "That's the door to the left," she added. "Please keep away from the window, Mr Carey, even though the curtains are drawn."

Perhaps he should have knocked before entering, but the prospect of seeing Alex again, even after such a brief period, was too much for Harry. He found her sitting beneath a standard lamp, the glow of which highlighted the face of the woman he had come to adore. She rose at once and flew into his arms. They clung together for several moments, exulting in each other's embrace.

Eventually Alex reached up and held his head in her hands, searching his face for confirmation he was all right. Then she kissed him full on the lips and squeezed him tighter.

"I thought you'd never get here," she told him. "Are you all right? Are the others OK?"

"Everything's fine," he assured her. "How has it been for you?"

Before she could reply, a knock at the door followed by the sound of someone entering the room, caused them to separate, like a pair of embarrassed schoolchildren.

Pete coughed twice before intimating that he would be on night duty and wondered where he might be able to get some shut-eye, before taking up his watch.

"You will be sleeping in the blue bedroom," Alex replied. "I'll take you there now if you'll follow me upstairs. Will you come with me, Harry, and I'll introduce you to my father?"

They followed Alex upstairs, where she pointed to Pete's bedroom. "Your colleague is in the room next to yours," she continued. "The door opposite is the bathroom if you want to get freshened up first."

Pete said that he would like to do that, but did Harry want to go first?

"Mr Carey will be sleeping downstairs in another bedroom, which is ensuite, so you have free use of the upstairs rooms."

Pete entered the bedroom and deposited an overnight bag.

"I've left your case downstairs, Harry," he informed him as he made his way to the bathroom.

"Dinner will be at 7.30," Alex added, as he went to close the bathroom door. "We'll be eating in the kitchen, which is in the basement."

They left Pete and went downstairs together, Alex leading him by the hand towards another door opposite the lounge.

"This is Dad's room. He's been looking forward to meeting you. He's not at all well and doesn't have a great life expectancy, so don't be too surprised to see him as he now is. Asbestosis was the cause of his condition, and he tires very easily. Talking takes such a lot out of him but he's mentally as sharp as he ever was. Just be your normal self, Harry, and don't be too sympathetic. He hates people feeling sorry for him."

Alex's father was propped up on a bank of pillows, in a room lit only by a bedside light and the flickering of a television set tuned to the Heritage Channel. He wore a face mask connected to an oxygen bottle at the side of the bed.

Harry said hello and went to the bedside, offering his hand as he approached. He was greeted by a wry smile as the invalid gingerly removed the mask from his face, extending his other hand as he did so. There was little warmth in the papery, thin skin that Harry held between both of his hands.

"I'm so very pleased to meet you," he said haltingly, "Alex has told me so much about you. I'm afraid my condition will not allow me to converse with you for very long as I tire easily but I'm sure we'll have a chance to get to know each other better over the weekend."

"I'm very pleased to meet you too, Mr Green. Thank you for allowing me to visit you. I hope we'll be able to spend some time together but only if you feel well enough for that to happen."

"Alex has regaled me about your remarkable abilities,

Harry. I know that she is very impressed by you, and I can see why – not just because of that but also because I think she likes you for other reasons," the old man chuckled before lapsing into a fit of coughing which only began to subside after he had restored the mask to his face. "Please forgive me," he eventually wheezed when he regained composure. "I'm afraid that without this oxygen mask, I would not be able to survive."

His breathing sounded like a death rattle. Harry was unsure how best to respond but simply smiled, nodding understanding.

Alex intervened. "Dad," she said, "we're going to leave you now until you've had a chance to recover and will look back after dinner. We'll have plenty of time to chat before Harry has to return home."

The old man attempted to smile and nodded. "Till then," he whispered as he struggled to regain control of his breathing.

CHAPTER 142

Jones felt things might be coming to a head following receipt of an email from Control. He was requesting a car number check, which also came with a photograph of the two men that had been tailing Harry's van. Could he identify them? He discovered that the vehicle was registered to the brother of one of the men. Both were on the police's wanted list. Jones's interrogation of the system also revealed that the men were associates of a Manchester gangland boss.

He communicated the information back to Control and waited for his response. It wasn't long in coming.

"We're shadowing them and will be following them back to Manchester to determine who and where they report to," Control informed him. "We'll keep you posted on progress, and I thought you might like to brief your colleagues in Manchester that they might want to apprehend them later, at a time of our choosing. Do not action any arrests until I give the go-ahead, please."

Jones confirmed that he would only move once he'd received the OK from Control.

"I take it that Harry and the others are safe and well?"

"You can set your mind at rest on that score," Control assured him before ringing off.

Jones wasted no time in contacting his colleagues in Manchester. They were very interested in what he had to tell them, confirming they would be ready to act when he got back to them.

Meanwhile, Harry's van was sitting in the secure car park of a Glasgow hotel. Across the road from the exit gates, a black BMW with two men waited. The passenger got out of the car and made his way to the hotel entrance. At a discreet distance from the BMW, another man emerged from a Subaru car further along the road and followed him into the hotel.

They were to learn later that the BMW passenger had enquired if Harold Carey had arrived. The desk clerk confirmed that he had but had left by another entrance to meet with someone in town and would not be returning until later that night.

He then tried to book a hotel room but was told there were no vacancies. Clearly upset at receiving this information, he turned and stamped out of the hotel.

The two agents who had driven Harry's van to Glasgow watched with amusement from their room, which overlooked the car park, as he returned to the car, gesticulating wildly to the driver. A lot of animated discussion ensued until finally and seemingly reluctantly, the driver produced a mobile phone, into which he spoke with an apparent air of apprehension. Whatever the person on the other end of the line had to say caused the driver to wince. There was a lot of arm waving and nodding as the conversation continued. The passenger, although he did not speak, could also seem to be affected by what he was hearing.

"Just wait until tomorrow when they see what else we have in store for them," one of the agents chuckled.

CHAPTER 143

Alex led Harry through to the kitchen, inviting him to have a glass of something while she prepared dinner. As he waited for a glass to be filled, Alex pointed to a recipe book lying on a worktop. She opened the book and pointed to the handwritten words that lay just inside the front cover.

DO NOT DISCUSS ANYTHING THAT MIGHT BE PICKED UP BY HIDDEN MICROPHONES!

She then turned the page where a further message was scrawled in equally large letters.

I PLAN TO TAKE YOU AWAY TOMORROW, ON THE PRETEXT OF CONDUCTING TESTS AT THE UNIVERSITY. WE CAN TALK IN CONFIDENCE THERE.

Harry nodded his understanding. Alex removed the notepaper and fed the pages into a paper shredder.

She poured herself a drink and held the glass up in a toast.

"Here's to the future, Harry."

"The future," he replied, clinking glasses as he did so. "Let's hope it turns out like I hope it will."

"From what Beverly was telling me – we speak on the phone every day – you have some very ambitious plans for the farms, Harry."

He was clearly surprised to hear that Beverly and Alex talked to each other so frequently but did not comment.

"Yes, they are quite ambitious but realistic, I'm sure. It will only be achieved as finances allow. The main aim is to provide work and business opportunities for the local economy in a way that reflects the unique character of the area."

Alex smiled as he went on to tell her his plans. This was a different Harry from the one she had first met. Instead of the reserved, indecisive individual introduced to her just a few days ago, she marvelled at the positive and dynamic persona that was emerging. She wondered if she might play a part in the vision, which so clearly excited and enthused him.

CHAPTER 144

It had been a cold and uncomfortable night for the occupants of the BMW. The displeasure of their employer added to their mood, having heard what would happen if they did not get the result expected of them.

Both were suddenly alert as the backs of two boiler-suited figures made their way to Harry's van. They were to be frustrated once again, however, when a large removal van stopped adjacent to their vehicle blocking their exit. Four men got out of the van and proceeded to the front of the removal van. All entreaties to move were dismissed by the four burly men who alighted from the van. There was a mechanical problem, which prevented it from moving, they informed the occupants of the BMW. One of the four men appeared to be tying his shoelaces and ducked out of sight as he knelt in front of the BMW. He was using the diversion to attach a magnetic tracking device, which would lead them to their Manchester base.

Meanwhile, Harry's van had left the car park and was disappearing into the distance. It was a full fifteen minutes before the removal van was able to continue on its journey.

In a vain attempt to locate Harry's van, the thugs took off

in the direction it had departed, but despite travelling miles around Glasgow, they could find no trace of it. Dejected, they returned to the hotel area, hoping above hope it would return.

Now parked inside an MOD garage, Harry's van would stay out of view until it was driven back home, with Harry and Pete transferring from the Ford Escort to the van at a prearranged location.

In Edinburgh, Alex and Harry travelled across town to the university with Pete in tow. They would be carrying out tests in a soundproofed laboratory room, Alex informed him. He would have to wait outside in the corridor until the tests were completed. Pete was not best pleased but agreed to take up a position in the adjoining waiting room until they had finished.

CHAPTER 145

Dalrymple was incandescent. Ruth had seen him like this before and knew when he got in a state like that, he was capable of unpredictable and violent actions.

They were in his inner suite along with Isaac Lipman, who was also aware of Dalrymple's extreme behaviour when he felt things were getting out of control. The last time he had witnessed such anger resulted in the extremely unpleasant end of a competitor who had refused to heed a warning not to intrude on Dalrymple's territory. He shuddered at the memory of the atrocities committed against the victim, later reported in one of the more salacious red-top newspapers.

"What the fuck is going on?" he repeated for the umpteenth time before picking up a brass ornament and hurling it at a wall. "It was a simple enough task. They only had to follow the bloody van to find out where Carey's bird lives. That's not rocket science, is it?"

Both avoided eye contact as he ranted on.

"They not only lost him last night but have now lost him completely! I was told these were two of his best boys. Christ Almighty, if that is his best, I wouldn't want to see the thick ones."

He was pacing up and down and decided to take a kick at a wastepaper basket. It barely missed Lipman's head. The lawyer cowered in his chair and longed for the session to pass. He abhorred violence, especially if there was any possibility of it being directed at him.

"So, what have we got? Carey has rejected our offer of a million pounds and is lodging his own plans for the development of the farms. He even had the cheek to tear up the offer papers in front of the solicitor guy you sent to do the deal. That really pisses me off, Isaac. If ever it gets out that this 'hick from the sticks' can turn up two fingers at Donald Dalrymple and get away with it, I'll be a laughing stock and you know it! If Carey can defy me, others might think that they can too."

"Nobody else knows that, Donald," Lipman ventured.

"Fucking Carey and his crowd might know," he responded. "That solicitor of theirs traced Wiltris to our premises, didn't he – and don't you think that will be something that can be kept quiet? It's not a great leap of imagination to connect that with me. I'll bet they're crowing about getting one over Donald Dalrymple, to anyone who cares to listen."

"But nobody knows you are involved, Donald. The offer was made in my name," Ruth reasoned.

"These things have a habit of getting out. That lowlife nobody, Jake Butcher, knew we were connected."

"I thought you said he'd been taken care of, Donald?"

"It's true he won't be able to talk to anyone from the depths of the North Sea, but it's not to say he didn't tell anyone about this before he got taken out. He could have shared that information with Tristram, for all you know?" he thundered.

Ruth was ashen-faced as she responded. "But Tristram's dead! He can't tell anybody."

"He might have been having you followed for long enough without you being aware of it, you stupid bitch! What's more, that alcoholic, Wyllie, might have picked up on us. That's just two more people who could know."

As Dalrymple became more agitated, Lipman suspected he would not listen to any reason, and would not offer any advice until requested to do so.

The brooding silence which ensued felt even more threatening than the tirade that had preceded it.

"No!" Dalrymple declared. "I can't let this get out of hand. I'm going to have to deal with Carey and his gang personally. Don't ask me how but be sure that it will not be pleasant for him or his chums – you can be sure of that. Now get the hell out of here, the pair of you, and don't get in touch with me again, unless you have something positive to tell me!"

Neither Lipman nor Ruth delayed their departure, relieved they did not have to endure any more of Dalrymple's anger.

CHAPTER 146

Alex peered into the waiting area from the glass partition. Pete was casually flicking through dog-eared magazines with a bored expression on his face. Reassured that he would not be able to hear what they were about to discuss, she turned to Harry.

"I've been working things out and I have to confess that the reason for your minder being here, along with all the other measures that have been taken recently, was probably my fault."

"How so?" he enquired. "You have nothing to do with Donald Dalrymple, surely?"

"I think Dalrymple's involvement is simply coincidental. I'm inclined to think that the real reason for all the protection you are receiving was triggered by my accessing the website Professor Hart created and was somehow picked up by the security services when I visited it."

Harry cocked his head to one side, prompting her to continue.

"I believe Dalrymple is merely an opportunity for government agents to pretend they are part of a police operation tasked with safeguarding you from him. The number of personnel they have assigned to protect us is more than police budgets could ever support."

"But why would they want to do that? I have nothing that could be of the slightest interest to them, surely?"

"Oh, but you have, Harry! You could be one of the most important people in the world as far as espionage is concerned. Don't you see? Your ability to memorise information rapidly and accurately would be invaluable to any spy organisation. That, in my opinion, is why you are so important to them and why you have to be protected."

"But I'm not a spy, Alex."

"Nor ever will be, I hope. What they are most interested in is discovering if your abilities can be learned and transferred to their operatives."

"I know this may sound a bit thick, but how can my ability to memorise antiques be relevant to spying?"

"It's your ability to memorise things that is exciting them, Harry. They believe that the programme devised by Professor Hart might be used to condition others to retain different sorts of information. It would then be possible for an agent to absorb and memorise data without requiring photographic or other recording equipment. That would be a terrific skill for intelligence operatives to acquire."

Harry was beginning to understand the implications of what Alex was suggesting but could not make the link between what he was capable of doing as being relevant to the world of intelligence gathering and said so.

"You are the prototype, don't you see?" she responded. "Once this business with Dalrymple has been concluded, they will want to explore every aspect of how you came to develop the powers you have acquired."

"And…?"

"They will make your life a misery. You'll be subjected to all sorts of tests and processes under the supervision of a team of psychiatrists. I'll likely be 'obliged' to be part of that."

"That doesn't sound too bad to me," Harry quipped. "How sure are you of this, Alex? What caused you to think they are interested in me in that way?"

"I was suspicious about things before the woman who shadowed us at the auction, and now my minder, came to stay here. It was only after looking for some papers in my bureau that I discovered they had been filed out of sequence. I'm sure it's not how I'd left them. There were also other things that caused me to believe that my papers and CDs had been disturbed. I guess she had been trying to locate the tape that programmes your mind. We know it has no effect on others like it has had on you, but they might not want to believe that."

"It's strange that it only works on me, isn't it?"

Alex considered what he said before replying. "I believe," she began, "that it worked with you because your body had shut down so completely you were essentially at death's door then, and in an ideal state to accept suggestions."

"You mean, if I understand you correctly, for the system to be effective, a subject would have to be in an almost terminal condition for it to be effective?"

Alex nodded. "Yes, that's the conclusion I have arrived at. It would be virtually impossible for a patient to be reduced to that level of existence without endangering life."

"So how did it work for me, if I was so far gone?" Harry queried.

"Doctor Dixon told me when Mark and he stood at your bedside, discussing your ability to memorise music, he did not have the heart to tell Mark he did not expect you to last the night. He remembers Mark saying something about how good it would be if you could memorise something profitable, like antiques, he recalled."

"This might sound strange, Alex, but I seem to remember

Mark saying something like that but later believed I'd imagined it."

"It's quite possible that you did. When the body is close to death, as yours was then, people who have survived often recall a sense of euphoria and of being hyper-aware of things around them. It seems that they are far more sensitive to stimuli in that state."

"I've heard of people having out-of-body experiences. Would it be something like that which happened to me?"

"Quite possibly," she conceded. "We simply do not know enough about the phenomenon. It is believed the brain produces chemicals that give a heightened sense of well-being and acute sensitivity just before the point when death is imminent."

"So…" Harry speculated, "if it hadn't been for Mark getting through to me somehow, I might not be here today!"

"That's my theory, for what it's worth."

"How did they get to know about me?"

"They have ways of finding these things out. Secrets are what they trade in, and believe me, something as sensational as what you are capable of doing is likely to get out. Foreign spy networks may already know about you."

Harry was quiet for a few moments as he absorbed what Alex had said.

"You, then, by association, will be vulnerable because of your earlier work and knowledge of Professor Hart's methods, I'm thinking."

"Probably," she conceded. "That's what's been preying on my mind since it first occurred to me what might be happening. I may be wrong, of course, but I don't think so. Don't worry about me, though, you are the one most at risk here."

"What can we do, Alex? I'm completely at a loss to know how we can overcome this. Do you have any ideas?"

"Maybe – but they all involve a good deal of risk for you, Harry. I'm going to have to do a lot more research before coming to a decision. You're going to have to trust me when the time comes. I'm afraid it may mean taking a great leap of faith on your part and might even result in life-changing effects that could be irreversible."

"I'm completely in your hands, Alex, whatever it is you decide I should do."

She held his hand, stared earnestly into his eyes and thanked him for his faith in her. He pulled her closer and whispered that was an easy thing for him to do.

They spent the rest of the time running tests, which only served to confirm that Harry's ability to memorise antiques was both instant and infallible.

CHAPTER 147

The following day, despite warnings it was unwise to be out and about, Harry insisted on going for a walk around Edinburgh with Alex. They took in the usual tourist sights, the security agents following discreetly behind.

Chancing upon an open-air market, Harry was intrigued by some of the stalls offering the kind of ephemera usually found at car boot sales. He pointed them out to Alex, fixing a price on each as they examined them, deciding to buy a few things as they flitted from stall to stall. Soon, Pete and his sidekick were carrying bags of items he had purchased. When Pete complained, Harry pointed out that it would make them look less conspicuous if they appeared to be bona fide shoppers.

One item that excited him was a pale green 19th-century Chinese jade bottle vase, with a prunus and rock-worked design, on a wooden base. The stall holder was asking a mere £50 for something that Harry recognised to be worth in excess of £2,000. He bought the vase and was about to leave when he noticed a dark green dish. It was being used to display some trinkets and costume jewellery. On closer inspection, he identified it as a Chinese 19th-century jade spinach dish. He went through the details in his mind. Yes, he decided, it had all the necessary features, but did not share the information with anyone, having trained himself not to utter information that had been dredged from the deep recesses of his memory bank.

"How much is the dish?" he enquired.

"You can have that and its contents for thirty quid," was the reply.

Believing the dish would probably fetch around £1,000, he bought that too. Both of the items should excite Ralph, he predicted.

If it had not been for Alex reminding him they needed to be making moves to return home, he would have liked to spend more time in the market but decided to take her promptings and made for the exit. The agents looked relieved as they trailed behind, clutching the bags of goods he had purchased.

"You'll be leaving soon, Harry," she reminded him. "I'd like to have you to myself for a while before you set off. Do you have any idea when you might be able to return?"

"It won't be any time soon, I guess, or at least until the Dalrymple business is sorted. They weren't happy about me coming to see you this weekend. I had to insist."

"I'm glad you did. It's been great having you here. I know Dad enjoyed his time with you last night. Thanks for that."

"It was good hearing everything he had to say, Alex, particularly about you when you were growing up."

She laughed before responding. "Don't believe everything he told you. He's inclined to exaggerate."

Harry wondered if he should mention what Alex's father had told him in confidence. The old man had revealed his life expectancy was not great. The doctor had warned he had maybe a month or even less before succumbing to the illness. He had also said how pleased he was that Alex had found someone like Harry to care for her before he passed away.

"I've not known you for very long, my boy," he wheezed,

"but I'm content and assured that you are very well suited to each other. I'd very much like to be here when you decide to make things permanent but very much doubt that I'll be able to witness that moment. You will take good care of her, won't you, Harry?"

"You can be sure of that, Mr Green. If Alex will have me, that is," he quickly added.

"I don't think you can have any fears on that score," he confided, smiling coyly as he spoke.

The memory of that conversation caused him to frown as they trudged back to Alex's house. How long would it be before he could safely return to Edinburgh? Alex could not come to him without becoming a target for Dalrymple's thugs, he reasoned. Besides, she could not leave her father, especially now, when the end was near. The thought of Alex being alone with her father troubled him. There might be no one there to comfort her or share her grief when that moment arrived.

Alex had noticed the change in his expression and asked if something was troubling him.

"I'd love to stay with you forever," he admitted, searching her face to see how she reacted to what he had said.

"What are you saying, Harry?"

It was surprisingly easy to reveal what had been exercising his mind from the moment he had first met her. He stopped in the middle of the street to blurt out, "I would like you to be my wife, Alex Green. That's what I'm saying."

The blaring of car horns drowned out her reply as the agents hustled them towards the opposite pavement.

He looked at her anxiously with a questioning look on his face. "What did you say? I couldn't hear you for the traffic," he complained.

"She said 'yes'," Pete impatiently informed him, before Alex could reply.

Alex nodded enthusiastically before throwing her arms around him.

"Are you sure?"

"If you hadn't asked before you left, I was going to ask you to marry me, even though it's not a leap year."

They both laughed as the two agents looked on, clearly anxious to have their charges returned home safely.

A few short minutes later, they entered the downstairs bedroom to find Alex's father propped up on pillows, the flickering television screen illuminating his sallow features.

Before they could share their news, he removed his air line and spoke.

"You don't have to tell me," he said triumphantly. "I can tell by your faces. Congratulations. I'm sure you'll both be very happy together."

CHAPTER 148

Beverly was the first to know about the engagement and excitedly relayed the news around the friends, following a telephone call to Alex. She was delighted to learn that things had developed so quickly. They then went on to discuss what had happened during the weekend, but Alex resisted telling her about the theories she had revealed to Harry. Agent John listened in on his earphones, in the next room, and wondered if Control would find the information useful. More importantly, he hoped he had devised a plan to bring the operation to a conclusion. He was bored with being stuck at the farmhouse and wanted to be involved in some sort of action because that was what he enjoyed most.

A tap on the kitchen window made him start. Ralph Fortescue was peering in at him and motioned he was going to enter. John wondered how he had managed to get there without him being aware of his arrival but was soon to find out as Ralph entered the kitchen.

"I walked through the fields from Joe's place," he informed him. "Has Harry returned home yet?"

John was relieved Control had not been there to witness his dereliction of duty. He would have to be more alert, he told himself. It was a serious breach of duty, he realised.

"Tomorrow night, I believe," he replied.

Ralph appeared disappointed it would not be sooner but asked John if Beverly could ask Harry to get in touch before then. He had tried several times to ring him and had even sent a couple of texts but had received no reply.

John knew Harry's phone was switched off and locked in a drawer in the kitchen but wasn't going to share that information with Ralph.

"It's kind of urgent," Ralph continued. "I've got buyers for some of the items I photographed when Harry and I were at the repository. The total amounts to about £68,000. I think he would like to know about that sooner rather than later, I'm sure."

John promised to pass the message on to Beverly, who he could hear giggling in his headphones as she conversed with Alex. He told him that she was on a call right now and would not want to be disturbed. Reluctantly, Ralph said goodbye and returned to Joe's farm the way he had come.

John watched him mount a gate before trudging through the meadow that led towards the garden centre. Ralph's colourful attire intrigued him. He was certainly a flamboyant character and would be easy to pick out in a saleroom, he reasoned.

He was also easy to spot from the car, which had just pulled into the lay-by along from the entrance to Harry's farm. The driver, a private detective hired by Isaac Lipman, reported in and was instructed to find out what relationship existed between Harold Carey and Ralph Fortescue. There had been rumours the latter had found a rich source of antiques, which had been selling well throughout the county, Lipman had learned.

The antique-dealer community was littered with less than honest traders, who were always quick to spot any developments in their line of business. One such dealer had recently required Lipman's services, Friday past, over a fake antique that a disgruntled buyer was suing him over. It was during the consultation that the trader had commented on Fortescue's sudden and uncharacteristic success in locating items of much higher value than he could normally acquire. He speculated that this might be connected with Carey's recent emergence in the antiques market. Lipman had tucked this information away in his head before contacting Dalrymple, to see if it might be a possible way of getting to Carey.

Fortescue, Lipman had heard, was a very knowledgeable and reputable dealer. He had never achieved the kind of success other dealers enjoyed, mainly because of his inability to keep quiet about potential deals he was hoping to achieve, especially when plied with alcohol. Lipman told his gumshoe to keep an eye on him but nothing more. He then contacted the dealer who had come to him over the fake-antique problem and asked him if he would like his legal fees waived in return for a small favour that Lipman would like him to carry out on his behalf.

"All I want you to do is to take Fortescue for a drink," he began. "I'd like to know where he is getting his merchandise from. Let's meet up at ten in my house on Saturday. I'll tell you how I'd like you to handle it. Tell nobody about this or our deal is off," he warned, before ending the call.

CHAPTER 149

Harry and Pete enjoyed an uneventful journey home, although his minder was constantly scanning the rear-view mirror for signs of anyone tailing them. They arrived home just as darkness was falling. Pete was interested in the car parked in the lay-by near the farm road end. John had already clocked it, he told him so, when they later liaised in the farmhouse.

"We are aware of that," John confirmed. "It belongs to a local private detective. He's been parked there at various times during the day and just left seconds after you arrived back here."

"Any connections to Dalrymple?"

"Yes, Control confirmed that he had been given a watching brief by Dalrymple's legal eagle, Lipman."

"Does he pose a threat to our man?"

"Control doesn't think so but believes that there are other moves afoot, although he did not say what."

John then went on to complain about how bored he had been and told Pete he had requested that he swapped roles with Pete for a few days.

"What did he say to that?"

"He said he wanted continuity and wouldn't be changing

things in the immediate future, but I got the impression things are likely to take off soon."

"I hope so," Pete agreed. "I'd like to get back to some real intelligence work and not have to act as a nursemaid much longer. What did he say that gave you the impression things were about to kick off?"

"He asked me to stress we should both be super vigilant over the next few days."

"Sounds like things are moving along then," Pete agreed.

Both agents, like so many others in the organisation, were former SAS personnel, selected because of their high IQ ratings, along with the ability to carry out orders without question, in support of Queen and country. In a crowd they would not have attracted much attention as their ability to blend into any social situation was something they had acquired through careful observation and training. Only the constant scanning of areas they found themselves in gave away the fact that they would never allow themselves to be taken by surprise. A closer inspection would also have chilled an onlooker to note the cold ruthlessness that emanated from their eyes. They had come to develop a sense of confidence in each other from special assignments they had collaborated in since joining the organisation. Occasionally it had resulted in the termination of enemies of the state. In every instance, they had carried out such missions without compunction or any pangs of conscience, having both been selected because of their psychopathic personality ratings. The death of an enemy, of any age or gender, would never cause either of them to lose sleep.

CHAPTER 150

Mark was in the kitchen when Harry and Pete arrived back at the farm; partly to welcome Harry home but also to check that Beverly was OK.

They were joined by Chris and Joe. Chris had been spending Sunday with the old man, helping out in the garden centre as one of Joe's assistants had been taken ill. An upsurge in trade had meant that several items needed restocking. The auction had put the garden centre back in people's minds, resulting in a healthy increase in sales, which pleased Joe no end.

Liam and Sally were not far behind. Sally came carrying a cake she had baked, to accompany the champagne that Mark and Beverly had been keeping on ice as soon as they learned that Harry and Alex had decided to make a go of things.

Despite all the congratulations, teasing and laughter, Harry found it difficult to shake off the realisation that he did not know when he would see Alex again. While he knew she understood the situation, probably better than he himself did, he couldn't ignore the feeling of emptiness following his departure from Edinburgh. Knowing that her father could die at any time troubled him even more. How would she cope if the worst came to the worst?

He smiled politely and thanked everyone for coming but

found that he could not bring himself to celebrate in a way that was expected of him. He cursed Donald Dalrymple and vowed that if he could, he would find a way to deal with him that would be both effective and maybe even terminal.

After everyone left, Beverly sensed he had been holding back and said so.

"What's troubling you, Harry? I thought you would have been more upbeat considering that Alex and you have put things on a more permanent footing."

He admitted he couldn't be happier about that but then went on to list all the things that had been troubling him, including not being able to be with her when her father was so close to dying.

"Then there's the Dalrymple business and these bodyguards that are supposedly here to protect us. It must be awful for you too, Beverly. I'm so sorry to have subjected you to this."

She assured him it might not last much longer, considering a conversation she'd overheard between John and Pete, when she'd been in the laundry room, next to the kitchen.

"They seem to think that something will soon bring the Dalrymple affair to an end."

Harry replied he hoped that might be the case but confided that, even with Dalrymple out of the way, it might not be the end of the matter. When Beverly asked why he thought that he declined to elucidate, merely replying that a conversation he'd had with Alex caused him to think otherwise.

Although she wanted to press him to say more, Harry lifted his hand and touched his nose, winking as he did so while making his eyes dart around the room.

She cottoned on quickly, recognising that he did not want to discuss things further for fear of being overheard.

"I'm going to bed now," he told her. "The weekend was quite tiring as you can appreciate."

"Oh, I forgot to mention, Ralph Fortescue wanted you to get in touch as soon as possible. He has buyers for some of the antiques he photographed and mentioned a figure of £68,000 when he spoke to John. It seems like you are going to be very rich, dear brother."

"And you too, darling sister," he reminded her, before planting a kiss on her forehead and making for the stairs. He paused halfway and returned to the holdall he had dumped in a corner of the room.

"I picked these things up from a flea market in Edinburgh," he revealed, unwrapping some of his purchases as he spoke. "The two most interesting and valuable ones are these two Chinese items. I haven't really been looking for new stock, considering how much we have in store, but these just sang out to me. They are only a fraction of what I believe they may be worth. Ralph will know better when he sees them, I'm sure."

Beverly examined them as Harry retrieved his mobile phone and texted Ralph to drop in past the farmhouse at ten on Monday morning.

CHAPTER 151

Ralph arrived early, just as Harry was finishing breakfast. Not known for early-morning appearances, unless there was an auction to attend, Harry noted the kitchen clock chiming nine as he bustled into the room, his face flushed with excitement.

"Great you're home again, Harry," he began. "Have I got news for you? You'll remember those pictures I took at the warehouse – well, I've found buyers for all sixteen of them! What's more, some of them got even more than I had valued them at."

He listed the items he had sold as Harry and Beverly listened with interest. John and Pete were also intrigued to hear his news, as both had been having morning coffee in the kitchen when he arrived.

"What's more," Ralph went on, "I've been inundated with requests from other dealers who want to know what else I can offer. You know how word gets around when desirable items come onto the market. Just last night Alexander the Greek called to ask if I could meet with him. It seems that he has a customer interested in acquiring anything in bronze. I never saw what was in that container, Harry, but seem to remember you saying there were a few odds and ends that might be of interest."

Slightly out of breath, he paused for a moment before continuing. "I'm afraid everyone seems to have guessed you've been supplying me. I've denied it, of course, but wouldn't be surprised if you start getting approaches from some of the trade. Something like this was bound to get out, despite my denials."

Harry conceded that other antiques dealers would have quickly worked out that Ralph was fronting for someone else.

"What are you doing this morning?" Harry enquired.

"Why, nothing. What have you got in mind?"

Harry turned to Pete, suggesting that they should collect the items Ralph had sold. They could also inspect the containers, which held the bronze figurines, metalware and militaria artefacts.

Pete thought that it would be all right but went into the next room to notify Control of their plans.

While he was next door, Harry asked Ralph what he thought of the 19th-century Chinese jade bottle jar and green spinach dish.

Ralph examined them carefully before enquiring how much they had cost.

"Fifty pounds for the jar and £30 for the dish," he replied.

After a few moments in which he seemed to be having difficulty forming words to respond, Ralph finally spoke.

"I'm afraid the dish is a rather crude copy, Harry, and probably only worth what you paid for it. I'm surprised that you would have bought something so obviously fake."

Harry now appreciated that, while his memory skills were unquestionably accurate, his ability to differentiate between genuine antiques and fakes was something he was unable to do.

Beverly then posed the question that Harry didn't ask, as he did not want Ralph to be aware of his shortcomings.

"How do you know it's a fake?" she enquired.

Ralph pointed out what was wrong with the dish,

explaining it had probably been produced in the sixties for the tourist trade.

"There's a lot of that going about," he went on, "but the jar is another thing all together. You should get anything between two and a half and three and a half k on a good day," he enthused. "Were you testing me, Harry?"

Harry merely smiled and was saved from responding, as Pete returned to the kitchen, declaring they could leave whenever it suited them.

"There's some other stuff in my holdall that you might like to take a look at, Ralph, but there's no great value in them – just basic stock items that every dealer is expected to keep. You might care to look at them when we return. Do you have your camera with you or is it in the car? I thought we could all travel in the van to check the stock your clients might be interested in buying."

As they pulled out of the yard, Pete noted that the car parked in the lay-by on Sunday had been replaced by another vehicle but with the same driver sitting behind the wheel. He believed John would have clocked him too but sent a voice message to make sure. Ralph and Harry, being too involved in conversation, didn't notice what he had done.

CHAPTER 152

Lipman listened intently when the private eye phoned in. He instructed him to follow Harry's van and report back when he discovered where they were going and what they were up to.

"Knowledge is power," he said to himself before placing another call to Alexander the Greek.

"Are you all set for your meeting with Fortescue?" he enquired without preamble.

"Yes," came the terse reply. "Tonight."

"Call me early evening before you see him," he instructed before ending the call.

He then telephoned Dalrymple and asked if they could get together that night, following the Greek's meeting with Ralph Fortescue.

CHAPTER 153

Pete waited outside while Ralph and Harry went to collect the items that had been sold and to inspect the items in which Alexander the Greek had shown interest. He noted that the car parked at the end of Harry's drive had followed them and was now entering the parking area at the repository. He used his mobile phone to take a picture of the vehicle and its driver before patching it through to Control.

A few minutes went by before a police car entered the compound and parked directly alongside the private investigator's vehicle. He left immediately on seeing the police officers getting out of the traffic car, apparently unwilling to be found in the private car park of a high-security firm.

The two officers crossed to where Pete was waiting in Harry's van to enquire if there was anything required of them as they had received a call from DCI Jones requesting they contact Pete asap. He replied that everything was under control, but it might be an idea if they could identify the owner of the vehicle, which had just left, and to notify Chief Inspector Jones of their findings. He passed them a piece of paper with the licence details and thanked them for appearing so promptly.

Inside the warehouse, Harry and Ralph had selected the

ordered items and were now examining the crates in which the copper and metalware items were stored.

Ralph's exclamations as each item was uncovered bordered on orgasmic proportions.

"This is amazing," he kept marvelling. "Where did you get all this stuff, Harry? It's not stolen, is it?"

"I'm surprised you could think such a thing. I thought you knew me better than that, Ralph."

"Sorry, Harry, it's just that I've only seen a small sample of what you've got stashed here and can't help wondering how you managed to acquire all this stuff without anyone noticing."

"The things stored here were acquired over the last thirty-odd years by my grandfather. He started assembling the items when I was only five years old. Some, I guess, he picked up for pennies when shifting stuff from salerooms when they didn't find a buyer."

"I guess that figures. Some of the stuff would have gone out of fashion as people replaced them with newer, more-fashionable goods. But some of these antiques must have been purchased, surely?"

Harry told him that most of the things contained in the crates had receipts which listed the dates and prices paid. When he showed Ralph the entries relating to the items he had just photographed, he was even more amazed at the prices paid for them.

"Looks like your grandfather had a good eye for things that would appreciate over the years. How long is it since he passed away, Harry?"

"I was just turning nineteen when he died. That was sixteen years ago. I never took much interest in what he had been doing. He didn't like banks, you see; didn't have much trust in them and preferred to invest any spare cash he had in antiques and collectibles. I had no idea what he'd been doing."

"And now you've got all this! You must be worth a fortune!"

"This is only part of it. He stashed stuff in different places around the country, I just barely remember taking stuff to them when I used to help him in the van. There's a jotter I found stuffed inside a bedpost that lists it all. With everything that's been happening recently, I had forgotten about them and must take time to go and check them out."

Ralph was incredulous. "You mean there's more? What are you going to do about that? Do you think they'll still be there after all this time?"

"I don't know," he admitted. "We could maybe check that out sometime soon, but it will have to wait, as there are a few things holding me back from doing that just now. Maybe once I've got planning permission to convert Joe's old watermill and the other developments that's planned for the site will be the right time to see what's been stored."

"I knew you had bought Joe out, Harry, but I don't really know what you're planning to do there."

"It will be common knowledge soon, I guess. What we're planning is an antiques centre that will act as a marketplace for not just our stuff but will also showcase items that other dealers can offer. I'd very much like you to be part of that enterprise if you are interested."

Ralph thought it was a great idea. "I'm with you," he confirmed enthusiastically. "You don't even need to ask."

CHAPTER 154

They had decided to meet in Dalrymple's private suite to discuss what had been gleaned from the meeting between Alexander the Greek and Ralph Fortescue.

Lipman informed Ruth and Dalrymple that Fortescue had avoided all attempts to get him to drink alcohol and turned up with Harold Carey in tow. One of Carey's van boys also sat in, so Alexander had been less able to probe Fortescue as much as he would have liked, Lipman informed them.

"A waste of time then!" Dalrymple exploded.

"Not at all, Donald," Lipman replied. "We have learned a great deal that could be turned to your advantage," he declared.

"How so?" Ruth enquired.

"Well, we now know that Carey has access to some very impressive antiques he is interested in selling. Where or how he acquired them is unknown."

Lipman went on. "We don't know where he got them, but I do know that Wyllie tried to get tax inspectors to investigate him when he cleared his debts with the bank. I know that happened because your husband told me so. He even watched as they visited Carey's farm. Butcher reported that the inspectors spent a lot of time going through Carey's outhouses before visiting Liam Forbes' offices. He followed them there, Tristram told me, but they did not stay very long. Afterwards, out in the street, Forbes was seen to shake hands with them and was heard to say that he would be ready to collaborate but was pleased to learn they would not be pursuing matters further."

Dalrymple absorbed all that Lipman had said before he continued.

"It seems, then, that Carey has acquired a valuable and legitimate stock of items he is now offering for sale. It will probably be needed to finance the purchase and development of the Burns' property, I'm thinking."

"How does that help us?" Dalrymple cut in, rather impatiently.

Ruth was quick to appreciate the opportunity and said, "If Carey is trying to raise capital by selling his stuff, it would be easy to arrange a meeting with him to do a deal. Serious collectors are notoriously secretive about buying antiques. It would be entirely normal for clandestine deals to be carried out in such circumstances, especially if it was a cash purchase and the client was seeking to launder money they did not want the authorities to know about."

"That's right, Donald," Lipman continued. "It's up to you how you do it, but it would be a chance for you to have a conversation with him at some safe place to let him know, that unless he agrees to sell, just what sanctions you might resort to if he continues to decline your offer."

The idea clearly appealed to him. Ruth understood the way his mind worked and speculated about the actions he was contemplating. She would not want to be in Harry Carry's shoes or anyone that was associated with him.

"It would have to be Carey on his own," Dalrymple finally decided.

"I get the impression that he will not meet with anyone

without his van boy tagging along," Lipman informed him. "The private detective I've had following them says he never goes anywhere without him. He accompanied him to Scotland at the weekend and I'm told he is living in Carey's house."

Dalrymple continued to quiz Lipman about what he had learned and finally asked him to arrange a meeting with Harry through Alexander the Greek. "I'll tell you where and when," he said finally, before dismissing them.

CHAPTER 155

Jones and Black travelled to Manchester at Control's request. He would meet and brief them there, regarding a series of arrests that would be of interest to them, Jones learned. It would now be appropriate for his sergeant to know about what was happening, he added, believing that events would soon lead to a satisfactory conclusion. Jones knew better than to enquire what that might be but was relieved that he could now inform Black about the events that had led up to the trip. He was reminded to emphasise what he told Black was highly confidential, however, and must not be revealed to anyone else, unless authorised by Control.

They met in a hotel room on the outskirts of Manchester. Jones was surprised to see that his chief constable was already there in the suite where they were meeting. Another high-ranking Manchester officer and his assistant also attended.

After thanking everyone for attending, Control came quickly to the reason for the meeting.

"My people identified and determined the location of two members of a gang we want to interrogate concerning the importation of illegal weapons. They are part of an organisation that Manchester police would like to round up for a variety of criminal activities, but so far have been unsuccessful in bringing them to justice. We have obtained intelligence that they have paid informants within the force who alert them to police investigations and have identified some of the officers involved."

The Manchester police officer looked uncomfortable at this disclosure.

"Our operation is designed to apprehend the people that comprise that organisation. Some are based overseas, and our colleagues abroad are awaiting our signal for them to act."

He looked around the room and then focused on Jones and Black.

"You will not be involved directly in the arrests, gentlemen," he advised them. "Your role will be simply to observe the interview process and eventually spend time with the officers we suspect are in the pay of the criminals. Any questions so far?" he invited.

"What are we supposed to do when the suspects approach us?" Jones enquired.

"You will feed them information, Detective Chief Inspector. I'll brief you both about that after this meeting ends," he replied.

When the briefing had concluded and the others had departed, Control addressed the two officers in the presence of their chief constable.

"We anticipate rounding up around twenty gang members in Manchester. Another five will be captured abroad with the exception of the head of the organisation and his personal minders, of which we believe there are six."

Black wondered why they should be excluded, but on Jones's advice remained silent.

Seeming to interpret Black's thoughts, Control continued.

"We want the gangland boss to be free to act following the apprehension of his minions," he explained.

Jones and Black immediately understood what was planned and thought it a clever ploy that should yield results.

Jones, in particular, felt a sense of elation that maybe – just maybe – Donald Dalrymple's reign might be about to end. He listened with growing interest as Control laid out his plans.

CHAPTER 156

The meeting with the unidentified buyer had been arranged for Friday night following a call from Alexander the Greek, Ralph informed Harry. The items he had shown were of great interest and his cash buyer had offered to pay well over the odds for what he thought they were worth, Ralph enthused. It was a condition that the transaction must be kept secret, with only Harry and the buyer being present when the deal was done, he added. The time and place would be confirmed after 6pm on Friday.

Pete was suspicious and notified Control. Harry received a telephone call from DCI Jones minutes later, warning that on no account should he agree to any appointments with anyone until he returned home.

Harry immediately called Ralph to cancel the Friday night arrangement, until a later date, saying that something had come up.

Ralph was dismayed, as he considered the possibility of losing 15% of the money that had been agreed for the sale but reasoned that the buyer would just have to like it or lump it.

Dalrymple was apoplectic when he learned of the delay.

"What the fuck is he playing at?" he yelled down the mouthpiece.

It took some time for Lipman to placate him, but eventually, and ungraciously, Dalrymple rang off, vowing that Carey was really going to suffer for messing him about like this.

Lipman was in no doubt Harold Carey would greatly regret his dilatory behaviour, in delaying the tryst with Dalrymple, in a manner that he did not care to contemplate.

Harry, however, was elated by the news that his initial planning application would go forward. Liam had telephoned to tell him the application had gone through to planning without any queries. The sale of Joe's farm had also been concluded, he added.

"It looks like everything's coming together, Harry," he remarked before ringing off.

CHAPTER 157

Jones and Black sat in on various interrogations the Manchester police conducted over the next forty-eight hours. They attended interviews separately and were restricted to an observer's role. Some of the interviews were straightforward in the sense that they dealt with wanted criminals who had evaded capture for some time. Others were more searching where they had resorted to using search warrants at various locations, which produced more incriminating evidence previously unknown to the police. There was a sense of jubilation amongst the officers involved in the operation. All believed that the success of the operation was down to the intelligence supplied by Jones and Black.

It was on the third day Jones and Black were approached by a superintendent and one other officer while lunching in the police canteen. He seemed a friendly sort of man who, after introducing himself and his colleague, enquired if they might join them at their table. Jones said they were very welcome. After the usual exchanges when strangers meet for the first time, the superintendent enquired if they had been successful in their collaboration with the Manchester force.

Jones pretended to be very pleased with the way things

had gone, especially considering the number of prosecutions which had resulted from the exercise. Had the superintendent not been briefed on the operation, Jones queried, in apparent ignorance.

He admitted that he had known, but only after the event, he conceded. How had the intelligence to mount such a major investigation been acquired, he wondered?

It was then that Black developed a new insight into the behaviour of his boss.

He could not be specific, he said, but a certain Donald Dalrymple, who he might have heard of, had been indiscreet, was how he put it – or maybe not, he added quickly.

When pressed to continue, Jones went on to say he suspected Dalrymple had designs on creating a presence in Manchester. The current gang, now under arrest, would have represented a deterrent to him achieving that, he suggested. He speculated that Dalrymple had provided the information through a third party.

When they finished lunch, Jones and Black watched with interest as their Manchester colleagues made a rapid exit, talking animatedly as they hurried from the canteen.

Black looked at Jones, who merely nodded.

He then proceeded to send a text message, which merely stated 'Contact made'.

"I guess we can go home now, sir," he suggested.

The DCI confirmed that perhaps they could but waited for a reply to check first with Control, before returning to base.

CHAPTER 158

Harry had been experiencing mixed emotions. It was good to know the plans for the garden centre would go forward. It was also comforting to know that, through Ralph's efforts, more money was rolling into his bank account from the recent sales he had achieved and only a few of the invoices that Beverly and Sally had issued remained unpaid.

The threat of Dalrymple hung over him like a dark cloud, however – not that he cared so much for his own safety but more in relation as to what might happen to his friends if Dalrymple decided to go after them to get at him. Uppermost in his mind were the measures that Dalrymple might adopt if he ever targeted Beverly or Alex.

He kept in touch daily, through Beverly's phone, and always felt a great sense of emptiness when they finished speaking. It was the frustration of not being able to provide protection for the two women who meant everything to him that troubled Harry most and wondered what he could do to change that.

Alex was dismissive when he voiced his concerns, stating she was well protected by her minders.

"I can't even go to the loo on my own," she informed

him. "My bodyguard waits outside for me, when I'm at work – having first checked there's no one else in there when I spend a penny."

Learning that her father's condition was deteriorating only added to his concerns. During their last conversation, she told him he had been taken into hospital. She suspected the end was near. He decided that he would make his way to Edinburgh, with or without Control's permission, but asked Pete to let him know what he was going to do.

The message which came back was that on no account could he make the trip. He did not have the personnel to guarantee a safe journey.

"I've already contacted my solicitor," Harry responded defiantly. "He has told me that there is no way you can prevent me from going."

Pete looked perplexed for a moment before relaying Harry's ultimatum. A long monologue ensued, in which Pete merely listened, occasionally nodding his head, then terminated the call and said, "He's very unhappy about this development and is concerned that you are taking unnecessary risks when we are so close to finding a solution to your problems. He appreciates you feel obliged to be with Doctor Green at this time, however. We'll work something out between us, Harry. When did you plan to go there?"

"Right away, Pete, and I want to take Beverly with me if she'll come. That would allow John to come with us, if that is OK with your boss?"

A further telephone call eventually confirmed he was agreeable to that happening. They decided to leave within the hour.

Harry telephoned Mark to ask if he could borrow his car for a few days. The plan was simple. John and Pete would drive to Mark's hotel with Harry and Beverly travelling inside the van, hidden from view. Once they arrived at the hotel, Pete would reverse into the garage and close the doors, after which he and Beverly would exit from the rear of the van. Along with the two agents, they would exit by the rear garage door, where Mark's car was waiting for them. They would leave the hotel by a back lane that connected to the main road. Harry and Beverly would be concealed, crouched down in the back of Mark's SUV.

Despite the agents' misgivings, neither detected signs of anyone tailing them. After about ten minutes on the road, John suggested it would be all right for Harry and Beverly to adopt a sitting position. They did not stop again until reaching Edinburgh, except to top up with fuel at a village just off the motorway.

In the hospital car park, Pete contacted Alex's minder to ascertain that she was satisfied no one had been paying them any special attention. Minutes later, Beverly and Harry entered the room to find Alex sitting by her father's bedside, holding his hand against her cheek, sobbing quietly.

Beverly, being first into the room, went immediately to Alex's side and flung her arms around her. Harry, unsure how to conduct himself, gently placed his arm on Alex's shoulder. Seeing them both there caused her to break down completely. What had been a brave attempt to control her feelings gave way to unrestrained weeping. It took a few minutes before she regained composure.

Beverly said the things that Harry would have liked to have uttered but was unable to find the words that would provide the comfort he so wanted to convey. Eventually, he was able to say how sorry he was that her father had finally passed away but also that he would not have to suffer any more. In a husky voice he did not recognise, he apologised for not getting to Edinburgh sooner.

That they had both managed to make the trip was more than she could have hoped for, she replied, before burying her head in his chest.

The rest of the day was taken up with the usual things that need to be done when someone dies. They returned to the house in Edinburgh, where Beverly, with Alex's approval, dealt with some of the arrangements while Harry simply held Alex in his arms on the sofa, allowing her to talk about the memories and special occasions she had shared with her father. The outpourings that follow death are usually about coming to terms with the finality and sense of helplessness survivors have to deal with, Harry acknowledged. He knew that it was the best therapy Alex could indulge in and encouraged her to talk it out, with occasional questions about things that would help her deal with her loss.

He also came to understand that when his grandfather passed away, he did not allow himself to grieve. All the years he'd bottled up those feelings of loss came home to him then. He found he was also weeping in a way he'd not imagined he could ever allow himself to do before.

Alex became concerned when she noticed his distress and wondered if she had caused him to weep.

"I'm deeply sorry for your loss, Alex, believe me," he said haltingly as the words were hard to articulate, "but I was finally mourning my grandfather, who never got to know just how much I loved him. He went to his grave thinking I hated him. I've never really come to terms with that until now."

Despite her own sorrow, Alex realised this was uncharacteristic behaviour. This was not the repressed individual she had been analysing, understanding now that he needed to unburden himself fully.

"Tell me all about it, Harry," she coaxed. "It will be good for you to do that, believe me."

It all came pouring out, along with the memory of how he had confronted the old man while travelling in the van. How the distraction led to the accident that had left him in a coma. She listened patiently, not wanting to disrupt the flow of words that were slowly and painfully emerging, speaking only to give encouragement to continue, or to gently probe the things he had revealed.

By the time Harry had finished speaking, darkness had fallen. They both remained silent for some minutes before a knock on the door preceded Beverly enquiring if it was all right to come in. She entered carrying a tray, immediately aware that something significant had occurred.

"It's all right, Bev," Alex assured her. "We've both made great progress today."

Despite the sad occasion, the rest of the evening was relatively light-hearted, filled with reminiscences of their previous lives. The only dampener occurred when both John and Pete came into the kitchen requesting a word with Harry, as Control had been in touch. There had been developments, John informed them, which they needed to share with Harry and hoped that he could travel back next day, or at the very latest, Sunday morning.

"Why the urgency?" Harry wanted to know.

Pete replied that he did not know, only that something major was afoot, and it was essential Harry was more visible back home. His absence had made certain parties nervous, making them likely to behave unpredictably, he informed him.

"I think we might be getting near to achieving closure," John added by way of encouragement.

Although clearly anxious at hearing this, Alex was reassured by Beverly's offer to remain until Harry could return for the funeral on Friday.

"Can you guarantee that?" Harry challenged them.

Moments later, Pete had contacted Control, who confirmed he would honour that request.

"If it brings things to a conclusion, I'll do that," he responded, "but only if you can guarantee that Alex and Beverly are protected while all of this is going on."

"You can be sure of that," Pete told him. "Another agent will be assigned here in Edinburgh when John and I return with you."

Alex was unsure about what they were proposing and said so.

"Although you are giving assurances about our safety, I'd like to know what danger Harry might be exposed to. Can you guarantee his safety?"

Both agents looked uncomfortable at Alex's query, but John eventually admitted there might be some element of danger, but felt sure Harry's well-being was uppermost in Control's mind.

He quickly realised that he had probably said too much as Pete shot him a warning glance.

The information was not lost on Alex, however, as she became more convinced that Harry was the main focus of their interest.

It was agreed he would stay over until Sunday morning, with both women exhorting him to be ultra careful and to avoid being drawn into any situation that might put his life in danger.

That night, Alex snuggled into Harry's arms, absolutely convinced of his importance to the secret services. She worried about how that involvement might affect him once they had disposed of the threat posed by Donald Dalrymple.

CHAPTER 159

They left before daybreak and were turning into the hotel car park just as the town clock chimed nine. Approaching from the lane that connected with the rear of the hotel, they quickly parked Mark's car behind the garage.

Harry had telephoned ahead, warning that they should arrive within the next ten minutes, enquiring if it was safe to return. Mark confirmed that everything seemed to be fine and that as far as he was aware, nothing suggested anyone knew of his absence via the hotel.

They entered through the kitchen, where Mark was waiting for them.

He was disappointed Beverly had not been able to return with Harry but understood that she would be a comfort to Alex in Edinburgh.

A new kitchen worker overheard the conversation as the four men proceeded through to the restaurant. She listened with interest, her ear to the door, as they continued to update Mark on what had occurred up north. The arrival of another hotel worker prevented the woman from hearing all that was being discussed as she dumped a tray of breakfast dishes on the draining board.

"Come on, Alice," she urged. "You're falling behind with the washing up. Chef will get annoyed if he can't get those casserole dishes through in the next five minutes. You've only been here two days. If you don't buck your ideas up, you won't last three more minutes!"

"I was only closing the door," Alice retorted, annoyed that she would not be able to eavesdrop any longer. They were joined by a receptionist, who wanted to discuss the lunch menu. She returned to the sink, cursing her luck but was also pleased to be able to report Harry's whereabouts. The knowledge he had been in Edinburgh, not Glasgow, as had been previously believed, would be of interest to Donald Dalrymple.

When left alone again, she returned to the restaurant connecting door, only to find Mark waving them away, as they departed in Harry's van.

CHAPTER 160

Neither Pete nor John seemed surprised to find Control waiting for them in Harry's yard. He was sitting in a water company van, behind an outhouse that concealed it from the highway. He left the van and quickly made his way to the kitchen, where he waited impatiently until Harry located his house keys.

Once inside, he said he was sorry to hear of Doctor Green's bereavement before coming to the reason for his visit.

"A lot has been happening since we last spoke, Harry. We anticipate that matters will come to a head very shortly. I am telling you this because we expect Dalrymple will make a move within days, if not hours. All our operatives have been briefed to be extra vigilant and that also applies to our Edinburgh personnel."

"What do you think is going to happen?" Harry asked.

"We're not sure," Control admitted, "but from intelligence received, it seems you should be prepared for Dalrymple to try to persuade you to sell your farms to Ruth Grant or suffer the consequences of noncompliance."

"How am I to respond?"

"Quite simply, do not go anywhere or agree to see anyone without Pete or John knowing what you are doing, even if they are accompanying you. That applies to everyone in your circle of acquaintances. They will report back to me, to authorise your movements. We do not want any unexpected developments. Matters are at a very critical stage, which is why we are being ultra careful. I'm sure you'll appreciate your compliance with this request is vital in bringing this situation to a satisfactory conclusion?"

Harry nodded agreement.

"We know that Ralph Fortescue has been attempting to set up a meeting with a prospective client earlier. Do not agree any meetings without first sharing the details with us," Control emphasised.

How did he know about that? Harry wondered but made no comment.

"Fortescue was unknowingly being used as a go-between to entice you to a meeting with Dalrymple. He has no connection with Dalrymple, but the other party involved in the deception is linked to an associate acting on his behalf."

Harry was relieved to hear that Ralph was not colluding with Dalrymple but made a mental note not to share information that could be used by the crime boss.

Control interrupted his thoughts by asking if he had any questions.

Harry shook his head, saying he had none.

"Stay safe, Harry," Control warned as he made for the kitchen door.

CHAPTER 161

A Spanish flight landed at Luton Airport. Seven of the passengers were travelling on forged passports. They had been followed by a couple, apparently returning from a package holiday. After exiting the airport terminal, four of the men were picked up by a driver in a black car. The three remaining men entered a similar vehicle, which followed on behind.

Their movements were communicated, by cell phone, by the holiday couple, to two plainclothes policemen, waiting in an unmarked police car, who set off in pursuit of the two vehicles, maintaining a discreet distance as they travelled towards Manchester. Three other unmarked police cars took turns at tailing the two vehicles, as they proceeded towards a location in Moss Side.

DCI Jones turned to Sergeant Black when the text came through from their Manchester colleagues. It simply read 'They've arrived!'

CHAPTER 162

Alexander the Greek, when informed of Harry's decision not to meet, was disappointed, as was Isaac Lipman. Dalrymple, however, was furious beyond reasoning. Neither Lipman nor Ruth attempted to appease him in his anger. He was going to have Carey's guts for garters, he vowed – and that was going to be sooner rather than later.

When they had gone from his office, the phone rang. He answered it gruffly but then listened attentively as Slack Alice told him what she had learned that morning. He questioned her for some moments before ringing off and sat for several minutes pondering what he had just learned. Firstly, Carey had been in Edinburgh, visiting the woman he'd been told was somewhere in Glasgow, according to the Manchester mob. Although he did not know where, Carey was not to know he didn't possess that information. Alice had also suggested there had been a death, probably the girlfriend's relation, and also that his sister, Beverly, was staying with her until Carey returned north for the funeral, on Friday. As this was already Monday, he would have to act quickly. Tonight was too soon, he reasoned, but maybe Wednesday would be a better time to put a plan into action? Alice ended her report, casually mentioning that Mark had insisted Harry should join him for dinner every night until Beverly returned. It gave Dalrymple cause for thought. He sat back in an armchair and considered his options.

Both the private eye and Alice had reported that Carey was never alone. He was always accompanied by a van boy, who sounded like he could take care of himself. There always appeared to be someone occupying Carey's house, he also learned. Whatever plan he hatched would have to be carried out with his own men. Maybe they should be armed for the caper?

Without further thought, he pressed a button on the desk intercom to summon the security staff who lived in the casino. They appeared within seconds, as the signal was one he only used if they were needed urgently.

Six heavily built individuals stood before him in his office, in varying states of dress. One was in underpants, shaving foam covering one side of his face.

Dalrymple surveyed them thoughtfully, before instructing them to listen carefully to what he was going to tell them. They hung on to his every word, nodding vigorously when asked if they understood what he'd said. When he finished speaking, he asked for questions. Only one of the thugs enquired if they would be acting on their own.

"Oh no, I'll be with you every step of the way on this one," he told them.

CHAPTER 163

Nothing much happened on the Tuesday following Harry's return. He spent most of the day on the internet, searching for antiques that he had not viewed before. Realising he was not as knowledgeable as he needed to be concerning the authenticity of antiques made him feel inadequate. He spent the rest of the day seeking information that would help identify what was real and what was fake. The more he learned, the more he appreciated how scant his knowledge really was. As with anything of value, there would always be those who would seek to earn a dishonest living by creating fakes and forgeries. The more valuable the item, the greater the appeal to the faker, he realised. As soon as he could rid himself of his current problems, the sooner he could spend time with someone like Ralph, to guide him through the pitfalls of the antiques world, the better.

He also appreciated how discerning his grandfather must have been. Sheer bloody-mindedness on his part was at the root of his ignorance. When Grandad Carey had tried to educate and interest him in antiques, he was simply ignored out of childishness on his part. What a fool he'd been! It must have pained the old man to lose his grandson's respect, but most of all, his affection, following the accident. He sighed, acknowledging that he could never make amends for those wasted years or thank the old man for providing for him so generously. Harry vowed that, in future, anyone he cared for should never be in any doubt as to how much he loved them.

CHAPTER 164

Wednesday dawned bright and clear. Harry decided to continue his investigations on the web. He ordered various catalogues and reference books, which would help him improve his knowledge of antiques.

Pete and John seemed to be on edge, he noted, when he paused in his research to share a mug of coffee. They were continually listening to messages on their earpieces, occasionally leaving the room or going to the kitchen window to check that no one was approaching the farmyard.

They became very excited when Chris turned up mid-morning in a new car he'd just bought. It was enough for the two agents to draw pistols from their shoulder holsters, Harry noted, until satisfied that it was actually Chris approaching and that he was alone. He'd never been aware of either of them being armed before, so it must be getting near to the time they expected Dalrymple to make a move, he reckoned.

Chris didn't stay long. He just wanted to get an update as to what had been happening since he had last seen Harry. They exchanged news, before Chris looked at his watch and informed him he was taking Joe for a spin in his new motor and then having lunch with him at the Crown. Would Harry be dining there tonight, he enquired.

Harry said that until he returned for the funeral, Mark had offered to feed him at the hotel.

"I might join you then for a proper catch up," he said as he made to leave. "I guess Mark will have set a table aside for you. Could you maybe call him to keep a place for me? I just came through the town and the place is swarming with strangers. Is there something special happening today?"

Harry said that he wasn't aware of anything. He also noted John and Pete exchanging looks, which suggested it was something they were expecting.

When he telephoned the Crown to ask for a place for Chris, the receptionist said she would note the booking and inform Mark, when she caught up with him, when lunch was over. They had been unexpectedly busy, she told him, although why today, she could not fathom.

CHAPTER 165

Dalrymple's plan was simple.

It would be a four-car operation. When Carey left the farm to go for dinner at 7.30, one of his drivers would cut in front of Harry's van, while a second would box him in from the rear. A third car would pull up alongside, preventing the van from moving to the opposite side of the road. Two passengers in the front car would approach the van with pistols raised. They would pull Carey and his van boy from the vehicle, forcing Carey into the fourth car containing Dalrymple, his driver and two heavies accompanying him. The van boy would receive a heavy blow to the head and Carey would have chloroform held to his face. Dalrymple's men would then proceed to the garage where he had met with Ruth a few short weeks ago.

That was the plan. He had schooled his men repeatedly, to ensure there would be no mistakes. He sat back in his favourite chair, savouring the moment he would have Carey delivered into his hands. "Say no to ME?" he fumed. "The bastard will wish he had never been born by the time I've finished with him," he vowed.

Only one thing troubled him, Lipman was not returning his calls. The solicitor's receptionist didn't know where he was but would be sure to let him know he had called and was wanting to speak to him urgently.

The clock on the wall showed it was almost 6.30. "We'd better get going," he told himself as he went to join his men, waiting in the compound below.

Jones and Black waited patiently in an unmarked police car. They were radio-linked to other police vehicles. A SWAT team awaited orders. To the rear of the casino car park, seven men had arrived in three cars. They quickly made their way on foot to the compound where Dalrymple and his cohorts were illuminated by a security floodlight, triggered as they crossed the compound to their cars. The sound of an approaching helicopter might have alerted Dalrymple to proceed with caution, but so intent was he on exacting revenge on Harold Carey, he was barely aware of its approach.

Control listened intently, by radio link, as information was relayed from his agents, who had been stationed at various locations around the casino. Suddenly, it became impossible to hear any spoken messages. The unmistakable sound of machine-gun fire rang out from the casino car park. It lasted for several minutes and then subsided before being replaced by shouting. The agent Control had been talking to announced that the SWAT team had been deployed and were ordering Dalrymple's attackers to throw down their weapons. More shots rang out. The Manchester mob had elected to shoot it out, but the cessation of gunfire was followed by more shouting.

When he was again able to get his agent's attention, Control demanded to know what had happened.

"Dalrymple is believed to have been killed, along with four of his men. Others have sustained injuries, but some are showing signs of life. All have surrendered."

"What about the Manchester contingent?"

"They seem to have fared worse. All are lying on the

ground. None are moving. The medics should arrive soon. You can maybe hear them approaching?"

Control detected the clamour of emergency vehicle sirens approaching, but he pressed the agent for more information.

"Did we sustain any injuries?"

"None of our people, sir, but one of the SWAT team copped a bullet in his leg."

"What's happening now?"

"The SWAT team are entering the casino to make sure it is secure. More police officers are arriving as I speak."

"Has anyone checked the Manchester gang's vehicles?"

"Yes, two of our men are doing that now with DCI Jones and his sergeant."

"Have they found anything?"

"I can't see very well from here, sir. I'll go and take a look."

All the cars were empty except for one where a bound and gagged individual was lying in the boot.

When the agent reported the discovery, Control had already assumed that Isaac Lipman would be the person they had found in the trunk.

"Is he still alive?"

The agent confirmed he was, although there was evidence he had sustained several cuts and bruises. All of his fingernails had been removed, he added.

Control allowed himself a smile as he digested the information. It couldn't have gone much better, he muttered, before ending the call.

His cell phone started to beep. It was an incoming call from DCI Jones.

"Are you pleased with how things are going?" he enquired, pre-empting the policeman's salutation.

"Only partly," Jones admitted. "I would have liked to have seen Dalrymple suffer more as we dismantled his empire, but you can't have everything. At least he's not going to be a problem for us now he's dead. We've got Lipman too, as you know from what I heard one of your men tell you a few minutes ago. He'll sing like a canary, now that Dalrymple's gone. We should be able to uncover a lot of things that were hidden from us before, I suspect. I did wonder how the Manchester crew got to hear that Lipman would provide the route to them, knowing Dalrymple's movements so intimately but have worked that one out for myself."

Control did not respond. Jones was smart enough to know that the friendly Manchester policeman he and Black had spoken to in the police canteen would have been fed that information by his agents.

"Talking of the Manchester end," Jones continued, although they had not mentioned any connection. "Several arrests have been carried out in the area. I know you won't be surprised to learn that three of our Mancunian colleagues are currently helping with enquiries relating to the Manchester crime family. Forensic teams are searching their homes for evidence of collusion. It's going to be a lengthy job but will produce a great result, I'm sure you'll agree."

Control did agree.

"Before I ring off," Jones continued, "can I now let Harry, and his friends know they are safe from any danger?"

"Yes but keep it as brief as possible. Tell him we will arrange a full debrief within the next twenty-four hours."

Once again, Control ended the call without further discussion.

CHAPTER 166

Mark had invited Liam and Sally to join them at the hotel, along with Chris and Joe, to act as a diversion for Harry. He suspected he would be worrying over Alex's and Beverly's welfare in Edinburgh.

They were chatting in his private lounge when Jones's call came through on Harry's phone. He listened intently as the policeman relayed the news that Dalrymple would not bother them anymore. He couldn't give any details at present. Could he please share this information with the others? On no account must they tell anybody what they knew until he could provide a more detailed debrief tomorrow.

Harry's relief was obvious. "We're all right!" he blurted out before telling the others what he'd just learned.

He was about to telephone Alex to share the news, but before he could do that, Pete and John, who had been standing guard outside, entered the room. Pete told the friends they had been 'stood down' and ordered to report to another location.

Everyone spoke at once after the agents left, speculating as to what might have happened. Then Chris, who had been staring vaguely in the direction of the mute television screen, noticed a newsflash was interrupting the main broadcast. His curiosity was greatly increased to see the figure of DCI Jones appearing on screen, flanked by Sergeant Black and an excited news reporter, in a location he recognised. Ambulances, police cars and fire engines provided a backdrop to the three figures all patiently waiting for a signal to speak. The reporter put a finger to his ear as he listened to an instruction on his earphone. Chris increased the volume until it drowned out the babble in the room.

"Look who's on TV," he yelled as the sound of shouting and sirens filled the room. The others looked on in astonishment as they took in the scene. Paramedics were rushing around with stretchers, while police assisted walking-wounded casualties into police vans.

"Good evening, Inspector Jones," the reporter began, only to be corrected by DS Black.

"It's Detective Chief Inspector," he growled, somewhat self-consciously, remembering he was on television.

"I'm sorry, Chief Inspector," he replied apologetically. "Can you please tell the viewers what has been happening here tonight?"

Jones hesitated for a moment as the reporter moved the microphone under his chin. Jones waited as an emergency vehicle siren began howling as it sped away into the night.

Jones spoke in a measured way, which suggested he was recalling a script already composed prior to when the event had occurred.

"This was a joint police operation, mounted as a result of information received. A possible territorial battle between two criminal gangs was predicted. We deployed a SWAT team to intercept the conflagration but were unable to prevent an exchange of firearms between the two groups involved. As a consequence, there have been several fatalities, and some gang members have received life-threatening injuries while others have suffered flesh wounds."

The reporter could not contain himself and pressed the DCI for the number of deaths sustained.

"I cannot give you any details at this time," Jones replied, "but we expect to be in a position to provide more information at a press conference – sometime tomorrow."

Undaunted, the reporter continued to query how many fatalities there might be.

"An onlooker said that he counted seven bodies lying under canvas sheeting. Was he correct in that assessment, sir?"

"I'm not at liberty to give that level of detail just now. This particular incident is part of a wider police investigation being undertaken in different locations as I speak."

"We are standing outside the premises of an alleged gangland boss," the reporter paused and consulted his notebook, "believed to be Donald Dalrymple. Is that correct? Was he one of the casualties?"

"I'm afraid that I cannot divulge more information at this time."

"Was it connected with terrorism?"

"As I said earlier, this was a falling-out between two alleged criminal gangs, which resulted in the deaths of some very dangerous individuals. We do not believe this has any links to terrorism at this time."

"But there might be? You can't rule it out completely," the reporter persisted.

"That's all I'm able to convey to you just now, other than that there was never any danger to members of the public. I would also like to stress that everyone can sleep soundly in their beds tonight. We are satisfied that the matter has been effectively dealt with by colleagues, who acted with great bravery and professionalism. Thank you!"

The reporter tried to follow DCI Jones as he moved off camera but Black stepped in front of the eager newshound, preventing him from pursuing his boss. Disconcerted by the policeman's departure, he seemed to be at a loss to know how to continue. Touching his earpiece again, he nodded before summarising the information he had received from DCI Jones.

The friends listened intently as the report continued with the studio presenter quizzing the onsite reporter in the hope of uncovering more details not discussed in the interview.

Harry's mobile started ringing. It was Alex, wondering if they had seen the television report.

"Yes," he replied. "If we can believe what Jones just said, it seems like our troubles are over, Alex."

CHAPTER 167

Rather than returning to the farmhouse, Mark insisted that Harry slept at the hotel. He was jerked awake as his mobile clamoured for attention at 7am exactly. DCI Jones wished him a perfunctory good morning before enquiring if he could be available to go to rendezvous with Control at eight o'clock.

Jones sounded as if he had been up all night. Despite the apparent tiredness in his voice, Harry detected a note of triumph as the officer continued to speak.

"I'll send a car for you, Harry, and will also pick up Liam Forbes on our way to get you."

"I'm not at home," Harry informed him. "I stayed overnight in Mark's hotel. Can you collect me from there?"

Jones said that would be fine, before ringing off.

Harry's regular morning routine was to consult his iPad to scan and memorise information from websites he regularly visited to ensure that he kept up to date with new entries and other developments. Today, however, he would postpone that ritual until later. Previously, it had been an almost overwhelming urge to follow the routine but was now diminishing as the days went by. He realised that this coincided with Alex's arrival.

Liam was already in the unmarked police car with Jones

and Black when they collected Harry from the hotel. Black drove quickly to Control's operational headquarters. They were escorted to the room where they previously met. Even before they sat down, Control began to speak. It seemed he was in a hurry to get on with matters in hand.

"Good morning, gentlemen. Thank you for coming. Please make yourselves comfortable.

"Last night was a triumph for law and order, which DCI Jones will brief you on presently. Several undesirable members of the criminal fraternity have been eliminated, while others are in captivity, awaiting charges and court appearances. Some of the criminals involved were known gun-runners who were not too discerning about who they would supply with illegal firearms and explosives. From that standpoint, you can appreciate that the department of Her Majesty's government my team represents is very pleased with last night's results."

He turned to Jones, inviting him to speak.

"As you may have deduced from my phone call, Donald Dalrymple was killed in the exchange of gunfire. We are delighted to report that organised crime has suffered a major setback in the area and much further afield. We owe you a great debt of gratitude for helping us to achieve that, Harry. The activities of the two gangs involved in last night's operations have been virtually eradicated, some terminally, while others will face lengthy jail sentences, following due process in the courts."

Liam interjected before Jones could continue.

"Can you assure us now that we are free from any threats or reprisals, considering what happened?"

Control responded before Jones could speak.

"As sure as we can ever be. You were only ever threatened by Donald Dalrymple and Tristram Grant – both now deceased. Jake Butcher, who we believe set fire to your Portakabin and was also involved in the slurry incident prior to the auction, is

480

also believed to be dead. Dalrymple, we are fairly convinced, ordered his killing to prevent Butcher incriminating Dalrymple in conspiring to force Joe Burns and you to sell your properties to Ruth Grant."

He looked again at Jones, inviting him to continue.

"We also have evidence that Ruth Grant was involved in the plotting that went into wresting ownership of your farms. She was arrested on charges relating to conspiracy to defraud and money laundering. A local solicitor is also in custody, assisting the police with enquiries relating to corruption, money laundering and attempting to pervert the course of justice. Two other associates of the solicitor, one member of his legal team, and an accountant are also being interviewed in connection with his firm's activities."

Liam nodded sagely on learning this. He had noticed police activity outside Lipman's offices as he travelled in the police car to collect Harry from the Crown.

"Others have been implicated in crimes connected to Dalrymple," Jones continued. "You might also advise your friend Mark that his new scullery maid will not be reporting for work today, following enquiries into various services she has performed for Dalrymple."

"It should be understood that the police operation was not confined to this area alone," Control added.

Jones spoke again.

"As a result of information gained through the Dalrymple investigation, we identified other criminals from the Manchester area, whose leader controlled operations from abroad. He came with colleagues – all wanted men – seeking revenge because he believed Dalrymple was attempting to take over his area. Through your problems, we were able to acquire intelligence that enabled us to confine the resulting shoot-out, but not without loss of life, I'm afraid."

Ever watchful, Liam noticed Jones sneak a glance at Control, who retained an impassive expression. I'll bet I know where that intelligence came from, he speculated.

"We also unearthed information that suggested police corruption in another force – out with our area – I hasten to add. As far as we are concerned, therefore, we are convinced that any threat that might have been targeted at you and yours has been eliminated, Harry."

Always focused on detail, Liam enquired what had happened to William Wyllie.

"Wyllie has recently admitted to crimes of a sexual nature which we cannot discuss at this time. It seems that Tristram Grant latched onto Wyllie because of his gambling losses and somehow came to learn about Wyllie's unnatural practices. He then coerced him, through threat of blackmail, to collaborate over the acquisition of the farms. He does not present a threat to you. While receiving help with his alcohol addiction, Wyllie has been diagnosed with pancreatic cancer. It seems he does not have a great life expectancy and may not survive long enough to make a court appearance," Jones added.

"And will any of us be required to testify in any court proceedings?" Liam queried.

"That should not be necessary," Jones assured him. "We are confident of securing convictions without any of you having to give evidence."

Up until this point, Harry had remained silent but now enquired if this was the end of the matter.

Control elected to reply.

"I mentioned earlier that I work for the government security services," he admitted. "I understand that you have already deduced this from conversations overheard by our operatives. You are of great interest to us, Mr Carey, because of your ability to memorise information. I'm sure you will appreciate how valuable that skill can be in terms of counter-intelligence in so many different ways. If we are able to implant your memory skills to other agents, it will be an invaluable tool in preventing the kind of atrocities our enemies would seek to perpetrate against our nation."

So, Alex was right, Harry thought to himself.

He decided not to reveal she had warned him that this was the reason for their interest in him but said instead, "If I can help at all, I'll do whatever it takes."

Control smiled. He was not guilty of revealing how he felt but, on this occasion, it was evident this was what he had hoped to hear.

"I'm very pleased to hear you say that," he replied. "There is a problem, however. We will require both you and Mr Forbes to sign the Official Secrets Act."

Liam and Harry agreed to do that and were informed that Doctor Green would also need to be involved in subsequent investigations and tests.

"DCI Jones and Sergeant Black will have a watching brief while investigations are continuing, in order to ensure your safety during that time."

Harry had another question for Control, "As you may know, Doctor Green's father is due to be buried on Friday. I would like to travel to Edinburgh today, to be with my sister, Beverly, and Doctor Green. Is there anything preventing me from doing that?"

"Nothing at all," Control confirmed.

Jones also nodded assent.

"I will, however, want to meet with both Doctor Green and you to discuss how we should proceed. I would like that to be a week on Friday, if Doctor Green is able to receive me then. Would you be kind enough to mention that request, at an appropriate time following the funeral?"

Harry said he would.

Having signed the Official Secrets Act papers, Harry and Liam returned in the police car with Jones and Black.

As they got out of the car, Jones also stepped out and took Harry's hand in his.

"You have no idea yet how much we appreciated your co-operation, Harry. You have been instrumental in putting very nasty individuals behind bars. Thanks again!"

CHAPTER 168

Mark drove to Edinburgh with Harry.

After the funeral, the couples decided to go for a meal in a restaurant that Alex regularly visited. They discussed the events of the day, along with other practical matters relating to things that needed attention following her father's death.

At length, the conversation turned to what Control had requested.

"I'm afraid I can't say too much," Harry apologised. He explained that what they suspected concerning the involvement of the security services was true. "Liam and I have both been required to sign the Official Secrets Act, so I'm unable to say more. I'm to undergo clinical and various other tests in the weeks ahead."

"Not if I can help it!" Alex vowed. "I'll do everything in my power to prevent that."

Beverly pressed her to explain but Alex would not be drawn on the subject. "I'll explain later, to Harry, but the plan is not without its dangers. He will have to be sure he wants to expose himself to the risks involved before we attempt anything."

Beverly reached over and held both Alex's and Harry's hands.

"Please be careful," she pleaded. "I would hate for any harm to come to either of you."

CHAPTER 169

Mark and Beverly returned home on Sunday, leaving Harry in Edinburgh with Alex. He would help her attend to a few matters before the meeting with Control.

Alex had arranged a fortnight of compassionate leave and was planning to spend all of it with Harry. They had discussed what she would do now that there was no need to remain in Edinburgh other than for her work commitments. Being the sole beneficiary of her father's estate, she was financially independent and did not need to earn a living. They agreed that she could either rent or sell the Edinburgh house and live with Harry. If he was looking for an investor in his scheme, she would like to contribute to the new enterprise, she told him. He replied that as they were to get married, she would immediately become a shareholder without having to inject any funds into the business.

Harry received several phone calls while in Edinburgh. Liam called to tell him that the architect had drawn up more detailed plans for the conversion of the watermill into an antiques emporium. They had also extended the building by adding an annex, constructed with stones from a disused steading. It would incorporate craft shops and the restaurant. It looked magnificent, he enthused.

The only negative information was that Sally had been appointed acting manager at the bank but learned that it might close in the near future. Harry was pleased to hear Sally might need a job. He would talk to her first but felt sure that she would be an ideal candidate for financial controller of the complex.

Ralph phoned several times during the week with news that items he photographed in the repository had nearly all found buyers. He was pleased they had not needed to involve Alexander the Greek or his mystery buyer. It seemed that every dealer for miles around had learned of the items Ralph had marketed on Harry's behalf. They were clamouring for more and he wanted to know if he would be coming home any time soon.

Beverly called every day and spent most of the time in conversation with Alex. Like most men, Harry was not a good telephone conversationalist and left them to exchange information about what had been happening in his absence. He learned that Beverly had stayed with Mark after returning but visited the farmhouse daily to collect mail and flick a duster around the house. Knowing that Alex would be coming to stay for a few days, the bedding had been laundered and she had bought in a store of groceries. She'd also filled the freezer with some meals she'd prepared, to save them having to cook while Alex was staying.

Everything seemed to be going well in every aspect of his life, but Harry noticed Alex often looked distracted. Was she merely going through the inevitable process of grieving? He decided not to comment but was soon to learn what was troubling her.

"We're meeting this Control person on Friday, aren't we?" she began as they motored back to Millfield.

"Yes," he replied.

"I've been thinking a lot about that, despite all the things that have been happening lately."

When he didn't comment, she stumbled on, trying to form the thoughts that had been preying on her mind since she first suspected Harry was the focus of the security services' interest.

"It's got me worried, Harry. I fear you are more in danger than before."

He looked at her questioningly. "How so?"

"Well, if British intelligence has identified you as being a powerful weapon in their fight against enemy states, you can be sure other regimes will have caught wind of what you are capable of doing."

"But surely my ability to memorise things will only be known to our people, Alex?"

"You are assuming that no foreign agents have infiltrated our security service. I think it entirely reasonable to believe that each spy network, anti-terrorist agency or other secret service branch based in our country is constantly monitored by other nations. Dozens of agents have been deployed to protect you. It will not have gone unnoticed by the foreign intelligence organisations that spy on our spies."

"You think that I am now likely to be threatened by the Russians, or whoever?"

"'Whoever' is right, Harry. If they can apply your skills to their own operatives, it gives them a tremendous advantage. Imagine, for example, if they could train their people to memorise data as quickly and as accurately as you can do that with antiques, the need to carry incriminating cameras or other recorders becomes unnecessary."

"Surely gaining access to our country's secrets will be very difficult, if not impossible?"

"They are called sleepers, Harry. Professor Hart used to tell me about them. He used to work for some obscure part of the security services and warned me about never divulging anything about his work to anyone."

She paused before continuing. "He told me one of his students had been recruited by the security services. After about ten years in the branch he was working, he landed in a sensitive area of work when it was discovered he was acting as a double agent, not for Russia but America."

"The Americans spy on us – their allies?"

"In the world of espionage, everyone gathers intelligence on everyone else. They're a very distrustful group of people."

"I can't believe that the Americans would be a danger to me, surely."

"Any power that gets their hands on you will subject you to all sorts of pressures and techniques to discover how you do what you do. That would be true of any of them, whether a friendly or hostile organisation."

"What are we going to do, Alex? I now understand that your association with Professor Hart and me also makes you a target."

"I'm working on a plan. It could be extremely dangerous for you, Harry, and I have to tell you that when the time comes, you will have to be convinced you want to go through with it."

"I'm entirely in your hands, Alex. Tell me what I have to do."

"The first thing is, not to discuss this conversation with anyone else – not Beverly – not Mark – nobody. Secondly, never talk about it with me, unless we are absolutely certain we cannot be overheard."

CHAPTER 170

Control came to the farmhouse. He entered through the kitchen before they were aware of his presence. As usual, he came straight to the point without preamble.

"As you have already deduced, my colleagues and I work for British intelligence. It is not necessary for you to know which branch that is, only that you can be confident we are primarily concerned with the fight against terrorism, in all its forms."

When neither Alex nor Harry questioned that, he went on.

"Professor Hart, who you collaborated with, Doctor Green, was seeking to develop a mind-programming system that would enable our personnel to develop rapid and accurate memory recall. It was always something we looked upon as being highly unlikely but when Doctor Green visited the covert website she and Professor Hart had shared, it triggered a warning that there might have been developments we needed to investigate."

Alex bit her lip, acknowledging the statement with a nod of her head, while staring fixedly ahead.

"While sceptical about Harry's ability to memorise facts, we now know that he can indeed do that with apparent accuracy. How do you explain this amazing development, Doctor Green?"

She thought for a moment before answering.

"Prior to Harry's ability to memorise facts about antiques, he had already developed a near-photographic memory for music. This skill first originated after a period spent in a coma, following a road traffic accident. When he fell down the stairs in Professor Hart's house, he lay unconscious there for some hours. A tape created by Professor Hart had been set playing while Harry was descending. It played repeatedly on a loop as he lay there unconscious until his friends came looking for him."

"So, the suggestions on the tape were being played to him as he lay there in an unconscious state?"

"Yes, it was still playing when he was discovered in Professor Hart's house."

"May I ask why Harry was in the house?"

"I was clearing it for his daughter, who had decided to sell the property," Harry informed him.

"And how did you come into contact with Doctor Green?" Control queried.

"I had been a bit negligent in my business affairs. Accounts hadn't been issued for several months. The bank was calling in a loan, which threatened to ruin me. My sister, Beverly, and Sally Smith took matters in hand and started issuing accounts. It was then that Professor Hart's daughter, Amelia Hart, was identified, because of an outstanding bill that needed paying. The others, wondering how I had become able to memorise facts so easily, decided to contact her."

"So, Amelia Hart, I am guessing, put you in touch with Doctor Green?"

"That's correct."

"You must have been intrigued but also sceptical, I'm guessing, Doctor Green?"

"Yes, of course. We hadn't tested the programme with any

degree of success, and I wasn't very hopeful of it being any different with Harry. Neither did it have any effect upon his friends when they listened to it."

"So, what, from your initial findings, do you believe enabled this phenomenon to work so successfully in Harry's case?"

"Several things, really. The first is that he was already a suitable subject, as it had happened previously in respect of his ability to recall music and lyrics. Secondly, Harry is very receptive to hypnotic suggestion. People with very high IQs are particularly good subjects, given the right circumstances for that to happen."

Harry showed some surprise at Alex's statement.

"He is a very intelligent man," she revealed, "which I feel sure he has never appreciated. The tests I ran place him in the higher levels of intelligence quotients, which apply to less than 3% of the population."

Control looked impressed. Harry looked astonished.

"Concerning the tests you were able to conduct during your last visit – what conclusions did you come to, Doctor Green?"

Alex produced some notes, which she passed to Control.

"He is able to memorise data, rapidly and accurately in relation to antique and collectible products."

"Does that apply to other data?" Control cut in.

"No. His ability to memorise facts is exclusively programmed to antiques and collectibles."

"Have you tried other subject areas?"

"Yes, of course, but with no success so far," she admitted.

Control was silent for a moment, considering what he had just learned.

"I'm afraid that my ability is limited to absorbing written and visual information," Harry cut in. "I've since come to realise that I'm not able to determine if the information I have assimilated is reliable. Last week, I purchased an item that I thought was a genuine antique, only to discover it was a crude fake. I don't have the ability to discern if something is genuine or not."

"Could the problem be addressed, Doctor Green? Could he be programmed to memorise other information?"

"Probably," Alex responded thoughtfully. "What I'm not sure about is whether or not the conditions that led to Harry developing his super memory powers can ever be achieved again, without that process being life threatening for anyone subjected to it."

Although Control had been concentrating hard on what she said, this latest revelation produced a visible result.

"That's a very strong statement, Doctor Green. Why do you think that?"

"Part of my investigations required me to establish the condition Harry was in when he started receiving suggestions. I consulted with the neurosurgeon, Doctor Dixon, who cared for Harry while he was in a coma, during his last time in hospital. He tells me that on four occasions, while under his care, he had to be resuscitated. Harry, too, has recalled 'out-of-body' experiences while in hospital, which is common amongst patients who have been clinically dead but have come back to life, usually through clinical intervention."

"What exactly are you saying?"

"I believe for anyone to acquire Harry's capabilities, they would need to be in an induced coma for several hours – if not days. Also, there would be no guarantee the same results could be achieved."

"If I understand you correctly, you are saying that the danger of placing a subject under such a deeply induced condition could result in death?"

"That is correct. It might also result in brain damage to the subject undergoing that process."

"Why didn't it happen to Harry?" Control countered.

"I don't know," Alex replied. "It would be an extremely dangerous process, however, that much I'm sure. When I discussed the matter with a colleague, in the university where I work, she was quite adamant it was not something that should ever be attempted again. I can give you her contact details if you want to discuss the matter directly."

Uncharacteristically, Control showed displeasure at what he had heard. He eventually regained composure and enquired how Alex proposed to continue with her investigations.

She said she had no intention of subjecting Harry (or anyone else for that matter) to anything that extreme, as it could be life threatening or debilitating.

"We could test Professor Hart's programme on volunteers, but it would have to be under strict medically supervised conditions – and not down to the deeply comatose state that Harry experienced," she stressed.

After more consideration, Control queried if tests could be carried out in the presence of his colleagues to demonstrate his abilities. If there was any chance a way could be found to transfer this ability to other subject areas, without any danger to Harry, they would like to explore that possibility.

She had been anticipating his query and said that possibly it could, but only under the circumstances she had previously stipulated.

Control turned to Harry at this point and asked if he would be willing to do that for his country?

He looked at Alex before replying, noticing that she gave an almost imperceptible nod.

"Yes," he replied. "When do you want to do this?"

Control thanked him for his patriotism before asking Alex when the tests could be conducted.

She paused to consult some papers before replying.

"I could arrange for that to happen in a fortnight from now in Edinburgh. You will no doubt want to include your own personnel, in addition to the medical team I will assemble to conduct the tests?" she suggested.

Control said he was comfortable with that and would consult with colleagues to determine who should attend.

Seemingly at a loss for anything more to say, he thanked them for their time and departed as promptly as he had arrived.

Harry opened his mouth and was about to speak. A warning look from Alex reminded him not to discuss anything until they were sure they would not be overheard.

"Let's go and meet Mark and Beverly for lunch," she suggested, winking conspiratorially as she spoke.

CHAPTER 171

The rest of the week was spent visiting places and sharing precious moments together alone and with the friends.

They took a trip to the repository with Ralph to inspect antiques requested by prospective clients. Alex, who had never seen any of the items, was impressed by what she saw. The sales Ralph had made since acting as Harry's representative now amounted to tens of thousands of pounds. The pot was building up nicely for them both.

Later, when they were alone again, Harry revealed there were more sites where his grandfather had stored things he had purchased years ago. They had gone out of fashion, or not found a buyer at local auctions. When Alex enquired what the items might be, he was unable to tell her.

"With everything that's been happening lately, I've never got round to looking," he admitted.

They decided to spend Saturday locating and investigating the sites that had not been visited. Ralph would come with them in Harry's van in case there were items that might need to be moved to a more secure location.

There were seven sites in all to visit.

The first four sets of keys had the same address.

"That's where my place is!" Ralph marvelled.

It was also where Sally had identified council tax was being levied but had not got around to querying the charges. It was later discovered that the garages had been purchased by Granda Carey. They had been disposed of by a housing developer who had acquired them as part of a deal with a local landowner. The garages did not figure in his plans and were acquired for a pittance.

The lock-ups were situated just two doors down from Ralph's premises.

"Well, I'll be darned!" he exclaimed. "When I think about it now, I have a faint recollection of seeing you both unloading stuff there, many years ago. Don't you remember being here, Harry?"

"Vaguely, I guess," he replied. "I wonder what's stored in them?"

Each of the garages held a jumble of stuff, piled on top of each other. Unlike the sheds at the farm, there appeared to be no order to what was contained in each. The variety of items in the respective garages defied categorisation, ranging from vases to prams, sofas to lawnmowers.

"I guess most of this stuff was just considered junk when he acquired them," Alex observed.

"Worth money now, though," Ralph enthused. "What are your plans for this, Harry?"

"Let's lock it all back up again and fix a day or two to put it on an inventory list. This stuff will be ideal for stocking the emporium when it is ready to start trading, or at least suitable for another auction."

The three other sites were located in a private estate belonging to Sir George Mackenzie, an impoverished, elderly landowner.

He was confused by their approach. Gladys, his

housekeeper, reminded him that this was Harold Carey, whose grandfather used to sell antiques for him about thirty years ago, when death duties had threatened to force him into disposing of the estate.

"Ah yes, I remember Mr Carey with great fondness," he suddenly recalled, "and you too, if I'm not mistaken," he recalled, giving Harry a searching look. "If it hadn't been for him discreetly finding buyers for some of our heirlooms, we would not have been able to hang on to the old bricks and mortar, I can tell you."

He appeared to reminisce about the past but was dragged back to the present by the housekeeper.

"They've come to inspect the stuff that Harry's grandfather stored here," she reminded him. "Will I take them over to the stables where it's kept, Sir George?"

"That will be fine, Gladys, but I'll come with you as I've not been in there for years. I was never away from the place when they were filled with horses – before we had to let them go," he added bitterly.

None of the stables were locked. There seemed to be little need when they discovered what was housed in each stall. In every available space, statues, birdbaths, sundials and other garden paraphernalia were revealed, some covered in bird droppings while others had cobwebs linking them. There were stone pillars, recumbent lions, birds of prey, cherubs and Greek and Roman figures scattered amidst other stone sculptures, some of which appeared to be water fountains.

"Architectural salvage!" Ralph breathed in wonder. "Where did all this come from?" he wondered.

"Some of it was from properties on the estate, removed before we had to sell them off," Sir George informed him. "Your grandfather made me an offer for them, and we agreed that he would sell them off at some time in the future. That was about twenty years ago but it never happened because of his untimely and regrettable demise. I had forgotten all about them."

"Did he own them outright, Sir George?" Harry enquired.

"Yes, but he did say he would give me 10% of what the items realised," he added hopefully.

"I'm sure we can honour that agreement," Harry assured him. "But what about these other two keys I have labelled as being in your estate, Sir George?"

"Ah, one would be for the barn. Come this way. It's just round the corner."

It was a large stone and lime building fronted by two large sliding doors. The heavy padlock eventually opened, after several applications of penetrating oil were squirted into the mechanism. What they discovered when the doors finally slid back resembled a museum of vintage agricultural and horticultural machinery. All had been restored, although it was clear from the dullness of the paint the work had been completed many years ago.

"Wow!" was all that Harry could say. His grandfather's love of all things mechanical, particularly vintage agricultural vehicles, came flooding back to him. He even remembered watching him patiently renovating some of the implements as a child. It caused him to feel a lump forming in his throat and it took an effort not to shed the tears that were threatening to form in his eyes.

"Of course, there's still the garage," Sir George interrupted.

Once they had taken a cursory look around the barn, Harry re-locked it and followed Sir George to where the garage was located. It was a building capable of holding several vehicles, typical of estate garages of that era. There were four sets of swing doors along its breadth. The nearest set hung open on sagging hinges. It looked as if it had been that way for several years. A mud-spattered Land Rover stood at the mouth of the doorway, looking more like it had been abandoned than parked. Behind the Land Rover, a racing green Mark 10 Jaguar rested on a flat front tyre.

"I should get that seen to someday," Sir George said, "but I'm getting very forgetful about such things," he admitted.

"Are these my grandfather's cars or do they belong to you, Sir George?" Harry asked.

"Oh, these are mine. The other vehicles belong to you."

When they got nearer, they could see other areas inside the garage contained four vintage cars and nine motorcycles. Apart from the dust that covered them, all appeared to be complete in every aspect.

"These are all mine?"

"Yes. I'm sure they will be worth a pretty penny now," Sir George responded.

Harry and Ralph took a closer look at the vehicles, astounded by what they had discovered. Alex, too, was lost for words.

"So, this key is for the garage, is it?" Harry queried, holding it up for Sir George to examine.

He agreed that it was, although obviously redundant now, considering that one of the doors would not close, let alone lock.

Alex gave Harry a nudge. When once she got his attention, Alex followed up with a meaningful look.

"Don't you have a handyman that could fix the garage doors and change that tyre, Harry?" she enquired.

He caught her drift immediately and turned to Sir George. "Would you allow me to send someone up to attend to those matters? It would be at my expense, of course. It's the very least I can do after storing my grandfather's stuff after all these years."

Sir George looked relieved that he would not have to pay for the work and accepted graciously.

Harry went on to say that with time he would arrange to identify and sell the items that Sir George was entitled to receive a commission for and that perhaps an additional bonus might be paid on the items he had held in store, as compensation for their safekeeping.

"That would be very generous of you, Harry," the old gentleman replied. "And as you have keys to the areas in which your artefacts are held, there is no need to contact me when you visit, although we would be delighted to have your company if time allows. Isn't that right, Gladys?"

The housekeeper smiled benignly and agreed that there would be tea and cakes if they would let her know when they might be dropping in.

Returning in the van, Ralph looked almost stupefied. They had travelled a good distance before he finally spoke.

"What else are you going to come up with? There's all the stuff in the repository – that I know a bit about, as they're all antiques or collectibles – but this other stuff is something else. I might be able to give you a steer on the stuff in the stables, but the machinery, cars and motorbikes are out of my ken."

"I guess they will be worth quite a bit?" Alex enquired.

"You can take that to the bank," Harry replied. "I wonder where Grandpa kept the logbooks and other papers relating to the ownership of the goods we have just discovered."

He was later to learn that Gladys had kept them in a box file in her pantry, as they contained receipts for the items her employer had sold to his grandfather.

Later that night, when Alex and Harry hosted a meal for the friends in the farmhouse, Chris was beside himself with excitement. Being a petrol-head, he declared he was dying to get an eyeful of Harry's latest acquisitions. It was encouraging to know he also had contacts through various car clubs that would have knowledgeable people who could value the vehicles and get them into running order.

CHAPTER 172

They drove to Edinburgh on Sunday. Alex wanted to ensure all the procedures and tests she was going to subject Harry to would be in place. She warned him he would be on his own during working hours, while she consulted with colleagues who would help her conduct the tests. She would not be drawn on what she planned to do because it might affect how he might behave while undergoing the tests. It was best that he had little knowledge of the process, she emphasised.

He passed the days walking around the city, poking about in junk shops and antique sellers' premises, picking up items, which he took back to Alex's house. One of the revelations of his meanderings was that charity shops were selling items that had high value but were on sale for just a few pounds. These he purchased, ensuring that each item acquired was clearly marked with the name and address of the charity concerned. He planned to sell them for their true value before passing the proceeds back to the shop from where they had been purchased.

At night Alex and Harry took to going out, partly for exercise, but also to ensure they were not bugged. On Wednesday night, prior to when the trials would commence on the Friday, Alex outlined the programme.

"I have to tell you about what has been arranged for the days the tests will be conducted with the security services," Alex began. "There will be Control and two agents, who I believe you have met before. Their names are Charles Whyte and James Melville. Both have volunteered to undergo hypnotic programming on Professor Hart's tape."

Harry recalled the agents who had masqueraded as the water company workers and had later identified as being at the auction.

"I will have a colleague from the university inducing each of them into a deep hypnotic trance. He will then subject them to Professor Hart's recorded suggestions. It will be repeated over a twenty-four-hour period, after which they will be prompted to memorise various pieces of written and visual data. Each will be allocated a word prompt that they – and only they – will be able to respond to. The idea is that they will then be able to trigger memory retention, as and when they need to do so."

"How do you think it will go?"

Alex pursed her lips as she considered her answer. "Both have very high IQs just like you, Harry, but I'm a bit sceptical about how effective the tape will be. Firstly, they will not be reduced to such a low level of consciousness as you were when in a coma. Secondly, unlike you, they have demonstrated no previous ability to memorise data, as you did previously when you became absorbed in memorising all things musical. By the way, can you still do that?"

"I don't know," he admitted. "I've not been listening to much music since all this began. Before my last tumble, it was all I ever did. I don't seem to have the same interest in that now. It also seems like a long time since I jammed with the others in the band."

She looked at him quizzically before going on. "You may have heard of the amazing things some people can do following

505

a traumatic event or by some other incident that gave them incredible abilities. There is, for example, a man who almost drowned but when revived was able to play the piano like a virtuoso, although he'd never laid hands on a keyboard in his life!"

"I'd heard about that. It must be a very rare occurrence, I'm thinking."

"There are other examples of people being able to do the most remarkable things, although it is very rare for that to happen. We're not yet able to comprehend how such phenomena could have occurred. I'm pretty sure you are one of those exceptional people who have been affected in that way."

They walked on silently before she spoke again.

"Three other people will accompany Control. I do not know their specialities, but it is likely that they will have medical qualifications necessary for determining the reliability of the testing methods."

"So, how is this all going to be scheduled?"

"You will be supplied with information about antiques you will not have seen before. It will be presented on video, and you will then be asked to provide answers to questions from the security services people regarding the information viewed."

"Will you be there when I'm doing that?"

"Yes, but in a glass-partitioned area, to ensure that there is no collusion between us. I've no doubt you will be able to provide them with a faultless recollection, which was not what I have planned."

"What have you planned, Alex? You said that it might be quite dangerous for me."

She looked thoughtful for a while before answering. "I was considering faking another head injury, having first injected you with a substance that would cause you to suffer memory loss and mental confusion. It appears that, after having consulted with colleagues, the process might be irreversible, so we won't be doing the injection bit."

Harry waited for her to continue.

"Drugs that begin with the word 'anti' such as antipsychotics, etc., affect your acetylcholine levels. Acetylcholine is the primary neurotransmitter involved in learning and memory. When someone is low in acetylcholine, they become forgetful, can't concentrate or think of the right word to use. These deficiencies are associated with people suffering from dementia."

"And you were thinking of giving me that?"

"It was a long shot but not one that we could have employed, considering the potential dangers it might have triggered," she conceded.

"So, what will happen now? Have you got a plan B?"

"Of sorts. These are smart people who will not be easily taken in. What I have in mind will depend upon several factors. You do not need to know what that involves, yet. It will, in fact, be better if you don't know what is planned, so you will not be seen to be complicit in the scheme that I've devised. Almost certainly it will need to involve you sustaining another head knock."

Harry looked appalled at this latest revelation.

Noting his reaction, Alex was quick to reassure him. "You will not actually suffer any impact, Harry. It will be stage-managed, just before you are due to go into the cubicle where you are to be tested."

"Tell me how you plan to do that."

Alex counted the process off on her fingers. "First of all, a technician will be engaged in setting up the room for the experiments. She will be transporting equipment into the area and will 'accidentally' knock you over with her trolley – or at least that will be how it will appear to the security services people – just before they enter the room. She will be kneeling over where you will be lying on the floor. Her story will be that you lost balance and suffered a head knock against a table when you fell. You will not be unconscious but give the impression of being a bit groggy. When you get back on your feet, you will insist on going on with the tests and enter the cubicle set aside for that purpose."

She looked for comprehension before continuing.

"Secondly, all you have to do is memorise the information that will be fed to you on the monitor inside the cubicle and commit it to memory. A separate monitor, outside the cubicle, will present the same information to the security people observing the test. You should shake your head every now and again and give the impression that you are still a little dazed."

"How will that work, Alex? If I don't get a head knock, I won't be able to resist memorising the information they will be feeding me."

"That's the third and most important element of the process. Just memorise the information you are fed, exactly as you would normally do that. Afterwards, when questioned about what you have been asked to memorise, just answer as accurately as you can remember."

"Surely that will only confirm I am capable of total recall. I thought the idea was to give the impression that the head bang would affect my ability to do that?"

"That's exactly right. Do that exactly and leave the rest to me."

Harry looked puzzled but realised that whatever Alex had in mind for him, she wasn't going to reveal it then.

CHAPTER 173

Control didn't reveal the names of the colleagues who accompanied him but waited for Alex to explain how the tests would be conducted.

She went through the programme, step by step, beginning with introductions.

A white-coated man stepped forward.

"This is Doctor Jones, who will take Mr Whyte and Mr Melville to a consulting area in the building. There he will subject both gentlemen to hypnotic suggestions, to prepare them for receiving Professor Hart's recording. They will receive the same stimuli that Harry was subjected to for the next twenty-four hours."

Doctor Jones invited the agents to follow him and departed from the room.

"My other colleague, Miss Gray, is our college technician. Alison will operate the audio-visual equipment when we carry out the tests on Harry."

She paused to allow the visitors to take their seats in front of the cubicle in which Harry would be presented with the information and would also be simultaneously beamed into the outer-room monitor, where the security services entourage would observe the process.

Alex then enquired if Control could pass the DVD his people had compiled to Alison Gray.

He produced a sealed package, which he opened in front of everyone. The technician inserted the disc in a DVD player and switched on the monitor. She then excused herself to check that the monitor in the cubicle was functioning correctly.

At this point, Alex continued her briefing.

"I have to warn you that the exceptional circumstances that enabled Harold Carey to acquire the ability to memorise antique, vintage and collectible artefact information are probably a one in a million occurrence. Although we will seek to replicate the conditions in which this resulted in his ability to recall data, it is highly unlikely we can replicate that situation again, if ever."

She paused to seek eye contact with the assembly before continuing.

"As you may have learned, Harry had previously developed a remarkable ability to recall all things musical. This occurred as the result of a period in deep coma following a road traffic accident. He had been in a highly emotional state prior to the RTA. He was also suffering mental anguish just before he fell in Professor Hart's house – briefly, his state of mind was adversely affected by the prospect of losing his home, as Control will be able to confirm."

Control nodded.

"The greatest difficulty we have in trying to replicate the conditions under which Professor Hart's tape can be employed is due to the depth of unconsciousness Harry achieved while receiving hypnotic suggestions. His doctor informed me he had to be resuscitated several times while in hospital. Consequently, we will not be able to achieve that level of unconsciousness, without endangering the lives of our two guinea pigs, Melville and Whyte."

She handed out some papers to the gathering before going on.

"As you will see from the notes in front of you, Doctor Dixon, the neurosurgeon who attended Harry in hospital, provides details of his condition and subsequent recovery."

She allowed them a few moments to absorb the information before enquiring if anyone had any questions. When no one responded, she continued.

"Today, we will provide you with a demonstration of what Harry is capable of memorising in just a few minutes of exposure to data. I should stress that his abilities are restricted to antiques. He doesn't appear to have the ability to recall any other kind of information."

One of Control's colleagues interrupted. Why did Alex think that it was confined in that way? Did she think that other data could be incorporated into his ability to remember things?

"Hypnosis is about suggestibility. For that to be successful, the individual concerned would have to achieve a state in which the suggestions are acceptable to them. We cannot, for example, hypnotise someone to carry out an act like murder, if they are morally opposed to killing someone. The recipient of hypnotic suggestion would also need to achieve the same level of consciousness Harry experienced," she replied.

The men exchanged glances but did not speak.

"Regarding our guinea pigs," Alex continued, "the trials may be successful, but I am not hopeful they will attain the levels of recollection that Harry has achieved, for the reasons I have just mentioned. However, it would be good to discover if Professor Hart's programme has any significant effect upon your personnel."

Further discussion was interrupted with the return of Alison Gray, who announced that the trial could commence. She beckoned to Harry, who made his way to the room that led into the cubicle. The technician was heard to warn him that he should watch where he was going as the room light had just blown.

Seconds later, the sound of something metallic falling prompted the security service contingent to follow Alex into the room where Harry had gone with Alison Gray. With the entry door wide open, exterior light streamed into the room to reveal Harry lying face down on the floor beside an overturned equipment trolley. The technician was kneeling over him, asking if he was all right. He eventually stirred and tried to adopt a sitting position while gingerly rubbing his head.

After continued entreaties to speak, he eventually managed to say that he thought he had tripped over something. The others noted that a piece of electrical cable was snaked around his left ankle.

Alex kneeled and put her arm around him. "Are you all right?" she repeated anxiously.

"I think so," he eventually replied, "but I think I might have passed out when I fell."

He tried to get into a standing position, aided by the women but had to steady himself against the wall, as he appeared to be in a dazed state. They found a chair for him and a glass of water, until minutes later he declared he felt fine and wanted to go on with the experiment.

The technician escorted him into the cubicle and checked with the observers that they were ready to commence with the trial.

From the other room, the onlookers saw Harry sit down in front of a monitor, the back of which faced the observers. As the screen in the viewing room came into life, Harry's face illuminated simultaneously. He was the picture of concentration as different colours reflecting from the screen gave his face a variety of hues. Every now and again, he would shake his head as if trying to clear his thoughts. Fifteen minutes later, the screens went blank.

"Please fetch Mr Carey," Alex requested. The technician, clearly upset by what had happened, took Harry by the arm and led him back into the viewing area, apologising repeatedly for what had happened.

"Are you able to continue, Harry?"

The question came from Control.

"As I ever will be," he replied emphatically.

"All right then. If you are ready, my colleagues will ask you to repeat some of the information you saw on the video."

What happened then clearly caused dismay.

Harry had no trouble in identifying the items they questioned him about, but the information he gave to each question was clearly incorrect.

After several mistakes, Alex was able to identify the problem.

"It seems that the first piece of information he provides is correct but what follows appears to have been taken from another description of a subsequent or earlier item."

After some checking, everyone agreed that this was what seemed to have happened.

"I think the blow to the head might have been the cause of that," one of Control's colleagues suggested.

They all looked at Alex for confirmation.

"Perhaps," she conceded, "but let's not come to any conclusions just yet. How are you feeling, Harry?"

"I'm still a bit groggy," he admitted.

In the silence that followed, everyone's eyes were on Alex.

"I think we should abandon this test today," she concluded before addressing Control.

"Would you be able to provide us with a different set of data tomorrow when we could run the tests again?"

After some thought, he agreed that he could do that.

"We could hold them just before we subject Whyte and Melville to their tests," she suggested.

Everyone agreed that it might be the best plan, since the fall Harry had suffered might be the cause of the problem. "Maybe a good night's sleep might resolve matters," Alex suggested.

CHAPTER 174

There was no improvement, however. It seemed that any information Harry articulated was mixed up, out of sequence or juxtaposed.

Control was dismayed, as were his colleagues. Harry, too, appeared genuinely upset.

The security service personnel were similarly disappointed to note that the agents, Melville and Whyte, were only partly successful in recollecting the information they were subjected to.

In the debriefing that followed, Alex was asked to give an analysis of what had happened, along with what might be possible with ongoing research and investigation.

Her response was thoughtful and measured.

"It seems," she began, "that the knowledge Harry has already acquired prior to these tests is retained and uncorrupted. Anything that he has been asked to memorise following the head knock is gobbledegook. That may change, but it would not be through intervention in a clinical way, I'm thinking. However, it might be possible that, with further hypnotic intervention, the condition might be corrected."

"How likely do you think that might be?" Control interjected.

"I think it is very unlikely, but you never know."

"Would you be prepared to continue with your investigations if results are inconclusive?"

"Are you offering me a job? I am contracted to the university here for another six months."

"I'd have to clear it, of course, but yes, that is what I am suggesting."

"We can discuss that in more detail. I would be interested, of course, but it would depend on a lot of factors," Alex replied. "As I'm sure you know from what your agents overheard two weeks ago, Harry and I are emotionally involved and have decided to get married. That might be seen as a problem with any future investigations."

"I was thinking more in terms of you heading up a team that would investigate the efficacy of Professor Hart's programme, involving other subjects. I accept that Harry is unique, and you would not want to expose him to any unnecessary risk by subjecting him to further experimentation."

Although she could not be sure, Alex thought she detected a flicker in Control's right eyelid. Had he just given her a knowing wink? Was he aware that she had sought to deceive him?

"In that case, I am very interested," she replied.

He did not say goodbye, only that he would be in touch, shook Harry's hand and departed without a backward glance, with the others following on behind.

Harry had been listening intently to what had been discussed and now wanted to know why he had made such a hash of memorising the data he had been given.

"You probably recalled it absolutely perfectly," she told him.

"How come it was different from what Control and the others questioned me on?"

Alison had returned to the room carrying two DVDs which she brandished theatrically.

"She's a genius, our Alison," Alex enthused. "The videos were supplied by Control as you know, and what they saw on their monitor in the viewing area was an exact copy of what was on their screen. The ones you viewed were from the same video but had been fed through a computer linked to your monitor. It scrambled the information that you were asked to memorise."

"So, what I saw and memorised on my screen was tampered with, meaning that I wouldn't be able to provide an accurate report to the security services people?"

"Correct! Now you'll have to find some way of unlearning the nonsense that Alison contrived to hoodwink them."

"Does this mean that I am still able to memorise things like before, Alex?"

"Why don't we find out? Will you run the DVD again, Alison, only this time on the viewing-room monitor only?"

She did, and Harry was relieved to discover that his powers had not abandoned him.

"I think we owe you a drink, Alison. Thanks for doing that," he concluded, mightily relieved.

EPILOGUE

Almost a year had elapsed since the Edinburgh trials. Alex Green became Mrs Harold Carey, eschewing the current practice of retaining her maiden name, as so many of her professional contemporaries had elected to do.

The security services requisitioned the Grant estate. Police investigations discovered it was actually owned by Donald Dalrymple, acquired through the proceeds of crime.

At Harry's suggestion, the main house was turned into a respite centre and nursing home. A row of four unoccupied houses, previously the homes of estate workers, were converted into a research facility occupied by the security services. The facility was to be known as the 'Institute of Cerebral Studies' headed by Doctor Alex Carey. The research centre, it was stated, would seek to find solutions to eliminating memory loss brought about by ageing and Alzheimer's. The centre's title was, of course, a cover for research into memory programming and training systems.

Ruth Grant was currently serving a five-year custodial sentence for her collaboration with Dalrymple in his money-laundering activities.

Isaac Lipman was struck off for unethical behaviour and, like Ruth Grant, was imprisoned for his involvement in various crimes including money laundering and tax evasion.

William Wyllie passed away in three short months after being diagnosed with pancreatic cancer and never appeared in court.

Work at the garden centre commenced four months after Harry underwent the Edinburgh trials and was trading as an antiques emporium. Several artisan and craftworkers were renting space in other converted buildings. Monthly auctions drew large crowds, which had the effect of swelling the number of customers that became regular visitors to the restaurant. The garden centre, too, had benefited from the increased footfall at the site. Joe still had a presence in the shop, although the increase in trade necessitated the hiring of additional staff. The site had become a tourist attraction, with bus parties visiting throughout the year.

As expected, Sally was offered another post in a nearby town when the local bank closed. She decided to accept Harry's offer of becoming the centre's financial director.

Mark and Beverly named the day and were due to get married in the spring. Beverly was the centre's commercial director and revelled in the job.

Liam assumed the role of legal and corporate director while Chris, who retained his DJ role with the radio station, headed up the marketing and sales promotion function.

Joe, too, had a title. He would be responsible for overseeing the development of the horticultural projects. He also had the responsibility of being the facilities director.

Ralph Fortescue invested some of his newfound wealth in the centre. He managed the acquisition and retailing of antiques, vintage and collectible items, along with two assistants recruited from the local area. It suited him well, as it brought him into contact with all sorts of objects he could only have dreamed of handling in his previous existence.

Alex did not have a role in the business because of her full-time involvement in the institute. The security services came to accept that the phenomenon that was 'Harry Carry' was probably unachievable, so her work focused upon developing techniques that would enable agents to develop memory skills already developed and tested elsewhere. She continued the process of analysing why Professor Hart's programme had been so successful in Harry's case. The work, however, was merely a token activity as justification for the institute's establishment.

Harry continued to surprise everyone, as his personality continued to revert to how it had been before the motor accident. His previously polite but introverted persona was gradually replaced with a charisma which those who knew him in earlier years remembered. He seemed to have unbounded energy and enthusiasm for everybody and everything he embraced.

As they relaxed on the couch one evening by the farmhouse fire, Alex asked if he was pleased with the way things had turned out.

"Of course I am," he replied. "What's not to like? Everything is going great! Are you concerned about something, Alex?"

"No. I couldn't be more contented," she assured him. "Sometimes I wonder if things are going too well. I'm probably just being silly," she said, as she snuggled closer.

There was nothing to worry about, he told himself. While the world of antiques was infested with rogues and cheats, there couldn't be anyone as dangerous or threatening as Donald Dalrymple, could there?

This book is printed on paper from sustainable sources managed under the Forest Stewardship Council (FSC) scheme.

It has been printed in the UK to reduce transportation miles and their impact upon the environment.

For every new title that Troubador publishes, we plant a tree to offset CO_2, partnering with the More Trees scheme.

For more about how Troubador offsets its environmental impact, see www.troubador.co.uk/sustainability-and-community